Christmas
with
the
Queen

Christmas with the Queen

A Novel

Hazel Gaynor and Heather Webb

WILLIAM MORROW
An Imprint of HarperCollins*Publishers*

CHRISTMAS WITH THE QUEEN. Copyright © 2024 by Hazel Gaynor and Heather Webb. All rights reserved. Printed in the United States of America. No part of this book may be used or reproduced in any manner whatsoever without written permission except in the case of brief quotations embodied in critical articles and reviews. For information, address HarperCollins Publishers, 195 Broadway, New York, NY 10007.

HarperCollins books may be purchased for educational, business, or sales promotional use. For information, please email the Special Markets Department at SPsales@harpercollins.com.

Originally published in the United Kingdom in 2024 by HarperCollins Publishers.

FIRST US EDITION

Library of Congress Cataloging-in-Publication Data has been applied for.

ISBN 978-0-06-327621-5 (paperback)
ISBN 978-0-06-341114-2 (library edition)

24 25 26 27 28 LBC 5 4 3 2 1

HR 09 12 2024 0833

To all who believe in the magic of Christmas.

And to Lucia Macro, for everything.

"I will honour Christmas in my heart,
and try to keep it all the year."

—From *A Christmas Carol*,
by Charles Dickens

1952

"Wherever you are, either at home or away, in snow or in sunshine, I give you my affectionate greetings, with every good wish for Christmas and the New Year."

Queen Elizabeth II, Christmas Day 1952

Queen Elizabeth II

Buckingham Palace, December 1952

December arrives with a blanket of thick fog and a flurry of activity as the staff begin their preparations for Christmas. I am reassured by the familiar traditions—the arrival of the trees, the planning of menus, the many cards to be signed—and yet even in these well-worn tasks there is change.

I feel my father's steady hand guiding me as I carefully sign my name beneath the Christmas wishes. *Elizabeth R.* My new signature feels as strange and unfamiliar as the person I have become.

Elizabeth Regina. Elizabeth II. Queen.

I glance at Grandpa England's coronation photograph on the desk, and then at Papa's beside it, and imagine the weight of the St. Edward's crown on my head. I smile lightly, remembering the time Papa let me try it on. I can hardly believe he won't be with us this Christmas, can hardly believe such a vibrant happy life was taken by the cruelest of illnesses, leaving me, his eldest daughter, on the throne far too soon. "You can do this, Lilibet," I hear him say. "And you will be wonderful."

I dip my head in silent acknowledgment. I can, and I will.

A light knock on the door catches my attention, and one of the groundsmen steps inside. "They're here, ma'am."

I put down my pen and stand. "Jolly good. Do they look nice?"

He smiles. "Rather splendid this year, ma'am."

A sense of childish anticipation washes over me. "Come along then, Susan, Sugar! Time to inspect the trees!"

My dear corgis stir from their slumber beneath the desk at the sound of their names. I rub their velvet-soft ears and take a treat from my pocket as they follow me along the corridors. I hum Tchaikovsky's *Nutcracker Suite* under my breath, the music still in my ears after a recent trip to the ballet. How can one not be infected by the magic of Christmas, even when one is filled with sorrow.

Downstairs, we are met with a bustle of activity.

The trees are, indeed, magnificent. Three noble firs, grown on the grounds at Windsor Great Park, ready to be decorated in lights and colorful baubles. Holly boughs, fragrant evergreen wreaths, and garlands already drape the fireplaces and the grand staircase. Soon, stuffy old Buckingham Palace will glow with Christmas cheer and sparkle with hundreds of glittering ornaments. A smile crosses my lips.

Philip arrives in a burst of cold damp air, arms full of books on flight and air travel.

"There you are, Lilibet." He plants a kiss on my cheek.

"Yes. Here I am."

"This bloody fog is exasperating," he says. "Damned impossible to fly."

"Dangerous, too." I frown as I walk to the window. The government has issued an instruction to the public to remain indoors as much as possible, but many have ignored the plea. There have already been a number of horrible accidents. "I do hope it blows over soon."

"They expect it to last until the end of the week, at least." He sighs as he drapes an arm around my shoulders. "Might as well get on with it then, I suppose."

I look at him. "With what?"

"Your speech, darling."

My stomach cartwheels at the prospect of the message I am to deliver over the wireless on Christmas Day. I am far more nervous about it than I thought I would be. How truly awful it must have been for poor Papa every year as he tripped and stumbled over his words. "Won't Tommy handle all of that?"

"Given half a chance, yes. He'd probably read out the bloody thing, too."

"Philip!" I scold, but I can't suppress a smile. My husband is wary of certain members of the household staff that I have inherited from my father.

"You must write your own message, before your private secretary puts words in your mouth. Say what *you* want to say, not what the establishment thinks you *should* say."

He's right. As usual. "Very well," I concede. "But perhaps a spot of lunch first. I work better on a full stomach. Speaking of which, I still need to decide on the Christmas menus for Sandringham."

"What's the decision? Powdered egg or Spam? How many dishes will be comprised mostly of potato?"

I laugh. Rationing is still making formal meals and menus very tricky to plan. The kitchen staff certainly have their work cut out for them. "I think we can do a little better than that. We have some new staff joining the Sandringham team apparently. Maybe they will find something inventive to do with whatever supplies they can acquire."

Philip laughs. "Inventive? At Sandringham? I'm not sure they've even heard of the word. Anyway, come along. I'm famished."

But that is precisely what we all need to be now: inventive. Traditions may lend us comfort, but as I look out again at the fog obscuring the view of London I know so well, I am also aware that traditions will have to change as we navigate our way through the unfamiliar path that lies ahead.

Chapter 1

Jack

London, December 1952

Sandringham!

I stared at the word written on the kitchen calendar, circled with a heart, and smiled. Only one more week and we'd be there. I couldn't believe I'd soon be working in the royal kitchens for Christmas. Though a temporary position—and a risk—I'd taken my wife's feverish encouragement to heart. It was a chance for a fresh start, a new world of possibilities, she'd said with that effervescent enthusiasm of hers that I could never resist. I knew she was right.

We'd both come to resent my dead-end position at Maison Jerome with little chance to move up, a poor salary, and a boss who berated me every time the chiffonade of herbs wasn't chopped to his liking. Andrea frequently reminded me that I was an excellent chef and deserved much more. A head chef position, or better yet, my own restaurant. That was the ultimate dream. For now, if I did my best work for the royal family, perhaps the temporary position would become something more permanent, at least until the next door opened.

I whistled merrily as I dipped a teaspoon into the rich gravy boiling on the stove and scooped it into my mouth. It was as silky as it should be, with a fullness that meant I'd gotten the fat-to-flour ratio perfect, but it needed a healthy dash of black pepper. I never, ever skimped on the pepper. My grandpa had taught me that. I smiled as I pictured him at the stove in his beloved restaurant back home in the French Quarter in New Orleans. It felt like only yesterday that we were cooking side by side, tasting another of his new dishes.

I churned the pepper grinder over the pot, gave the gravy a good stirring, and turned off the burner. Sometimes it was hard to believe it had been eleven years since my beloved grandpa had passed away and I'd left New Orleans, or that I had spent seven years in London, married to the woman I loved, with the beginnings of a new dream.

I glanced at Andrea, her head bent over a shoebox filled with postcards, letters, and photographs. Wrapped in a green woolen sweater, a red scarf tucked artfully beneath her chin, my lovely English wife looked like a Christmas present.

I grinned as I walked over to her.

"Why are you smiling?" she said, brushing her lips against mine.

"No reason, darlin'." You look like a Christmas present is all."

"'Darlin'.'" She mimicked me with a grin. "I don't know if I'll ever get used to your sweet southern accent."

"I don't know if I'll ever get used to how beautiful you are."

"Flattery will get you everywhere, Jack Devereux!"

I was rewarded with another lingering kiss, and I felt like a foolish young buck again, falling in love with his English rose.

"I thought you were packing anyway? Looks more like you're unpacking," I teased.

She stuck out her tongue, eyes filled with mirth. "My suitcase is ready to go. But I've just found this box of old photographs tucked away with our jumpers." She smiled as she flipped through them. "Look at this one," she said, laughing. "It's the old gang! I wonder what everyone is doing now. We seemed to drift apart as quickly as we'd come together."

I studied the photo. Andrea had taken it on Victory in Europe Day. As I looked at our old group of friends, it seemed like only yesterday. My best friend, Ryan; Peter Hall, whom I'd never been close to and, frankly, didn't miss; Rosie May, the life and soul of the party; and there on the end, in a lemon-yellow dress, Olive Carter. I remembered her most of all. "Look how young we were," I said, pushing Olive and her bright smile from my mind.

Andrea returned the photograph to the shoebox. "We were children who thought we knew it all, but knew nothing." We both laughed at that. "Speaking of children, I have some last-minute shopping to do."

"What can you possibly have left to buy? There are already a hundred packages under the tree."

She swatted my arm playfully. "I need a few more things for the boys. And some of those peppermint lollipops they love."

Andrea doted on our nephews. She wanted nothing more than to have a large, rowdy family of our own, but after several early losses, we'd almost given up hope.

"I also need to stop by the shop to drop off a gift for Mrs. Howard," she continued. "It was so kind of her to let me take the next few weeks off at our busiest time of year. You can't imagine how many Christmas arrangements I've made this week."

"I can." I scooped her hand in mine and kissed her battered fingertips. "All of those rose thorns leave their mark."

"Indeed," she said with a sigh. "But what could be more romantic than making beautiful bouquets and putting a smile on someone's face?" She pulled on her coat. "I'll only be gone an hour. Promise."

"I'll finish making lunch and start the Christmas pudding while you're gone," I said. "We can bring it with us to Sandringham."

Andrea reached for her handbag. "Do you need anything?"

"Another bottle of brandy wouldn't hurt." A good Christmas pudding required tending, as if it were a living creature. Feeding it every so often with a splash of brandy or rum was the key to its moist, dense texture.

"Done." She planted a ruby-red kiss on my cheek and pulled her scarf up over her mouth.

"Be careful out there," I said, as we stood on the doorstep amid the persistent gray mist shrouding the street. It was what the English called a real pea-souper: a yellow fog with a foul odor, the air heavy with soot. It still showed no signs of lifting. I ran my fingertip across the glass panel on the front door, leaving behind a clean streak amid the grime. There were reports of cows choking in the fields, and people becoming ill in the East End where the factories were greatest in number. The government advised everyone to stay inside as much as possible, but that hadn't stopped anyone from doing their usual holiday chores—least of all Andrea. Her nephews would be waiting for firecrackers and toy trucks and the big striped peppermint sticks they loved, and a fog wasn't going to keep her from making her nephews happy.

"We survived a war, remember?" she said with a wink. "I think I can handle a little fog."

I watched from the doorstep until she disappeared into the murk, her bright red hat the last I could see of her.

While Andrea was gone, I busied myself with the Christmas pudding: dried fruits soaked in brandy mixed with flour, sugar, and breadcrumbs, that would later be steamed. It would take weeks to mature properly, and I was already starting it much later than usual. When the day's work was done, I'd wrap the pudding snugly and let it rest until Christmas Day, when I'd flambé it and serve it with a rich brandy butter.

I wondered what Grandpa would have to say about my pudding.

It was so very English. For the hundredth time, I wished he was still alive, that he could meet Andrea. At least I had become a part of her very large, fun-loving family. I was an only child, an "oops baby," as Mom had always called me. She'd gotten pregnant after one night with a man she'd never heard from again and who I could never call a father. My grandpa had been my hero instead. With a smile, I added my recipe for the Christmas pudding to the pile of Grandpa's recipes and notes.

Once the pudding was steaming, I moved on to lunch, and soon lost myself in the cooking, as I so often did. When the mantel clock chimed, startling me from my thoughts, I realized it was getting late. Andrea had been gone for nearly two hours. I frowned and peered out the window at the pernicious fog, searching for her familiar red hat in the dim light.

I glanced at the clock again and turned off the oven, leaving the roast inside to keep it warm. Perhaps I should walk toward the market, catch Andrea on the way home.

Outdoors, I was assaulted by the fog. It coated my face and hair and chilled my hands. It was even worse than the day before, if that were possible. I looked ahead to where I'd normally see a cherry-red telephone box standing like a sentinel at the edge of the sidewalk. It was invisible now, shrouded by a curtain of gray.

Wrapping a scarf over my nose and mouth, I walked quickly past the grocer's and the bookstore, past a couple of pubs and a pharmacy, and on to Richmond Street, where I paused, as always, to admire a two-story red-brick building. *Our building*, one day. The "For Sale" sign had been up for months, and still it sat empty, the windows shuttered, the painted trim peeling. Soot stained the roof near the trio of chimneys.

But I could see past the grime to a new slate roof, imagine window boxes bursting with flowers in the spring, white linen and candlelight. One day, Andrea and I would run the place together;

she'd take care of the front of the house while I ran the kitchen. The menu would be exciting and fresh, not the usual predictable classics I'd been forced to make at Maison Jerome. It was nearly impossible to become head chef there—or anywhere—unless you'd attended one of the prestigious culinary schools—at least, that was what I was told over and over again. But I would change the game. *We* would change the game, Andrea and me.

Mrs. Howard, the elderly woman who ran the florist's next door where Andrea worked, waved to me through the window as she took a few sprigs of holly and a cluster of mistletoe from a display. "It's still for sale," she said, peering around the door.

I smiled. "And I'm still dreaming about buying it."

"Make a wish," she said. "It's nearly Christmas. Who knows what magic might happen."

"I'll need a miracle if I'm ever going to afford this place, never mind magic! But no harm in dreaming."

She smiled and passed me the mistletoe. "Here, for Andrea. She stopped in earlier and forgot to take it with her. But first, let me steal a kiss." She dangled the sprigs above her own head and puckered up her lips.

I laughed and pecked her on the cheek. "You're a saucy one, Mrs. Howard!"

"Andrea got everything she needed, did she? I told her she was mad going shopping in this."

"I'm headed to meet her now. I'll surprise her with this mistletoe on her way back. Happy Christmas, Mrs. Howard. We'll see you in the new year."

As I turned away, my smile faded. I sounded more confident than I felt. No doubt Andrea had simply met someone she knew, or was waiting in a lengthy queue somewhere, but still, I couldn't help worrying.

I tried to push the unease away and headed back out into the fog.

Chapter 2

Olive

It was three weeks before Christmas, and I was determined to retain my enthusiasm for my favorite time of year despite the less-than-festive weather. I'd always felt there was something magical about London in December. Like roast goose and stuffing, or Christmas pudding and brandy butter, it was the perfect combination. There was nowhere I'd rather be when the shop windows gleamed with toys and decorations, and frosty breaths were lit by the low winter sun that painted the Thames golden. London at Christmas was a Dickens novel, a Turner painting, and a Victorian Christmas card all rolled into one, and I adored it.

Except that it was none of those things as I rubbed my glove against the bus window and peered out at the awful fog that hadn't lifted for days.

I turned to the woman beside me. "Excuse me. Do you know where we are?"

She smiled. "Not sure the driver even knows, love."

The bus crept along at a snail's pace, headlamps seeking the right direction on a usually familiar route. It was as if all the London landmarks had simply disappeared—the Houses of Parliament, Big Ben's clock tower, the dome of St. Paul's—concealed behind the miserable gray gloom. We'd all seen pea-soupers before, but this was different. According to my mother, who now considered herself an expert on the weather, as well as any number of other topics, something called an anticyclone was causing the fog to hang over the city, suffocating everyone below. "They should declare an emergency and force everyone to stay indoors before we all drop dead," was her cheerfully optimistic opinion on the matter.

Fog or not, I was eager to get to work. After several years in the typing pool, I'd recently started a new position as a trainee reporter in the BBC home affairs department, and I couldn't wait to be given some proper assignments of my own. At least the fog gave us some interesting stories to cover. It was all anyone seemed to talk about.

"Oxford Circus, next stop," the driver called. "Or, at least, I think it is."

"Excuse me," I said to the woman beside me as I stood up. "This is my stop."

She swung her knees to one side so I could get past. "Good luck, love. I hope you find what you're looking for out there."

"Oh, I'm just heading to Broadcasting House. Straight up Regent Street. I think I could find my way blindfolded from here!"

"I meant, what you're *really* looking for." She smiled. "Happy Christmas, love."

I hesitated for a moment, puzzled by her words. I wished her a happy Christmas in return before I jumped off the back of the bus. I stood for a moment as I watched it pull away, the lights quickly swallowed up by the fog.

I *was* looking for something, all right. I was looking for excitement and new opportunities. And, of course, I was looking for someone, too. Life always ended up messy and complicated when I was with a man, and yet I lived in hope that there was someone out there who was neither messy, nor complicated, and wouldn't mind too much that I was both. I'd been on my own for so long I could hardly remember what it felt like to fall in love, and Christmas felt like the perfect time to do exactly that.

I pulled my scarf over my mouth and nose and made my way tentatively along Regent Street, past the familiar facade of Maison Jerome, toward BBC Broadcasting House. I could barely see my feet. The intermittent sounds of car horns, police whistles, ambulance bells, and my own coughs broke the muffled silence. It was confusing and disorienting, and absolutely freezing. I hurried on, as quickly as I dared, glad to eventually see the lights of Broadcasting House looming through the murk.

People were easily impressed by my job, especially my mother, who liked to brag about it to her friends at the bingo. "Olive works for the BBC! With Charlie Bullen!" But the reality was far from the glamour they imagined. Even as a trainee reporter, I spent most of my time at my desk, in front of my sage-green Royal typewriter, writing up the reports of more senior staff, and attempting to write something of my own that might, one day, make the bulletins.

As for Charlie Bullen, he was the BBC's senior royal correspondent, reporting on state banquets and official engagements and royal tours. My mother's generation adored him. To me he was an ancient relic, part of the old guard from a generation of stuffy old kings; completely out of touch with our new royal family. Our young Queen Elizabeth was an unfamiliar species to people like Charlie. He had no idea how to talk about her in his reports, no idea that women were as interested in what she was wearing as they were in whatever ceremonial event she was attending, and above all, far more interested in what she had to say. What I wouldn't give to step into his shoes, but, like the fog, Charlie

Bullen was going nowhere. He was a permanent fixture, a toxic threat to everyone in his path.

I darted through the office and hurried to my station, bumping my knee painfully against an open filing drawer and hobbling the rest of the way to my desk. I was glad to see that Alice, Bullen's secretary, wasn't at her desk, ready to snigger at me with her perfectly painted red lips and haughty ways.

"Late again, Carter?" My manager was onto me like a hawk stalking a mouse.

"Detour, Mr. Maguire. The fog's as thick as bunions this morning."

"Thick as *what*?"

"Bunions. You know, those horrible hard lumps old people get on their feet. My nana had them. It can be very painf—"

"Yes, yes. I know what bunions are." He waved me on, his dislike for bodily descriptions outweighing his fondness for reprimanding me.

Rosie laughed as I took my seat beside her. "Calamity Carter strikes again! You'd get away with actual murder, you would!"

I glanced back at Mr. Maguire, with his thin lips and sharp elbows. "Don't tempt me."

I took the cover off my typewriter, pulled my notepad from the desk drawer, rolled a piece of paper onto the drum, and clicked the ribbon back into place with a sigh.

"Oh, dear. The siiiiiigh is back. What's wrong?" Rosie asked.

"Nothing."

"Liar!" Rosie May was one of my oldest friends and could read me like a book. We'd started at the BBC within a few weeks of each other several years ago and had both recently escaped from the typing pool, our sights set on bigger things. "Everything all right at home?" she asked. "Is it Lucy?"

"Lucy's fine. Everything's fine, apart from Mum and Dad."

"Still not getting on?"

I shook my head. "Bickering like a pair of old fishwives. I'm not sure they even like each other anymore."

"That's what thirty years of marriage will do to you. It all turns sour in the end."

I glanced at the wedding band on my finger and lowered my voice. "Yes, well, I wouldn't know about that, would I?"

She offered a sympathetic smile. "No. I suppose not."

Apart from my parents, Rosie was the only person who knew my true story: the unplanned pregnancy, the shame of being an unmarried mother, the imaginary deceased husband to cover my sins. Rosie had never judged me about any of it. It wasn't unheard of for a married woman to work under her maiden name, so I went by Miss Carter at the office, and, with a fake wedding ring on my finger, most people didn't ask questions if I mentioned my daughter, which I was mostly careful not to. But it was always there—the trail of lies and pretense, waiting to trip me up.

Rosie offered me a mint imperial. "Chin up! It's payday. I'll take you to the pub later. We could do with a bit of Christmas cheer in this bloody fog."

I was glad of Rosie's understanding. She saw life in simple straight lines, never questioning or complaining. I wished I could be more like her, but that wasn't my way.

"Daydreaming again, Carter?"

I stirred from my thoughts as Mr. Maguire passed me a note.

"This is a priority," he said. "Have it on my desk in ten minutes."

I picked up the handwritten note. "But this is from Mr. Bullen. Won't Alice type it for him?"

"Alice is off sick. Along with everyone else, it seems. Ten minutes."

I began to type, hardly taking any notice of the words.

May it please Your Majesty,

I regret to inform you, with my humble duty, that I will not be able to travel to Sandringham to report on the Christmas preparations, as has been the tradition for many years now. This dreadful fog has left me feeling rather unwell, and my doctor has advised me to spend some time with my sister on the Sussex coast.

I was very much looking forward to seeing you and the Duke of Edinburgh (and the corgis), and I wish you all the very best as you prepare for your first Christmas as our sovereign. I will be listening keenly to your inaugural Christmas message. You will do marvelously well. I know your father would be very proud.

I have the honor to remain, Your Majesty's most humble and obedient servant,

Charles Bullen

I read the typed page to check for mistakes, and then read it again, and once more, as an idea lodged in my mind. A ridiculous idea. An exhilarating idea. It stayed with me all morning, long after I'd dropped the letter onto Mr. Maguire's desk, until I couldn't bear it any longer.

I found an excuse to take some paperwork to the boss's office and, heart in my mouth, took my chance.

"Where are you going now, Carter? Doesn't anybody do any actual work around here?"

"Lavatories, Mr. Maguire. Got my monthlies early."

He waved me on, a mortified flush blooming in his cheeks. "There's no need to announce it to the entire office."

I hurried up the three flights of stairs and knocked on the boss's office door. Mr. Harding waved me in without even looking up.

"Sorry to interrupt, Mr. Harding. Olive Carter. Trainee reporter."

"How can I help you, Carter? I'm afraid I'm rather busy. Is there something for me to sign?"

Tom Harding was an old softie, a veteran of two world wars who everyone loved. He'd appointed his son to run his newspaper, the *London Daily Times*, and had joined the BBC's home affairs department just after the war.

"I hear Charlie Bullen can't go to Sandringham," I said, keeping my voice as casual as you like.

Mr. Harding ran his hands through his hair and glanced up at me. "Yes. Bloody unfortunate, and everyone else is ill or has left the city to get away from the fog. And with this being the queen's first Christmas and everything . . ."

"*I* can do it."

He rummaged for something in his desk drawer. "Do *what*?" He stopped rummaging and looked at me. "Have we met before?"

"Yes. You hired me last month. I was in the typing pool previously." He nodded, although I wasn't entirely convinced he remembered me at all. "I can go to Sandringham. Cover the royal Christmas piece for Mr. Bullen." I sat down in the chair opposite him. "I mean it, Mr. Harding. I can do this! I adore Princess Elizabeth—*Queen* Elizabeth. I've been fascinated by her for years. I know it sounds silly, but I feel like I understand her."

He laughed. "Those are not exactly compelling journalistic credentials."

"I mean that I understand her as a woman, not just as a queen. I can look at her differently. See another side to her. A more feminine side. Who *is* the young woman beneath the jewels and tiaras? What does Christmas mean to her as a wife and a mother—and a grieving daughter—besides all the formal business of being a queen?"

That got his attention. He leaned back in his chair. "Hmm. That might be an interesting angle, I suppose." He paused for a moment as he studied me. "It's a very important piece, Carter. Listeners look forward to it every year. I'm just not sure you're . . ."

"Ready? I *am*, Mr. Harding. I *am* ready. I'll be a breath of fresh air. Just what we need. Maybe what the queen needs, too? Someone more like her? Well, not *very* like her, but more like her than Mr. Bullen." The question and hope in my voice hung in the air between us, entangling with the smoke from his cigarette.

Harding's face softened. "You talk rather a lot, don't you?"

"Afraid so. But I'm a good listener, too."

"Well, I don't have anyone else I can spare, so I suppose it's you or nothing."

"Really? I can do it?"

He leaned forward, resting his elbows on the desk, his hands steepled at his chin. "This is important, Carter. Essential, in fact. You are there only to gather notes on the preparations, so that Charlie can record the Christmas special. How the trees are decorated, what traditions they follow, what they will be eating for Christmas dinner—that sort of thing. Nice and light. Nothing too serious. And keep out of everyone's way. You are *not* going there to become the queen's best friend. Understood?"

I nodded. "Absolutely."

"Our association with the royal family is very finely balanced. One wrong word, one foot out of line, and we may not be invited back."

"Believe me, if you let me go to Sandringham, I will do everything I possibly can to make sure I am *always* invited back."

At this, he burst into laughter. "I have to hand it to you, Carter. You have the confidence and self-belief of someone far more experienced than you."

I leaned forward and shook his hand. "Self-belief is the only way to get experience, isn't it? Thank you for the chance. You won't regret it." I bumped my hip off the filing cabinet as I made to leave his office, sending a potted plant rocking.

"I'm already regretting it," he said. "Now get out of here before I change my mind."

I hurried back to my desk, a grin stretching across my face, my mind awhirl. What would my mother say? And Lucy? She'd be so excited. Rosie would be sick with envy when I told her. She was as obsessed with Elizabeth as I was. We'd already picked out our coronation outfits from the Dior collection. Rosie's mother was a dressmaker and was making us a replica each.

"What's got into you?" Rosie asked when I slid into the chair at my desk.

I grinned at her. "Christmas spirit, Rosie! One has had a bit of good news."

"Is one going to tell one's best friend?"

"Later. Now hush. You're distracting me, and I'm terribly busy." I winked at her, eliciting a soft laugh.

At the end of the day, we pulled on our coats, hats, and gloves and made our way out into the gloom. It was worse than it had been earlier. The fog was now laced with smoke from the factories and coal fires burning across the city against the freezing tempera-tures. We could hardly see our hands in front of our faces as we made our way slowly toward our favorite pub. Everything was muffled by the thick fog, and the roads were almost empty.

As we hurried across the road in front of the pub, we came across a small group of people gathered around a stationary taxicab.

"What happened?" I asked, turning to a newspaper seller beside me.

"Some poor woman got knocked down. Looks to be in a bad way."

Rosie pulled me away as a bell sounded through the murk and

an ambulance approached, but as I stepped around the crowd, I couldn't help but take a quick glance. All I could see were a woman's shoes, several Christmas parcels strewn nearby, and a number of striped peppermint lollipops, crushed against the tarmac. But it was a bright red cloche hat in the road that left a lasting impression on me—a burst of color among all the dark and gray.

As we walked away, I wondered who the poor woman was, and who might be waiting for her, peering out into the fog, desperate for her to come home.

Chapter 3

Jack

London, one week later

My darling wife hadn't been delayed by a neighbor, or by long queues at the shops. She'd simply been crossing the street, arms full of presents, and hadn't seen a taxi coming around the corner.

She hadn't come home—and never would again.

Her life had been taken far too soon, and mine had come to an abrupt halt.

The funeral was a blur—something I participated in but couldn't fully understand. It inched by, one painful moment at a time. The packed church, the hastily chosen hymns, the hugs and kindness and conciliatory handshakes, the Christmas roses that Mrs. Howard had arranged. Andrea's usually cheerful nephews with their tearstained cheeks. They were sorry. Everyone was so terribly sorry.

I couldn't sleep. Guilt and grief tormented me. If I had only gone with her that day, if only I had been the one to cross that street.

It seemed impossible that her vibrant light had gone out, that my darling girl would never smile at me or take my hand again, that I'd never again trace the curve of her lips with my fingertip or feel a rush of warmth as her infectious laughter filled the room. I squeezed my eyes closed against the pain as the memories flooded in, of those first hopeful months when we'd met and fallen in love, our wedding and the bliss that had followed. Our hopes for our future together. The dream of children, of a true home, of our restaurant. It was gone, like a trace of perfume or a puff of smoke, there for an instant and vanished the next as it dissipated on the wind.

I couldn't bear it. I didn't know how to go on without her.

I lost hours and days, time becoming liquid. But time didn't care about my grief. The days peeled away, one by one, just as they always had, just as they always would.

The only thing I'd managed to do was telephone my new boss, to explain that I couldn't take the job at Sandringham and wouldn't need the little cottage we'd been assigned on the Sandringham Estate after all. After the call, I disappeared down a well of grief, surrounded by the echo of my sorrow, entirely and utterly lost.

Days passed in a blur until the incessant chime of the doorbell interrupted my pain. When I heard my name being called, I pulled myself from the bed and stumbled to the front door. A figure waited patiently on the other side.

"Jack!" The man shouted my name again, and I knew then it could only be one person.

"Ryan?" I said, as I opened the door. "What the hell are you doing here?"

We'd met during the war and had become fast friends. Ryan Harris was possibly the only person I could stand to be around at that moment.

"Good to see you, too!" He threw his arms around me in the familiar bear hug of his that I'd relied on many times before. "I've been waiting for you to arrive at mine. I invited you to stay with us for a while, remember?"

"Did you?"

"Yes. After the funeral?"

I shook my head. I didn't remember much about that day.

"When you didn't answer the telephone, I thought I'd better check on you. And before you make excuses and send me away, I'm not leaving without you."

"I don't have excuses," I said tiredly. "I don't have anything."

"You have me, Jack. Now, are you going to let me in, or what? It's a long way from Norfolk. You look like absolute hell by the way."

I showed him into the narrow hallway. "I can't promise I'll be much company."

"You never were." He offered a tentative smile.

We talked for a while. Ryan had an easy way about him that had always made me feel comfortable. It was good to see him, and I felt guilty for forgetting his invitation, but I just wanted to be alone. The conversation soon stalled.

"Look, I know you'd rather I buggered off and left you to wallow," he said. "But I'm not leaving you here alone, not with Christmas coming. Not this year, Jack. You need a friend more than ever. Come and stay with us for the rest of the month. Pack a bag. I've already booked your train ticket."

"I don't know . . ."

"Spend Christmas with us. Maggie and Ivy love you, Jack, and they haven't seen you since August. We have a room ready. You can stay as long as you like."

Ryan and Maggie had lived in Norfolk for years. When I'd accepted the temporary position in the royal kitchens, being near my best friend had been a part of the appeal. "I canceled the job at Sandringham." I rubbed a hand over my tired eyes, over my mussed hair. "I was going to—"

"Well, *we* need your help. You know how Maggie hates to cook, and I'm hopeless."

The thought of the Christmas cheer in their home, the gifts and laughter and love . . . I didn't know if I could stomach it. And yet, I couldn't stand to be here, in our neighborhood, passing the building Andrea and I had hoped would become ours, staring at the door of our flat, waiting for her to come home from work with a kiss and the day's gossip, the scent of lilac in her hair.

"Come to Norfolk, Jack. There's nothing for you here."

As I took in the days-old dishes on the countertop, the Christmas pudding dry and hard as a brick, and the wilting fir tree in need of watering, I squeezed my eyes closed. How could I stay?

"When does the train leave?" I rasped.

"In two hours."

"Two hours!" I repeated. "Didn't give me much time, did you?"

"Do you need it?" Ryan asked, voice soft.

He knew me too well. I glanced at my suitcase, still packed for the original planned trip. "No," I said. "I suppose not."

Norfolk county formed part of England's east coast and was about a hundred miles from London. The last time I'd been, lush green grass had carpeted the landscape and honeysuckle vines had infused the air with their sweet perfume. Now, winter had brought its browns and grays, and clumps of melting snow, which did little for my mood. And yet, as the city streaked by and buildings turned to open sky and pasture, I exhaled a deep breath. The houses we passed were quaint and beautiful with their golden sandstone, ribboned wreaths, and festive garlands. Despite the darkening sky, every windowpane glowed cheerily in the gloom. Though the ache in my chest still throbbed, there was something soothing about being closer to nature. Away from the important, imposing bustle of city life. For now, that was good enough. It was all I had.

Ryan's wife Maggie met us at King's Lynn station with a

tentative wave. At her side, their four-year-old daughter, Ivy, showed me the gap in her smile.

"Uncle Jack, look! I lost a tooth! Daddy said the tooth fairy will leave me a surprise under my pillow tonight."

In spite of myself, I felt the urge to smile and crouched down to eye level to greet her. "Well, Ivy, I'd say you're lucky." I touched the end of her freckled nose with my index finger. She giggled and threw her arms around my neck.

"I'm so glad you came," Maggie said, kissing my cheek in greeting as I stood again. Her belly had grown round since I'd last seen her; baby number two was well on the way. "I'm so sorry, Jack. I wish I could have attended the funeral." Ryan had rightly protected his family from the train delays and, more importantly, the deadly fog, by asking them to remain behind in Norfolk. "Andrea was such a dear woman."

Pain gripped me at her name, and all I managed was a hoarse "Thank you."

Relieved the requisite condolences were behind me, I followed them to the car.

We drove the short way to Ryan's modest cottage, had a simple meal of stew and fresh bread, then settled on the sofa with a brandy while Maggie wrangled Ivy into bed.

As Ryan finished stoking the fire, his brother, Mason, joined us. Mason was a chef, too, though he'd advanced at a decidedly faster pace than me. He'd worked in the prestigious kitchens at Buckingham Palace for the past two years and had clearly made himself indispensable enough that he'd been chosen to join the select group of kitchen staff who traveled to Sandringham for the Christmas holiday. It was through him that I had first become aware of the opening at Sandringham for a temporary chef.

"Jack. It's been a while." Mason shook my hand. "Good to see you again, though I wish the circumstances were better."

"That makes two of us. How's work?" I asked, desperate to steer the conversation away from another litany of "I'm sorry"s.

He swirled the brandy in his glass and took a sip. "Hectic. Half of the kitchen staff are out with the flu. We're really behind on the Christmas preparations. We've sent for two others to join us from London, but we still need more hands."

His unspoken words hovered in the air between us: that I'd bailed on the job, albeit with good reason, and had made their situation worse.

"I know Max would have you in a heartbeat if you changed your mind," Mason added.

And then my gaze flicked to Ryan. When he wouldn't meet my eyes, I realized he'd not only invited me to stay for Christmas as a gesture of kindness, but also to tempt me back to the role at Sandringham.

"You think I should take the job, don't you?" I said.

"It could certainly help to distract you a little," Ryan said. "Besides, Andrea would hate to see you miss this opportunity. Who knows where it might take you." He took a drink. "Of course, it's your choice. That's all I'll say about it. I'm here for you either way."

I sank into the cushion on the armchair, his words washing over me. He was right. Andrea wouldn't want me to give up on this opportunity to expand my experience and skills, not after I'd worked so hard. Taking a job with the royal family was a chance to enhance my reputation, and, more importantly, might be a stepping-stone to eventually owning my own restaurant. Still, I found it hard to muster even the faintest interest in anything.

I sighed heavily. "I don't know if I can."

Mason gave me an encouraging smile. "If it becomes too much, you can always walk away."

I looked at Mason, thoughtful, as firelight flickered across his face.

Ryan leaned forward. "I really think you need this, Jack."

Again, he was probably right. I could see Andrea's face alight with excitement when I told her I'd been offered the job. I could hear her, urging me to take it, not to stand still. I sat quietly for a moment, gazing into the glowing embers of the fire. *"Do it for me, Jack. Do it for us,"* her voice echoed in my ears.

After a long moment, I drained the rest of my brandy, and looked up. "What time should I arrive?"

Chapter 4

Olive

The day I found out I was going to Sandringham to report on the Christmas preparations had ended so horribly with the poor woman's accident that I saved my happy news to share with my family at teatime the following day.

"Something exciting happened at work," I said. "Who'd like to guess?"

Lucy stuck her hand in the air. "Can I guess, Mummy? Was it somebody's birthday party?"

I smiled. Lucy loved nothing more than a birthday party. She'd even given herself a second birthday, like the queen. "No, darling. Even more exciting than that. I've been asked to go to the Sandringham Estate, to make a report on the royal preparations for Christmas!"

My mother's fork froze halfway to her mouth. My father nodded in his proud fatherly way. Lucy asked what the Sandringham Estate was.

"It's a big house where the royal family sometimes goes for their holidays, and for Christmas."

She was beside herself with excitement. "Will you meet the queen? Really and truly?"

"I hope so!"

"How on earth has this come about?" my mother asked. "I thought Charlie Bullen always covered the royal family. Has he retired?"

"You almost sound disappointed, Barbara." My father winked at me.

My mother gave him a withering look.

"Charlie's not well," I explained. "Taken ill with the fog. Gone to stay with his sister at the coast, or something."

My mother looked visibly shocked. "Good God. The poor man. I hope he doesn't die."

I stared at her, incredulous that *this* was her reaction to my news. "Anyway, the *point*, Mother, is that *I'm* covering the royal Christmas preparations in his place."

My father put down his knife and fork. "It's bloody marvelous, love. Isn't it marvelous, Babs? I think it's marvelous."

My mother, still shaken by news of the possible demise of Charlie Bullen, at least managed a token, "It is. Congratulations, love."

"Can *I* come, Mummy?" Lucy looked at me with her chocolate-brown eyes. "Please!"

I tweaked her nose. "I'm afraid not, darling. Anyway, it will all be terribly serious and boring. Lots of curtseying and 'one must not step on the grass,' and whatnot." Lucy laughed at my upper-class accent. "But I'll tell you all about it when I get back." I looked at my parents. "I'll only be gone for the day. Will you be able to collect Lucy from school?"

My father nodded. "Of course, love. Take all the time you need. We'll be fine, won't we, LouLou."

Lucy adored her grandpa. Spending extra time with him almost made up for not seeing the queen.

My mother studied me through narrowed eyes. "When do you go? You need a haircut. And what on earth are you going to wear?"

I was on the train to Norfolk by the end of the following week. The fog had finally lifted after a devastating week during which thousands had lost their lives, and countless more had been left severely ill. It was a relief to see the sky again as life returned to something like normality, although setting off for an appointment with the queen was anything *but* normal.

After much deliberation, I'd eventually settled on wearing a sensible knitted twin set my mother had suggested. Half a size too small, it pinched my waist and clung apologetically to my bottom, and the buttons strained against my bust, but it was the best thing I owned. My hair had been cut and styled, a loose button had been stitched back onto my best coat, and my shoes were polished until they looked like glass slippers. I'd added my grandmother's locket necklace at the last minute, for luck. I checked my makeup in the mirror of my compact and added a little pressed powder to cover the high color in my cheeks. I was almost sick with nerves.

My stomach churned at the prospect of what—and who— would be waiting for me at Sandringham. Doubt and worry battled with my sense of excitement and ambition. What had I done? What ridiculous situation had I got myself into now? I'd taken a chance, grabbed an opportunity, and I could no more stop the train as it hurtled through the Norfolk countryside than I could stop the chain of events I'd set in motion the moment I'd stepped into Tom Harding's office. It wasn't the first time my life had felt wildly out of my control, and, knowing me, it wouldn't be the last, so I took a deep breath and held on to see where it would spit me out next.

As unprepared as I was in many ways, in another way I felt as if I'd been preparing to meet the queen for half my life. Apart from her wedding day, when I'd seen her several times but only from a distance, I had seen her up close once before, as we'd danced in a conga line around Trafalgar Square on VE Day. I knew it was her I'd seen that night—Princess Elizabeth—although Rosie didn't believe me then, and still didn't now.

From the moment I'd heard young Princess Elizabeth speaking on the wireless for *Children's Hour* during the first year of the war, I'd been fascinated by this regal young girl, so composed for her age. My sister and I had spent the better part of a week mimicking Elizabeth's clipped pronunciation, pretending to be Lilibet and Margaret Rose, until our mother couldn't stand it anymore and insisted we give it a rest or she would have to evacuate the two of us overseas.

My first scrapbook about the princess had quickly developed into a second, and then a third as her engagement to the handsome Prince Philip of Greece and Denmark was announced. When Elizabeth Windsor had the world at her feet, I'd found myself with a two-year-old at mine, and while I wouldn't change a thing—I couldn't imagine my life without Lucy—it certainly hadn't been easy. At times, it had been nearly impossible. A fake wedding ring on my finger and a deceased "husband" provided a sufficient explanation for the inevitable questions about Lucy's father. There were, after all, too many women raising their children alone in the aftermath of war. But *I* knew I was different to them, and the deep sense of shame and the scornful judgment I'd faced in the months during my pregnancy still lingered painfully. As did the memories of Lucy's real father. I'd always felt I had something to prove—to him and to myself, but mostly, to Lucy. Perhaps this chance appointment at Sandringham would allow me to do just that.

I took the opportunity to prepare even more for my report as the train clattered along the tracks. On paper, my brief was simple. I was to observe in detail—*and without getting in the way of* (this part Mr. Harding had underlined)—the preparations for Christmas at Sandringham. How many staff were there, and what was everyone's role? How was the place decorated? Which members of the royal family were there, or expected? What traditions did the family follow? When were gifts exchanged, and by whom? What was everyone eating? Did the corgis get a gift? (This last question, I'd added myself.) I was to write up my findings into an entertaining and informative three-minute report, which would be recorded for broadcast by Charlie Bullen as part of a Royal Christmas Special. This was my chance, and I was determined to make it count.

Eventually, the train deposited me at King's Lynn station, where I was met by a driver who went by the name of Evans and who was to take me on to Sandringham.

"I've never had a driver before," I said, nervous energy making me talk too much as usual.

"Mr. Bullen always has a driver, miss. We presumed the same would apply to his replacement."

"Temporary replacement," I emphasized. "I mustn't get used to this sort of life! Do I sit in the front or the back?"

At this, Evans smiled. "The back, miss." He held the car door open for me. "All aboard!"

Once we'd left the town behind, it was a pleasant drive along narrow country lanes, through pretty villages and past stone cottages. As we got closer to Sandringham, I noticed that many of the homes had their doors painted the same shade of blue.

"What does the blue door mean?" I asked.

"Those are estate houses, miss. Any building with a light blue door is owned by the king. I mean, queen! The shade of blue is a nod to the queen mother's racing colors. Many are lived in by estate staff. I have one myself."

Everything was immaculate, the front gardens tidy, not a dustbin or pigeon to be seen. I felt a million miles from London.

"It's all so pretty," I said.

"Wait until you see the main event! Here we are, miss. Enjoy the view."

I peered out of the window like a child staring into a sweet shop as he turned the car through black wrought-iron gates with gilded royal crests. Uniformed policemen stood as stiff as toy soldiers on either side of the posts. I showed the papers I'd been given and held my breath as they were inspected and my name checked against a list. I breathed a sigh of relief when we were waved along.

Evans continued up a vast sweeping driveway, passing immaculately manicured lawns and frost-dusted trees and borders. There was a different feeling in the air here, a wonderful sense of space and serenity. No wonder the royal family loved it so much. No wonder they traded their palaces and castles for this peaceful sprawling home in the countryside. And what a home it was!

I gasped when I saw a beautiful building emerge through the trees.

"Not been here before, miss?" Evans asked.

"Never. It's bloody enormous!" I clapped my hand over my mouth. "Oops. Sorry. I mean, *very* enormous."

He laughed lightly. "And yet it's one of the smallest royal homes. You'll be surprised when you see inside."

I could hardly wait to see inside. I could hardly believe I was here at all.

"You'll be in good hands with Mrs. Leonard," he continued. "She probably knows more about the house than anyone else, the queen included!"

"Who is Mrs. Leonard?"

"The housekeeper. She'll give you the tour."

"The tour?"

"She'll show you the bits of the house you're allowed to access. Give you a few quotes for the report. The usual stuff."

My shoulders slumped. I didn't want a tour, or the usual stuff, or pre-prepared quotes. I wanted to see what it was *really* like to be part of a royal Christmas. I wanted to put it into my own words.

Evans pulled the car to a stop and opened the door for me.

As I stepped out, I took a deep breath, filling my lungs with the crisp clear Norfolk air. For the first time in weeks, I felt as if I could breathe properly. It felt wonderful, magical, and it was exhilarating to be somewhere new, where nobody knew anything about me, and the mistakes of my past were a secret I could keep hidden away.

I looked at the wedding ring on my finger and wished I could take it off, wished I could be free of the need to make up a husband in order to save my reputation. I held my head high and straightened my shoulders. Mrs. or Miss, wife or widow—those were just titles. All that mattered was the truth. I was Olive Carter. BBC reporter. I had nothing to hide, nothing to be ashamed of, and *everything* to prove.

Chapter 5

Jack

Norfolk, December 1952

I changed my mind three times as I lay in bed that morning, turning my thoughts and feelings over and over, trying to find some enthusiasm for my impending new role. In another life—a life where Andrea had not crossed that road—I would have been excited, if a little nervous, to get started. As it was, all I felt was an overwhelming desire to hide beneath my bed covers and fade into oblivion. But that wasn't possible here, with Maggie and Ivy bustling about, and the constant gentle encouragement to face another day. Eventually, I dressed and made my way downstairs to wait for Mason to arrive. I'd finally decided I'd rather be in a kitchen than anywhere else—the place where I was most comfortable, most myself.

Mason pulled up outside the house just before seven, as arranged.

"Ready?" he asked as I opened the car door.

"Ready as I'll ever be. I guess." I gave a shrug and tried to smile, but what emerged was more of a grimace. Mason kindly pretended not to notice my reserve, my hesitation, and general disposition.

We didn't talk much on the way. The silence suited my mood and the peaceful morning.

As we approached the gates to the estate, a mist arose from the immaculate lawns. We were met instantly by a guard, who checked our names and papers, after which, we were waved inside the gates. The house had a red-brick facade with cream trim, dozens of windows, and several small pointed roofs in the Dutch style. The sprawling grounds were beautiful even in winter, intersected with winding paths and bordered by evergreens and holly bushes. Acres of woodland were scattered beyond the gardens that hugged the house. Sandringham was so different from the colder, stately grandeur of Buckingham Palace in the best way possible, and despite my unshakable sadness, I found myself warming to its charm.

Mason parked near the stables and showed me to the eastern-most wing of the house, where the kitchens were located.

"The kitchens are quite far from the dining room," he said as we walked. "The Duke of Edinburgh often complains about the food being cold. Takes a while to ferry all the dishes on trolleys and lay it out on the buffet. I don't know what we're to do about it." He shrugged. "It's an old house. The Victorians certainly didn't think the way we do."

The main kitchen itself was definitely in need of updating, the appliances and pots and pans were heavily used and worn. The few newer contraptions looked ill-fitted in the cramped room. The staff clearly made do with what they had, including separate workstations, much like those at Maison Jerome. It appeared they operated with the same French hierarchy as Jerome's as well. I felt the smallest sense of relief. One less thing I'd have to learn.

"There's talk of renovations," Mason added. "But who knows when that will be. I'm sure it would cost an absolute fortune. Now, let's get you kitted out, chef!" He sorted through the linens and handed me a freshly starched double-breasted chef's jacket and a pair of trousers, along with a crisp white apron and hat.

"Thanks," I said, suddenly overwhelmed at the prospect of finding my place in a new team, learning the rhythm of an unfamiliar kitchen.

I clung to Andrea's encouraging words, repeating them in my head like a mantra.

The air was thick with the smell of bone broth boiling away on a gas burner. The music of the kitchen that I knew as well as my own heartbeat swirled around me. There was nothing I loved more than the clang of pots and pans, a chorus of voices shouting orders, a chef singing to the roasted duck as it was stuffed and trussed and sauced. The rhythm never failed to sweep me into its current as I plated a tender pork loin, or arranged a fan of crisped potatoes dusted with flake salt and chives.

Something sparked inside me for a moment before flickering out again.

"You'll report to Max Barrington," Mason said. "He's the head chef." He pointed to a man with dark hair and a barrel chest. He wore a pristine white chef's coat with miniature Union Jacks on both sides of his collar. His face was cragged from age and hard work; his hands were thick with muscles forged over years of chopping vegetables and whipping eggs and sugar. His toque blanche—the familiar pleated chef's hat—made him appear ten feet high.

I paused, unsure how to proceed.

Mason clutched my shoulder with brotherly affection. "Max will decide what you'll be doing each day. I'll be around if you need anything, too, but I'd better get to it." He joined the crowd of kitchen staff.

I took a deep breath and scooted expertly around the others, busy at their stations, racing back and forth for ingredients, or carrying dirty dishes to the sink. The place whirred like gears in a well-oiled clock.

At Max's prep table, I paused, watching as he plated scrambled eggs topped with smoked salmon before someone—presumably a butler, or a footman—whisked the plate immediately away to a cart already laden with a teapot, sugar and milk, a silver rack with delicate triangles of toast, and small silver dishes filled with preserves. In an instant, breakfast was wheeled out of the kitchen and down a long corridor.

"That's it, then," the head chef said, exhaling. "We'll start on lunch prep in fifteen minutes."

I cleared my throat. "Pardon me, chef. I'm Jack Devereux." I extended a hand. "A temporary hire, for Christmas."

Max raised an eyebrow at me. "*Very* happy to have you here, Jack." He wiped his hand on his apron and shook mine firmly. "You're American?"

"Yes, chef."

"Southern, by the sounds of it." He smiled warmly. Judging by the laugh lines around his eyes, I got the sense he smiled often.

I nodded. "New Orleans, but I've lived in London since the war ended."

"New Orleans!" Recognition lit his dark eyes. "Spent some time there myself—a long while ago, mind. My mouth was on fire the whole time. Loved every minute of it!"

I felt my shoulders relax. "We do love our spices and peppers."

"What kitchen experience do you have?"

"I've worked at Maison Jerome for the past seven years. Galley cook in the US Navy before that. And a childhood spent at my grandpa's side—he owned his own restaurant."

At this, he smiled again. "No better teacher than a grandfather! As for Jerome Laurent —you must be classically trained, I imagine. And sufficiently shouted at."

I felt heat around my collar. This was the part I always dreaded, explaining my lack of a formal culinary education. At least Max knew what a bully Jerome could be. "I was shouted at plenty, but I'm not classically trained, chef."

"I see." Max eyed me a little more closely. "Well, we don't need a Michelin-star chef to help for the next few weeks. We're happy to have you."

I liked this man instantly. If he had the arrogance of most head chefs I'd met, it was hidden beneath a warm nature and perpetual grin. The exact opposite of Jerome. Something about that pleased me.

"I was sorry to hear about your wife," Max added. "Bloody awful news. Hopefully a busy kitchen will help to distract you."

I stiffened at the mention of Andrea, her presence conjured instantly, hovering and cloying like a cloud of perfume.

I choked out a "Thank you, chef."

"Right. There's plenty to do. Come, I'll show you around."

I followed him, lump in my throat, but grateful for his stiff British ways and his reluctance to dwell on my emotions.

He took me on a tour of the kitchens, pointing out the various stations and the storage cupboards. He also underscored the kitchen rules before setting me loose. For the next three hours, I ferried vegetables, cheese and cream and dozens of other items to the chefs' and sous-chefs' stations; washed dishes, scrubbed tabletops and butcher blocks, emptied buckets of carrot ends and pepper husks and onion skins that would be fed to the estate pigs. In short, I was an errand boy. Under any other circumstances, I would have been irritable at the barrage of simple tasks, but today, I was thankful for the mindless work.

I lost myself in the work and the sea of new faces, watching my temporary boss alternate between barking out orders and sharing jokes with his staff. It was clear they respected him, and that he respected them. As I heard his belly laugh echo against the cabinets and the gleaming windows, I realized why I liked him so much: he reminded me of my grandpa.

Pascal Devereux had shared Max's jovial nature and friendly—if firm—way with his staff. I remembered how he used to bustle around his restaurant kitchen in the French Quarter, a quaint little place down the road from our home, cooking up turtle soup, game pies and oyster gumbo, candied fruits and eggnog, and small fried cakes dusted in sugar. He'd dance along with the jazz band that played on Friday nights, pulling customers from their chairs to join him. Grandpa knew nearly everyone who walked through his door, and those he didn't, he'd made into friends by the end of their meal. He was a man who inspired joy in everyone he met. It felt like only yesterday that we were cooking side by side, tasting another of his new dishes. "You need to feel the recipe, boy," he'd say as he took a bite and closed his eyes. "Stop trying to be so exact about everything." And I *was* exact about everything—I liked things orderly, logical, and as presentable and predictable as possible—a habit born of an absent father and a flighty mother never at home.

As I ruminated on my dear old grandpa and lost myself in memories, I slid into the rhythm of this new kitchen. And silently, I thanked Ryan and Mason for being good friends—for throwing me a life raft when I needed it most.

Chapter 6

Olive

Sandringham Estate, December 1952

The exterior of the house was as impressive as I'd imagined, but not as old and palatial as I'd expected. There was a sense of welcome about it, a homeliness and warmth that made me feel a little less anxious about making a good impression. While my driver, Evans, spoke to someone making a delivery, I took the opportunity to check my reflection in the wing mirror of the car. The cold had brought a healthy glow to my cheeks and nose. My hair still looked nice. The winter light was flattering. I straightened the locket that hung from my necklace; something old for good luck. I rehearsed a confident smile, determined to make this unexpected opportunity count for something.

I watched as a rather sour-faced man dictated orders to a pair of young porters struggling with a Fortnum & Mason hamper that had just been delivered.

He eyed me warily and began to walk toward me. "Can I help you, miss?" he asked. He carried the same look Charlie Bullen gave to people he considered his subordinates.

"Oh, I'm with Evans. Well, not *with* him! He drove me from the train station. We're to find a Mrs. Leonard, I believe?"

"And you are?"

"Olive Carter, sir. I'm with the BBC. I'm here to report on the Christmas presents—I mean, *preparations*." I laughed at my mistake. "Sorry. I'm a little nervous!"

Mr. Sour-Face looked over my shoulder. "Is Bullen joining you?"

I leaned forward and lowered my voice. "I'm afraid Mr. Bullen is unwell. I'm here in his place."

Sour-Face stared at me. "I see. I presume you're his . . . secretary, perhaps?"

A little piece of my festive bubble burst. It was always the same—the assumption that a woman's only possible role could be to support a more important man. I wondered if the queen had to put up with this tiresome attitude.

"Actually, I'm a reporter. The BBC is modernizing, Mr. . . ."

"Andrews."

I held out my hand. "Well, Mr. Andrews, it was very nice to meet you." He shook my hand, although I could tell that it almost killed him to do so. "Are those two all right, by the way?" I asked, peering over his shoulder. "Did Fortnum and Mason send a hamper of bricks?"

The hamper was now firmly wedged in a narrow side door. The two porters had decided to assess the situation over a cigarette.

Just then, Evans made his way back over to me. "Sorry about that. Old pal from the war. Haven't seen him in an age!" He looked at Sour-Face and offered a curt greeting. "Andrews."

"Evans."

The frostiness between them was painfully evident and terribly awkward.

"Ah, and right on cue, here's Mrs. Leonard." Evans called to a woman passing by the open door on the inside. "BBC for you, Eleanor! Shall I send her in?"

The woman peered around the door. Finally, a friendly face. "If she can *get* in. Yes!" As she spoke, two dogs barreled past her. "Susan! Sugar! Honestly, these two are like giddy children! If I don't trip over one of them and break my neck, it will be a Christmas miracle!"

"Hectic today, isn't it?" Evans called back.

"When is it not?"

The two of them exchanged a shy smile that suggested they wanted to chat further.

Sour-Face huffed out a breath, muttered something, and strode away. I wondered if Mrs. Leonard was the source of their disagreement, and, if so, I immediately took Evans's side.

"Right then," Evans said, turning his attention back to me. "I'll leave you in the very capable hands of Mrs. Leonard. And try to relax, miss. They don't bite!"

"The corgis?"

"The royal family!"

I stepped, inelegantly, over the stuck hamper, exchanged a flirtatious smile with the better-looking of the two porters, and finally, I was inside. I was actually inside Sandringham House!

I'd expected stuffy silence and footmen carrying gleaming trays of champagne, but what I found was bustle and noise as a heavy-set woman pushed a noisy vacuum cleaner over a large rug, and other staff putting up curtains and tending to arrangements of flowers. It was a house in disarray, just like every house in the run-up to Christmas. I stood to one side to make room for a large portrait being carried by two men in gray aprons and flat caps. Perhaps not so much like every house after all.

Mrs. Leonard offered a welcoming hand. "Eleanor Leonard. Frazzled housekeeper! Very pleased to meet you, Miss Carter. We were expecting you."

"You were?"

She smiled. "Of course, dear. The palace press secretary informed us yesterday evening that you would be covering the BBC piece this year instead of Mr. Bullen. Poor Charlie. I do hope he recovers. He'll be terribly missed. It seems as if everything will be different this year, but nothing stands still, does it, even if we might dearly wish it to." She seemed to get lost in her thoughts for a moment. "Anyway, it's lovely to have you, and we'll make the best of it. Please, follow me."

We walked through several rooms, all tastefully furnished with comfortable-looking chairs and elegant sofas. My eyes flitted from left to right, mesmerized by enormous gilt-framed portraits of deceased royals and an entire cabinet of gleaming jade ornaments and Fabergé eggs. Next, we passed through a room that resembled something belonging to French aristocracy, decorated in delicate pastel colors of greens and pinks and furnished with ornate chairs and settees, then continued through a corridor filled with cabinets of guns. It was an intriguing mixture of country house and museum.

I imagined Lucy beside me, armed with a barrage of questions. She was such an inquisitive child, keen to understand the world and all its mysteries. I always answered her as honestly and fully as I could, partly because I'd been an inquisitive child myself and understood her thirst for knowledge, but mostly because I knew the inevitable day would come when I would have to tell her the truth about her father. And when it did, I'd promised myself I would answer all the questions she might have.

"It's not a bit like I'd expected," I remarked, turning my focus back to my present surroundings.

Mrs. Leonard laughed. "Not quite the grand palace or turreted castle, is it! Catches everyone by surprise."

We had just reached a room Mrs. Leonard called the Long Library, when a rather harassed-looking young woman hurried over to us.

"'Scuse me, Mrs. Leonard. Could you spare a minute? Nancy's taken a tumble off the ladder."

"Heavens! I told her to wait until I got back!" Mrs. Leonard turned to me. "Take a seat in the library, Miss Carter. I'm so sorry. I won't be long."

She was an age. I twiddled my thumbs until I was convinced she'd forgotten about me, then decided to go and look for her.

I wandered back through several rooms, until I came across the woman with the vacuum cleaner. "Excuse me. Hello! I'm from the BBC! Do you have a moment?"

I had to shout above the noise of the vacuum cleaner until she switched it off. "What's that you say?"

"I'm from the BBC. I'm doing a report on preparations for Christmas at Sandringham—for a special program on the wireless. What is it you do here?" My pencil was poised over my notepad.

She stared at me as if I were the Ghost of Christmas Past. "What do I do here?"

I nodded encouragingly. Perhaps she was hard of hearing. "Your job? What is it like to work here? Have you ever met the queen?"

She shook her head and switched the vacuum cleaner back on as I jumped to one side to stop her vacuuming my shoes.

I tried again with the florist. "Hello! I'm with the BBC. I'm doing a piece . . ."

She turned to me and smiled. "Sorry, love. I'm ever so busy—have to get these finished and then a dozen more to do. You couldn't pass me that spray of eucalyptus, could you?"

I wasn't sure which was the eucalyptus—flowery things all looked and smelled the same to me—so I passed her a few green things, wished her a happy Christmas as an afterthought, and wandered back to the safety of the library, my notepad blank.

This wasn't going to be as easy as I'd thought it would be. Not getting in the way was virtually impossible, and everyone was too busy to explain what they were doing. I was also starving. Deflated and tired from the journey, I sank into a chair in a little alcove beside the fireplace and waited for something interesting to happen.

Mrs. Leonard eventually returned, full of apologies and a rather grim story about Nancy's broken ankle. She tipped her head in the direction of another door. "Have you eaten? Or been offered so much as a cup of tea?"

I shook my head. "Neither. But I don't want to intrude. Everyone's clearly very busy."

"I'm so sorry. You must think us terribly rude. It's been one of those days, I'm afraid. Come with me. We might as well start in the kitchens. Truth be told, that's where the heart of this home sits anyway. Same as any other, I suppose. If you want to know about the royal family—about *any* family—you need to start there."

I smiled. It was true. All the Carter family dramas seemed to play out in the kitchen. It was the place where we came together, where we sat down to eat, where we talked about our day, where new boyfriends sat through their first agonizing experience of a Carter family gathering. It was where we laughed and cried, where birthdays were celebrated, where friends and neighbors gathered during happy moments and sad ones. Above all, our kitchen was the place where I had shared a pot of tea with my father and listened to his warm gentle wisdom as I nursed a hangover or a broken heart.

While I didn't expect to find the queen in Sandringham's kitchens having a heart-to-heart with someone over a pot of tea, I still hoped to find some insight there into her tastes and traditions, and into the hearts and minds of the men and women who worked in the royal kitchens. What did it take to cook for the queen?

I would take the required notes for Charlie Bullen's predictable report, but there was nothing to stop me preparing a separate piece of my own. A short piece on the queen's dining choices would keep Tom Harding happy, but an inside scoop on the royal chefs would surely be more interesting for our listeners. As I followed Mrs. Leonard down a long corridor, I scribbled a note on my pad: *A MENU FOR A MONARCH—Olive Carter discovers the secrets of the chefs behind the royal Christmas feast.*

Chapter 7

Jack

After luncheon had been served to the family, it was the staff's turn to break, so I joined Mason at the table. We ate our fill of a simple vegetable soup with bread, tea and biscuits, and headed outside. Cool, damp air swirled around us, a nice change from the heat of the kitchens.

Mason shook loose a cigarette from a half-empty packet. "How's it going?"

"Fine, fine," I said. "Max seems like a nice guy."

"He is," Mason agreed, blowing a stream of smoke through his teeth. "He has high standards, but he's the salt of the earth."

"He reminds me of my grandfather," I said, leaning against the outer brick wall.

"Oh yeah? The one who owned a restaurant?"

"The one and only," I replied. "He was good-natured. An enormous man, with a booming laugh. He taught me everything I know about the spice and flavor combinations of Creole cooking, and the way it melds many kinds of cuisines together."

I looked out at the thick carpet of grass that still glistened with dewdrops. Blue sky peeked between the dissipating clouds. I missed Grandpa so much, missed his steady guidance and encouragement. I thought of Andrea then, and how she'd never had the chance to meet him. She would have loved him so much. The hollow ache in my chest began to spread again.

"I joined the US Navy soon after he died," I added quickly, forcing down the emotions before they threatened to overwhelm me. "Haven't been back home since."

"Let me guess. You were running away. Putting some distance between you and your memories of him?"

"Something like that, yes."

I hadn't expected to find my calling in life peeling mounds of potatoes during a war, but I'd found it there, wedged between the mess hall tents at camp and aboard our ship. I should have known that I would eventually follow in the footsteps of the man who'd guided me for most of my life.

My world had upended when Grandpa died of a heart attack. Mom had closed his restaurant instantly, said it must be sold because we were steeped in debt. Whether it was her, or Grandpa, who was steeped in debt was unclear. She sold the restaurant and his home without consulting me—and set me adrift. I'd wandered aimlessly from job to job, until one particularly swampy summer day I found myself on the doorstep of the US Navy recruitment office, volunteering for the construction and support unit, the Seabees. I was quickly relegated to cooking duty. It was hard to believe I'd spent four years cooking for the US Navy and seven more cheffing in London. I'd always been a cook, just like Grandpa, and I always would be.

"And London after the war?" Mason dragged on his rapidly dwindling cigarette.

I nodded. "I didn't intend to stay, but life has plans for us all, doesn't it."

I'd been glad to settle across the ocean, as far away as possible from the reminder of what I'd lost and the disappointments of a mother who cared about no one but her latest sponge of a boyfriend. And then I'd found a new family with Andrea and thought I'd never have to doubt or worry again.

"Our gain then."

I warmed to Mason's kindness. We weren't exactly friends, but we had known each other for years through Ryan. "Thanks," I said. "Mine, too."

He flicked his cigarette butt to the ground and crushed it with his shoe. "I started out as a dishwasher, then somehow wound up at a culinary school in Paris, like the rest of that lot in there." He motioned to the building behind him. "After the war, I applied to join His Majesty's staff, and next thing you know, it's been seven years."

"Ever wanted to work somewhere else? Have your own place?" I asked.

He shrugged. "Wouldn't that be the dream! I don't know where, or how I'd ever manage the costs though."

"Restaurants don't come cheap. Grandpa was always struggling to make ends meet. I still have his recipe books. I'd hoped to have my own place one day, give his dishes another try."

"Hoped?"

I nodded. "A lot of things have changed recently."

Andrea had been such an integral part of my dreams. It felt as though they had all died with her.

I turned my face to the sun, closing my eyes. I didn't know where I'd go from here, after Christmas. The thought of returning to my old life in London paralyzed me. Walking the same streets where I'd held Andrea's hand, passing the flower shop where she'd worked, seeing my own grief reflected in Mrs. Howard's eyes—it would be too much. But neither could I imagine returning to New Orleans, a place that had lost all meaning for me since Grandpa's passing. Both former iterations of my life felt impossible.

After meeting Andrea, I had never imagined that I'd feel lost again, and yet, here I was, as lost as ever. What I wouldn't give to talk to Grandpa now, about all of this; about Andrea. If he were here, he'd tell me what to do, show me the way through.

I swallowed hard against the grief that hovered at the edge of every conversation, every thought. Suddenly overcome, I leaned against the brick wall for support.

Mason studied my face and reached out, cupping my shoulder for the second time that day. "Take a moment. I'll see you inside."

I wiped at my eyes and worked to steady my breathing, forced myself to think about the tasks ahead. Eventually, my hands stopped shaking. With a deep breath, I joined the others indoors.

Over the next few hours, I busied myself in the steamy kitchen, doing every task asked of me with precision and diligence, moving from the sandwiches for afternoon tea to the dishes on the dinner menu. I focused on my work, kept my head down—even when a visitor arrived.

The woman and her escort were an unwelcome interruption when we were all so busy. They seemed to be in everyone's way, and the prattle of her endless questions clearly irritated everyone, given their clipped answers. I hoped she'd take the hint and not bother me.

I was glad I was a nobody, a temporary if helpful pair of hands, not a person worth interviewing. The last thing I wanted was to force polite interactions with this stranger, especially when I scarcely knew the operations of the kitchens myself. Besides, I didn't have the wherewithal. It was hard enough keeping myself together as it was.

Eventually, I heard Max take charge in a firm but fair tone, letting them know it really wasn't a good time for visitors.

"Good luck, miss, and happy Christmas," Max added as the woman left the kitchen.

I glanced over my shoulder at her retreating back, glad to be left to the rhythm of my work.

Chapter 8

Olive

We left the kitchens within five minutes, finding everyone far too busy to answer my questions. We'd only been under everyone's feet. Far from the inside scoop I'd imagined, I'd barely written a handful of notes. For all of Sandringham's warm welcome, procedures and protocol were closely guarded secrets. Far from impressing Tom Harding and proving something to Charlie Bullen, I would be lucky if I returned with anything more than a summary of Charlie's pieces from the last few years, but with "the queen" substituted for "the king."

Mrs. Leonard apologized for the brusque manner of the kitchen staff. "I'm very sorry, Miss Carter. They take their work ever so seriously, and don't take kindly to strangers wandering around. They're usually a little more accommodating, but they're very short-staffed at the moment, so their time is precious."

"Are all chefs so grumpy and serious?" I asked as Mrs. Leonard deposited me in front of a crackling log fire in the library.

"Most I've met, yes!" She fluffed a few cushions on the sofa. "The kitchen is like their church, their recipes and processes sacred."

I scribbled a note on my pad. *Kitchen = church. Recipes = sacred. Chefs = insufferable.*

"Now, you make yourself comfortable here. I'll send someone out with that tea, and some of those delicious scones that have just come out of the oven. We'll finish the rest of your tour once you've had a chance to revive yourself a little."

I tried to forget where I was and concentrated on writing up my notes, sparse as they were. I scribbled a few sentences about the busy atmosphere in the kitchen, the inviting warmth of the house, the pristine whites the chefs wore, and then I added some of the details Evans had told me about the estate's small army of gamekeepers, gardeners, and farmers, as well as workers on the sawmill and its apple juice pressing plant.

If I couldn't get any real insight into the royal family, I wondered if there might be some interest in a piece about how Sandringham supported the local community. That it wasn't all "them and us" and that there was more of a sense of collaboration here, not simply the formality and distance we'd come to associate with the royal family. I filled a page, so lost in my thoughts that I didn't hear someone enter the room.

I nearly jumped out of my skin when a cough came from behind me. Presuming it was Mrs. Leonard returning with the tea and scones, I turned.

But it wasn't Mrs. Leonard.

It was her.

Queen Elizabeth.

My heart raced beneath my cardigan. I stood up and attempted a curtsey, which ended in an ungainly wobble. "Ma'am. Your Majesty."

Without missing a beat, she offered a polite "Hello," and proceeded to look for a book.

I tried desperately not to stare at her. She was dressed in a sensible tweed skirt, biscuit-colored jumper, and simple flat shoes. She was far more beautiful in person than in the many photographs

I'd seen in which she looked regal, but distant and cold. Up close, she radiated the beauty of a young woman in her prime. She carried a surprising warmth and a vibrant energy.

"I don't believe we've met," she said as she ran her fingertips along a row of spines. "It's hard to keep track of everyone at this time of year."

I wanted to tell her that we *had* met, for the briefest moment, on VE Day, but I knew that she wouldn't even have noticed someone like me.

"Olive Carter, ma'am," I said. "With the BBC."

At this, she glanced in my direction. "I see. Are you doing a piece on me?" She pulled a book from the shelf and thumbed through it.

"I'm doing a piece on the Christmas preparations," I offered. I was so stunned to be in her company that I could hardly speak. I started to fiddle with my necklace. A nervous habit.

"Oh yes. They do that every year. They usually send a man, though. Bullen, isn't it?"

"Yes. Charlie Bullen. Unfortunately, he's unwell. Struck down by the fog."

At this, she looked up. "Oh dear. I am sorry to hear that. Most unfortunate for him, but it is always rather nice to have another woman about the place."

"Yes, ma'am. I expect it is."

She called the corgis after her and left as quickly as she'd arrived. "Do make sure they show you the tree," she added over her shoulder. "It really is a beauty this year."

I nodded. "I will. Thank you, ma'am."

I sank down onto the chair and quickly scribbled some notes to capture our interaction, her mannerisms and demeanor—and yet, having imagined this moment so many times, I couldn't help feeling a little deflated by our brief interaction. She'd been perfectly polite, but had maintained a clear distance, physically and emotionally. It was going to be much harder to crack the hard shell of royal formality than I'd imagined.

I took a few deep breaths to calm down, and checked the clasp on my necklace to make sure it hadn't become loose again after all my fiddling.

I'd had little more than a few minutes to process what had just happened when I heard more footsteps approach and someone clearing their throat as they entered the room.

"They asked me to bring you this."

The accent was instantly familiar. My stomach lurched; my heart began to race. It couldn't be him. It couldn't possibly be him.

Not here. Not now.

I turned around. "Jack? Jack Devereux?"

He stood in the doorway, dressed in chef whites, carrying a tray of tea things. I couldn't believe he was standing there, right in front of me. After all the years, all the hours I'd spent thinking about him, wondering and questioning—and here he was, as if he'd always just been in the next room, waiting to bring me tea and scones.

"What on earth are you doing here?" I asked.

His face was a picture of shock and disbelief, as I knew mine was. "Olive Carter? I don't believe it! What the hell are *you* doing here?"

I stood up, my heart racing beneath my cardigan. We looked at each other for what felt like an age, memories and surprise filling an awkward silence as time seemed to slip away and a handsome young man in uniform was asking me to dance on VE Day. He was still handsome, but he looked different. Older, definitely. Dark circles beneath his eyes carried a trace of too many late nights. There was a weariness about him, his shoulders hunched, his eyes reluctant to meet mine.

"You first," I said. "What *are* you doing at Sandringham?"

He placed the tray on the table in front of me. "Serving tea to the visitors apparently."

"You've gone up in the world then," I said with a touch of a smile. "You were peeling potatoes and washing dishes the last I heard." I took a deep breath, desperate to compose myself. I couldn't let him see how much his unexpected appearance had unsettled me. So many thoughts raced through my mind as I poured myself a cup of tea and spilled half of it on my skirt in the process.

"Still as clumsy as ever, I see," he said.

"Still as annoying as ever," I countered.

At this, he cracked a half smile. I remembered Jack's smile, although it had usually been aimed in Andrea Keane's direction.

He pulled a cloth from the belt of his apron. "Here. For the spill. White vinegar will get out the stain. Stop by the kitchen later. I'll fix you up with some."

I took the cloth and dabbed at the tea stain on my skirt, embarrassed. "Thank you."

"It's really good to see you, Olive. It's been . . . what, six, seven years?"

"Seven," I replied. The dates were imprinted on my mind.

"A long time, anyway," he said.

"A long time," I agreed.

Long enough to believe that I'd left those years—and him—behind forever. Long enough to leave me questioning everything now that he was here again.

"So, what brings you to Norfolk?" I asked. "Got tired of cooking for the peasants?" I was nervous and fidgety and found myself playing with the locket on my chain.

"I'm just helping out for the Christmas season," he said. "All very last minute. You?"

"Same. I'm filling in for someone. The man who usually covers the royal family at Christmas is laid up sick. Lungs affected by the fog. Awful, wasn't it." I poured milk into my cup. "I'm writing a piece about the Christmas preparations. Any juicy tidbits you can share with me? Shocking secrets? Scandalous gossip? Secret recipes? A quote from famous royal chef, Jack Devereux?" I was talking too much. "I'm at the BBC now," I added.

"The hallowed BBC. You got there after all. You always said you would."

He'd remembered. He'd remembered our conversations, the hopes and dreams we'd shared in companionable moments.

I wondered what else he remembered. How much he remembered.

I poured milk into my cup and added a lump of sugar, even though I didn't take sugar. Stirring the tea gave me something to do with my hands. "How's Andrea keeping?" I asked as I took a sip of tea and almost burned my mouth in the process.

At this, Jack seemed to falter.

I took another slurp of tea. "Is she still pretending to be Eliza Doolittle? Selling 'er flowers?" I laughed at my cockney accent, trying to break the unbearably awkward silence.

"Andrea passed away earlier this month."

My hand flew to my throat. "What? Oh God, Jack. I'm so sorry."

Andrea was dead? I couldn't believe it. I hadn't been especially close to her during the brief time I'd known her, but it was shocking to hear, nonetheless. Now I understood why he no longer resembled the assured Jack Devereux I'd known. He was a man haunted by grief. A man mourning his wife—the woman he'd loved from the moment he first set eyes on her.

"That's terrible news. Was she ill?"

He shook his head. "A traffic accident. In the fog."

To lose his wife in such a tragic way . . . my sympathy deepened.

"I'm so sorry," I said, stumbling over my words. "You must be devastated. I know how special she was to you."

He looked at me for a moment as he cleared his throat. "She was special to everyone who knew her. She had a sparkle about her . . ." His words trailed off. "Anyway, I'd better get back to it."

I nodded. "Of course." I returned the cloth to him. "It's good to see you again, Jack."

It really was, and yet I was so muddled and confused. I'd often wondered what I would say if I ever saw him again, what I would feel. But now I only had more questions than answers.

"It's good to see you, too, Olive." He turned and made his way to the door, where he paused and looked over his shoulder.

Before I could say anything else, he rushed off.

I sank down onto the sofa, all thoughts of my piece on the royal preparations suddenly irrelevant. Jack was here, and Andrea was dead. I couldn't believe it—couldn't believe any of it. Mostly, I couldn't believe that Jack Devereux had waltzed back into my life as suddenly and unexpectedly as he'd waltzed into it all those years ago.

Chapter 9

Jack

London, 8 May 1945

After three long and tumultuous years with the Seabees' construction battalion of the US Navy, the glorious news finally reached us that Germany had officially surrendered. As luck would have it, we were docked for repairs in Portsmouth when the news was announced. A group of fellow Navy boys and I took no time to rush to London after the announcement. Soon, we joined the mass of humanity gathered in Trafalgar Square. Victory in Europe Day, in London—it was a day I'd never forget. Every person around me was delirious with relief and joy, coupled with a deep reverence—every toast, every grateful epithet dedicated to all the dear ones we had lost. We cheered, we cried, we prayed in thanks. At last, the darkest chapter of our lives was coming to an end.

We pushed our way through the crowd, carousing with people in the streets, making our way from pub to pub. Every place was packed; people clinked beer glasses or bubbling flutes of champagne; music blared from the wireless, and anyone with an instrument struck up a song.

Eventually, we found ourselves at The Pelican Club. A full

swing band played as couples crowded the dance floor. My friends flowed from our table to the bar and then to the main floor, dancing with this woman and that woman. I watched from a distance, envying their confidence. I was a quiet sort of person, serious and sensitive. Always had been, since I was a boy. My awkward invitations, and the likelihood of rejection, kept me firmly planted at the edge of the dance floor, and at the edge of all the fun.

Peter Hall, a lieutenant and a friend of a friend, found my hesitation amusing. "Go on, mate. Get stuck in. Why are you always such a chicken?" He enjoyed ribbing me for no good reason, and I avoided him as much as I could. "Ask a girl to dance. With so many here tonight, someone is bound to take pity on you and say yes."

I gave him the middle finger.

He laughed uproariously and sauntered off, quickly connecting with a brunette on the other side of the room.

I sipped my drink and looked out over the crowd. An auburn-haired woman in a lemon-yellow dress threw back her head and laughed at something her friend said. She was attractive, but the way she radiated joy made her absolutely captivating.

Ryan Harris, a Royal Navy boy and a buddy of mine, clapped me on the shoulder. "You should go and talk to her." He lifted two fingers at the barman, who rapidly pushed two pints in our direction.

I took a large gulp of my beer. I didn't know why I became so tongue-tied and stiff around women. I shrugged. "Nah, I'm fine here."

"Don't overthink it," Ryan replied and took a big swig of his pint. "She's looking at you. Now's your chance, old pal!"

I glanced her way several more times, but rather than approach her, I kept pace with the boys at the bar, following the pint with a gin and tonic or two. Eventually, my reserve grew fuzzy around

HAZEL GAYNOR & HEATHER WEBB

the edges. Emboldened by the booze and the exuberance of the night, I wound my way toward the girl in the yellow dress and tapped her on the shoulder.

"Hello. Want to dance?"

She laughed. "I *am* dancing."

"With me, I mean."

She grinned, reached for my hands, and pulled me onto the packed dance floor. "So, what's your name, sailor?"

"Jack. Jack Devereux," I shouted over the music.

"Olive Carter," she said, smiling again. "You a Yank?"

"How did you guess?" I grinned. "I'm from the south. A New Orleans boy, through and through."

"I've heard southern boys are gentlemen. Is that true?"

"I guess you'll have to see for yourself."

We danced to one song after another, occasionally bumping elbows with couples next to us, all the while trying to talk over the noise. She worked in a typing pool for some government ministry or other but had aspirations to work for the BBC. She talked a lot, and then apologized for talking too much and asked about me.

I told her I'd grown up in New Orleans, volunteered for the Navy as a Seabee, and now here I was and the war was over, and I had no idea what to do next. We laughed when I didn't turn her as tightly as I should, and when she stamped on my feet. She told me her nickname at work was Calamity Carter, on account of her clumsiness. I couldn't stop laughing around this woman, as bright as sunshine with her warm smile and red lips.

As we stumbled around the dance floor together, I felt a lightness I hadn't felt in so long.

"What are you grinning at?" she said, laughing.

"Not sure! I think I've forgotten what it feels like to be happy."

She leaned toward me to reply, just as a friend grabbed her arm and said everyone was going to Trafalgar Square to dance in the fountain.

"Come with us!" Olive said.

It was that kind of evening—impulsive and wild.

I was happy to tag along and see where the night, and Olive Carter, took me.

Chapter 10

Olive

London, 8 May 1945

Nobody could quite believe it when the news came down the wires that the war in Europe was over. We'd hoped for the moment for so long that, when it came, the reality seemed too impossible to fully trust.

Within minutes, the traffic outside the office windows came to a standstill. Drivers tooted their horns and ran into the street, abandoning their vehicles and throwing their hats into the air. Passersby stopped to ask what had happened and hugged each other as they were told the news. The joy was infectious. Even our miserable supervisor said we could finish for the day to celebrate. We didn't need asking twice. Typewriters were covered, handbags gathered, hats and coats pulled from the stand as we ran, laughing and nattering, heels click-clacking down the three flights of stairs at Whitehall Place.

Outside, I'd never seen such an outpouring of joy, never felt such immense relief or such a sense of hope and optimism.

"It's over, Rosie! It's finally bloody over!"

Rosie, my dearest friend, linked her arm through mine and planted a crimson kiss on my cheek. "Victory, at last! I need a drink! Come on."

The cautious grim stoicism of the last six years seemed to wash away in an instant. We laughed as men in military uniform and others in business suits grabbed our hands and twirled us around in an impromptu dance in the street. We had no plan, no curfew, nowhere to go and nothing to do but celebrate. Nothing was off limits. Everything was possible again.

A group of four Navy men insisted we accompany them to a jazz club where they bought us gin and tonics like they were going out of fashion. The music soared and the crowd swayed in a magnetic pulse. The gin went to my head as my feet led me to the dance floor.

We danced with anyone and everyone—jitterbugs and jives, fast and free. This was no time for a slow waltz. A tanned fair-haired American caught my eye across the bar. I smiled and twirled in my yellow dress. It was a tatty old thing, patched up and repaired more times than I could remember, but the color had always made me smile.

"He keeps looking at you!" Rosie said as we made our way back from the ladies'.

"He does, doesn't he!"

I was in a carefree, flirtatious mood. When the American eventually invited me to dance with him, I laughed and pulled him onto the dance floor and draped my hands loosely around his neck. I liked the way he smiled, the way he looked at me with his green eyes, the way we moved together, the way he spoke.

His name was Jack Devereux and he was from New Orleans. Head spinning, heart full, I wanted him to kiss me, but he seemed shy and a little formal as he told me about his role as a Seabee volunteer in the US Navy. I was about to tell him to shut up and kiss me, for God's sake, when Rosie grabbed my arm.

"We're all going to Trafalgar Square to dance in the fountain!"

She looked at me, and then at Jack. "Hello! I'm Rosie. And she's coming with me."

He laughed. "Hello, back!"

"Bring him along, Liv," Rosie said as we left the dance floor. "Everyone's going."

"Who's everyone?" Jack asked as I pulled him along with me.

"*Everyone!*" I laughed. "Come with us!"

In a few moments, half the club seemed to have been scooped up by someone or other, like links in a chain that moved as one.

Outside the heavy press of the club, London was intoxicating. The air crackled with exuberant singing, impulsive cheers and laughter. Thousands of people were gathered in Trafalgar Square. We kicked off our shoes and rolled down our stockings and ran through the crowds into the fountain. An attractive woman of around my age laughed as she slipped and grabbed my hand to steady herself.

"Whoops! Sorry! Nearly took us both for a swim there."

"Don't worry about it," I said. "Don't worry about anything, anymore."

We both laughed.

"I'm Andrea," she said, shouting above the noise. "I've lost my friends."

"Olive," I replied. "Stick with us. We're your friends now."

Eventually, a policeman ushered us out of the fountain. We put our shoes back on, stuffed our rolled-up stockings into our coat pockets, and set off in a conga line. Rosie's hands held my waist. In front, I held onto Jack Devereux. In front of him was the new girl, Andrea, and then others we'd collected along the way. At one point, the line fell apart. We all linked up again, grabbing the closest person to us—and when I turned to the person behind me, I gasped.

It was, unmistakably, Princess Elizabeth and her sister, Princess

Margaret, behind her. As a mad royalist, I'd know their faces anywhere.

"Is it really you?" I asked.

The young woman smiled, and then she was gone, swept up in the crowd as if she were any normal young woman, not the heir to the throne.

"Rosie! Did you see?"

"See what?"

"Princess Elizabeth! She was right here!"

Rosie laughed. "Don't be daft. You've had too much gin! Come on. We're going dancing again. Someone knows a place out Camden way."

We danced all night, moving among each other like moths fluttering between electric lights, drawn to the flicker and hum of everyone else. Somehow, six of us had ended up sticking together— Rosie and me, Andrea from the fountain, and Jack from the jazz club, along with two of his Navy friends. In the early hours, someone suggested we climb Primrose Hill to watch the sunrise. We made a rag-tag group by then—makeup smudged, hair asunder, ties undone, shirtsleeves rolled up.

At the top of the hill, we spread coats and jackets out like blankets and lay down to watch the sky. Someone had champagne. Someone else had cigarettes. We all had the infectious enthusiasm of youth and beauty, our optimism as wide and endless as the just-lightening sky above.

As dawn bloomed and the first amber rays of sun spread their fingers wide across Regent's Park and the city beyond, Rosie pulled a Kodak camera from her handbag.

"Come on," she said. "A photograph to capture a new dawn. The first day of the rest of our lives!"

Rosie took a few snaps, and then Andrea insisted she take a photograph of us all. We wrapped arms around each other's shoulders as we bunched up so that everyone could fit. It was such a beautiful moment, a snapshot of perfect happiness captured in the golden rays of a glorious sunrise.

"Everybody smile!" Andrea said.

As the camera shutter clicked, I glanced over at Jack, but his eyes were fixed firmly on the camera, or perhaps on the woman behind the camera, I wasn't sure.

"One more for luck!" Andrea called.

I held my shoulders back and put on my brightest smile. The war was finally over, and the rest of my life beckoned on the horizon.

Chapter 11

Jack

Sandringham Estate, December 1952

Icouldn't believe that Olive Carter was here. I hadn't seen her for years, and then, out of the blue, there she was, sitting on a sofa in the library at Sandringham as if she lived there. I'd always liked Olive. It was nice to see an old friend, a connection to happier days. I considered returning to the library to ask how long she was staying, but the clock was ticking, and I had plenty to do.

As I returned to the kitchens, I thought back to the day we'd first met all those years ago. A handful of months later, she'd vanished from our circle of friends, never to be heard from again. I wondered what her story was, how she'd filled the years since.

I paused outside the door to the kitchens, Olive's expression flickering behind my eyes. Shock and sadness had passed over her face when I'd told her about Andrea, but there was something else, too. A distant faraway look, as if she was staring into the past, even as she looked directly at me. Whatever it had meant, I pushed it aside, and tried to focus on my tasks.

But seeing Olive had stirred long-forgotten memories. As I worked, I couldn't stop falling back in time, remembering Olive and the circle of friends we'd made on VE Day, and those first weeks I'd spent with Andrea, so filled with hope and possibility. How happy we were. As emotion rushed up my throat, I squeezed my eyes closed, willing my thoughts elsewhere. I'd never get through the day if I dreamed of her, if I longed for her, if I allowed the pain to overtake me.

By the time I was finished with my duties for the day, it was late and I was exhausted.

Mason drove me back to Ryan's house. "Well, you survived day one! They're not a bad bunch really."

"I've worked with worse, that's for sure."

"See you bright and early tomorrow."

"Thanks for the lift. See you tomorrow."

I was careful to close the front door softly behind me so as not to wake little Ivy. On the table, Maggie had left a covered plate of meat pie made with potatoes and vegetables and stout, and a small serving of beef she must have bought with the ration coupons she'd been saving. Lately there had been talk of rationing coming to an end, and it would be a relief for us all. At Sandringham, things were more relaxed, although Max had told me the queen still insisted that formal meals—often comprising dozens of courses—be scaled back considerably.

"Hello there." Maggie trundled into the kitchen, already in her slippers and dressing gown. Ryan followed. "You must be exhausted." She put the kettle on to boil.

"I am," I said between mouthfuls of the pie. "I'm looking forward to a bath and a good sleep."

Ryan pulled out a chair at the table and sat beside me. "How did it all go?"

"Fine. I like the head chef a lot. Nice guy. I spent some time with Mason, too. At least during our breaks."

"Good to have a familiar face about the place, I'm sure."

"It is," I agreed. "He's a good man, your brother."

At this, Ryan smiled. "He's always everyone's favorite!"

Maggie leaned forward and kissed Ryan's cheek. "He's not *my* favorite."

Ryan laughed, reaching for her hand. "I should think not!"

"Eat," Maggie said, scooping another helping of pie onto my plate when I'd finished. "You're too thin."

I didn't argue. I'd barely touched the meal served for the staff earlier. I hadn't had much of an appetite since Andrea's death, but I found myself hungry after a long day's work.

"I bumped into an old friend today," I said. "Caught me completely by surprise."

"Anyone we know?" Ryan asked.

"Not sure you'd remember her. Olive Carter? She was part of the group in London after the war."

Ryan thought for a moment. "Olive? Wasn't she the girl who stepped out with Peter Hall for a while? What is she doing at Sandringham?"

"Peter Hall! I'd forgotten about him. Didn't much like him. Olive is working for the BBC, doing some story on the royal Christmas traditions. It was strange to see her after all this time. Strange, and . . ." I searched for the right word.

"And?"

"And nice, I guess. To see her after all these years. We exchanged a few pleasantries, she spilled tea on herself, and that was that."

Ryan laughed. "Calamity Carter always was a bit of a mess."

Calamity Carter. I'd forgotten the nickname. For the first time in what felt like weeks, I cracked a smile. "That she was."

"I'm glad it went well today. You look like you could do with a drink," Ryan said.

We sat by the fire and talked about old times: the pranks he'd play on his brother during their school days, and my life in New

Orleans. It was surprisingly soothing to reminisce, to think about the time before the war, when things were simpler, before we'd become adults with responsibilities and the kind of ambitions that drove us to distraction.

The day soon caught up with me, and before I knew it, it was midnight, and I couldn't keep my eyes open. Yet, as I laid my head on the pillow, my thoughts persisted. Chatting with Ryan, and seeing Olive earlier, had pulled me back to a time in my life when everything had felt so hopeful and new. Olive had been there that night when I'd first met Andrea. Seeing her again was a jolt, a painful reminder of how quickly the years had passed, and how suddenly life could change.

It was unbearable that Andrea and I had only been given seven years together. We should have had a lifetime.

I willed my mind to be quiet, for sleep to allow my grief to rest for a little while. It had only been such a short time since her death, yet it already felt like a lifetime. How could I possibly endure all the years that spooled ahead without her, without purpose?

I closed my eyes, and waited for the release of sleep, and for morning to come.

Chapter 12

Olive

London, December 1952

My visit to Sandringham wasn't the roaring success I'd hoped it would be, and I was disappointed that I hadn't found any interesting new angles on the royal Christmas. I had nothing refreshing and insightful to present to Tom Harding. Even my additional piece on the royal chefs was rather thin on detail. I should have been happy to have finally met the queen properly after years of sticking pictures of her into my scrapbooks, but even that had been something of a letdown. Even worse, I'd lost my grandmother's locket necklace somewhere on the way home and was annoyed with myself for fiddling with it.

At least Mrs. Leonard had given me some information I could use, and Evans had shared a few extra nuggets on the drive back to the station, although he mostly talked about how wonderful Mrs. Leonard was and how lucky the royal family were to have her.

But far more from anything I'd achieved professionally from my trip to Sandringham, it was my conversation with Jack Devereux that had left the most lasting impression. I still couldn't believe it. After all this time.

Our brief conversation had left me wanting to know so much more: where he'd been, what he'd done in the years since I'd last seen him, whether he and Andrea had a family. Seeing him again had brought everything rushing back: how much I'd enjoyed his company, how much we'd laughed together, the hopes and dreams we'd shared with each other. Jack Devereux was a loose thread on the end of a seam. If I pulled, I didn't know where it would lead, or what I'd unravel in the process. So, I decided not to try. Jack belonged in my past, and that was where he should stay.

Preparing my report for Tom Harding was a welcome distraction from any further thoughts of Jack, but even that wasn't enough to knock Rosie off the scent.

"You're acting funny," she said as I typed up my piece on Sandringham's kitchens and chefs. "What happened at Sandringham? You didn't kiss one of the footmen, did you? *Did* you?"

"No, Rosie. I definitely did *not* kiss one of the footmen!"

"Well, something happened. I can tell. You have that look about you."

I turned to her and pulled a silly face. "What look?"

We both laughed, which earned us a barking reprimand from Maguire. He was in a worse mood than usual.

"Nothing happened," I whispered. "I promise."

Rosie narrowed her eyes at me, clearly unconvinced. I could tell she wasn't going to let it go until I confessed.

"All right then. I bumped into an old friend."

"Which friend? How old? Who was it?" She stared at me, trying to work it out. It didn't take long. "Not . . . *him*?"

I nodded and struck the typewriter keys to spell out J A C K onto the empty drum.

Rosie reached for my arm. "Oh, Olive."

"Carter? Do you have that piece ready yet?"

I flinched as Maguire breathed down my neck, and turned in

my chair. "Just finished. I'll take it up to Mr. Harding now." I turned to Rosie as I gathered up the pages. "We'll talk later."

I was nervous as I knocked on Harding's office door and stepped inside.

"Ah, Carter. How did you get on? Managed to not get yourself thrown into the Tower, I see."

I smiled. "I had an interesting time," I replied. I put the typed pages on his desk. "I hope you like it."

He studied the pages for a moment before reading out the title. "*MENU FOR A MONARCH—BBC royal correspondent, Olive Carter, goes behind-the-scenes of the royal kitchens at Sandringham.*" He peered at me above his spectacles. "Royal correspondent?"

I bit my lip. "I meant to type a new title page. I'm afraid I got a bit carried away—I'm sorry."

He carried on. "*Christmas is about family and tradition: keeping old traditions and establishing new ones. And never has that been truer than for our new queen as she faces her first Christmas as our monarch and prepares to give her first Christmas message from Sandringham, just as her father and grandfather did for many years before her. And, let us not forget, that as well as being our queen, she is a young woman—a wife and mother—facing her first Christmas without her beloved father. But among so much change, some things remain reassuringly the same. The small army of chefs in Sandringham's kitchens are hard at work preparing the many meals the royal family will enjoy over the festive period.*"

Harding put the pages down on the desk. "Take some notes for Bullen. The usual format. Wasn't that the brief?"

"Yes, Mr. Harding, but I met the queen, you see, and . . ."

"You did?"

I nodded. "I felt it was important to emphasize the changes and challenges she faces this Christmas—as a young woman and

73

a new queen—rather than stick with 'the usual format.'" I knew I was on thin ice. Harding was a generous man, but he was no pushover.

"Well, I'll be the judge of that, shall I?"

"Of course. I added all my notes on the usual things at the back." I took a deep breath. "How is Charlie? Any progress?"

"Still sick as a dog."

"Oh. That's a pity." I waited a moment to see if Harding could guess what I was going to ask next. He looked at me, daring me to speak. "I was wondering who will record the piece for the broadcast in his place?"

"I'll find someone." He stood up and took his hat and coat from the stand. "I have to run, or I'll be late for a very important lunch appointment with my wife, and if I've learned anything over thirty years of happy marriage, it is to never leave your dear wife sitting alone at a restaurant table wondering where you are."

I thought about my parents, and how tired their marriage seemed in comparison. I couldn't even remember the last time they'd gone out together. I wondered what sort of marriage I'd have had if things had worked out differently. Would my husband still enjoy taking me out for lunch after thirty years, or would we sit in silence, hardly able to remember why we'd fallen in love in the first place? Rosie was of the firm opinion that it wasn't too late for either of us to find a husband, even though we'd fallen behind most of our friends, who were already married. But, unlike Rosie, my situation was complicated. Any man who fell in love with me would also have to love Lucy, too.

"Carter?"

I stirred from my thoughts and looked at Mr. Harding. He was holding his office door open, waiting for me to leave. "Sorry. I was miles away."

"Still at Sandringham?"

"Maybe?"

"I was thanking you for getting us out of a hole this week," he added. "It's always good to maintain our connections with the royal family."

"Will you use it?" I asked. "My piece?"

He ushered me out of the door. "That'll be all, Carter."

I couldn't shake off the sense of frustration after my meeting with Mr. Harding, or the creeping sense of dread I'd brought back from Sandringham after seeing Jack. As I got off the bus and walked down Buckingham Street toward home, I felt restless and anxious. I stopped to stroke a neighbor's cat, taking a moment to collect my thoughts. I'd made a promise to myself to always leave work behind so that I could give Lucy my full attention. But some things weren't as easily put away or ignored.

I took a deep breath and walked on toward our modest red-brick terrace—"a palace of our own," as my father always said. Number 25 was my safe harbor—the place I always returned to when life threw another storm my way. I envied my friends with homes of their own, but 25 Buckingham Street had become more than my childhood home. It was now Lucy's home, and for that I would always be grateful to my parents, difficult as it was at times to all share the same cramped space.

After chatting with Lucy and admiring some snowflake decorations she'd made out of old newspaper, I put the kettle on. My mother was at her sister's, so it was just the three of us.

"I was thinking earlier, Dad. You should take Mum out somewhere nice for lunch," I said as I added tea leaves to the pot. "Surprise her with an early Christmas present."

He laughed. "*Lunch*! I see. You spend one day at Sandringham and come back all lah-di-dah, with fancy airs and graces."

"Dinner then. It doesn't matter what you call it—I just think it would be nice to do something romantic."

He folded his newspaper over. "I'll take her to The Feathers for a pie and mash supper. How's that? Romantic enough for you?"

I sighed. "I'm sure you can make more of an effort than that. There's a French place near work called Maison Jerome. Why don't I book a table for you both?"

He peered at me over his spectacles. "What are you up to?"

I laughed. "Nothing! I was just thinking. That's all."

He reached for my hand. "I know you're only trying to help, love, but me and your mother are fine. Don't worry about us."

But I did worry. My mother was a difficult woman, but I knew she was doing her best. My father could be stubborn at times, but he had a big heart. Selfishly, I needed them to be happy, because my happiness depended on theirs. Between them, they walked Lucy to and from school, and took care of her when I was at work or when I went out with the girls. Without my parents' support, I would struggle to work, and without work, I would struggle to fulfill the promise I'd made to Lucy: that one day, we would have our very own home, with a tree for her to climb, and a dog to play with in the garden. The simple fact was that my parents allowed me to do a job I couldn't afford to lose, in order to keep a promise I couldn't afford to break.

I called Lucy downstairs. "Come on, you. We're going for a walk."

Lucy loved our evening walks when I got home from work, just the two of us. Well, almost just the two of us.

"Can Alfie come too?" she asked as she ran downstairs.

Alfie was Lucy's imaginary dog, conjured to replace the actual dog she desperately wanted and which we couldn't have on account of my mother being allergic to dog hair—or so she claimed.

"Of course he can." I made a performance out of fetching an

imaginary lead and attaching it to an imaginary collar. "Hurry up then. He's busting for a wee."

Lucy laughed, and my heart smiled in response. I wasn't good at many things, but being Lucy's mother was one of them, even if I'd once doubted myself and been terrified of raising a child on my own. I often wondered if she was missing out by not having a father in her life, but I did my best to fill the gap. I had never lied to Lucy about her father, reserving my "dead husband" story for nosy parkers, and those outside my close circle of immediate family—and Rosie—but she had said things once or twice that made me realize she assumed he had died. She knew plenty of children at school whose fathers had died in the war, so it seemed quite natural to her that if she had no father, that was the reason why. I knew she would inevitably ask more questions as she grew older, and might want to know more about him one day. It was a day I dreaded. A day that felt suddenly much closer.

Wrapped in coats and hats, gloves and scarves, we walked along the terraced streets and found our favorite bench in the park. We took turns to look for the constellations, tipping our necks back as we searched out the distinctive shapes.

"Do you think we'll see Father Christmas and his sleigh?" Lucy asked as she leaned into my shoulder.

"Not tonight, darling. It isn't Christmas Eve yet. He'll be getting ready at the North Pole. Wrapping up all the presents." I pulled her hat over her eyes. "And no peeking! Have you written your list yet?"

"I'm almost finished." She swung her legs beneath the bench, hesitating for a moment before she turned to look at me. "Can Father Christmas really bring anything you ask for?"

I chose my words carefully. "Well, he's very clever. I think he brings children the things they'll like the most, and maybe some of the things they need, too."

"I think I might have asked for something even Father Christmas can't bring."

I pulled her close to my side. "Oh? Well, let's make a wish and see what he can do."

Lucy wasn't the only one with a difficult request for Father Christmas that year. I closed my eyes and wished for my parents to fall in love again, for better opportunities at work, and, most of all, for someone to love me the way Tom Harding loved his wife.

And none of that could be easily wrapped and placed under the tree.

Chapter 13

Jack

Sandringham Estate, December 1952

The days passed in a blur as I raced around the kitchen at Sandringham for endless hours, barely noticing anyone, or anything, outside of my tasks. In the afternoons, I took lunch breaks with Mason, and in the evenings after dinner service, he'd drop me off at Ryan and Maggie's cozy cottage. Often, Maggie and Ivy were already in bed. I'd have a brandy by the fire with Ryan, or take a cold walk alone through the pretty village—thinking, remembering, allowing the emotions I'd buried all day to wash over me.

With a week to go until Christmas, I reluctantly rolled out of bed at dawn, finding the air as crisp as a fresh apple. I shivered as I dressed and peered out the ancient bedroom window that sat crookedly in its frame. The rain from the day before had frozen, coating the grass, leaves, and even the tree bark, in a dazzling, glittery sheen. It was breathtaking, and I found it hard to tear myself away.

Andrea would have loved it here in the countryside, especially during winter. It had been her favorite season. My eyes filled with tears as I realized I'd noticed something beautiful for the first time in weeks, and I felt the smallest inkling of hope steal over me.

Downstairs, I spent a few extra minutes with my porridge and tea, lost in thought. I didn't know whether I believed in fate or in the simple, chaotic, and cruel struggle of life. What I did know was that I was glad to be spending my days in Sandringham's kitchen, where I could work myself to the point of exhaustion.

Mason arrived half an hour later, and together we drove to Sandringham. He chattered like a happy bird and didn't seem bothered by my brooding silence as I watched the landscape unfold ahead. We pulled into the winding drive, parked the car, and made our way to the staff entrance. It already felt normal to be here; already felt like a familiar routine.

I was surprised to find Max waiting for me to arrive. He immediately ushered me into the dry pantry.

"Good morning," he said, sweat already dotting his brow. The man was a workhorse. I wondered if he ever slept.

"Good morning, chef," I replied as I tied my apron.

He met my eye. "You've been working hard, Jack, and you haven't complained. I'm impressed by your attitude. So, how about we see if you can really cook."

I nodded. "Yes, chef. What would you like me to make?"

"The staff meal. Something simple but . . . well, I'll leave it to you."

I nodded. "Thank you, chef."

He said nothing more and shouted for the grillardin, the cook in charge of the grill.

I spun to the pantry, my mind whirring with possibilities of what I might cook. The staff meal was the main meal of the day, eaten around one o'clock in the afternoon. Max wanted simple, and it had to be relatively inexpensive—something I was already accustomed to since I'd learned to cook during a time of strict rationing—and I had to make enough to feed the large staff that serviced the estate. I also needed to balance our rations with the types of dishes that would usually be served: classic French cuisine and traditional English favorites. Something told me I should save my more innovative ideas for another time.

Pies then. Pigeon pies and tossed salad. Simple, filling, delicious.

As I gathered the ingredients, an overwhelming sensation washed over me—that grandpa was with me, gently urging me to make this meal my own, despite what Max would expect. Invention had been one of our favorite games; Grandpa would gather basic ingredients for a particular dish and then he'd challenge me to make it unique, different, more exciting. Sometimes it was a disaster, but he never chastised me.

"Experimentin' is how we achieve genius, boy," he'd say in his thick Louisiana drawl. "Now, how do we fix this?" He'd explain why the flavors or textures didn't work, and we'd try again until I got it right. I didn't need formal training with him as my guide. He was the best kind of teacher.

I returned to the pantry, scanning the shelves of seasoning and spices until I found what I was looking for: a small cylindrical glass tube labeled "cayenne pepper." The lid was dusty and the fine crimson granules were packed nearly to the top. It seemed as if no one had been using it, at least not often. I returned to my station, a smile crossing my face. They were in for a surprise.

Pigeon pies were a lot of work, so I set about plucking and butchering the birds before pan roasting the breasts and sautéing mushrooms in butter and cognac. Once these were cooked, I added a healthy amount of cayenne pepper to the mixture. Rather than the pie crusts I'd originally planned, I pivoted to something more interesting . . . more *me*. Buttery, southern biscuits.

As I prepared the savory fluffy dough, a memory drifted through my head: Andrea's surprise that a southern biscuit wasn't a sweet confection—a cookie—but was closer in taste and texture to a savory scone, only better, lighter, and much richer. Her eyes had widened as she bit into the hot biscuit which I'd slathered with peppered honey butter. She'd pronounced it to be the best thing she'd ever eaten.

I poured the pie filling into casserole dishes and topped them with the biscuit dough. Once everything was in the oven, I tossed a few bowls of greens with olive oil, salt and pepper, and added a squeeze of lemon. I was careful with measurements, precise with chopping, rolling, and then cleaning my workstation. I bent over a stubborn spot on the countertop and scrubbed for some time.

"Jack." A hand gripped my shoulder.

I turned to see Mason. My mind had emptied of everything for a blissful moment, even if the ache in my chest knew otherwise.

"I think that spot's clean now," he said. "You've been scrubbing it like you're trying to rub away the varnish on the wood!"

I dropped the rag. "Sorry. Got lost in my thoughts for a moment there."

He smiled. "The pies smell great. Can't wait to try them."

The meal was a success. The staff were as surprised by the biscuit-topped "pie" as they were by my generous measure of cayenne.

"This is fantastic, Jack," Max said, filling his plate with another helping.

"Thank you, chef," I replied, feeling my first hint of pride since I'd arrived.

"I think it's time for a promotion from errand boy. I want you to help out at the pâtissier's station this afternoon."

Mason clinked his water glass against mine. "Well done. He isn't an easy man to impress."

"Thanks. I'm glad the cayenne didn't scare anyone off."

Later that afternoon I followed my nose to the pâtissier's station, where the smells of Christmas wafted all around. I admired the cakes spiced with cinnamon and nutmeg, the gingerbread men dressed for the holiday in piped white icing and sugar-coated red and green candy buttons. Sweet almond paste had been colored and molded into Christmas scenes of snow-coated evergreens, reindeer, and even a nativity scene complete with a baby Jesus and animals. I'd never been particularly talented at pastry work, but it wasn't too late to learn. I rolled up my sleeves and followed the pâtissier's instructions.

A few hours later, the housekeeper swept into the kitchen and pulled me aside. "Mr. Devereux, a message has come through for you. It sounded urgent." She gave me a folded piece of paper.

My throat tightened as I clutched the note in my hand. What could possibly have gone wrong now? "Thank you, Mrs. Leonard."

"And does anyone know who this locket belongs to?" she added, turning to address the whole kitchen. "Found it in the library. I've asked everywhere and nobody recognizes it."

I glanced at the gold necklace. "I think that belongs to the BBC reporter who was here." I'd noticed how Olive played with it while we'd spoken.

"Olive Carter? Oh, yes. That would make sense. I bet she's missing it," Mrs. Leonard said. "I'll telephone Broadcasting House, see if they can get a message to her."

"I'm sure she'd be grateful," I replied politely before dipping into the pantry to read my note: *Jarrod Waverly requests your immediate return to London to settle your wife's affairs. Please telephone at your earliest convenience.*

My solicitor. I sighed heavily. I'd been so devastated by Andrea's death that I'd ignored the formalities and the paperwork—death certificates and wills—and followed Ryan to Norfolk without a second thought. And now, I didn't have time to do it, not without throwing a wrench in the works at Sandringham. I cleaned my hands and headed to Max's station.

"There's a problem, chef," I said. "The solicitor handling my wife's affairs has called me urgently to London, to handle some paperwork. I know this is terrible timing, but it shouldn't take more than a couple of hours if you can spare me."

Max lightly clapped his hands against one another to brush away flecks of breadcrumbs. "I can spare you for a few hours tomorrow morning. But I'll need you to return as soon as you can. The schedule will be especially tight for the next few days. In fact, I've arranged for you to stay in one of the estate cottages until New Year's Day. We'll be working long hours—early and late—and it's best you're here. Even the short drive to the village where you've been staying will feel far when you're exhausted."

"Yes, chef. Thank you. I really appreciate it."

I returned to my station, mind racing, my heart filled with dread at the prospect of the next day's chore and the finality it would bring.

Chapter 14

Olive

London, December 1952

After another restless night turning everything over in my mind, I was glad of the crisp December air that settled over London a week before Christmas.

As we did every year, Lucy and I went out to admire the Christmas trees in the front windows of the houses along our street. At the park we threw stale bread to the ducks, laughing as they slid and stumbled on the icy water. We collected fallen pine cones and took a few sprigs of berry-laden holly to make a table decoration. We sang our favorite carols and called in at the shop on the corner to buy sugar mice and the week's *Radio Times*. We stayed out until our cheeks and noses were pink with the cold, and we couldn't feel our toes in our shoes. For all the fancy extravagance of Sandringham, I much preferred our simple family Christmas traditions. There was nothing I loved more than being outside with Lucy, wrapped up in our coats, hats, and gloves, a rosy winter sky promising snow. Everything else melted away when it was just the two of us.

Back home, I gave the *Radio Times* to my mother.

"Pass me a pen, love," she said as she sat at the kitchen table. "I'll circle the programs we don't want to miss."

This was my mother's Christmas preparation. A religion all her own.

For a family who only went to church for obligatory weddings, christenings, and funerals, the *Radio Times* was our equivalent of the Bible, a sacred document to treasure, particularly when the special Christmas edition went on sale. The wireless cabinet was the pulpit from which those we idolized preached, providing endless entertainment from early morning until midnight when the programs ended and the station fell silent.

As children, my sister and I used to sit with the magazine and scrutinize the schedule, circling programs we planned to listen to, especially at Christmas. Sitting cross-legged beside that heavy old cabinet was one of my fondest memories. I felt safe there, even during the war, while voices as familiar to me as those of my own family soothed and distracted us with stories and comedy sketches and songs. Perhaps it was inevitable that I would follow those voices to the BBC, and that was why it mattered so much to one day see my name in the program listings in the *Radio Times*.

Charlie Bullen's annual *A Royal Christmas* was on air later that day. His name was still listed in the magazine that had been printed long before he'd disappeared to the coast. I wondered who Tom Harding had chosen to read the broadcast on Charlie's behalf.

As I settled on the sofa to listen, Lucy snuggled into my side.

My mother stood at the back door and called for my father, who was keeping out of everyone's way by being very busy in his shed. "Bob! It's starting! Hurry up. You'll miss it!"

He rushed into the front room and sat down beside me on the sofa.

"What were you doing out there?" my mother griped. "You've been in that shed for hours. Are you building the Ark?"

The poor man couldn't win. If he was in the house, he was under her feet. If he went out to the shed, he faced the Spanish Inquisition.

Whatever he'd been doing suddenly didn't matter as the announcer introduced the next piece—the one we'd been waiting for all day.

"*And now, in what has become a much-loved Christmas tradition here on BBC radio, we hear about the preparations for Christmas with the royal family, and how everything is just a little different this year . . .*"

The program opened with classical music. I sat, sulkily, wishing it could have been my name in the listings and my report to follow.

"*Christmas is about family and tradition: keeping old traditions, and at times, establishing new ones. And never has that been truer than for our new queen as she faces her first Christmas as our monarch, and honors the royal Christmas traditions established during the reign of Queen Victoria . . .*"

I recognized the voice: Archie Maguire, my boss. But as he continued, I also recognized the words.

My words.

"*But as well as being our queen, Her Majesty is a young woman—a wife and mother—facing her first Christmas without her beloved father. Things will be very different for her as she prepares to give her first Christmas message from Sandringham, just as her father and grandfather did for many years before her. But among so much change, some things remain reassuringly the same. The small army of chefs in Sandringham's kitchens are hard at work preparing the many meals the royal family will enjoy over the festive period.*"

I grabbed Lucy's hand as I leaned forward. "I wrote this! He's reading the piece I wrote for Tom!"

My mother shushed me.

Good old Tom Harding had used my report on the royal kitchens and the chefs after all!

I listened intently, a sense of pride blooming in my chest as I turned to my father. "I wrote this!" I whispered.

"That's wonderful, love," he said, giving my arm an affectionate squeeze.

My mother shushed us again.

"*In the royal kitchens at the Sandringham Estate, preparations have been underway for many months already, planning the various meals the members of the royal family will require over their festive stay, and of course, on Christmas Day itself. There is a great reverence for the processes and recipes that are used. The kitchen is like a church, the recipe books the chefs' bibles.*

"*Under the careful eye of head chef, Max Barrington, a small army is hard at work to make sure everything is just right. Soups and sauces, pastries and pies, and the traditional yule log will all be enjoyed by the queen and the royal family over the festive period. Cooking for the queen is considered a great privilege—a chance to be part of royal traditions that go back many years.*

"*Christmas is a time for celebration, and for family, but it is also a time for remembering. The late king will be in everyone's minds as we gather around the wireless to await the traditional Christmas Day message at three o'clock. Our young queen has addressed the nation and the Commonwealth twice before: once during a* Children's Hour *broadcast in 1940, when she spoke to displaced British evacuees around the world, and then on the occasion of her twenty-first birthday when she committed her lifelong service and duty to the nation. Nobody, least of all young Princess Elizabeth herself, could ever have imagined just how soon that service and duty would come to bear.*

"*We wish you well, Your Majesty.*"

The radio announcer's voice came next. "And that was Archibald Maguire, reading a special report by Charlie Bullen. We wish you well in your continued recovery, Charlie."

"*Charlie!*" I felt my face flush with anger as I stood up and glared at the wireless cabinet. "But that wasn't Charlie's work! It was mine! How dare they!"

"Well, I thought it was *lovely*," my mother said. "A shame Charlie wasn't reading it—he has such a soothing voice—but a lovely piece nevertheless."

I was furious. "Yes, Mum! *My* lovely piece."

"Yes, dear. You've said that."

"Aren't you annoyed? Don't you think it's unfair that someone else gets to take the credit for my work?"

"Does it matter who gets the credit?" she said. "*You* know those were your words, and just think how many people heard them! Millions! And your boss knows. Even the man who read it knows, and Charlie Bullen knows. Who else needs to know? Who else matters?"

I felt tears prick my eyes. "*I* matter, Mum. This is precisely why women have so much trouble being taken seriously—we are never given the credit where it is due." I sat, then stood again, so angry and hurt I didn't know what to do with myself. "I'm going for a walk," I said at last.

Just then, the telephone rang. I picked it up on my way past to get my coat.

"Hello. Clapham, 31874?"

"Oh, good evening. I'm so sorry to bother you. Could I speak to Olive Carter, please?"

"Speaking. This is Olive."

"Oh, Olive. Hello, again. Eleanor Leonard. From Sandringham House. I think I have something here belonging to you."

"Oh?"

My mother arrived in the hallway. "Who is it?" she whispered.

I covered the receiver. "Housekeeper from Sandringham."

"Really?" She turned to my father, who was now also in the hallway. "Sandringham House, Bob!"

Mrs. Leonard went on to explain that one of the cleaning staff had found a locket in the library. "The new American chef recognized it. He said he'd seen you wearing it when you were here."

89

"Jack?"

"Yes. Mr. Devereux."

My mind spun. How had Jack known it was mine? "I thought I'd lost it on the way home. The clasp is loose. I really should get it fixed."

"Well, it's safe now in my desk drawer. Should I pop it in the post?"

I thought for a moment. "Actually, would it be all right if I came to collect it?"

"Come all the way to Sandringham?"

"Yes. It's very precious, you see. It was my late grandmother's. I'd hate for it to get lost in the post."

"Of course. I quite understand."

"Tomorrow's Saturday, so I have the day off work. Could I come then?"

"We'll see you tomorrow. Just ask for me when you arrive."

I hung up and put on my coat.

"What was all that about?" my mother asked.

"They found my locket. I can go tomorrow to collect it, if you can watch Lucy?"

"A second trip to Sandringham! They'll be giving you a key next."

I stepped outside, glad to have a chance to clear my head. I was so furious about what had happened with my radio piece, but Granny's locket gave me the perfect excuse to go back to Sandringham. I was relieved to know the locket was safe, but I was also pleased to have a chance to try again, to find inspiration for a piece that wouldn't work with anyone else's name attached to it but mine.

And there was another reason I was keen to go back to Sandringham. I needed to talk to Jack. I needed to tell him something I should have told him a long time ago.

Chapter 15

Jack

London, June 1945

Victory in Europe Day had changed everything for me in the most unexpected ways. Though I missed the camaraderie with the Seabees after being discharged from my voluntary duties, within a few short weeks in London, I'd already made a new group of friends. I moved in with Ryan and quickly found a position in a kitchen, frying greasy piles of fish and chips. Though far from a dream job, it paid the rent, and until I figured out where I would land for good, I was happy to live a simple life, having fun. When the group of us gathered together, every night felt like a party.

We were an unusual mixture of personalities, but somehow the combination worked. Ryan was the salt of the earth, a good guy in every way, and very soon he was like a brother to me. Peter Hall was the life of the party—when he decided to show his face—and Rosie was great to talk to, if a little "too much fun" at times. Olive was always up for anything, and no one could help but be drawn to her effervescent energy. I often thought about the night we'd met, our dance on VE Day, and the laughter that had followed.

"Are you ever going to ask Olive out?" Ryan teased one evening. "You two have a spark. Anyone can see it."

"She's interested in Peter," I said, glancing at the two of them, cozy in a booth, despite the fact that Andrea and two of our other friends were jammed in beside them. Peter was an on-again off-again part of the group. Truthfully, I found I preferred the off days. Everyone else seemed to like him, but I found his constant need to be the center of attention a little tiring.

"You're reading too much into it," Ryan replied. "You know how Peter is. He chases every woman in the room. Give it a chance with Olive, you'll see."

But it was Andrea who I ended up talking to every time the group met up at our favorite watering hole, The Thirsty Dog. Andrea was sensitive and on the quiet side, but endearing and sweet, and I found her the easiest to talk to among the crowd.

"Time for another, ladies?" I pointed at Olive's and Andrea's empty glasses.

"Yes!" they said in unison.

"Make mine a stout, will you?" Olive added. "This lager tastes like yesterday's bathwater."

I headed to the bar, thinking about how much Olive made me laugh.

When I got back to the booth, Peter had already slung an arm around both Andrea and Olive. He read my expression. "You can't hog all the beautiful women, Jack!"

Peter was all dark good looks and charisma. He could have any woman in the room, and he knew it, and not only that, he had a way of making me feel more awkward with women than I already was.

Olive offered me a smile. "Thanks for the beer, Jack."

"My pleasure." I put the other beer in front of Andrea and squeezed in beside her. "For you, madame."

"Thank you," she said, bumping my right arm as she reached for her own glass. "Sorry, it's so crowded in here tonight!"

"Don't be sorry," I said, glancing again at Peter and Olive chattering happily, all smiles. "We're packed in like sardines."

Andrea wasn't as confident and vivacious as Olive, but I was drawn to her elegant beauty, her vivid blue eyes, and her calm demeanor.

The next thing I knew, we had talked the hours away, and when we all left the pub to move on to a dance hall Olive knew, Andrea and I stuck together. Eventually we ended up on the dance floor. Around midnight, someone spilled an entire tray of pints as they passed us. We avoided the spray, laughing as we bumped into each other. As I smiled at Andrea, she reached for me, wrapping her arms around my neck and pushing her lips gently against mine.

I was stunned. I hadn't known her long and yet, here we were, kissing. "Well. That was . . . something."

She laughed. "Something? You have quite a way with words."

I grimaced. "Sorry, lots going on up here," I gestured to my head. "My brain doesn't always connect with my mouth!"

"You do just fine with your mouth."

"Oh yeah?" I leaned in for another kiss, and this time no words were needed at all.

When we returned to the others, Peter made a big show of the fact we'd been gone so long. "You two took your time. Found a good dance partner, did you? Hot and sweaty, is it?"

Andrea blushed and laughed. "Peter! Stop!"

"Nobody else dancing?" I asked. My eyes met Olive's.

She looked at me, and then at Andrea, and took a sip of her drink.

"Too bloody right." Peter stood up and pulled Olive to her feet. "Might I have the pleasure, Miss Carter?" He dipped her dramatically, and held her against him.

93

She laughed. "Of course, Mr. Hall."

I leaned toward Andrea. "Want to get out of here? Go some-place quieter?"

"I thought you'd never ask."

When she smiled, I knew that whatever was brewing between us was worth following.

Chapter 16

Olive

London, June 1945

Our circle of friends, formed in the heady celebrations of VE Day, melded together into an inseparable group over carefree nights of drinking and dancing. Although the awful impact of war was all around us—London's streets badly damaged from the bombing raids and rationing still in place—we had reason to hope again, and to look forward to the future. There was plenty of flirting, and more than a few drunken kisses, but nothing serious developed between any of us.

My position at the War Office continued, with documents to be filed and all manner of correspondence to be typed up, but I had my heart set on moving into more exciting surroundings. I had a wild dream of working at the BBC, and since the war had ended, I knew it was time to take a chance. I applied for a position in the typing pool in the home affairs department and hoped for the best. Rosie decided to apply, too, declaring that she couldn't possibly bear it if I left her at Whitehall for a glamorous life at the BBC.

After work one evening, Rosie and I hurried to meet the others at our favorite pub, The Thirsty Dog.

"I wonder if darling Jack will be there," she said as we ran up the steps from the underground.

She insisted that Jack liked me, and that the attention he gave to Andrea Keane was his way of making me jealous.

"I keep telling you, Rosie—Jack had his chance on VE Day and he blew it! We're just friends." I tried to sound convincing but didn't even manage to convince myself. I *was* attracted to Jack, but he wasn't as confident, or as easy to get to know, as the other boys in the group—Peter, especially. Jack had also started a new job in a scruffy restaurant in the East End, and worked odd shifts which meant he wasn't always with us when we got together.

"You can deny it all you want, Olive, but I see the way the two of you look at each other." Rosie grabbed my arm. "You should flirt with Peter. Make Jack jealous."

I laughed. "I won't need to try hard to flirt with Peter Hall. He'll flirt with anyone."

As it happened, I ended up sitting beside Peter in the pub that evening. He was dark-haired and even darker-eyed and handsome as hell. There were worse ways to spend my evening than flirting with him.

"So, are the two of them a couple, or what?" Peter asked later that night, when we had moved to a dance hall and Jack and Andrea had made their way to the floor together.

"Looks like it," I said.

Rosie leaned forward. "Although he secretly likes Olive."

I dug her in the ribs with a sharp elbow. "He does not! Jack's a friend. We enjoy each other's company," I added. "That's all."

Peter looked at me, his eyes studying mine. "I enjoy your company, too, but with less talking and more of this." He leaned forward and brushed his lips against mine. "You're a firecracker, Olive Carter. If Jack's too stupid to make a move, then I sure as hell will."

"Don't mind me," Rosie said, laughing as she kicked my feet under the table.

I ignored her. Peter tasted of whisky and tobacco and delicious things, wild and dangerous. Jack and I talked a lot, but with Peter, conversation was entirely unnecessary. He was the perfect antidote to the long difficult years of war.

When Jack and Andrea returned from their dance, Jack seemed a little uncomfortable and Andrea was embarrassed by Peter's teasing. They soon finished their drinks and said their goodbyes.

As they left arm in arm, Jack turned to look over his shoulder, and our eyes met. I pulled Peter toward me and kissed him, and hoped that Jack would realize he was leaving with the wrong girl.

Chapter 17

Jack

Sandringham Estate, December 1952

I woke at dawn the next day in the little cottage I'd been allocated on the Sandringham Estate, and dressed hurriedly. I met one of the royal family's many chauffeurs, a friendly Welshman named Evans, who was kind enough to drop me at the train station for my quick trip into London.

Lulled by the gentle motion of the train, my eyes soon became heavy, and I fell into a deep sleep, exhausted by the demanding schedule in the royal kitchen and the emotional fallout of Andrea's death.

The next thing I knew, we had arrived in London and a conductor was shaking my shoulder to wake me.

It was a short walk to the solicitor's office, where I signed various distressing forms relating to Andrea's death. I didn't even read the words. I simply signed where I was told to sign. When I'd finished, I breathed a sigh of relief and all but sprinted for the door.

Outside, sluggish gray clouds crowded the sky and a damp wind whipped off the Thames. I huddled in my jacket and, chest tight, began to walk to the flat. I took my time, watching harried shoppers and eager children stream by on either side of me. Every shop or pub window was decorated for Christmas, and festive merriment bubbled in the air. I could sense it, even as I moved outside of it, my palms sweaty as I drew nearer to my neighborhood. *Our* neighborhood.

I climbed the steps to the flat and let myself in. The mat was so thick with mail that I had to shove the door hard before it opened. As I gathered up the pile of bills, Christmas cards, and condolences, I was hit with the odor of stale air.

The Christmas tree sagged limply in the corner of the living room. A few baubles had dropped and rolled across the floor. I walked numbly to the bedroom and stood in the doorway, desperately seeking any sign of her—an indentation on her pillow, her favorite perfume still uncapped, her dressing gown crumpled in a heap on the floor. It was all there, just as I'd left it. Just as she'd left it. I could sense her, hear her bright laughter in my ears. The way she'd tease me about my favorite sweater with the holes in the sleeves. How she'd straighten my shirt collar before planting a kiss on my nose.

I didn't know how I could ever move past the excruciating ache of her absence.

I sat for a while in the kitchen, not bothering to turn on the lights, wearily opening the stack of bills and Christmas cards and condolences. *To Jack and Andrea, Happy Christmas. Dear Jack, We were so sorry to hear about your terrible loss* . . . I couldn't bear to read them. As I tossed them into the garbage can, my eye caught the familiar spine of a well-loved notebook. Grandpa's recipes.

I took the tattered old notebook in my hands, thumbing carefully through the worn pages, running my fingertip over his scrawled notes in the margins. For a moment, the ache in my chest eased as a sense of nostalgia washed over me. Grandpa always knew how to make me feel better. Whether it was a pile of sugar-dusted beignets, a fatherly hug, or a story from when he was a boy, he always knew what to do. I held the book to my chest. I would take it back to Sandringham. It was a little like taking Grandpa himself, and I needed his soothing presence now more than ever.

As I blindly gathered my things and locked the front door behind me, another pang hit me. I wanted to see her, to tell her I loved her, that I was thinking of her wherever she was. I glanced at my wristwatch. I had enough time to stop by the cemetery—Max would understand. I walked to Mrs. Howard's flower shop to buy a posy for Andrea's grave, and to see a friendly face, too.

"Jack! My goodness, aren't you a sight for sore eyes. I've missed you," Mrs. Howard said with a kind smile. "Give us a hug, won't you."

I embraced this sweet lady who had been such a friend to Andrea. I was grateful for her in this moment. "It's good to see you."

"How are you doing, dear? I've been thinking about you." She reached for a handkerchief and wiped a tear from her cheek.

"I'm taking things one day at a time." I glanced around the shop, wondering what I should bring to the cemetery. Nothing too big or flashy, but something pretty and seasonal, just as Andrea would have liked.

"Going to see her?"

I nodded, relieved I didn't have to explain myself.

Mrs. Howard led me to a corner of the shop and selected a posy of red and white Christmas roses. "Consider it a Christmas gift."

"That's very kind of you, Mrs. Howard, thank you."

"Nonsense. You've given me plenty over the years. The lovely cakes and biscuits, the Sunday dinners when I was all alone. I was very fond of her, you know." Her voice wavered a little. "You're a good man, Jack. You deserve every happiness. I know you'll find it again, in time. Now, come here." She raised her hands to my face, and I bent down to her height so she could place a motherly kiss on my cheek.

"How about I stop by again," I said. When I'm back from San-dringham in the New Year?"

"That sounds perfect."

Outside the shop, I paused to stare up at the building next door with its red brick and faded white trim, as charming as ever, even if it needed sprucing up. *Our* building. Our restaurant. Our dream. I couldn't imagine it without Andrea, and I didn't have the energy to try.

I walked to the bus stop and traveled the few stops to the cemetery, where I walked past centuries of worn headstones, trying to return to the numbness that had shored me up the past couple of weeks.

When I reached my darling wife, I laid the bouquet atop her grave and stared at her headstone. A thousand emotions and memories swept through me as I crouched down beside her. It was agony to be there, but it felt unbearable to leave.

After some time, the cold seeped into my hands and feet, and I began to shiver.

"Until we meet again, my love," I whispered. "Merry Christmas."

I walked from the solemn cemetery and hailed a cab to take me to the train station, to return to Sandringham. I was needed there, and for now, that was all I had.

When the train pulled into King's Lynn station, I breathed a sigh of relief. I'd done it; I'd signed the necessary paperwork and visited the cemetery. Two tasks I'd been dreading.

Evans chattered away on the drive back to Sandringham, oblivious to my thoughts. "I'm like a spinning top today, back and forth!"

"Lots of new arrivals?" I asked, not really caring for conversation but making an effort to be polite.

"Plenty. It'll be hot in the kitchen tonight, I'd say! I'm not long back from dropping another visitor to the house. Actually, you know her, I think. Olive Carter? With the BBC? She's very pleased her locket was found. Must be pretty special, what with her coming all the way from London."

I was mildly interested to hear that Olive was back, and glad to have reunited her with her necklace.

At the house, I dressed quickly in my chef whites and was immediately swept up into the dinner service. I barely had time to think until we'd finished and the cyclone of activity began to wane. Exhausted, I wound through the kitchen to the back door, only to be met by an unexpected face.

The Duke of Edinburgh. Philip. Standing outside the staff entrance in a pristine suit, a cigarette in hand. He was staring up at the stars.

"Your Highness. Apologies. I didn't mean to interrupt." I bowed my head awkwardly and turned to step back inside.

He put the cigarette to his lips, inhaled, and blew out a stream of smoke. "Not interrupting. Yet." He winked in a friendly way. "I've escaped from the women. So many of them in there. What are you escaping from?"

"A very long day," I said. "A very long month, in fact."

He offered me a cigarette. "A fellow doesn't like to smoke alone. Care to join me?"

I took one though I rarely smoked. "Very kind of you, sir. Thank you."

"You're American," he said. "Where are you from?"

"New Orleans. Louisiana."

"You are a long way from home."

"I sure am. I was a Seabee for the US Navy. Worked in the mess hall and, when the war ended, landed in London."

"Ah. A Navy man." His face lit up. "Served in the Navy myself." He leaned closer. "I miss it a great deal, but don't tell anyone."

"Your secret's safe with me, sir. I don't miss the war, of course, but I miss being at sea. The endless horizon, the sensation of being at one with nature, the cycles of sun and moon and tides, the feeling that everything is inconsequential out there. There's something calming about it."

"That's exactly it. You have captured it perfectly." He looked at me and tapped his cigarette, sending a scattering of ash to the ground. "What brought you to London then? A beautiful blonde, perhaps?"

A small smile tugged at my lips as an image of Andrea flashed through my mind. Victory in Europe Day. That first carefree night of cocktails and dancing and new friends.

"A beautiful brunette, actually. Now I consider England home."

"That makes two of us then."

"Isn't England your first home, sir? Sorry. Your Highness."

"You seem like a decent sort—no need to get hung up on the formalities. Us Navy chaps have to stick together! It is a complicated thing, loving two countries," he continued. "Serving one in deed, and one with your heart. My mother and sisters are in Greece. That was my first home."

Of course. I remembered Andrea saying something about Philip's Greek heritage when she'd dragged me to the Mall to celebrate their wedding and catch a glimpse of the happy couple on the balcony at Buckingham Palace. I studied his lean face and sharp cheekbones, his bright, intelligent eyes. He was much more than the papers made him out to be.

"Well, I'd best get back inside," he said, crushing the stub of his cigarette into the ground. "No doubt Lilibet will be looking for me. She is still grappling with the bloody speech she has to deliver on Christmas Day. At this stage, I think she would be as well to wish everyone a merry Christmas and be done with it!" He offered his hand. "Merry Christmas to you . . ."

"Jack," I offered. "Jack Devereux."

"Merry Christmas, Jack."

"Merry Christmas, Your Highness. And thank you for the cigarette."

He turned back. "And thank *you* for a few moments of normality! Did you make that sauce we had with dinner tonight, by any chance?"

"I did, Your Highness."

"Delicious. I enjoyed the spice. It's rather nice to have something different for a change." With that, he waved a hand over his shoulder in farewell and disappeared into the night.

I shook my head, unable to believe I'd had a conversation with the Duke of Edinburgh—with a member of the royal family. I wished I could tell Andrea. She'd been beyond excited when we'd decided I should take the position here—in part, I knew, because the thought of being near the royal family had delighted her.

Heart in my throat, I gazed at the infinite night sky and thought about all the things she was missing and how very much more she would miss as life carried on without her.

Chapter 18

Olive

It was strange to find myself back at Sandringham so soon. I'd presumed my previous visit would be the first and last time I would step inside a royal household, but life was full of surprises lately, and maybe fate was playing a hand, too. The locket had given me a second chance to find inspiration for an irresistible piece for Tom, and to prove that I was worth ten Charlie Bullens or Archibald Maguires. It would also give me a chance to see Jack again, if I could find an excuse to get back into the kitchens.

The temperature had dropped overnight, and a hard frost made the lawns sparkle like diamonds. Evans drove carefully from the station, avoiding treacherous patches of black ice.

"Watch your footing," he said as I stepped out of the car when we reached Sandringham. "Those flagstone paths can be lethal."

I assured him I would be careful.

Mrs. Leonard ushered me inside out of the cold. "It would cut you in two," she said. "Come and get warm by the fire. I've ordered tea and scones."

"Oh, you really didn't have to go to any trouble," I said, but I was glad she had. Maybe Jack would bring them out like he had last time, although I didn't know what I would say to him if he did.

"I'll run and fetch the locket," Mrs. Leonard said. "Make yourself at home."

And there I was, back beside the fireplace in Sandringham's library, with a curious sense of déjà vu. It was strange to know that Jack was so close by. I checked my face in the mirror of my compact and fidgeted in my chair. I was nervous—anxious—conscious that I had to make this visit count.

Mrs. Leonard returned shortly afterward with the necklace and a tea tray. "Now, here it is. Thank goodness Mr. Devereux recognized it."

I took the locket from her. "Yes. It really was fortunate."

"Is he a friend of yours?"

I thought for a moment, unsure how to describe our connection. "An old friend," I said. "We haven't been in touch for years."

"Ahh. I see." She raised an eyebrow.

"Oh no, I don't . . . he isn't . . ."

"He's terribly handsome, don't you think?" She fanned herself theatrically.

I didn't know what to think. Seeing Jack again had been so unexpected and unsettling. He'd brought my past roaring into my present, and I wasn't ready, for any of it.

I turned my attention back to the locket. "This was my grandmother's," I said. "A family heirloom. I hope to pass it on to my daughter, one day." I hadn't planned to mention Lucy and was annoyed with myself for doing so. I was usually so careful. Talking about her only led to awkward questions and difficult explanations.

Mrs. Leonard looked momentarily startled. "Oh, I hadn't realized you were married," she said as she poured the tea. I saw her eyes flick to my wedding ring.

"Widowed," I said quietly, well-rehearsed in the charade. "I tend to use my maiden name at work."

Mrs. Leonard nodded. "Just have the one child, do you?"

I opened the locket to show her the photograph of Lucy I kept there. "One is more than enough!"

"She's a pretty little thing." She glanced at me and back at the photograph. "She must miss her father."

"We both do." I closed the locket and returned it to my purse, conscious, as ever, of the question of Lucy's father hanging in the air.

"I'm very sorry for your loss," Mrs. Leonard added. "I understand the pain of losing a husband."

I felt like a fraud accepting her sympathies, so I quickly offered my own in return and changed the subject.

"Do you mind me asking: what is it you think people want to know about the queen? I'd like our listeners to get a sense of who she really is, but it is proving difficult."

Mrs. Leonard thought for a moment. "Well, I know there's a great deal of interest in the Christmas Day message. Everyone is keen to hear the queen—a woman—speak to them for the first time. Between you and me, she's rather nervous about it."

"Really." At this, I pricked up my ears.

"Her Majesty worries that her way of talking is a little, shall we say, stiff. That she comes across as . . . detached."

Here was my chance to strike. "Yes, I can imagine that's a concern. Radio isn't an easy thing to get right," I said. "And the Christmas Day message is such an important moment in family traditions. I can't remember a Christmas Day without listening to the king's speech. We always turn the wireless on at three, pour a sherry, and eat our Christmas pudding in bowls balanced on our knees."

Mrs. Leonard laughed lightly. "His Majesty would have rather liked that. He worried so much, hoping he would get through it without stuttering too much. It was always a relief when it was over." She thought for a moment. "I'll mention your Christmas pudding tradition to Her Majesty. She'll be pleased to hear it.

Tradition is very important to her—that's why it matters so much to her that she gets this right."

I admired the way Elizabeth had stepped into her father's shoes and taken on such enormous responsibility. Though I was only four years older than her twenty-six years, we were both women finding our way in a man's world. Admittedly, that was where any and all similarities stopped, because while the queen's future was shaped by the traditions she'd been born into, mine would be shaped by the chances and opportunities I did, or didn't, take.

Opportunities such as this.

"I'd be happy to . . . help?" I said.

"Help?"

I swallowed hard. It was now, or never. "I could . . . listen to a read-through. Of Her Majesty's speech. Before I head back to London? Offer some technical advice, suggest some ways to soften her edges? Of course, this sort of thing comes up often in my line of work and . . ." I trailed off, not wanting to suggest I had more experience than I did, but eager to seize the chance. "My train isn't until four."

Mrs. Leonard frowned in thought. "I suppose it isn't every day we have someone visiting from the BBC. That's an interesting idea, Miss Carter. Would you wait here a moment?"

I finished my tea and scones and tried to remember anything I'd ever heard or learned about presenting a program on the radio. There was something about speaking slowly. Holding your chin up to enunciate clearly. Effective use of pauses. Surely, I could make up something plausible. Most of all, I needed to carefully explain to Her Majesty that she should try to relax, that this would allow her characteristic charm to come through, even over the radio. That was what people wanted: a glimpse of the real woman behind the crown.

Before long, Mrs. Leonard returned. "You're in luck, Miss

Carter. Her Majesty has just finished working on a revised draft. She would be very grateful for your advice. Although she doesn't have long, so it will have to be now."

My stomach filled with butterflies. I had to get this right. I drew in a deep breath. "Now is perfect."

"The duke has been helping with the content of the speech," Mrs. Leonard said as we walked briskly along a corridor. "I don't suppose every husband would be as interested in their wife's work, would they?" She chuckled lightly at her little joke.

"I suppose not."

The issue of my "husband" danced around us again.

"But, I suppose the war changed the way we do lots of things," she offered. "I try to remain open-minded about the more modern ways of the world, but tradition clings on stubbornly here."

"Everything must be very different for you all this year," I said. "A new queen, after so many kings."

Mrs. Leonard offered a small dip of her head. "Indeed. Christmas is a time for reflection, isn't it. Old traditions lost. New traditions beginning."

I wanted to scribble a note on my pad: *Old traditions lost/new traditions beginning*—that could be the perfect angle for a piece for Tom. But we had reached the end of the corridor, and the conversation.

Mrs. Leonard knocked on a door and stepped inside. "Olive Carter, ma'am."

A familiar voice replied, "Very good. Show her in."

I stepped into the room and curtsied as the queen rose to her feet.

"That will be all, Eleanor," she said.

Mrs. Leonard nodded, whispered a "Good luck" to me, and stepped outside.

"You are from the BBC, I believe?" the queen said, addressing me directly.

"Yes, ma'am." I hoped she couldn't tell that my knees were shaking.

She looked at me carefully. "Have we met?"

"Briefly, ma'am. I was here a week ago."

"That's right. Bullen's replacement. And back so soon! Fortuitously, it seems—they tell me you can help with my radio voice."

"I hope so, ma'am."

"Well, shall we?" She motioned for me to take a seat on the other side of the desk. "Did Mrs. Leonard explain?"

"She mentioned that you are keen to rehearse your delivery, ma'am." I decided it was best not to specify that I was to help her sound less stuffy and regal.

"Precisely. Why don't I read what I have written so far? We shall see how it sounds."

I found it impossible to concentrate as she spoke. I saw her as both our new queen and as a daughter, sitting in the same chair where her dear father had sat and her grandfather before him. There was so much history, so much tradition to carry on her narrow shoulders.

My eyes wandered around the grand room, taking in the portraits of the kings and queens I'd learned about at school. I couldn't silence the voice in my head that kept telling me I shouldn't be here, that I didn't deserve to be here.

"Was that all right?"

I pulled my attention back to the issue at hand. "It was lovely."

"Lovely? Or adequate? One would appreciate your honesty, Miss Carter."

I took a deep breath. "I find it helps to smile as you speak."

"Smile? But nobody will be able to see me."

"When we smile as we speak, it comes across in our tone. It makes us sound as though we are smiling. It's a trick shared among the regular presenters at the BBC."

"Really? How interesting. Very well."

She cleared her throat and started again, a wide smile on her face. This time, I gave her my full attention, listening to the cadence of her voice, the beats and pauses, where she stopped to take a breath, how she started and ended her sentences. I scribbled notes and made subtle suggestions when she was finished.

She did it again and again, until I forgot that she was the queen and I was Olive Carter who had bluffed her way into this entire situation. We were just two women, sharing a productive half hour together.

Eventually, she seemed satisfied. "You have been a great help, Miss Carter."

"I'm sure you'll be wonderful, ma'am. We are all on your side. Cheering you on." The words were out before I could stop them.

She studied me. "Well, that is jolly reassuring to hear."

"It will make a nice change to hear a woman's voice."

"Yes, history in the making, as everyone keeps telling me." For the first time, I saw the flicker of nerves. "Mrs. Leonard mentioned your family's tradition of a sherry and Christmas pudding while my father delivered his Christmas Day message."

"Yes, ma'am. Nobody would miss it. My daughter is especially excited to hear the queen—you—speak this year."

She smiled. "Well, I must do my very best for your daughter then."

She rang a bell on the table and asked the footman to show me out.

I curtsied, wished her a happy Christmas, and before I'd fully processed what had happened, I was back with Mrs. Leonard.

"Well?" she asked. "How did it go?"

"Very well, I think. She seemed to find it helpful."

"Well, isn't that wonderful. A bit of Christmas magic. Maybe your grandmother had it planned all along!"

At this, I smiled. "Maybe. It would be just the sort of thing she might have done!"

"Now, Evans is ready with the car to take you back to the station. The poor man is like a yo-yo today, coming and going!"

I noticed a slight blush in her cheeks as she mentioned Evans.

"Actually, could I use the lavatories before the journey back?"

"Of course. Would you mind using the facilities in the kitchen block? Just out of the door, turn right, and you'll see the building ahead of you. I've to rush off, I'm afraid. Never a moment's peace."

I stepped outside and hurried along, ready to burst after all the tea I'd drunk. In my hurry, I forgot about the icy flagstones, and as I rushed around the corner, my feet went clean out from under me and I landed awkwardly, twisting my ankle painfully beneath me.

My shriek drew the attention of a passing gardener, who came to help. "Don't move, miss. Are you hurt?"

"It's my ankle," I gasped. "I think I might have broken it."

Within minutes I was surrounded by several members of staff, who helped me up and carried me inside. I was given a brandy for the pain and settled on a sofa with my foot elevated on a mound of cushions.

The doctor was summoned, and within the hour, he'd diagnosed a badly sprained ankle. "Needs to be kept elevated and rested as much as possible," he said.

"But I'm traveling back to London today. I have to get home." I'd promised to make paper chains with Lucy and hated to let her down.

He smiled. "I'm afraid you're going nowhere today, miss."

"You can take one of the cottages in the grounds," Mrs. Leonard offered. "Stay and rest your ankle overnight."

There wasn't much I could do, other than quietly admit defeat. It was decided.

I would stay.

I telephoned home, glad to get Dad rather than Mum, who would have made an enormous fuss. Lucy was perfectly happy to make paper chains with Granddad, and was far more interested in the fact that I was staying at the queen's house. Then I telephoned the office to explain the situation to Maguire who told me to "bloody well make the most of it then."

I'd already planned to do exactly that.

I was escorted to a lovely red-brick cottage on the grounds of the estate. Christmas roses bloomed in planters beside a gravel path that led to a blue front door, a wreath of glossy green holly leaves adding a festive welcome. Above, pink clouds promised snow. It felt magical, like something drawn into the pages of a storybook.

I was given everything I could possibly need and encouraged to relax and make myself comfortable for the night.

Before Mrs. Leonard left me, I asked her if there might be a typewriter I could borrow.

"A typewriter?"

"I'd like to write a piece for work. I might as well make myself useful while I'm laid up."

Mrs. Leonard smiled. "Of course. I'll see what I can do."

I had an idea for a piece that couldn't come from anyone but me: CHRISTMAS WITH THE QUEEN—Olive Carter reflects on the importance of the Christmas Day message and speaks to the queen as she prepares to take her place in the history books.

When Mrs. Leonard had left, I looked around the room and hopped toward the window. Sandringham House gleamed in the afternoon sun. Despite my throbbing ankle, a wide smile spread across my face. I was a guest of Her Majesty, Queen Elizabeth II. At Sandringham. This was the best Christmas gift ever!

I reached for the locket at my chest. "Thank you, Granny," I whispered.

Chapter 19

Jack

I was grateful that Max had insisted I stay in one of the cottages on the grounds. My four-thirty morning alarm woke me horribly early, and I was scarcely awake enough to get ready for the day. As I closed the front door and headed across the park, I noticed the cottage next to mine was dark and silent. When I'd finally fallen into bed the night before, I thought I'd heard the clack of typewriter keys through the shared wall and wondered what in the world could be so important that my neighbor was still writing at eleven o'clock.

When I joined the rest of the staff in the kitchen, we instantly busied ourselves with the day's tasks. With only a few days until Christmas, more guests had arrived and our work had tripled overnight. I was glad to be assigned the kitchen staff "family" meal again later that day. It was a pleasure to be helpful to Max, who I'd grown to truly respect. He ran an efficient and orderly kitchen that produced some truly delicious dishes, and I wanted to impress him. I'd already made plans for what I'd cook next—and it would knock their socks off.

I pivoted to the dry pantry and the ice box and busied myself peeling shrimp and roasting tomatoes. Mason was working the station beside me.

"Did you hear about that woman from the BBC who was getting under everyone's feet the other day?" he asked as he reached for a pot and lid.

I looked up from a fistful of shellfish. "Olive Carter?"

He shrugged. "I didn't catch the name. You know her?"

"She's an old friend, from a long time ago. We hardly know each other now. Ryan used to know her, too. Why?"

"She was here again yesterday. I heard that she fell on the ice and twisted her ankle. Now she's laid up in one of the cottages until Evans can drive her back to London."

"Sounds about right. She was always clumsy, but a good sport. We used to tease her, all in good fun. Too bad about the ankle."

Max stopped and peered over my shoulder at my work. "I can't wait to try that."

"Shrimp and grits," I replied. "A poor man's food, but it's delicious. It was one of my grandpa's favorites." This time, I hadn't bothered to make a classic French or English dish with a twist. I was feeling emboldened by Max's comments on my flavor combinations, so I figured it was high time I shared some recipes I'd grown up eating. Grits and polenta weren't common in England, but cornflour was. Though it was ground finer than polenta, it would substitute nicely in a soft creamy base for the shrimp.

I laid out bowls for each of the staff and, moving left to right, carefully ladled the shrimp mixture over the cornflour and broth mixture. I'd made do without andouille sausage—too difficult to come by from our suppliers—and substituted a fresh fennel sausage with roasted chilies, a bit of smoked bacon, and added the must-have smoked tomatoes. I sprinkled each dish with a bright green mix of herbs and a healthy dash of black pepper.

When everyone was seated, Max reached for a clean spoon and scooped up a large bite. His eyes widened. "Good God, man. It's rich. And delicious."

I nodded. "Thank you, chef."

Some really liked the meal, some were surprised by the spice, but I enjoyed watching everyone's faces as they registered the flavors.

Mason grinned at me in a conspiratorial way. "You keep me on my toes, Jack. You need to teach me about your spice combinations."

"Not a chance! They're top secret," I said, eliciting a laugh.

After the meal, Max motioned for me to follow him outside.

"You're doing fine work," he said. "In fact, I'd like to offer you a permanent position."

My eyebrows shot up. "Really?"

"Yes, a permanent job on my staff. You'd be in line behind two others in terms of rank, but there's room to move up. I could teach you a few things. You have some natural abilities and do really interesting things with spices, but it's clear that you lack professional training. Bed and board are included, and the pay is decent."

I was taken aback by the offer, and flattered. It was a far cry from being at the end of the line at Maison Jerome. Jerome hadn't liked having an ambitious American in his kitchen, and he'd never taken the time to show me a damn thing. It was nice to be wanted.

"I'm really honored you should ask, chef."

He smiled. "You should be."

The knot in my stomach eased ever so slightly for the first time since Andrea's death. "Would the position be here in Sandringham all year, or . . . ?"

"No. We work at Buckingham Palace most of the year, and then a provisional staff stays behind in November when the rest of us retreat to Norfolk and prepare for Christmas."

I shook my head in disbelief. I immediately thought of Andrea, of what she would say, the way the light danced in her eyes when she was excited.

Max narrowed his eyes. "Is that a no?"

"No! No, I mean, it isn't a no. I'm surprised is all."

"Think about it for a few days."

"I will. Thank you, chef."

I headed back to my station, mind racing. It would certainly be a fresh start, but I found the fussiness and the emphasis on proper procedure in the royal household a little stifling. It couldn't be more different from the way I'd grown up, in my grandpa's boisterous and messy kitchen, which had still managed to put out one perfect steaming plate of food after another. I didn't know if I belonged here, working for the royal family with all their formalities and traditions.

And yet, if I worked at the palace, I could leave the London flat behind. Start again. Somehow, I had to close a door on the life I'd built with Andrea and begin a new one.

Perhaps this was the way.

As the day drew to a close, the housekeeper popped her head into the kitchen. "Excuse me, gentlemen, but could someone prepare a dinner plate for a guest in one of the cottages? She's twisted an ankle and can't get around, poor dear." She directed her gaze at me. "I believe she's staying in the cottage next door to yours, chef."

So Olive was the one typing into the night? It was strange that our paths kept crossing after all this time. "I was just about to head back," I said. "I'll drop by with a plate."

"That would be very kind of you," the housekeeper replied.

I made up a plate of leftover shrimp and grits and added a bit of fruit and cheese, then headed back to the cottage. Rather than stop immediately at Olive's door, I went to my cottage first. Inside, the smell of wood polish greeted me, along with the faint scent of lavender soap. I bathed quickly, combed my hair, and pulled on clean clothes. When I was convinced I looked slightly less grubby and disheveled, I gathered the plate and knocked at Olive's door.

"Jack!" Leaning on a crutch on her left side, she looked down at the flannel pyjamas someone had clearly lent to her. Her face reddened. "You're . . . umm . . . here."

"I was told you might be hungry? I've brought you a plate from the kitchen."

Her eyes lit up. "I'm starving! I had a bit of tomato soup earlier, but somehow I've managed to work up an appetite since. All of this hobbling around takes it out of you. Would you mind carrying it inside for me?"

I closed the door behind me and followed as she hopped to the table and sat down.

"That looks painful," I said. "Heard you slipped on the ice?"

"You know me! Clumsy as ever!" She smiled a little shyly. "It's more inconvenient than painful. I really need to get back home to . . . Well, I need to go home."

"It's freezing in here," I said as I put the plate down. "How about I light a fire?"

"Would you mind?" she replied. "I couldn't get it to catch. My dad always does it at home."

I crumpled newspaper and lined the bottom of the fireplace grate, made a tent of firewood, and fished my silver lighter out of my pocket. I carried it with me, always—a gift from Andrea for my occasional cigar habit. I avoided reading the inscription that I already knew by heart.

The paper lit instantly and soon, the fire crackled and roared.

"Thank you for helping to reunite me with my locket," Olive said as I put the dinner plate in the oven to warm. "I was so worried about it."

"It's a good thing I'm observant," I said. "I'd noticed you fiddling with it when we met in the library."

"Nervous habit," she said.

"Nervous? Around me? Surely not!"

At this, she laughed, but there was something about her that still seemed a little anxious.

"It was my grandmother's," she said, quickly changing the subject. She popped the tiny clasp and the delicate silver face opened to reveal a photograph of a little girl about four or five years old. "This is my daughter, Lucy," she said.

I peered at the picture. I remembered a rumor that Olive had taken up with some new guy, and that was why she'd disappeared suddenly from our group all those years ago. I hadn't heard that she'd married and had a child.

"She's cute! No wonder the necklace means so much to you."

"More than you'd ever know."

As she closed the locket my eyes fell on the wedding ring on her finger. In my mind, I'd been calling her Olive Carter, but she was clearly a Mrs. Somebody now. "You're . . ."

"I'm . . . widowed," she said, biting her lip.

She was definitely a little nervous.

"I'm so sorry," I offered, although I knew well how hollow those words were.

"I go by my maiden name at work. It seemed easier . . ."

Of course. I remembered Mrs. Leonard calling her Olive Carter. "There's no need to explain."

A moment's silence expanded around us, neither knowing quite what to say next.

"Do you have any children?" she asked at last.

I shook my head. "Andrea desperately wanted a family, but it never worked out for us."

"I'm sorry to hear that." She looked at me for a moment. "I'm so sorry again, Jack. I can't imagine how hard it must be for you."

"Impossible, really. But life goes on, somehow." I let out a long breath.

Another strained silence washed around us.

"What a pair we make," Olive said. "Full of Christmas cheer." She offered a tentative smile. "How about a drink? There's a bottle of whisky on the counter if you fancy a drop. Evans brought it over. He felt guilty about not being able to drive me home today, what with all the guests arriving and then a flat tire. It seems as if everyone is conspiring to keep me here!"

I poured us each a splash of whisky.

She took a glass and clinked it against mine. "Cheers. Hopefully it'll numb the pain."

I raised my glass in return. "Amen to that."

Olive ate while I sipped my whisky, and the strains of an Andrews Sisters' Christmas song drifted from the wireless. I caught myself looking at Olive over the edge of my glass. She'd hardly changed at all.

"Can you believe we've run into each other, after all these years?" she said between hungry mouthfuls. "This is delicious, by the way. Did you make it?"

"All my own work. It sure is a surprise to see you again. Have you seen the others from the old gang? I haven't talked to anyone but Ryan in a long time."

"Only Rosie," she admitted. "She's still my best friend. The rest fell out of touch over time."

She wouldn't meet my eye. I had the distinct impression she was a little uncomfortable around me.

"So, tell me more about your job at the BBC. What's it like?"

"I've only just started in this role. I worked in the typing pool for some time and recently worked up the nerve to interview for a position on one of the news teams. I'm hoping the pieces I've been researching here will gain my boss's attention. It can be hard, working among so many men—they don't trust that women can do what they can. I'd like some proper assignments, and this is the first that fits that description."

CHRISTMAS WITH THE QUEEN

"I've no doubt you'll succeed. You always had a way of getting to the heart of a story."

At this, she smiled. "And what about you? Do you like working here?"

"You know . . . I do, actually. It isn't my dream job, but I like working with the head chef. He's a good man. Matter of fact, he's just offered me a permanent position at Buckingham Palace, when the staff returns to London after Christmas."

"Congratulations! That's quite a job title: royal chef!"

I smiled faintly. "Thanks. I haven't given him my answer yet, but I'm flattered." I swirled the remaining liquid in my glass, creating a tiny amber whirlpool before I drained the last of my drink. "Thank you for the whisky, Olive. And the company. It's been nice to run into you again. Twice."

"It has been nice."

"Well, I'd better head to bed. I have a busy few days ahead of me."

She struggled out of her chair.

"You don't need to get up," I said.

"I need to head to bed myself, soon. Can't lie on the sofa all night! It isn't the comfiest, if I'm honest."

She hobbled with me to the door, where I paused for a moment, not quite ready to go. Perhaps it was her open, honest face. Perhaps it was because she'd known me before it all, and because she'd known Andrea. Or perhaps I just didn't want to go back to my cottage and be alone with my thoughts.

"Thanks again for bringing me the dinner plate," she said.

We looked at each other for a moment, both of us lost for words.

"Well, if we don't bump into each other again, happy Christmas, Jack."

"Happy Christmas, Olive."

As I stepped out into the bone-chilling air, snow began to fall. In a few short strides, I had crossed the lawn, but rather than going inside, I turned to look out at the clutch of trees waving in the cold wind, fluffs of snow floating to the ground, and the lights of Sandringham House twinkling just beyond.

I was so relieved to have a busy schedule ahead, where I could escape from my thoughts and memories in the company of new friends and new tasks, spending Christmas doing what I did best. Cooking had been my only way forward in the past and suddenly I knew it would be my only way forward again.

I would accept Max's offer in the morning.

Chapter 20

Olive

I woke early the next morning. The swelling on my ankle had come down a little and the pain wasn't as bad. I washed and dressed, tidied away the few things I'd used, and sat by the window to wait for Evans to arrive as I read over the piece I'd typed up for Tom.

I was pleased with it. I'd focused on the monarch's Christmas Day message and the important role the BBC played in broadcasting this, and other historic moments, to the nation. And I'd shared an intimate portrayal of the queen, and how much it meant to her to honor her father's legacy, and to speak to the nation. All I needed to do now was prove to Tom Harding that I could deliver the piece for broadcast as well as I could write it.

I used the telephone in the cottage to place a call to Broadcasting House. I'd realized that if Rosie could get me a dictation machine, I could record my piece and present it to Harding in a way that would be much more powerful than giving him a typed script.

"Rosie. It's Olive."

"Olive! I thought you'd been kidnapped! Where are you?"

"I'm still at Sandringham. It's a long story. I'm heading home today but I need you to do me a favor."

I explained about the dictation machine and arranged to meet her later, in reception.

"Anything else happen?" she asked. "Did you see Jack?"

"Yes, actually, I did."

"And?"

"And nothing. It's too late, Rosie. He's a grieving widower. And even if he wasn't—that ship sailed a long time ago." There was no sound from the cottage next door. Jack must have left early for his shift. Neither of us had asked for the other's telephone number or address last night, so we had no way of keeping in touch. It had been a fleeting reunion. That was all. "It's probably best if I forget I ever saw him again."

"But don't you think you should—"

"I'd better go. The driver is just here. I'll see you later."

I'd written a powerful piece for Tom Harding, so even if I hadn't done everything I'd come back for, I had that, at least. Now, I just wanted to get home to Lucy and have a quiet family Christmas.

As I hobbled to the door, I saw an envelope on the doormat. My name was written on the front. I opened it and pulled out a page of writing paper with the Sandringham Estate header. On it was written *Recipe for Shrimp and Grits* with a list of ingredients and instructions. *It was good to see you again! J*

I returned the page to the envelope with a smile. Jack had clearly forgotten I was a terrible cook. I could barely manage to make an edible tomato soup, let alone shrimp and grits, but I was touched that he'd thought about me.

Evans helped me into the car and made sure I was comfortable before we set off.

"Now, miss. I finally have a bit of time, so if there's anything last minute you need to pick up, let me know and we can make a detour."

"Well, this is very presumptuous of me, but would it be possible to stop by Broadcasting House when we get to London? There's something I need to drop into work. I won't be long."

"No problem at all. As a matter of fact, it gives me the perfect excuse to pop to Hamleys and pick up a few things for the grandchildren. I spoil them rotten!"

I hadn't been back to the office since I'd heard my piece credited to Charlie Bullen, and I was still furious about it. I hobbled inside on the crutch I'd been given, met Rosie, and found a quiet room to record my new piece before making my way to Tom's office.

"Carter! What are you doing here? I thought you were out of action."

"I was—I am. But I wanted to give you this."

"What is it?"

"A piece I worked on while I was at Sandringham. Since my last report was considered so helpful, I thought you might like another. I'd be perfectly happy for my own name to be attached to it. Unless Charlie would prefer to take the credit again?"

Mr. Harding at least had the grace to look embarrassed. "Ah, yes. About that. It was all very last minute. We decided to use your report after all, and it was too late to change the listings and . . ."

"You don't need to explain, Mr. Harding. I understand exactly what happened." I took a breath to stop myself saying something I might regret. "This new piece is about traditions and the importance of the Christmas Day message, and how the monarchy and the BBC help us come together as a nation—and as a family—in these historic moments. In fact, I spent some time with Her Majesty. It's all here, in my report. I've also recorded it on the dictation machine, in case there was any doubt about my ability to be put in front of a microphone." I placed everything on his desk. "I suspect it's far too late to be useful for this year, but I wanted to give it to you, nevertheless. I'm ready to do more, Mr. Harding."

He looked at me a moment and smiled. Harding was an intensely private man. Rumor was he'd gone through hell in the Great War when he was young, suffered from shell shock for a while, but he had a good heart and a soft center. "You remind me a little of my wife, you know. Just as stubborn and absolutely determined to get your way."

"I'm honored," I said. "I've read all her Genevieve Wren pieces." "A Woman's War" had been a very popular and—for the time—ground-breaking column Evie Elliott had written under the pseudonym Genevieve Wren during the Great War. She was considered a trailblazer for women in journalism and had a legion of admirers—myself included.

"Is that so? I must tell her!"

He picked up the items I'd placed on his desk. "Very well, Carter—I'll listen to your recording, but I don't know that I have space for it in this year's Christmas schedule, even if I like it."

I was disappointed to hear that, but at least I'd gained his attention. "But if you like it, I could record another piece, for another occasion? The coronation is coming in June."

"Let's not push it, shall we?"

I smiled and hobbled to the door.

"Happy Christmas, Carter. Enjoy the few days' rest. We've a busy year ahead with the royal family. First the coronation, and then there's talk of an ambitious overseas tour."

It was a busy royal year I fully intended to be part of. "Happy Christmas, Mr. Harding."

Christmas morning started, as usual, with Lucy bounding into the bedroom and bouncing up and down on the bed.

"Wake up, Mummy! It's Christmas! Father Christmas has filled my stocking by the fireplace. Come and see!"

I pulled her into me and gave her a hug. "Happy Christmas,

darling bear. Are you sure it's Christmas morning? It's still very dark outside." I reached for my watch. It wasn't yet six. "Why don't you try and sleep a bit more? Tell me when you see the first bit of daylight."

She was restless and excited and fidgeted beside me as I dozed. "Mummy! Mummy! It's daylight. Look!"

I gave up, hauled myself out of bed, threw a blanket over my shoulders and trudged, bleary-eyed, downstairs, where we followed our tradition of sharing an orange while Lucy opened her stocking. No pony had arrived down the chimney, but there was a special note from Father Christmas to tell her she would be starting riding lessons, which was the next best thing. My heart burst as I watched her. My gorgeous girl. My precious gift.

There was a lovely simplicity to our family Christmas, especially after all the rigid formality of Sandringham. Breakfast in our pyjamas, a walk before our slightly chaotic lunch of goose and all the trimmings—overcooked sprouts, slightly soggy swede, almost burned roast potatoes—then Christmas pudding and Harveys Bristol Cream as we settled in front of the wireless for three o'clock.

I was so nervous on the queen's behalf. Now it was my turn to shush my mother as the national anthem played and we waited to hear her voice.

"*Each Christmas, at this time, my beloved father broadcasted a message to his people, in all parts of the world. Today, I am doing this to you, who are now my people. As he used to do, I am speaking to you from my own home, where I am spending Christmas with my family. And let me say at once I hope that your children are enjoying themselves as much as mine are . . .*"

As she spoke, I followed the words quietly along with her, willing her to do well, to not stumble as her father had so agonizingly done. Her voice was a little higher than when she'd rehearsed, lifted a tone by her nerves. She sounded so young, vulnerable in a way, and yet serene.

I needn't have worried for her. For the full six minutes and eight seconds of the broadcast she was pitch perfect, relaxed, and yet perfectly regal. She was a triumph.

My father patted me on the arm. "Well, love. Whatever you said to her worked a treat."

"I can't really take any of the credit, Dad! I only gave her a few bits of advice."

"But it's not everyone who can say they advised the queen, is it? Give yourself *some* credit. Your mother certainly will. She'll claim it was *all* down to you."

My mother told him to stop being silly.

While my parents dozed that afternoon, and Lucy played with her presents, I took a moment alone. I added the latest newspaper clippings to my royal scrapbook, along with the cutting from the *Radio Times* for the piece I'd written that Maguire had presented. It might have had Charlie Bullen's name attached to it in the listings, but I was determined that next year it would be *my* name, *my* voice.

While I didn't envy the queen her grand homes or her Dior dresses or jewels, I did envy the sense of purpose she had and the path that was mapped out for her: a husband, two children, a carefully managed schedule, a diary full of appointments, a lifetime role of queen stretching ahead. I seemed to have only questions: What would the new year bring? What would I be doing this time next year? I certainly hadn't expected this year to end with Jack Devereux strolling back into my life, and I wondered if there was more yet to our story, more surprises for the new year to deliver.

As I tipped the contents of the satchel I used for work onto the bed, a pocket lighter tumbled out—the lighter Jack had used to start the fire in my cottage. I must have picked it up when I was gathering the rest of my things. As I turned it over in my hands, I noticed an engraving on the back. *To darling Jack. The light of my life. Andrea. X*

My breath caught in my throat as the words engraved themselves onto my heart in sharp, painful scratches. I'd made the best of things, but sometimes I longed to be the light in someone's life, to be loved, and to love in return.

And, although Jack didn't know it, there was another light in his life.

I took the locket from my bedside table and opened the catch. The photograph of the little girl inside, the little girl Jack had admired was, in fact, his daughter.

Our daughter.

The light of my life.

1953

"Of course, we all want our children at Christmas time—for that is the season above all others when each family gathers at its own hearth. I hope that perhaps mine are listening to me now and I am sure that when the time comes they, too, will be great travelers."

Queen Elizabeth II, Christmas Day 1953

Queen Elizabeth II

Royal Yacht SS *Gothic*, South Pacific, December 1953

ondon's stuffy obligations and gray winter skies feel like a distant memory as I gaze out from the deck of SS *Gothic* and see nothing but sparkling blue water and cloudless skies. I capture the view on the cine camera dear Papa gave to me as a wedding gift, "to capture life's happiest moments." I sometimes imagine myself as a much older woman, looking back on these films of Philip and I, in the flush of our youth. I wonder what lies ahead for us. The death of my dear grandmother, Queen Mary, earlier in the year, was another great loss to the family. The old guard are slowly departing, and I must press on, without their steady hands to guide me.

I close my eyes and let the warm sun flood my face. Despite the approach of Christmas, there is no mention of steamed puddings or hearty stews and soups, no familiar festive scent of cinnamon or ginger. Here, we dine on freshly caught seafood, vibrant salads, and platters of exotic fruit. I must have lost a stone in weight already, despite eating heartily to sustain the energy needed for all the shaking of hands and smiling and polite conversation.

Dear Philip is in his element, back on the water where his soul belongs. He is proving to be a wonderful support. Charming as ever, if a little unpredictable at times in his chosen line of conversation. I remind him, occasionally, that we are always being watched, the press waiting for the slightest misstep. And he reminds me that he doesn't give two figs about the press. "Damned vultures, circling a kill." Philip hates the intrusion my unexpected ascension has brought into our now very public lives. Being at sea gives us both a chance to escape from it all for a while—until the next port of call, at least.

We have already covered so many miles, across the crystalline blue-green waters of the Caribbean, through the Panama Canal, and along the bottom of the world toward Fiji and Indonesia. I have learned so much about the people and nations of the Commonwealth. Our next stop is New Zealand, where I will broadcast my Christmas Day message from Government House in Auckland. I will be the first monarch in history to visit the country, which lends its own particular excitement and anxiety. We will visit some forty-six towns and cities, and have over a hundred scheduled functions to attend. I've heard they are even dying the sheep red, white, and blue to mark the occasion.

I have been working on my speech for several weeks, but I fear I have yet to hit the right note. It is difficult to concentrate when one is so consumed with learning the latest country's customs and culture, so as not to offend or embarrass. Besides, it is hard to think about Christmas while I gaze out upon tropical seas and feel uncommonly warm.

I find myself wishing that a younger woman, perhaps someone like Olive Carter from the BBC, could be with me again. I found her practical manner and steady encouragement most fortifying at Sandringham last year. Instead, I am accompanied by a pack of press men of a certain age, most noticeably Charlie Bullen. My father always found him quite amenable, but I must admit that I struggle to like him. It is very trying at times to be around the old establishment, but as Philip reminds me, they will not be here forever. "Stay on the throne long enough, darling, and you will have your pick of who you want around you."

A light cough behind me interrupts my ponderings, and I glance over my shoulder.

"Penny for your thoughts," Philip says as he joins me at the railing and places his arm around my shoulders. "You look nice."

"Do I? I feel rather dull compared to the photographs of Margaret they keep putting in the newspapers."

"Margaret is Margaret. Don't compare yourself. Besides, the sun on your cheeks suits you. You are positively glowing." He thinks for a moment. "Bloody hell. You're not expecting again, are you?"

I laugh. "No. A woman can glow for other reasons."

"Evidently." Philip gives me that look I have come to recognize, a twinkle in his eye that makes my pulse quicken a little.

I smile and rest my head on his chest. "The ocean is so beautiful, isn't it? No wonder you loved being in the Navy."

"Shall we stay here?" he says. "Run away. Leave crumbling old Buck House and the crown jewels to the rats?"

"Tempting, isn't it? But I rather think we should go back, for the children at least." I smile.

He lights a cigarette and leans against the railing, his back to the ocean, his face turned to mine. "Must we? I'm sure they can manage with Nanny Busybody and their aunt Margaret to corrupt them."

"Philip! It's Nanny Lightbody. You mustn't call her that!"

I scold him playfully, but I love him with all my heart. I would happily run away with him. I would go anywhere with my darling Philip by my side.

Although I know it is impossible for the children to be here,

I still feel a nagging seed of guilt at being away from them. Six months is such a long time when they are so very small. Philip says I worry too much, that they'll be having a marvelous time being spoiled rotten and eating far too many cakes, especially if Margaret has anything to do with it. Philip doesn't worry as much as I do, having had a rather disrupted childhood himself.

Mine, on the other hand, could not have been happier. I have such fond memories of playing with Mummy and Papa at our beloved family home at 145 Piccadilly, how Papa would chase me and Margaret around the garden, and pull us along in the little trolley Grandpa England gave us for Christmas. Of course, our governess, dear Crawfie, was always on hand, but it is our family time with Mummy and Papa I remember the most. I hope my children will have the same lasting memories of happy, carefree days with Philip and I.

"Well, let's enjoy it while we can," he says as we steam ahead. "We can just be Philip and Lilibet again, for a while."

I loop my arm through his. "Lilibet would like that very much."

The gong rings for dinner.

"Best not keep the chefs waiting," I say. "You know how precious they are about their creations."

Philip taps me on the rear as I turn toward the stairs.

"Philip! Behave!"

He roars with laughter.

I do love him so, the silly old thing.

Chapter 21

Jack

Royal Yacht SS *Gothic*, South Pacific, December 1953

I maneuvered expertly around Max as he shouted for the next dish. Pulling the venison off the grill, I ladled a wine reduction sauce over the tenderloin. Two plates, three, four, five, in quick succession, passing them forward to Max, who finished them with a sprig of rosemary and an eagle eye. The familiar clatter of clanging utensils, pots and pans, and hurried voices was a symphony I'd grown as used to as my own heartbeat. I'd even adjusted quickly to the cramped galley kitchen of the SS *Gothic* and the swaying motion of the ship, my body remembering the sensation of cooking at sea. Formerly a merchant vessel, adapted for the royal tour, the *Gothic* didn't exactly have restaurant-standard facilities, but it was much better than the galleys I'd cooked in during the war.

"Three more venison, Devereux!" Max shouted.

"Yes, chef!"

I rushed to fill Max's order—and bumped into Mason for the fifth time that day.

"Jesus, Jack!" he said, his tasting spoon falling onto the stainless-steel countertop with a loud clatter.

"I'm sorry. I'm in my head too much today."

"If you bump into me again, I'll toss you overboard!"

We had a good laugh at that and went about finishing the dinner service.

Mason had become a real pal this past year. Along with his and Ryan's help, I'd packed up my life on Richmond Street and given Andrea's things to her family in the second-worst goodbye of my life, before moving into the staff quarters at Buckingham Palace. I still thought of Andrea every day, still missed her in a way I couldn't measure, but I found myself breathing a little easier.

It was hard to believe that nearly a year had passed since I'd joined the royal kitchen staff. The days and weeks had slipped away in the busy kitchens, the calendar full of official state dinners, the sumptuous coronation banquets for Her Majesty, and the far simpler family meals and teas dotted in between. It was a whirlwind, a constant cycle of pressure that suited my state of mind. When the overseas Commonwealth tour was announced and I was assigned to the SS Gothic's crew, I was proud to be selected, and more than happy to leave London behind for six months. I had nothing else in my life beyond work and a few friends, and truthfully, there was a part of me that missed the Navy days of sea, sky, and sun.

"I need more creamed potatoes!" Max called.

I reached for a clean serving bowl, spooned a heap of the silky potatoes onto it, and passed it to Max.

"That's the last of them," he said, blowing out a breath and mopping his brow. Between the ovens and unrelenting sunshine of the South Pacific, it was hot as Hades in here.

I cleaned down my station thoroughly, as always, and gulped a glass of cold water. I was looking forward to a little star-gazing on deck later—and a chance to rest my aching feet. The ship was like a small battalion, and there was an endless list of people to feed: the queen and the duke themselves, and their personal staff, comprising two ladies-in-waiting, three private secretaries, a press secretary, the Master of the Household and two equerries; twenty other officials and staff; seventy-two naval staff, as well as a band of the Royal Marines. Last came the nine members of the press who had been invited to join the tour to report on it for the newspapers, newsreels, and radio programs back home.

I scrubbed my hands clean and removed my dirty apron, thrilled to be done for the day.

"Jack! Look lively!" Mason called as he crossed the short distance from the preparation area to the back sink. "The duke is here."

I shrugged. "And?"

"He's asked for you. Wants you to meet him upstairs in his salon."

"He asked for me?" I was pleasantly surprised. We'd had a nice exchange at Sandringham a year ago and had spoken a couple of times since, when he'd popped into the kitchens at Buckingham Palace, and at Balmoral that summer. I was always surprised when he remembered me.

"Go on then," Mason prompted. "Don't keep him waiting!"

I made my way to the duke's salon, where I was shown inside by one of his staff.

"Devereux, sir," the equerry announced.

I stepped forward and cleared my throat. "You asked to see me, sir?"

The duke looked up from his desk and smiled broadly. "Ah, yes, Devereux. There you are. Good man. Look what I found!"

He held out a handful of black and white photographs. I took them and studied them, feeling a smile come to my lips. Sailors posed for the camera in some of the pictures. In others, they were boarding a ship before setting sail, or setting up mess halls in the driving rain. I flipped through two more photographs of men peeling mounds of potatoes, and serving the soldiers.

I looked up. "The Seabees?"

"Indeed." A hint of a smile curved at his lips. "I had a little time to look through my naval memorabilia and came across these. I remember for one campaign, our resources were running low, so we joined the Allies for meals. The Seabees were there. I thought you might like to see these."

"Thank you, sir. That's very kind of you." I peered at one of the photographs. "Look at this guy—he's staggering under the weight of that pot. He looks like he's about to drop it!"

"What do you suppose would be the punishment for wasting all that food? Fifty push-ups and run laps on the deck until you vomit?"

I laughed. "That seems pretty likely to me, sir. Or clean-up duty, maybe."

"Good grief. The horror of it all!"

I liked the duke's sense of humor. Sometimes I thought he didn't quite fit within the stiff formality of royalty, but he seemed to charm everyone he met, and Elizabeth clearly adored him.

I missed the closeness a marriage brought. Missed having someone to share things with, or to laugh with in silly moments.

The duke tucked the photographs back into his pocket. "But, bloody hell, I do miss it—the boys, the camaraderie, and all the raucous games! At least we're at sea again. That does something for the spirit, doesn't it?" He clapped me firmly on the shoulder. "It's good to have someone here who understands. Anyway, must get on. There is always something for one to do. And no doubt you're dead on your feet after another dinner service."

"I'm a little tired, sir. Yes."

The equerry opened the door.

"Thank you again, sir," I said. "It was good to remember the old times."

I headed back to the kitchen, where Mason was finishing the last of his duties.

"What was that about?" he asked.

"The duke wanted to share some pictures from his time in the Navy."

"Well, aren't you the favorite! It doesn't hurt to have the queen's husband as an ally, does it?" He grinned.

"I suppose not," I said, still surprised that the duke had not only remembered me but had gone out of his way to share his photographs.

"Game of cards on deck, and a nightcap?" Mason asked.

"Sounds perfect."

A sense of contentment washed over me as I realized how much I enjoyed my job and the company of the people I worked with, and for. We headed up on deck to the balmy air and clear star-studded skies, and for the first time in a year, despite the lingering sadness that colored each day, I felt as if I truly belonged.

Chapter 22

Olive

London, December 1953

Christmas carols rang through the crisp afternoon air as I darted out of the tube station and ran along Bedford Street, sidestepping people who seemed to be in no rush at all. I'd promised Lucy I wouldn't be late for her nativity play, and I already was. Of all the traditions December brought, the school nativity was among those I enjoyed the most. Finally, I rounded the corner and sprinted toward the church hall.

Gasping, I pulled the door open and skittered inside, bringing a blast of cold air and a swirl of dry leaves with me. Several people tutted. Others shushed me. I made my way to an empty seat at the end of a row toward the front, sat down, and tried to steady my breathing so that I didn't sound like a steam train.

"Just in time," the woman beside me whispered. "They had a bit of a delay. One of the shepherds got stage fright."

I stifled a laugh as the curtains were pulled back to reveal Joseph, a heavily cushion-pregnant Mary, and a rather tattered-looking toy donkey. Lucy was an angel. She'd told me she wouldn't be on stage until "the shepherdy bit."

As I settled in to wait for her big moment, I glanced around at the other parents—mothers mostly—waiting for their own children to make an appearance. For once, I didn't feel out of place without a husband by my side. The sad truth was that many women in the church hall had lost their husbands during the war, meaning that many of the children on stage didn't have a father watching, or waiting at home. It was only the circumstances of my past that separated me from these other women.

"And lo! The Angel Gabriel appeared."

There she was. My angel.

I leaned forward in my seat. "That's my daughter," I said to the woman beside me. Tears pricked my eyes as I watched my beautiful girl, arms spread wide in her bedsheet angelic robes, a halo of golden tinsel around her head. She waved as she spotted me, before she remembered that angels weren't supposed to do that and returned to her stiff pose.

"And that's my young lad beside her," the woman replied. "The tall one at the back. His father would have been so proud. Thick as thieves they were before the war stole him from us." She turned to me. "Doesn't get any easier without them, does it."

I looked at her a moment before shaking my head. "No, it doesn't."

My heart ached to acknowledge the truth: that Lucy had never known the proud gaze of her daddy. My thoughts turned to Jack as I tried to imagine him beside me, but the image didn't fit, didn't work. Just like me and Jack had never worked. He and I were the opposite of a happily-ever-after fairytale. We were a terminal case of being in the wrong place at the wrong time.

I took a deep breath as all the angels gathered at the front of the stage to sing their rendition of "Jingle Bells." My heart soared with love for Lucy as she sang her heart out. She didn't have a father to admire her, but she had a mother who loved her more than she would ever know.

By the time we got home, we were both exhausted. After tea, when Lucy was settled in bed with a book, I joined my father in the sitting room. I leaned back against the cushions and closed my eyes.

"How was our angel?" he asked. "I'm sorry I couldn't be there, love. Can't seem to kick this bloody awful cold."

"It's fine, Dad. She was brilliant. Word-perfect, which is more than can be said for Joseph who forgot all his lines, and the shepherd who dropped his lamb."

He laughed. "Don't suppose your mother made it along?"

I shook my head.

My mother was at Auntie Jean's, taking a few days "away from it all." She'd been at Auntie Jean's a lot over the last year. Neither of my parents wanted to discuss it, but it was obvious that their marriage was far from a happy one. There was no question of them getting a divorce—my mother couldn't cope with the scandal it would cause, not to mention all the legal upheaval—but it was also clear that they couldn't go on forever with my mother disappearing sporadically.

"Can I do anything?" I asked. "To help?"

He shook his head, got up, and turned on the television set he'd bought to watch the coronation that summer. I knew that was his way of telling me he didn't want to talk about it, or her.

"I'll make a pot of tea," I said and gave him a reassuring kiss on the cheek.

He reached for my hand and held it a moment—his way of letting me know he was grateful. "Mrs. Butler dropped in some Christmas cake."

I groaned. Our neighbor, Mrs. Butler, was renowned for her Christmas cakes, and for all the wrong reasons.

"It's as dry as dust," my father called as I busied myself in our little kitchen. "Approach with caution! I nearly choked when I had a slice earlier."

I laughed to myself. All the silly little habits and traditions of the friends and neighbors I'd grown up with were as reassuringly unchanged as the crown jewels. There was something comforting in things staying the same. Change wasn't always for the better.

After we'd shared the pot of tea, and watched an episode of *The Good Old Days*, I went upstairs to check on Lucy.

She was busy with her Queen Elizabeth II scrapbook, pasting in the latest pictures from the royal tour.

"Can we look at the map, Mummy?" she said. "See where the queen is now."

Lucy's latest obsession was the Commonwealth tour. We kept track of all the countries the queen had visited, and where she was going next. They were doing a project on it at school, not that Lucy needed any extra encouragement. I found it fascinating myself, not least because of the state-of-the-art Marconi radio and sound equipment SS *Gothic* had been kitted out with especially for the tour. There were twice-daily dispatches to keep the news desks at home up to date, and even occasional live broadcasts, which I'd had to endure the agony of listening to while wishing things were different and that it was me reporting on the latest state function.

"Look. I found another piece at work today, about the coronation," I said. "I thought you might like to add it to your scrapbook, if there's room."

It was a piece I'd written for Bullen to record as a headline broadcast for the coronation special—a series of programs about the historic event. Revived by a stint at the Sussex coast, Bullen had triumphantly returned to work just in time for the coronation. I, on the other hand, had been assigned a small job reporting on a local woman who'd dedicated an entire room in her house to the coronation and had decorated it in memorabilia produced for the occasion. The whole thing had given me a migraine.

In the end, the pieces I'd produced after my visits to Sandringham last year had counted for little. As Tom Harding had warned, my second piece on the Christmas message was too late to broadcast, although he'd at least offered to keep it on file for another year. Since then, I'd found myself assigned to the "and finally" items deemed too frivolous for serious reporters like Bullen or Maguire: the latest time-saving electrical appliance, a lost cat reunited with its owner after ten years, a heartwarming story of a helpful schoolchild.

Lucy flicked through her scrapbook. "I don't think there's space to add anything else about the coronation. Will you read it to me instead? Pretend you're reading it out on the wireless, like you will one day!"

I was used to the little tricks Lucy used to delay her bedtime. I glanced at my watch. "It's getting late."

"Pleeeeease, Mummy. I was a very good angel today, wasn't I?"

I smiled and tucked a loose curl behind her ear as I sat on the end of her bed. "You were the best angel. I'll read it once. But then, straight to sleep." I cleared my throat. "AN OCCASION FIT FOR A QUEEN—Olive Carter reports for the BBC."

Lucy laughed as I substituted Bullen's byline for my own.

I carried on. "*History was made today as our new monarch, Queen Elizabeth II, was crowned in a dazzling ceremony at Westminster Abbey. Over three thousand dignitaries from across the Commonwealth were seated inside the abbey, with millions of ordinary people able to watch the historic events unfold on television sets around the world. It is estimated that the dress weighs around eleven pounds. The coronation necklace is one that was commissioned by Queen Victoria. Our young princess looked every inch Elizabeth Regina as the mighty Prince Edward crown was placed on her head by the Archbishop of Canterbury in a most solemn moment. Back in the stateroom of Buckingham Palace, the guests were served an eight-course banquet, prepared by the talented chefs of the royal kitchens. Even the corgis were treated to the very best chicken and steak. On a day that saw the happy news that the British expedition party in Nepal have successfully reached the summit of Mount Everest, it seems fitting that our young queen begins her reign as our new monarch. No doubt she, too, carries a sense of embarking on a challenging expedition into uncharted territories. We wish you well, ma'am, in your own endeavors to reach the summit. God save the queen."*

I had read the piece and listened to Bullen's recording of it so many times that I almost knew it by heart. I found his pieces so dull and predictable. I'd started rewriting them with a fresher, more feminine slant, and left the alternative pieces on Tom's desk. I'd written an alternative coronation piece, focusing on the detail of the dress. I read it out now to Lucy.

"Despite the rain and drab skies, she was a vision of calm composure in her coronation gown that took eight months to make and was the eighth of nine designs proposed by Norman Hartnell, Her Majesty's preferred designer. The gown is made from duchesse satin and embellished in gold, silver, and pastel thread with motifs of the four national emblems, and emblems of the dominions of which she is now monarch. The intricate embroidery is arranged in scalloped graduated tiers. Gold beads, diamanté crystals, and seed pearls have also been added and shimmer in the lights of the television cameras, carefully positioned all around the abbey to ensure that every moment of the ceremony is captured and beamed around the world to an anticipated audience of some three hundred million viewers."

"Did the dress really take eight months to make?" Lucy asked.

"Yes. All that time. Imagine!"

"And she'll never wear it again?"

"Never. Isn't that silly!"

"If I had a dress that pretty I would wear it every day!"

Tom had at least admitted that my detail on the dress, and on the impact of television in bringing the event into people's homes, were interesting perspectives and ones that Charlie hadn't fully considered. I'd pointed out that this was because Charlie was a man and only saw things from a man's point of view, which had been fine when reporting on a king, but not when reporting on a queen. Mr. Harding had conceded that I had a point but had also emphasized that changing the opinions of people like Charlie Bullen wasn't something that could happen overnight.

It had been hard to watch Charlie stride back into his role. He hadn't once asked me about being at Sandringham, although I could tell he was dying to know how I'd ended up having a private audience with the queen to advise her on the delivery of her speech. He'd been reporting on the royal family for thirty years and had never had such a personal encounter with the reigning monarch. But, of course, it was Boring Bullen who'd been dispatched as part of the BBC team covering the Commonwealth tour.

While he was halfway across the world, I was stuck at Broadcasting House. Tom Harding knew that I would have loved a place among the press team on the ship, but he also knew that I couldn't have gone, even if the opportunity had arisen. It was one thing to ask my parents to mind Lucy for a few hours when I went to the pictures with Rosie, but it would have been out of the question to leave her for six whole months—even though that was precisely what the queen had done, leaving her young children behind with the nanny. Lucy was growing up fast—too fast—and I didn't want to miss a minute of it.

Tom Harding had promised me he would find me something else to make up for it, but so far, the best he'd been able to offer was a small legacy piece on last December's deadly smog and the government's promises to bring in a national air pollution law. At least it was a step up from reporting on the latest domestic appliances.

I kissed Lucy on the cheek and tucked the bedsheets around her. "Now, get to sleep, you. Remember Father Christmas is watching for good girls and boys."

She squeezed her eyes shut tight.

Heart full of love, I went to my bedroom and pulled an old shoebox out from beneath the bed. It was covered in dust, and full of memories, some of which I didn't want to stir up. I removed the lid and took everything out: Lucy's baby things, a few special letters and trinkets, postcards from my parents' holidays in Rhyl and the Cotswolds. And there, at the bottom, the photograph I'd kept all these years. A snapshot taken on the night we'd celebrated Victory in Europe. An impromptu party on Primrose Hill. Old friends, and new. On my left, with his arm draped casually around my shoulders, was Peter Hall. On my right, a bottle of champagne raised in joyful celebration, Jack Devereux.

I turned the photograph over: *8th May, 1945. Victory!*

Working on the Great Smog piece had sent my thoughts straying back to this time last year, and especially to when I'd bumped into Jack at Sandringham and learned of Andrea's tragic accident. I'd returned his lighter straight after Christmas, along with a note to thank him for the recipe, posting them to Mrs. Leonard at Sandringham House and asking her to forward it to him, if she knew where he was.

A note of thanks had arrived two months later, via Broadcasting House. I took it from the envelope now, and read it again. *Dear Olive, Thank you for returning the lighter. It seems we are quite a couple of magpies, finding each other's shiny things! It means a great deal to me, so I am very thankful, even though it took me all this time to say so. I've been busier than you can imagine in my new job at Buckingham Palace (yes, I accepted). You mentioned that the shrimp and grits hadn't gone well when you'd tried to cook it, so I've enclosed a simpler recipe for a spiced tomato soup. Hopefully this one will be more successful! J.*

I couldn't help being a little disappointed by his response—no invitation to meet; not even a cursory kiss at the end of the note—and it irritated me that I still cared. Jack was an itch I couldn't scratch. A stone in my shoe. Impossible to ignore and yet ever-present. But despite a few exchanged letters and the few recipes he'd sent on, it seemed we were destined to always circle around each other, moving in orbit, rather than toward each other. That was how it had always been with me and Jack. How it would always be.

Which was why I hadn't told him about Lucy. It was too risky; too complicated. Apart from the fact that he was still grieving for Andrea, his job didn't exactly allow for domestic harmony. Lucy and I were doing just fine, and the last thing Jack needed was another emotional bombshell. So I put him away, packed him into the shoebox of memories I kept beneath the bed, and tried to forget all about him.

Chapter 23

Jack

I watched as Ben, the pâtissier, pulled a tray of gingerbread from the oven. It smelled delicious—and festive—despite the oppressive temperatures.

"I can't get used to the summer heat at Christmas," I said.

"I know what you mean," Ben replied. "Who wants to eat turkey and Christmas pudding and then change into swimming trunks?"

We talked a little about the many colorful and fascinating differences from the English ways that we'd seen on tour already— different climate, the landscapes, cultural customs—and we still had months of the tour ahead of us.

Life at sea was turning out to be a real good time. The camaraderie among the kitchen staff and the rest of the crew felt like a brotherhood of sorts, like being in the Navy again. They were a lively bunch, and I finally started to feel my loneliness falling away. Had I been in London, I would have visited Andrea's grave with flowers and told her how much I missed her. Perhaps, after all, it was best that I wasn't there to mark the anniversary. Everyone kept telling me I had to move on, to live my life, as she would have wanted.

The kitchen prep for Christmas would be somewhat limited,

since the queen and the duke and the rest of the royal party would disembark for a time to celebrate with the governor of New Zealand and his wife. But the staff staying aboard had to eat, and though we wouldn't feast like royalty, we'd certainly celebrate. After we finished the lunch service, I tucked Grandpa's notebook under my arm, planning to check on a recipe to prepare for the next day, and climbed the steps leading to the upper decks. It was a beautiful golden afternoon. The white exterior of the ship gleamed so brightly that I had to shield my eyes. A handful of people were bathing in the sun, while others milled about, attempting to stretch their legs and get what little exercise they could.

The queen stood near the bow, filming the placid waters of the Pacific. She must have taken hours of footage over the last few weeks. Her fascination with documenting everything around her made me realize how little I'd documented my own life in photographs, drawings, or family portraits, let alone fancy new cine cameras like the queen's. Perhaps one day I'd regret it, but without Andrea—without a family of my own—I didn't see the point.

I flopped down into a deck chair and exhaled a breath. It was good to be outside, in the shade, with the wind on my face.

I thumbed through the recipe book, looking for a dessert I thought the crew might like, and settled on fresh bananas, whipped cream, and a rum butter sauce, perfect and light in the warm weather. As I skimmed the notes, voices drifted on a breeze from the pair of men standing at the railing.

I thought I recognized the older gentleman. He was part of the press, worked for the BBC, if I wasn't mistaken.

"Damned place is being taken over by women. A busy news desk is no place for a mother. She should be at home, looking after her child, not running around as a reporter, and a poor one at that."

My thoughts turned to a conversation I'd had with Olive last Christmas. She'd told me how difficult it was to be taken

seriously in such a male-dominated environment. After years at Maison Jerome, I knew, all too well, what it was like to work with someone with old-fashioned ideas. I turned my deckchair a little, straining to make out the rest of their conversation.

I had been pleased to hear from Olive soon after Christmas, when she'd returned my lighter, along with a note. When she said she'd struggled with the shrimp and grits, I'd sent her an easier recipe. After all, she'd admitted she was a terrible cook, and I thought she might appreciate a little assistance. She immediately wrote again to thank me, and since then, the cycle had continued. I tried to send her recipes when I had time, which admittedly wasn't often.

"You really shouldn't say things like that, Charlie," the younger man said now.

"It's the truth, and you know it. These women are taking our jobs. I'd fire the lot of them if I had any say. Tom puts up with too much."

"It's because of that wife of his," the young man replied. "She was a reporter, you know."

"At least she could write."

They both chuckled at his indirect insult to the rest of the female staff. I thought of Olive again, and frowned. I was about to say something as a shadow fell over me, and I glanced to my right.

"Mind if I join you?" Max asked, pulling up a chair next to me.

"Not at all."

We didn't often relax during the day, but we'd been hard at work for weeks, so he'd promised us a leisurely afternoon.

"You've been a real godsend this past year, Jack," he said. "You know that?"

I glanced at him, sprawled in the deck chair, lying back with his arms loose at his sides, his big barrel chest, his round but kind face. "How so?" I asked.

"For starters, this time last year, we were short-staffed and you stepped in, despite your own hardships. But you didn't act like a regular temporary hire. You worked as hard as three men, and you brought inventive recipes and ideas. Since then, you've continued to work hard. You never complain, regardless of the task. And you help others in the kitchen when they need it. I don't know how we got so lucky."

I warmed to his praise. "Thank you. I didn't set out to impress, but I like to work hard."

"That's what makes you special, Jack. You're unassuming. You come in, do your job, and do it well, and you help the rest of the crew do theirs, too. You know, you have real talent. And I've said this before, but if you dedicate yourself, I see you moving up in the ranks."

"Thank you, Max." I wasn't sure I wanted to move up the ranks in the royal kitchens, rather than striking out on my own one day, but I appreciated the praise and the support. It was a bright spot in my life.

He smiled. "You're welcome. I wanted to ask—do you mind if I look at that notebook of yours? Wouldn't mind checking out some of the recipes."

"Sure thing. Just be careful. It was my grandpa's, so it's pretty old. The pages are worn."

"Not to worry. I know how much it means to you."

Max thumbed through the recipes, commenting on this spice or that, the surprising combination of French, Spanish, and Creole flavors, the odd dish that seemed distinctly American in some way.

"What do you think?" I asked.

"I see you in these pages. His influence has clearly rubbed off on you."

That thought made me happier than he could know. "This recipe book is a piece of him," I said. "His whole life—memories and moments—marked by different dishes."

I thought back to the first time Grandpa had given me the notebook and told me to cook something from it, on my own.

"Choose something you want to make," he'd said. "That's the best way to learn. You have your eye on something delicious, and you attempt to recreate it."

I'd gazed at a picture of a beautiful soufflé pasted into the book. I'd never had one, but it looked puffy and light and crispy all at the same time, and my twelve-year-old self had wondered how I could make eggs do that. "I want to make a soufflé," I'd said.

Grandpa had nodded. "Gather the ingredients first. Next, read all of the instructions one time through so you know what to expect. After that, begin with step one."

I did exactly as he said, but the soufflé came out burned on top and soupy in the middle. The moment I'd removed it from the oven, it had collapsed. I was frustrated, disheartened. Though I'd followed the instructions, somehow I'd done everything wrong: I didn't whip enough air into the egg whites, and had used too much butter to grease the dish.

My grandpa had clapped me on the back. "Don't be disheartened, boy. It's all right to make a mistake. Listen, recipes—and life—don't always go the way we want them to go, even when we think we've done everything right. It's in the doing—and doing again—where the success lies. Keep at it, my boy."

He had been right that day and he was right now. I was glad I'd kept cooking and learning and trying new things. I wouldn't have ended up on the SS *Gothic* with the royal family had I not. I glanced at Max, who was caught up in reading some of Grandpa's notes in the margins of one of the recipes.

"This is a nice legacy to leave," Max said, snapping the book closed. "You should keep up the tradition."

"What do you mean?"

"Start documenting your own recipes. Where you were when you first cooked it. How it was received. How the recipe develops and changes."

I liked the idea. Rather than use a cine camera, I could record my life in recipes; write notes about textures and flavors and smells, divided by the chapters of my life. My years at home in New Orleans; my time in the Navy when recipes had been more about making available food palatable than anything else; and of course, the years with Andrea and her favorite traditional English recipes; then my time with Jerome; and now Max and his astute classical French training. The more I thought about it, the more the idea of my own recipe book intrigued me.

"Well, you've certainly given me food for thought," I said. "Literally."

Max smiled at my terrible pun. "You're the perfect man for it. Ever the ambitious one, you are. That's something I like about you, Jack. You're always looking for ways to challenge yourself. It makes you stand out, you know. You don't play it safe, and that shows in your cooking."

I'd never thought of myself in that light before, but I supposed it was true. In all ways but one: love. With the exception of Andrea, I'd never been brave about expressing my feelings. She had made everything so easy.

"Thank you, Max. You've been an excellent boss. I've learned so much from you and it inspires me."

He smiled. "Maybe one day you'll have your chance in the spotlight."

"Maybe." For now, I wanted only to work toward the things that made me happy, and as I looked down at my grandpa's recipe book, I knew I was on the right track.

"Good! Enjoy the afternoon off," Max said, standing. "We've a busy few days ahead until we reach Auckland."

I settled into the deck chair, face tilted toward the sky, and kicked up my feet for a long nap.

Chapter 24

Olive

London, December 1953

After a frustrating week at work, I was relieved when Friday evening came around. After tea, I buttoned my coat and stepped outside. It was a perfect winter night. Clear, frosty skies were peppered with stars and the pavement sparkled at my feet.

"Where are you off to anyway?" Dad asked as he stood in the doorway.

"To the pictures, with Rosie."

"I wish you'd find a nice young man to take you to the pictures."

I kissed his cheek. "Don't start that again, Dad!"

"I just want you to be happy, Olive."

"I *am* happy. I'll see you later."

But I couldn't help agreeing with my father. It would be nice to have a handsome man waiting for me at the tube station. For now, Rosie would have to do.

But even the latest film couldn't cheer me up. Somehow, the build-up to Christmas hadn't held the same magic as it usually did. Even the few flakes of snow that fell on my way home couldn't lift my mood. I found the crowded pavements irritating, surrounded by happy couples, arm in arm, laughing as they hurried through the snow, or stopped to steal a kiss. And if it wasn't happy couples in love, it was happy families carrying bundles of packages and stopping to admire the shop window displays. I was tired of always being the one to arrive home alone, and I was also tired of being given the least important assignments at work.

I went to bed in a bad mood and woke up in an even worse mood after a restless night.

Come Monday, I was irritable at work. I was distracted and tired and made silly mistakes. I was relieved when it was time for lunch.

Rosie leaned back on the bench and stared at me in that way she always did when she knew I was keeping something from her. "What's put you in such a bad mood today? And don't say nothing, because I can tell."

I sighed and took a bite from my meat paste sandwich. Rosie and I were having our lunch break in the park, despite the cold. It was her idea, and a good one as it turned out, despite my initial reluctance. It was lovely to be outside, to feel the nip of the December air on my cheeks, and to blow away the tired headache that had lurked at my temples all morning.

Rosie poured us each a coffee from her Thermos and added a tot of whisky. She took a sip and winced at the hit of alcohol. "Blimey! Might have been a bit heavy-handed there."

"You always are." I sipped my coffee and savored its warmth as it slipped down my throat.

"Let me guess. It's Jack *Devereux*, isn't it?" She always exaggerated the pronunciation of his surname.

"It isn't him exactly. It's just, well . . . Oh, God, Rosie. It *is* him. I can't stop thinking about him. Which is ridiculous."

"I don't see why it's ridiculous. He is the father of your child, after all."

"Don't remind me." I took another slug of whisky coffee. "I know it's silly, but when I saw him last year, I thought it meant something. You know how much I believe in fate and destiny and all of that. I thought there had to be a reason why I'd bumped into him again, but there wasn't. And now he's halfway around the world and I doubt he ever thinks of me at all."

"It's only been a year since Andrea died, Liv. Give him time."

"Time for what?"

"To move on. To see you as more than his old friend, Calamity Carter. If that's what you want?"

I wasn't sure what I wanted. "It's just all so complicated."

"Love always is."

"Who said anything about love? This connection—or whatever I have with Jack—doesn't even have to be about love, does it? Maybe I should tell him about Lucy, give him an opportunity to get to know her, regardless of what there could be between him and me."

"And what about Lucy? What if *she* falls in love with him and he decides he doesn't want to be a father to her?" Rosie looked at me, her understanding for my predicament clear in her eyes. "You can't rush it, Olive. Relationships are like a good Christmas pudding. They need time to steep and mellow, for all the spices and flavors to come together."

"Don't you go all cheffy on me, too. You sound just like him, turning all serious when he talks about food!"

"Maybe not now, not yet, but if it's meant to be with Jack, the time will come to throw some brandy on your feelings for each other and set them alight and then . . . whoosh!"

We both laughed as she threw her arms dramatically in the air to mimic flames of desire.

We talked over our plans—or rather, lack of plans—for Christmas, and then made our way back to the office, where Maguire was waiting with his usual welcoming scowl.

"Harding wants to see you, Carter."

"Did he say what it was about?"

"Why don't you go and find out? I presume you know the way. You've been up there often enough recently."

When I reached his office, Tom had a wry smile on his face. "Well, Carter, I promised you a good story since Charlie Bullen has the royal beat, and I think I have something that might put a smile back on your face." He indicated that I should take a seat.

I was intrigued. What could possibly be better than spending months with the queen and the Duke of Edinburgh in the South Pacific? "I'm all ears," I said.

"How are you with flying?"

"Flying?"

"As in, air travel."

"I'm not sure," I said, confused by the question. "I've . . . never been on an airplane."

At this, Tom laughed. "Well then, how about you start by flying halfway around the world?"

I leaned forward as he pushed a leaflet toward me. The words *SPEED AROUND THE WORLD WITH B.O.A.C.* were printed on the front, along with a map showing a route from London to New Zealand.

I looked up. "I'm not sure I understand."

"We've been offered a seat on the BOAC Speedbird flight from London to New Zealand, via Australia. BOAC want the press to raise awareness of the new service and assure people that it is all perfectly safe."

"Is it?" I asked. "Safe?"

He cleared his throat. "Of course. You will report on the experience of modern high-speed flight and send updates from each of the short refueling stops on the way. There will be just under two days of flying in total, each way. What do you say?"

I wasn't sure what to say. I had always wanted to travel, but had never been further than Cornwall. The invitation was a more than reasonable consolation prize for not being sent on the royal tour, and I could already see a way to deliver an entertaining report on the experience of taking such a long trip in such a short space of time. "Two days?" I said. "Each way?"

He nodded.

It was definitely manageable at home. My parents wouldn't mind looking after Lucy. My heart started to race with anticipation. I could do this.

"This is the perfect story for me, Mr. Harding. Thank you. I promise I'll—"

"And there's one other thing." He pushed his glasses up onto the bridge of his nose. "I'm not quite sure what witchcraft you're using to make this happen, or what sort of vendetta you have against poor Charlie Bullen, but we have been informed that Charlie took a nasty fall on the deck of the ship a few days ago and is now laid up with a broken leg. He needs surgery apparently. He'll be transferred to a hospital as soon as the *Gothic* reaches New Zealand."

"Oh dear." I bit my lip to stop a smile spreading across my face.

"Indeed. So that leaves us without a royal correspondent, during a very important royal tour, and an historic Christmas Day message due to be broadcast from Auckland." He looked at me and raised an eyebrow. "If you take the BOAC piece, you would arrive just before the *Gothic* is due to dock."

A smile finally escaped. "You want me to take over from Charlie? Cover the Christmas events in New Zealand?"

Tom nodded, then shook his head. "You're like a cat with nine lives, Carter—I've never seen anyone land on their feet so often."

My mind whirled. This was incredible. And yet, if I stayed on in New Zealand, it would mean missing Christmas with Lucy. "I really would love to, Mr. Harding, but . . ."

"Could your daughter manage without you?" Tom prompted, guessing the reason for my hesitation. "Just for one Christmas? It's a hell of an opportunity, Carter."

"Can I think about it?"

Tom leaned back in his chair. "For a couple of minutes, yes."

"That long? You're too kind." There was so much to organize, but I couldn't possibly let the opportunity slip away.

"I've a newsroom full of people who would bite my arm off for this chance."

I had to make it work somehow. "Then, my answer is yes."

"Good. I'm very pleased to hear it. Now go and get yourself organized. You leave in three days."

My head spun with ideas and excitement as I turned to leave his office.

"One more thing, Carter."

I paused in the doorway. "Let me guess. Don't mess it up?"

"Well, yes. That, too. I was going to say, happy Christmas. You've had a good year. Keep it up."

I smiled. "I absolutely will, sir. And a happy Christmas to you, too, Mr. Harding. Are you doing anything nice?"

He glanced at a photograph of his wife on his desk. "We are spending Christmas in Paris, as we do every year, to honor an old promise."

His words sent a prickle down my back. I had an old promise to honor, too. One I had made to myself, many years ago. That one day I would tell Lucy the truth about her father. I had thought this might be the year to do it, but now I was heading halfway around the world. The year would be almost over by the time I returned.

My father didn't see what all the fuss was about when I told him about the opportunity and how awful I felt about leaving Lucy.

"She's seven years old," he said. "You've dozens of Christmases to spend together. Leave her with me and your mother. We'll have a lovely time."

I still wasn't sure. "But you know how much Lucy loves Christmas, Dad. It feels wrong to not be here with her. It isn't as if she has a father to make up for it, is it?"

I didn't talk about Lucy's father often, but he had been on my mind a lot lately. Everything would be so much easier if he was around.

"She has her nanny and granddad, who love her as much as any father would," Dad said. "Talk to Lucy. She might surprise you."

Lucy couldn't believe I had even thought about not going. "You have to say yes when the queen invites you somewhere, Mummy. I think it's the law."

I didn't have the heart to tell her the queen hadn't invited me herself. "I'll miss you so much."

"I'll miss you too, but me and Nanny and Granddad will have a nice time. You can bring me some things back for my scrapbook."

Lucy saw everything through such a simple, uncomplicated lens. I often wished I could do the same.

"Well, how about we have Christmas before I go?" I said. "To make up for it."

"Really? Could we?"

"I don't see why not!"

"You're making a bit of a habit of spending Christmas with the royal family," my mother said later. She had returned from Auntie Jean's refreshed and less irritable, but she was still showing no real signs of affection or love for my father. "Oh, and there's a letter for you on the hall table," she added.

I padded through to the hall and opened the envelope, wondering who could be writing to me.

Dearest Carter,
I had a bit of bad news recently and find myself reminiscing about old times and old friends, so I'm writing on the off chance that you're still at your folks' place, or that they are and might pass this on to you. I'm back in London for the next few weeks, so how about a drink for old times' sake? If you're happily married, feel free to ignore this letter. If you're still single, or unhappily married, my telephone number is below.
Yours hopefully,
Peter Hall

Peter Hall was the last person I'd expected to hear from! I wasn't sure whether I was pleased to hear from him, or annoyed, or simply surprised. It was typical of Peter to be so impulsive, and so impossible to resist. Jack was a complication—always had been. Peter was just Peter, a bit of harmless fun. I wondered what he was doing now. Maybe a drink with an old flame for old times' sake was exactly what I needed, but I would have to put him off until after Christmas.

I grabbed my coat and went to the telephone box at the end of the road, preferring to keep my conversation with him away from my mother's wagging ears.

I put my coins into the slot and dialed the number at the bottom of Peter's note. My heart raced as the telephone rang at the other end, and then there was a click, and a voice I hadn't heard in years.

"Hello. Greenwich 38498."

"Hello, Peter."

"Carter? Is that you? Bloody hell. Didn't think you'd reply."

"I'm not sure I should have." It was surprisingly lovely to hear his voice, if a little annoying to admit how easily I knew I could fall for him again.

He laughed. "How the hell are you?"

"Not bad. You?"

"Middling. Better for hearing your voice. So, how about a drink? Browns in Bloomsbury? Tomorrow at seven? My treat."

"Actually, I'm about to go away for a while. With work. But maybe when I'm back, after Christmas?"

"Well that's a damned shame, but I've waited eight years to see you again—I suppose a few more weeks won't make much difference."

Had he really been waiting all this time to see me again? "I'll telephone when I'm back," I said.

"You'd better. And, Carter?"

"Yes?"

"It's good to hear your voice. Really good."

"Yours too, Peter. I'll see you soon."

I hung up the receiver and took a moment to catch my breath. What on earth had I just done? I didn't really want to rekindle things with Peter Hall? Did I?

That evening, I packed my suitcase and spent as much time as possible with Lucy. We looked through Dad's old atlas as I showed Lucy the route I would be taking, by airplane and ship. She couldn't believe how far away New Zealand was. I could hardly believe it myself. The furthest I'd ever traveled from London was to Cornwall, and that hadn't been somewhere I'd gone by choice. My thoughts clouded as I remembered those difficult months: the deep shame of my "condition," losing my job, being sent away to a distant relative where nobody would know me, the feeling of being so isolated and alone. And yet, when I looked at Lucy's face, I couldn't believe there had ever been any sadness or doubt about any of it.

"You get to sleep now," I said as I tucked the bedsheets and blankets around her, and kissed her on the forehead. "I love you, little bear. I'll be back before you know it."

She threw her arms around me. "I love you, Mummy. You're the best Mummy in the whole world."

My heart squeezed with affection. I hoped she would always believe that. Even when the truth about her father inevitably came out.

In the end, it was surprisingly easy to say goodbye to London and its cold gray December skies. As the airplane took off and climbed above the clouds, my life below already felt so far away. A thrilling adventure lay ahead, and I was ready for it.

Chapter 25

Jack

Royal Yacht SS *Gothic*, South Pacific, December 1953

Another week at sea had passed and Christmas was nearly upon us. We were to dock in Auckland in two days, where the queen and duke would disembark with the necessary staff for their tour duties. The rest of us would remain on the ship. We were looking forward to the ease of those days and a quieter Christmas.

We were winding down for the night after a difficult dinner service through choppy waters, when a surprise visitor brought us all to immediate attention.

The queen.

"Your Majesty, good evening," Max said. "Can we be of any assistance?"

"I should like to speak to Jack Devereux. Is he here?"

Max's eyebrows rose in surprise. "Yes, ma'am."

I jerked my head up from cleaning my station, surprised by her request. What could the queen want with me? I hoped I hadn't displeased her in some way. I hastily wiped my hands and walked toward her.

"How may I be of service, ma'am?" I towered over her petite

frame, but her presence emanated regality and importance and made me feel rather small beside her. I briefly wondered what the burden of such huge responsibility must be like for her.

She didn't so much as break eye contact.

"My husband is rather enamoured with the idea of a Cajun cook from Louisiana," she replied. "He's an adventurous man, you see—well-traveled—and he would be simply delighted if you could make a dish for him. Perhaps tomorrow for lunch service?"

"I'd be honored, ma'am."

A hint of mischief flashed in her blue eyes. "Be sure it has plenty of spice."

"I wouldn't make it any other way, ma'am."

At that, she offered a slight smile, before leaving through the galley door.

The queen continued to surprise me, as did the duke. They were both rigorously professional in their royal roles, but always kind. They didn't think twice about talking with their staff or crew. I'd grown to like them both during my time working for the royal family.

"What was that about?" Max asked as he wrapped up the leftovers and placed them in the refrigerator.

I explained the queen's request to make a Cajun dish for the duke. "Seems he's become quite a fan of the cuisine."

"Why don't you make the dish for the staff meal, too?" Max said. "Then we can all try it."

"You got it, chief," I said with a mock salute, drawing a smile from him.

"It's just as well you have that old book of recipes with you," Max said. "You're putting it to good use."

He was right. Although I'd brought Grandpa's recipes along for comfort rather than expecting to use them for inspiration, I was glad to have it with me. As I wiped down my station one last time, mind brimming with ideas of what to serve for lunch, I kept returning to Max's suggestion from last week: to create a recipe book of my own.

I removed my apron and tossed it, along with the dirty dish-cloth, into the laundry basket, then headed to my cabin. Max was right: I did have a great collection of recipes, my own ideas, my own techniques. The duke's interest in my food was proof enough. Perhaps there really was something to this idea.

I pictured Grandpa's face and smiled. I knew he would have been proud. I used to be wracked with sadness when I thought of him, but now, although I still missed him, all that remained were happy memories. Cooking had a way of doing that for me, each dish linking me to a moment in time. The seasons of my life entwined with taste and aromas and memories.

The idea of my own cookbook sparked something inside me. Suddenly, I latched onto the idea and began to parse through the cooking techniques, tips, and tricks I'd learned over the years, making lists and notes of my own creations. It would take quite some time to record and order everything, and of course I'd have to type up the pages, which I wasn't particularly good at—but I was excited by the idea. It felt good to have a project, a goal, and I hoped that one day it might become something special to look back on. Perhaps I might even try to get it published. For now, the book was for me alone.

That evening, when the dinner service ended, I pored over the notes I'd begun to collect for the cookbook. There was a lot to sort through.

"You writing in your diary again? Spilling all your secrets?" Mason asked as he sauntered into the room.

I laughed. Mason was good at that—making me laugh.

"Let's have a look," he said, as he sat down next to me.

Though a little apprehensive to share, I pushed my notes toward him. Mason was a good guy, a good friend, and I trusted his instincts. He'd made some of the best dishes I'd sampled at Buckingham Palace under Max's tutelage. Frankly, Mason was one of the most talented chefs on the staff and he'd deserved his promotion to sous-chef. I hoped I might be next.

Mason scanned the first page of notes. "May I?" He motioned to my pencil.

I handed it to him and watched as he scrawled several notes. *Add a pinch of this, trim that, cook five more minutes, baste at least twice.*

"You have a lot of thoughts."

He grinned. "You know I always do, but Jack, these are great. This is a good start. I think you really have something here."

"You think so?"

He nodded. "What do you plan to do with it all?"

I shrugged. "I don't know yet. For now, I just want to enjoy documenting it all. You know, what I've always really wanted is to run my own restaurant."

"Me too." He lowered his voice to make sure no one overheard him. "It's the dream, right? Nobody else to report to. Run things exactly as you want. Choose your own menus."

I thought of the red-brick building on Richmond Street, and all the plans Andrea and I had made for it, talking late into the night, imagining a dining room full of satisfied customers, reviews in the press, accolades and awards. "Andrea and I had this crazy dream . . ." I lost myself in memories, the grandiose ideas we'd held onto for years. "Anyway, it doesn't matter now."

"Doesn't it?" He looked at me. "I know it must be hell for you, Jack, but maybe you shouldn't abandon the idea entirely."

I hesitated for a moment. It was painful to go back there in my mind. "There's a building in my old neighborhood that we had our eye on for years. It's red-brick, two stories, white-trimmed windows with flower boxes, and a short winding pathway that leads to the front door. We imagined landscaping around the path, adding an elegant lamppost, perhaps. It's a little run-down at the moment, but it could be something really special. It's been on and off the market for ages."

"Sounds ideal."

"It does. It was."

"Have you thought about the menu?"

"Of course," I replied. "But I wonder how my Cajun dishes and southern country cooking would be received in London. I'd add some English classics with a twist, too, of course."

"I think the mix of traditional and new are a great combination. I've noticed some of your food has a French flair as well, which always does well in London."

The image of my dream bloomed behind my eyes. The elegant but cheerful ambience, the rave reviews in the newspaper, the kitchen staff working in tandem like a well-oiled machine.

Mason stood. "Well, if you're ever looking for a partner . . . ?"

I studied his expression, his serious brown eyes, the determined set of his jaw, and knew he meant it.

"We'd make good partners," I said. "My brains. Your brawn."

He laughed. "We'd make *great* partners, Jack. Think about it."

It was a nice thought, but neither of us had the time or the money to make it a reality. And yet, some part of me was hopeful. Maybe one day, the dream I'd harbored for the last decade would become a reality.

"Here's to thinking about it," I said, clinking my teacup against his.

"Cheers," Mason said. "To the future."

Chapter 26

Olive

New Zealand, December 1953

The flight to New Zealand went off without a hitch and despite the long hours of sitting, and the occasional bout of something dreadful called turbulence, I thoroughly enjoyed the experience. I felt like an intrepid explorer, and even managed to reference renowned female journalist and travel writer, Nellie Bly, in my report for Tom. It was the best piece I'd ever written, because there was so much I wanted to say.

Once in Auckland, I was transported by tender to board SS *Gothic* which was anchored offshore while the royal party prepared for their planned tours and official engagements. Their arrival was a source of immense excitement and anticipation throughout New Zealand. I'd captured the atmosphere as best I could on the journey from Christchurch and quickly dispatched a piece to Tom, taking advantage of the unique insight I had of the build-up and preparations for the queen's visit. I finally felt that I had something useful to contribute, a unique story to share.

On board SS *Gothic*, I was met with a wonderful lightness in the air that seemed to have infused everyone with good humor. From the news reports and photographs I'd heard and seen in

London, it was clear that even the usually stuffy royal family were enjoying a more relaxed atmosphere away from the demands of formalities at the palace. The queen and the Duke of Edinburgh, and their staff, spent sunny days on deck, playing cards and games and laughing with each other. I supposed it must be a rare treat for the queen to be out of the public's gaze during her time at sea.

The press team assigned to the royal tour consisted of a number of Fleet Street hacks and special friends of the monarchy from the more reputable magazines—*Tatler, Town & Country, Harper's*. On the long flight to New Zealand, I'd had plenty of time to worry about how I would fit in, anxious that I would be a spare part among the more experienced journalists, but I needn't have worried. Word about my involvement—albeit brief—in the queen's first Christmas message last year had spread beyond the walls of Sandringham, and several people mentioned it to me, impressed that I'd broken through the usually impenetrable division between her public and private self.

Getting people to open up to me was a talent I'd always had. People generally liked me. Olive, the dependable friend. Olive, who was always great fun. Olive, who would get the job done. Friendship had always been easy for me, but love was as elusive as an audience with the queen.

As I stood on the deck of the SS *Gothic*, exhausted after the long journey but elated to be there, I realized how much I'd missed having time to myself. Since Lucy's birth, life had revolved around her every need, and I had neglected my own. But now, with the breeze in my hair and a sense of adventure on the wind, I had time to think, to breathe, to process everything that had happened over the last few weeks.

I thought about Jack, wondering if he was here as part of the household kitchen staff. Part of me hoped he would be. Part of me dreaded seeing him again. And then there was also Peter, and the promise to meet up when I got back home. It was so strange that these two pieces of my past had come back into my life within a year.

I pushed all thoughts of them aside as I turned to see the queen walking toward me, a cine camera in her hand, color in her cheeks, and a lively sparkle in her eyes.

I curtsied. "Ma'am."

She stopped as she recognized me. "Miss Carter! What a pleasant surprise! Have you been here all the time?"

"I've just arrived, ma'am—reinforcements. There was an incident with another reporter."

"Oh yes. Poor chap. Well, it's jolly nice to have another woman on board."

Everyone in the press corps had remarked on the fact that the queen had been less reserved than usual on the tour. She certainly seemed in good spirits.

"What are you filming, ma'am, if you don't mind me asking?"

"Oh, anything really. Life on the ocean waves, the occasional dolphin, silly little films of Philip." She smiled as she glanced at her camera. "Clever little machines, aren't they?"

"Nice memories to capture."

She nodded. "Quite."

She was called away then by an equerry. I was about to return to my cabin when one of the other reporters appeared and called me over.

"Press briefing, Carter. Five minutes."

Inside, we were given details of the schedule and protocol for our arrival in New Zealand. It was the first time a monarch had visited the country, so huge crowds were anticipated. I was still suffering from the effects of the change in time zones and could hardly keep my eyes open.

After the briefing, I returned to my cabin to get some rest. I'd barely laid my head on the pillow when there was a knock on the cabin door.

I dragged myself up and opened the door. A member of staff offered a small smile.

"Sorry to disturb you, miss. Her Majesty would like to see you."

"Me? Now?"

"In her office, miss. If you'd like to follow me."

"Should I bring anything?" I grabbed my notepad and a pencil and hurried after the chap, more than a little surprised, thoroughly unprepared, but intrigued nevertheless to have been asked to visit the queen in her private office.

"Ah, Miss Carter. Take a seat."

"Ma'am." I sat in the Queen Anne chair opposite her in a pleasant lounge area away from her desk.

"Perhaps I could run my speech past you, as we did last year. I am afraid I have struggled rather to find the right tone."

I nodded enthusiastically. "Of course, ma'am." Not only was I eager to help, I was proud to have been asked.

I sat back, listening carefully as she read from the typed script. There was a lot of religious content, and details about the tour—where they had been, where they were going. It felt a little stiff and not at all Christmassy.

"What do you think?" Her eyes searched mine. "I felt it was important to emphasize the reason for this extensive tour, to remark on the opportunity it offers to reach all my subjects, not just those in Great Britain. It is a rather impressive schedule when one thinks about it. All those countries!"

I took a moment, wondering how honest I could be. "Perhaps there might be room for more about family in the speech, ma'am? Being away from loved ones at Christmastime can be hard, and I suppose it's often a difficult time for some people, as well as a happy time for others."

She thought for a moment and then made a few notes on the page. "Yes, quite. Thank you for the reminder."

I wondered if she was thinking about her children, and her sister, Margaret. The newspapers had been awash lately with stories of the love affair between the princess and Group Captain Peter Townsend—and the queen's refusal to approve their request to marry.

"Who is it you will miss this Christmas?" she asked.

I smiled. "My daughter, Lucy. It's my first Christmas away from her."

"Then we have something in common. I miss the children terribly."

Her words were unusually personal, offering a glimpse of the woman and the mother behind the crown. She seemed suddenly vulnerable and alone, with the weight of the world on her young shoulders.

"Your daughter's father is on hand back in England?" she continued.

I paused for a moment. "She's with my parents." I couldn't bring myself to offer my usual lie. Not to the queen.

She studied me for a moment, as if weighing up her response. "No happier times for a grandparent than those they spend with their grandchildren."

"No, ma'am." I breathed a sigh of relief, grateful for her diplomacy.

"Whether a mother, or a queen—or both—we must all make sacrifices at times. Face the difficult decisions." She returned to the script of her speech and made a few additional notes. "The crown is, both literally and figuratively, a heavy item to wear. One must rule with one's head, not with one's heart."

"But what if your head tells you one thing and your heart tells you another?" I asked.

At this, a light smile passed her lips. "Then one must choose and make peace with it. Life brings us many challenges and dilemmas.

Indecision and regret are where madness lies." She stood. "Quiet certainty, Miss Carter—that is the way we must all rule, however large or small our realms."

"Thank you, ma'am. I'll remember that."

She straightened her shoulders and smoothed her hair as she checked her reflection in the mirror above the mantelpiece. "And now, I must approve tonight's menu. Chefs really are unusual creatures—so particular, and so easily offended. I hardly dare make a single remark."

At this, I laughed. "They're an odd bunch, to be sure."

The queen picked up a pile of paperwork and sat down at her desk chair. "Duty calls, I'm afraid. I shall look at the speech again, see if I can add something a little lighter. And thank you."

I took my cue to depart. "No, ma'am. Thank *you*."

As I was about to leave the room, there was a light knock at the door, and a member of staff stepped inside. "Mr. Devereux for you, ma'am."

"Oh yes. Do show him in."

My stomach lurched. Jack *was* here.

As he stepped into the room, our eyes met. He did a double-take but then he quickly nodded his head and addressed the queen. "I have the menus you requested, ma'am."

I couldn't take my eyes off him. He looked so smart in his chef's whites, his face healthily tanned from the sun. He looked so much better than when I'd seen him last Christmas, when grief had hollowed his eyes and stolen his smile.

The queen seemed to catch the moment of surprise between us. "Thank you again, Miss Carter."

I dipped my head and dropped into a curtsey. "Ma'am." I looked at Jack as I rose. "Mr. Devereux."

He stole a wink and nodded his acknowledgment. "Miss Carter."

I walked out of the room with my heart pounding.

Chapter 27

Jack

Royal Yacht SS *Gothic*, South Pacific, December 1953

O live. On the ship. How had that happened? I did my best to appear nonchalant, but the truth was, I was happy to see her—happier than I would have expected.

I wanted to say something when our eyes met, but in the queen's presence, all I could do was wink and nod as she passed.

"Do the two of you know each other?" the queen asked as the door closed behind Olive.

"We're old friends, ma'am. We lost touch for many years, though our paths have crossed again recently." *And mostly when you're around*, I thought.

This time, she allowed her smile to show. "Sometimes, people are thrown into one's path for a reason. I find it best not to wonder why but simply to enjoy the meeting."

I nodded. "Very true, ma'am."

It was strange to see Olive again, never mind on a ship in the South Pacific. After Andrea's sudden death last year, life had seemed more capricious to me than ever. There didn't appear to be any rhyme or reason to anything . . . and yet, here we were once again, Olive and I, in service to the royal family at the same time.

"Mr. Devereux," the queen continued, "I wanted to personally thank you for the dish you made for Philip. He was surprised and positively delighted, although he did say that the—jambalaya, was it?—made his mouth burn."

I couldn't help but smile. "Yes, ma'am. Jambalaya. I'm very pleased he enjoyed it." I'd made the savory rice dish with sausages, shredded chicken, plump shrimp, and plenty of hot peppers. The staff had enjoyed it, too, although it was a spicy step too far for those with a more conservative palate.

"The duke also enjoyed the accompanying note about the origins of the dish. It adds something, I think, to know a little about what it is one is eating."

I'd written a short description about the dish's Spanish, French, and African roots from the notes I'd found in Grandpa's book. "I have to give credit to my grandfather for that, ma'am. It was his trusted recipe that I followed."

"How delightful. There is nothing so pleasant as a family recipe, or a piece of useful advice, handed down across the generations." She moved over to her desk. "Now, let us have a look at the menu, shall we?" The queen reached for the sheet, scanned it, crossed off a couple of items, and handed it back to me.

"Thank you, ma'am," I replied, bowing before I left the room.

Olive was waiting outside. Her lips spread into a wide smile when she saw me. "Surprise!" She seemed to hesitate for a moment, before leaning in for a slightly awkward embrace.

Surprise hardly covered it—I was stunned to see her. More than that, I was truly happy to see her. I'd often thought of the old group of friends in the months following Andrea's accident. I'd thought about Olive especially, after running into her last Christmas. The handful of letters we'd exchanged since had amused me, and I'd wondered if our paths might cross at Buckingham Palace one day. Now here we were, on the other side of the world, meeting yet again.

I laughed as I stiffly returned the hug. "Surprise is right! I was so shocked to see you, I almost forgot to address the queen!"

"I'm pretty shocked myself, to be honest. I was in London three days ago."

"What are you doing here?" I asked.

"It's a long story, but I presume you're busy, so I'll keep it short."

As we walked back toward the galley, she explained about her assignment on the new Speedbird flight, and about stepping in for Charlie Bullen.

"I heard someone had broken their leg—I didn't realize it was one of the reporters. Bad luck for him. Good for you, though!"

"Extremely good," she agreed. "I'm here for a week, to cover the queen's arrival in New Zealand and the Christmas Day message. Then I'll be headed straight home, back to—"

"Louise? Your daughter?"

"Lucy," she corrected, a slight flush rushing to her cheeks.

"Of course—Lucy. So you'll spend Christmas here?"

She nodded. "Christmas in New Zealand. It wasn't quite what I was planning a few weeks ago. I still can't believe I'm here."

We stopped outside the galley kitchen. I sensed a hesitation in her, a reluctance to leave.

"Listen, I have to get back to work," I said at last. "But we've made a habit of playing cards after the dinner service is finished, if you'd like to join us later?"

"Did you forget how dreadful I am at cards? My poker face is terrible!"

At this, I laughed. "That's right. I'd forgotten. Well, even better then. We'll take absolute advantage of it."

"How could I possibly resist?" she said, as she threw me a final smile and walked away.

As I watched her go, her auburn hair shifting around her shoulders, I felt a flicker of something long-buried spring to life; memories and moments resurfacing.

Chapter 28

Jack

London, August 1945

S ince VE Day, our new group of friends had stuck together like glue. Once a week, we met at The Thirsty Dog, a corner pub we'd grown to like, where we spent the evening catching up on everyone's news and having fun away from our responsibilities at work.

I finished my shift as a line cook in the worst fish and chip shop in London, changed clothes, and headed over to meet the gang. My routine was now so familiar, it seemed that I'd lived in London much longer than three months. I was a little early that night, but that suited me fine. A quiet pint sounded nice before the boisterous fun of the night began. As much as I'd been enjoying the group, I was really more of a one-on-one kind of man. I'd spent a little time alone with Andrea these past few weeks and enjoyed our time together more and more, but I still wasn't sure if things were progressing between us. I liked her a lot, but she was more reserved than I'd first realized, and I wasn't sure she felt the same way about me. VE Day had made all of us less inhibited than usual, but life was settling into a routine again. I suppose I was waiting for a sign from her.

When I ducked inside, I saw that I wasn't the only one to arrive early. Olive was already sitting at a table near the back of the pub with what looked like a fresh gin and tonic.

"Hi there," I said, sliding in next to her. "I guess we're early."

"I'm absolutely starved!" she replied. "I've ordered a ham sandwich to tide me over until the others arrive." She took a deep drink from her glass. "I've had quite the day at the office, working on a stack of the most boring papers imaginable. I think I could type in my sleep at this stage!"

"Do your hands ever get tired?" I asked, making polite conversation about her job.

"They did at first, but I'm used to it now."

The bartender arrived with the food and slid the plate in front of her. Olive refused the offer of English mustard. I ordered a pint of ale.

"I see you didn't want the mustard. You don't like spice, I take it?" I asked, once the bartender had left.

"Not really. I definitely don't like mustard."

"You probably wouldn't like my cooking then."

"Are you offering to cook for me?" She grinned playfully.

"If you play your cards right, maybe I will."

She laughed. "Well, I'm terrible at cards, so that definitely won't be happening!"

"Maybe I'll cook for us all. Ryan keeps badgering me to. Seems to think I have a bit of talent. I'll make something that will set your mouth on fire."

"I look forward to it." She sank her teeth into her sandwich. "I heard you were on the hunt for a better job? There's a new French restaurant looking for chefs. Maison Jerome. I pass it every morning on my way to work. I saw a sign in the window."

I nodded. "That's not a bad idea. I'll take a look. If I work at a proper restaurant, maybe I won't come home smelling like grease or looking like I crawled out of a dumpster."

"A *dumpster*." She mimicked my accent and laughed. "You couldn't look that way if you tried."

"Oh, but I could." I grinned and ran my hand over my still-damp, rumpled blond hair. And then it hit me that she was complimenting me, flirting a little, perhaps. I couldn't stop myself from doing the same. "And you look pretty as a peach tonight."

We talked easily and, before we knew it, an hour had passed. I glanced at the door.

"Where is everyone?" she said.

"You'd think we got the wrong day," I agreed.

"It's Thursday. We definitely don't have the wrong day."

We realized it at the same time.

Olive hit her forehead with her hand. "Peter said something about The Stag's Head, didn't he?"

"Damn. It's across town."

"And it's raining . . ." We both looked toward the window. The light mist that had persisted for most of the day had turned into a steady, soaking rain.

"It's awfully cozy in here where it's dry," I said.

"And there's good company," she added with a smile.

"You said it." We clinked our glasses against each other.

I thought briefly of Andrea, and then my thoughts turned to Peter.

"Peter will be waiting for you," I said. "Perhaps we should go?"

"It's fine. Peter will keep himself busy. He always does."

I smiled. "I've noticed."

Knowing Peter, he'd probably already set his sights on some other pretty young thing in the pub. He oozed charm and charisma. It was no surprise he'd swept Olive up so quickly, although it didn't seem as if things were serious between them. With Peter, it was doubtful.

"And what about Andrea?" she asked. "Won't she be expecting you?"

"She's with her family tonight," I said. "Having dinner with her parents and brothers."

"So, you're excused then."

I couldn't tell if Olive wanted me to say more about the situation between me and Andrea, but the truth was, I, too, wanted to know more—from Andrea herself. Perhaps I needed to be more like Peter, make a move and let the cards fall where they may. At the moment, I had no idea where we stood and if, or when, I should do something about it.

I bought another round of drinks, and, realizing I hadn't eaten, ordered a meat pie. The next thing I knew, we were several drinks in and couldn't stop laughing.

"Don't let anyone ever tell you that you're boring, Olive Marie Carter," I said, the beer going to my head a little.

"And don't let anyone tell you that you aren't charming, Jackson Devereux."

I grinned at hearing my full name on her lips. It sounded so different in a proper English accent rather than the thick southern drawl I'd grown up hearing.

"I should probably get home," she said, when the bartender collected our empty glasses.

I led her to the door, where we stopped to peer out at the sheeting rain.

"It's really turned nasty," she said. "Care for a walk, sir?"

"Since the weather is so grand? Sure. Why not! Let me walk you home, miss."

She took my arm. "That would be nice. A gentleman as well as a handsome and talented chef. You really are full of surprises!"

"My grandpa would've had my hide, should I even think of abandoning a woman at night in the city streets. He raised me well."

We strolled through the neighborhood, across the bridge to Bermondsey, to the flat she was sharing with Rosie. I was struck by how much fun I was having in her company, and I thought back to the night we'd met a few months ago. Olive in that yellow dress. Her ruby lips and big smile. How we'd danced and laughed half the night. And then Peter had stepped in, and I'd met Andrea, and that was the end of that.

Or, perhaps, it wasn't.

"Do you want to come in?" Mischief danced in her eyes. "I think we could both do with a coffee after that rain."

I hesitated. "I'm not sure, Olive. I . . ."

She turned the key in the lock. "I'll even use the fancy stuff!"

I smiled. "Coffee would be good."

After coffee, Olive poured us each a brandy, and we fell into another long conversation about our pasts, our friends, our hopes and dreams for our future. She talked excitedly about working for the BBC. I described the restaurant I hoped to own one day.

Some time later, warm with drink, I yawned.

"It's getting late," I said, standing to go.

"It is." Olive rose from her chair, facing me. "That was so much fun." She hiccupped and covered her mouth. "Too much fun! You're a bad influence."

"As are you."

I looked at her bright inviting eyes, her full lips, and thought again how beautiful she was. I fixated on a thought that had flitted through my head more than once that night. What if I kissed her? Just one kiss, to see if there was as much chemistry between us as I thought.

I moved toward her, pausing briefly to see if she would pull away. When she didn't, my heart skipped a beat. Just one kiss. Softly, I brushed my lips against hers.

And one kiss it was . . . at least, that was how it began.

Chapter 29

Olive

London, August 1945

Jack left before sunrise. He dressed in the dark, muttered something about getting home, and awkwardly offered to make me toast before he left.

"It's fine, Jack," I whispered. "You don't have to."

"I'm sorry, Olive. I really shouldn't have stayed. I shouldn't have . . ."

"Jack. It's fine. *I'm* fine. Just go, before Rosie hears you."

I listened as he crept downstairs, like a thief making his escape.

I lay in bed, my stomach churning at the memory of the night we'd spent together, the way he'd touched me, the way I'd responded. We should never have let it go so far, and yet how delicious it had been. I curled into a ball and squeezed my eyes shut, wincing at the thought of seeing Andrea, Peter, everyone. Would they know? Would they be able to tell? Somewhere in the middle of the night, we'd agreed it was a one-off. A mistake. Jack was with Andrea. I was with Peter.

So why had it felt so right to be with each other?

We couldn't avoid each other for long. The next week was Rosie's birthday and the whole group was meeting for a celebration. I couldn't stop thinking about the night we'd spent together. Things hadn't gone that far yet with Peter, despite him making several attempts, so it was Jack's touch I thought about, Jack's kisses I remembered on my lips, even when it was Peter's arm draped around my shoulders.

I tried to push it from my mind as the night went on, but when I was coming back from the ladies' and Jack was on his way to the gents', it was impossible to avoid each other.

We smiled a little shyly.

"Olive," he said. "Listen. I wanted you to know that Andrea and I had a heart-to-heart, and, well, we are officially a couple now. I wasn't sure where things stood between us the other night when you and me—and, well I wouldn't have, you know, if things had been clearer then. I'm not that kind of guy . . ." He shifted awkwardly from one foot to the other. "What I'm trying to say is, I had a great time with you, but—"

I forced a smile. "It's all right, Jack. There's no need to explain. We agreed it was a one-off. A mistake."

He smiled, showing the dimple in his cheek where I'd kissed him. "You're so great, Olive. Peter's a fool if he doesn't see what he's got in front of him. If things had been different, before, well . . . Anyway, I'll leave it there."

I laughed to cover my disappointment. "Go to the loo, will you? I'd better get back to the others. And Jack?"

"Yes?"

"Even if the timing was all wrong, I'm not sorry. About what happened."

He smiled and touched my arm. "How could anyone be sorry about that?"

We never talked about it again. I didn't even tell Rosie. It was a one-time thing. And although I wished it wasn't, Jack was with Andrea, and they were happy together, good together although I hated to admit it.

I tried to let Jack go and turned my attention to Peter.

Peter was attractive, but in a different way. He was always the one to come up with a plan, insisting we drive to Brighton for a picnic on the beach, or to Suffolk to taste the scrumpy cider. Peter was like a fever, infectious in the worst way. Rosie wasn't fond of him, but for once I didn't care what Rosie thought.

"I'm having fun, Rosie! It's not like I plan to marry the man. I haven't even slept with him."

"Good! And don't. Have some fun with Peter, but promise me you won't fall in love with him."

I promised her, and I meant it.

The truth was, I'd already fallen for someone else.

At first, I put my tiredness down to the after-effects of a virus, and my constant nausea down to a stomach bug that had been going around at work. I couldn't keep anything down and felt as if I had the most dreadful hangover even when I'd hardly touched a drop. My mother remarked on my gaining weight, but she was always remarking on my gaining weight. Although I had noticed that my skirts were tighter than usual at the waist.

It was Rosie who first made the connection. "Olive, you're not . . . you know? Are you?"

"Not what?"

"Pregnant?"

The word pierced my heart. It was every unmarried woman's worst fear. The greatest shame.

"I can't be. I'm just a little under the weather."

"When was your last monthly?"

I shrugged. "You know I'm useless at keeping an eye on all

that." I wasn't one of those girls who made a note in their diary. My cycle had always been erratic, so I'd given up trying to anticipate it. But Rosie was speaking aloud the nagging doubts and fears I'd been keeping to myself for the last few weeks.

"You should go to the doctor. Just to make sure."

"Do I have to?"

"Yes, Olive. You do." She reached for my hand. "I'll come with you."

I felt so ashamed and afraid as I waited for the doctor to assess my urine sample and for him to feel around my belly and breasts.

"Well, Miss Carter, there's no doubt about it. You are expecting a baby. Early days. You're maybe eight weeks along by my estimation."

His words buzzed like bees in my ears, my mind reeling. I felt as if I was swimming underwater.

"Your parents are aware of this?"

I shook my head.

"Well, the father will do the honorable thing, I'm sure," he added.

"Yes," I mumbled. "Of course."

"And, if not, there are several alternatives." He handed me a leaflet on a mother and baby home.

I burst into tears.

"There's no point crying now, Miss Carter. Your condition is easily prevented. Not so easily accepted, it seems."

"When are you going to tell Peter?" Rosie asked as we made our way home.

I stalled.

She stared at me, eyes wide. "Olive? Peter *is* the father, isn't he?"

Another month passed. I knew I couldn't hide my condition from my parents for much longer, but I couldn't find the courage to tell them. My mother would be so ashamed. My father, heartbroken. I couldn't bear to think about the mother and baby home, being hidden away with my shameful secret, but I couldn't possibly raise a child on my own, and—as Rosie had pointed out plenty of times after I'd told her who the father was—this was Jack's problem as well as mine.

"You have to tell him, Olive. Jack's a decent chap. He'll do the honorable thing, just as the doctor said."

"But he's with Andrea and they're madly in love. You know how they are together. How can I possibly tell him? 'Oh, hi, Jack. I know you're with someone else, but—surprise!—I'm having your baby!'"

"Jack and Andrea are a couple, yes, but it's not like they're married or anything. Tell him. Before it's too late."

I wrestled with it all week, and decided to tell Jack on Thursday evening as soon as I could get him on his own.

But the night went on and on, and still I hadn't managed to say anything. Rosie kept kicking me under the table and raising her eyebrows at me.

Finally, I grabbed an opportunity while Andrea was deep in conversation with Rosie.

I took a deep breath. "Jack, there's something I need to tell you. Could we step outside for a moment?"

He smiled at me. "There's something I need to tell you, too. Actually, something I need to tell everyone. But, you go first."

I took a sip of my drink. "You go first. It's fine. We can talk later."

He stood up and tapped the top of his glass with the end of a spoon. "Can I have everyone's attention, please?"

Andrea reached for his hand. "Jack, I thought we said . . ."

He leaned down and kissed her. "I know what we said, but . . ." He turned to the rest of us. "We have news! Andrea and I are engaged!"

He glanced at me as they were both engulfed by an outpouring of surprise and good wishes.

The room started to spin. My heart thumped in my chest. Engaged? They couldn't be. *Not now.* I heard myself offering my congratulations, joining in the clinking of glasses and hugs. Rosie looked at me, even as she offered her own surprise and congratulations. A wave of nausea washed over me, followed by panic and fear. How could I possibly tell him? What did this mean for me, now?

"So, you're making an honest woman of Andrea, are you, Jack?" Peter said, with a wry smile. "Why now, eh? Is there a baby on the way?"

Rosie batted his arm. "Peter!"

"What? We're all wondering!"

Andrea laughed and looked embarrassed.

Jack was offended. "Christ, Peter! No, there isn't a baby on the way—thank God!"

Thank God! I wanted to stand up and scream at him, "*But there is a baby on the way, Jack. It's too late. You're going to be a father.*"

"It *is* possible for two people to agree to get married because they love each other," he continued. "Not just because it's the decent thing to do."

For what felt like hours, the conversation revolved around the engagement news, until I couldn't bear it any longer and made my excuses to leave.

I somehow managed to congratulate them again as I put on my coat.

"She's a very lucky lady, Jack," I said.

"And I'm a very lucky man," he replied as he reached for Andrea's hand.

There was nothing else to say.

"You don't seem yourself tonight, Olive," he added quietly. "Is everything all right? What was it you wanted to tell me earlier?"

"It doesn't matter." Aware that everyone was looking at me, I smiled and planted a big red kiss on his cheek, as I'd done so many other times. "And that's the last time I'll ever kiss you, Jack Devereux, you heartbreaker!" I said dramatically, a smile forced on my face. "I hope you and Andrea will be very happy together."

Everyone laughed at my joke, but I felt as though I'd been stabbed in the heart.

Chapter 30

Jack

Royal Yacht SS *Gothic*, South Pacific, December 1953

Olive joined us for cards that night on the ship. She was a popular addition to our group, and we found ourselves laughing the night away. Mason and a few of the others joined in the stories we shared about our times at sea, and Olive entertained us with tales about some of the worst interviews she'd conducted for her job: rat-infested flats with negligent landlords, a new dog kennel opening, and a story on ladies' hosiery. All the while, Olive crushed me at cards.

"She's won again!" Max said. "You really need to catch up, Jack."

"Beginner's luck," I said, tossing my hand on the pile in the middle of the table.

Olive laughed. "I don't know what's happening. I've always been hopeless at cards. It must be something about the sea air."

"She's certainly better than you, Jack," Mason added, throwing his own cards on the pile.

"It's late," Max said, standing. "I'll call it a night and hit the hay."

"I'm exhausted, too," Olive agreed, smothering a yawn. "I feel half dead with the time change."

"I'll walk you to your cabin," I replied.

Mason nudged my leg, and we exchanged glances. I knew what he was thinking, but I wasn't about to make advances toward Olive. For one thing, she didn't view me that way—we were friends that had only just struck up an acquaintance again. For another, I wasn't ready for any sort of romance. It had only been a year since I'd lost my darling wife, and it still felt as if only weeks and, sometimes, only hours had passed. Grief was sneaky that way.

We threaded through the narrow corridors and down a series of ladders until we reached Olive's cabin.

"Thanks for tonight, Jack," she said, turning to face me. "It's been so nice seeing you like this."

"Seeing me like what?"

"Smiling. Laughing."

"It's been a tough year," I replied.

She laid her hand on my shoulder. "I can imagine."

"Well, goodnight then," I said. "Sleep well."

She paused, studying my face for a moment. "And you, Jack."

I turned to go, thinking about the look in her eye, and shook my head. It was still hard to believe she was here, but it was a welcome surprise to spend time with an old friend.

We were always good at being friends, Olive and me.

The following morning, the kitchen staff had a break for a couple of hours before we were needed in the kitchen again. I joined a few others on deck, hoping that perhaps Olive, too, would be there. Later that afternoon, she'd be off to follow the queen and her entourage around New Zealand for a few days, and then she'd return home. This would likely be the last time I saw her for many months.

And there she was, waving to me from near the railing. "Morning, Jack!"

"Good morning," I said, my broad smile a mark of how pleased I was to see her. "How did you sleep?"

"Like a log! There's something so soothing about the gentle list of the ship, isn't there? I've never spent time at sea before." She turned her face to the ocean, a contented smile on her lips. "I like it."

She was pretty when she smiled. I'd forgotten that about her, the way her face lit up. I'd forgotten nearly everything from those few months we'd spent together in the giddy aftermath of war. It was nice to remember.

"The ocean gets under your skin," I said. "A bit like food and cooking. Once you find a love for it, it's hard to let go."

She turned to face me, the early morning light casting a golden light onto her skin. She looked as if she wanted to say something, but her attention was caught by a noise behind us.

"Look at him." She pointed to the Duke of Edinburgh. "He's so alive out here on the water, don't you think? Less rigid."

Philip stood to one side, chatting with a few crew members. Everyone watched him intently, absorbed in his story, and after a moment, they all broke out into laughter.

"He is," I replied. "I think part of him will always long to be at sea. We've had a few nice conversations about our time in the Navy."

"You seem to be making quite a name for yourself here," she said. "Audiences with the queen, and friendly with the duke." She looked at me. "I'm pleased for you, Jack. You always said you would make something of yourself, and you certainly have."

I was touched by her words, touched by the fact that she

remembered the conversations we'd all had all those years ago, dreaming of our future lives. "Would you like to see what I've been doing?"

Her eyes filled with mirth. "I'd prefer to *taste* what you've been doing! I'm starving."

"Come on, I'll show you."

She followed me down the ladder and through the narrow corridors to the galley kitchen, where I pulled several covered dishes out of the refrigerator and set them on a long stainless-steel countertop.

"I've been working on some of my recipes, for a cookbook I'm writing."

"You're writing a cookbook? I'm impressed! Will you try to have it published?"

"I doubt it will be good enough to be published. For now, I'm just having fun with it, and thinking about what I'd like to cook if I ever have my own restaurant."

"Is that what you'd like to do?"

"Perhaps. I don't have any immediate plans, but maybe one day."

"I think that's wonderful," she replied, her tone earnest. "It's important to have dreams."

"Try this," I said, dipping a spoon into a pot of gumbo I'd be serving for the staff dinner.

She clapped a hand over her mouth. "It's spicy!"

"It's not all that spicy. I've toned it down quite a lot, for the English palate." My tone was sarcastic, but I found I was smiling. Again. It was a good day for smiling, it seemed. "Take another bite, with your eyes closed. Think about the flavors, and how they work together."

She closed her amber eyes. "I taste sausage, or bacon, is it? Peppers and onion?"

"Good. What else?"

"Some kind of seafood. Shrimp?"

"And oysters."

"There's a richness to it, too, something I can't name—but it's delicious! Once you get past the hot pepper, that is."

She licked the spoon and her lips. I couldn't take my eyes off her.

Next, she tried a brandied lobster cream sauce, pecan pesto, and the icing for a chocolate cinnamon buttermilk cake. She was a good sport and took her time to try and identify each flavor.

"I've never thought about food in terms of the separate ingredients," she said. "You're a great chef, Jack. I wish I had even half your talent."

"You do," I said. "In your reporting and writing."

She shrugged. "I'm not talented enough to be given the really meaty assignments."

"I'd say reporting on the royal tour is meaty, wouldn't you?"

"I suppose so, but I'd like to be given the job properly, rather than filling in for some man's illness or accident."

"I guess it's a tough business being a woman in a mainly male profession."

"Yes, but I mustn't grumble. Look where I am!"

As we joked and laughed and talked about our jobs and our ambitions, I felt something between us shifting. Whatever it was—this thing growing between us—I liked it. It felt good to connect with someone who'd known me before I'd become grief-stricken Jack, the poor man who'd lost his wife so tragically young. My friendship with Olive was a bridge between worlds, and it somehow made me feel a little less broken in two.

"Maybe we should do this again sometime, when we're both back in London?" I said.

Olive looked at me for a moment. "Do what? Test your recipes?"

"Perhaps. Or just . . . talk? Maybe you could do a piece about a young American chef making waves in the royal kitchens!"

She offered a small smile. "Maybe I will."

"We don't arrive home until May," I said as I began to put things away. "And then I'll be off to Balmoral for much of the summer, but we'll have to make a plan, one day."

A little of the light dimmed in her eyes. "Sounds like you have a busy year ahead. But, yes. I'd like to meet up again, one day, when you have time."

I held up a glass of water and clinked it against hers. "It's a date." The words were out of my mouth before I realized what I'd said. "I mean, not a date as such. But a plan. Between friends."

"Oh, Jack. You really must stop being such a romantic!" She placed her hand playfully to her heart and laughed lightly.

Mason and the rest of the crew trailed into the kitchen then, ready to start the next meal service. Mason caught my eye and raised an eyebrow as he glanced at Olive beside me.

I raised an eyebrow at him in return.

Olive knocked her glass against mine. "To plans. Between friends."

Chapter 31

Olive

S leeping on the job, Carter?"

I woke suddenly from a daydream in which Jack was kissing me. I sat up in the deck chair and shielded my eyes from the glare of the sun.

"Mr. Bullen? Cripes. Sorry, I must have dozed off for a minute."

"Yes, I heard some of you had a late night," Charlie Bullen said, with more than a hint of disdain.

"Late? Oh, that was an early night! All very tame."

He harrumphed and muttered something about showing some respect.

My cheeks were flushed, either from the sun or from the events of my daydream, I wasn't sure. And yet, even as Charlie Bullen's rotten old potato face peered at me from where he sat in his wheelchair beside me, his injured leg held rigid in a cast, my thoughts returned to my dream, and to the pleasant time I'd spent with Jack in the last twenty-four hours. Despite all the complications of being in his presence, and the constant questions in my mind, I still found him impossibly attractive. I wished we could spend more time together; wished I could experience that kiss of his for real once again.

I checked my watch. There was still an hour before we were due to leave the ship. "I was sorry to hear about your accident," I offered.

"Were you?"

"Of course! Hopefully they'll get you patched up in the hospital."

"It seems that you are always around to step in for me. I'd almost think you were planning these accidents."

At this, I laughed. "I do seem to be taking advantage of your misfortune, don't I? But, as long as the job gets done—and done well—I suppose it doesn't really matter which of us is reporting, does it?"

He frowned. "Make sure to include the duke in your reports, as well as Her Majesty. He likes to feel involved."

I stood. "Don't worry, Mr. Bullen. I know what I'm doing."

He didn't look convinced.

"And good luck at the hospital," I added. "I would say 'Break a leg' but, well . . ."

His face almost broke into a smile. "You'd better be getting down to the others. We'll be docking soon."

As I hurried to my cabin to get the last of my things, my mind returned to my daydream. Memories and moments with Jack swirled like oil in water: VE Day, when we had danced at the jazz club and drank champagne together on Primrose Hill; all the day trips and picnics and walks when he'd been there; that impromptu evening we'd spent together in The Thirsty Dog, an offer of coffee, a beautiful night of passion. Jack had always been there, and yet, our timing had always been wrong.

And here he was, inviting me to meet him in London—but he would be on the tour until May, and he might not have time to meet before he went up to Scotland with the royal family for the summer. At this rate, we might as well agree to meet once a year, at Christmas.

It was impossible to find a way to tell him about Lucy, and yet that was all I could think about whenever we spoke, always looking for a break in the conversation and searching for clues as to his feelings about children. Did he want them? Did he like them? How would a child affect his dreams and plans? Lucy had come so far without a father—and I had always carefully navigated around those who'd judged me or asked difficult questions about my life as a mother without a husband—so there was only one chance to get this right. There was too much at stake, too much to risk, too many people to hurt if I got it wrong. That was why I hesitated.

Tomorrow was Christmas Eve, and though I was excited to have stumbled my way back into this fascinating world of royalty—and was determined to grasp the opportunity—my heart was already counting the days until I could go back to London, to my daughter.

As I rushed along the corridors to the front of the ship, where the press had assembled, I heard a voice call out behind me.

"Happy Christmas, Olive! See you next year!"

I turned to see Jack smiling broadly, his dimples on full display, his tousled blond waves ruffled from running his hands through his hair. "Happy Christmas, Jack!" I called as I waved back to him.

Oh, Jack. If only you knew. If only I could find a way to tell you.

Our pre-arrival briefing had done little to prepare us for the size of the crowds and the sheer excitement of New Zealanders at seeing the queen and the Duke of Edinburgh. Everywhere we went, the route was lined with well-wishers, waving Union Jack flags and cheering as the motorcade passed.

At every stop, every tour and cultural event, every formal reception and dinner, the press area was like a rugby scrum, everyone packed in like sardines as they tried to get the best shot. This was an event of global interest. Most of the world, it seemed, had sent someone to report on it, not to mention all the local newspapers, radio, and television crews. Men teetered on stepladders with their cameras and flashbulbs poised. Cables and wires from television and newsreel teams snaked around our feet. Being small, I managed to tuck into gaps others couldn't reach, and I crept my way to the front like a mole burrowing its way out of the ground.

The queen was such a diminutive figure, dwarfed by the size of the crowds. I watched in awe as she took it all in her stride, passing bouquets of flowers to her ladies-in-waiting, shaking hands, stopping now and again to chat.

A man beside me spoke into a recording device, taking notes for later. "Nice dress. Off-white in color."

A woman beside him sighed. "It's a gown, not a dress."

I turned to her, and winked. "And the color is champagne," I added.

We exchanged a smile as she reached past him and offered a hand to me in greeting. "Angeline West. Fashion editor with the *Philadelphia Herald*."

"Olive Carter," I replied. "BBC."

The man ignored us both. "The *gown* has local New Zealand floral emblems sewn onto the skirt," he continued.

"*Embroidered*," Angeline corrected.

I snorted with laughter, turned on my taping device, and began to record my own notes.

"Our queen is a beautiful young woman, who the many well-wishers in the crowd are thrilled to see in person. For the first time, a monarch has stepped foot on New Zealand soil, and our marvelous Queen Elizabeth is perfect for this historic moment. She is very at ease among the huge crowds."

"What happened to that old dinosaur the BBC usually sends?" Angeline asked. "Awful man."

I laughed. "Had a nasty fall. Laid up with a broken leg."

She looked at me. "What a shame."

"Yes, isn't it! I shouldn't laugh."

"Well, it's good to see more women reporters. Madeleine Sommers is here somewhere, too. Do you know her?"

"Madeleine Sommers?" The name was familiar, but I couldn't remember why. "Didn't she write about the *Hindenburg*?"

"She more than wrote about it, dear. She survived it. I'll introduce you if I find her. Us gals have to stick together, make ourselves heard. God knows the men have been stomping around with their opinions for long enough."

She pulled a cigarette from a silver case and offered a "Good luck and merry Christmas!" to me over her shoulder as she rushed off to catch up with her cameraman.

Christmas. It was easy to forget, given the blue skies and summer sun.

And Christmas meant keeping up traditions, regardless of the fact that we were halfway around the world. The queen would deliver her Christmas Day broadcast from Government House in Auckland.

I wished I'd had more time here, more time with her. I felt that she liked me. Even though protocol dictated a certain stiffness and distance, I'd sensed a warmth from her this year that I hadn't felt the year before. Jack had remarked on how much more at ease she and the duke were at sea. I'd wanted to tell him how much more relaxed *he* seemed, too, but the best I'd managed was to tell him it was nice to see him laughing again.

It was hard to think about Jack so often and yet know that it would be a long time before I might see him again. What if he met someone in the meantime? What if he stayed behind on some Pacific island?

Suddenly, I felt a rush of panic. What if I never got the chance to tell him about Lucy, never got the chance to introduce her to her father?

At the hotel where we were staying for the night, I took a sheet of writing paper from the desk drawer and wrote a letter to Jack. I wasn't sure what I wanted to say, but I knew I had to say something before I returned to England. I agonized over the words for an age, then scrunched the page up and started again. In the end, I kept it short and simple. I would pass it to a member of staff to give to him back on the ship.

Just as I was done, the telephone in my room rang.

"Hello?"

"Miss Carter. This is Michael Charteris, the queen's press secretary. Sorry to disturb you, but Her Majesty has asked for your attendance at a final run-through of her speech for tomorrow. There'll be a car outside in five minutes."

"Five minutes?"

"Yes, miss. But if you could be downstairs in four, even better."

I was downstairs in three minutes.

The car took me to the official government residence, where the royal party were spending the night. I was shown into a surprisingly informal room and found the queen sitting behind a desk.

I was introduced. "Miss Carter, ma'am."

"Thank you." The queen looked up at me and smiled. "Thank you for coming, Miss Carter. This is becoming something of a tradition, isn't it. You and I."

"It is, ma'am."

"I shan't keep you long."

"Take as long as you need, ma'am."

Once I was seated, she cleared her throat and started to read her prepared script. It was a marked improvement on the version I'd heard a couple of days ago, and her delivery was so much more composed and confident than it had been the previous year.

I dared to tell her as much, offering my praise as respectfully as I could.

"I have had rather a lot of practice since last Christmas," she said. "I seem to give a speech about something or other almost every week. And the sunshine here helps, don't you think? It is a little easier to relax when one's shoulders aren't hunched against the cold draughts from the windows."

I smiled. "It's certainly very pleasant here, ma'am, although I must admit I miss the chill of an English Christmas."

I concentrated as the queen read on.

"So this will be a voyage right round the world—the first that a Queen of England has been privileged to make as queen. But what is really important to me is that I set out on this journey in order to see as much as possible of the people and countries of the Commonwealth and Empire, to learn at first-hand something of their triumphs and difficulties and something of their hopes and fears. At the same time, I want to show that the crown is not merely an abstract symbol of our unity but a personal and living bond between you and me."

Once more, I was struck by her sense of duty and certainty, and how she'd put her own hopes and dreams aside to take on this enormous role.

"It's perfect, ma'am," I said when she had finished her final read-through.

"Thank you. Philip helped—even though I didn't ask him to." She smiled to herself.

"It must be a great help, to have his support," I said, and then wondered if I'd overstepped the mark.

She looked at me, a little surprised by my candor. "Indeed. Life's experiences are always much better when shared, don't you think?"

Her words pricked my heart as I thought about Lucy, and all the moments we'd shared together, and all the moments she would never have with her father. Jack had whirled back into my life like a summer storm, and I was once again faced with the questions that had plagued me since my darling girl was born: was I wrong to have taken the years from them both? Was it too late to change things?

And most of all, would Jack ever forgive me?

Chapter 32

Jack

Christmas came swiftly once the queen and her entourage—Olive included—had disembarked for their planned events and festivities in Auckland. I wasn't ready to say goodbye to Olive yet. Her surprise visit had been a real treat, a breath of fresh air. She'd seemed to enjoy herself, too. She had a carefree way about her away from home and out on the water, and I couldn't help but see the young woman I'd first met on VE Day. Truth be told, I'd have liked her to stay with us for the rest of the tour, but she had her daughter to get home to. It was clear from the way she spoke about Lucy, that she was the most important thing of all.

I wondered, sometimes, what it would be like to be a parent, how that intense connection of love and responsibility changed a person. I'd witnessed it in my friends, and in Andrea's family. I'd never seen myself as a father until Andrea's longing to be a mother had consumed our lives. Now, I couldn't imagine the privilege would ever be mine.

We celebrated Christmas in our own way on the ship. The crew enjoyed the favorite traditional English dishes that Max, Mason, and I prepared along with the rest of the kitchen staff. We piled our plates with turkey, roast potatoes, braised carrots, and plenty of gravy, then rounded off the meal with a platter of local fresh fruits. When we'd finished, we poured coffees and took a brandy each to accompany our Christmas pudding.

"To our good health, first and foremost," Max said as we raised our glasses for a toast.

"Here, here," we replied and drank.

"To new frontiers and sunny horizons," Mason added.

I held my glass aloft. "To good friends. I don't know where I'd be without you."

"To good friends!" we all repeated and clinked our glasses together.

We drank and ate, groaning over our full stomachs, telling jokes and tall tales and laughing until our cheeks hurt. When we began to clear the plates, Mason cornered me.

"So?"

"So . . . what?"

"It was nice to meet Olive," he said, his face playful and teasing. "I'd heard a little about her from Ryan, but that was a long time ago now. She fit right in with us."

"She sure did," I replied, thinking again of her contagious laugh and her bright smile.

"She's rather pretty, too."

"She's a friend," I replied. "That's all."

"I know, I know." Mason waved his hand dismissively. "Just a friend. But one day, maybe more than a friend?"

I was about to reply that I didn't deal in maybes and was happy to take things day by day, when one of the crew stepped into the galley. "It's time!"

We set aside the rest of the dirty dishes for a moment and gathered around the wireless to listen to the queen's Christmas broadcast. One of the crew turned up the volume as we caught the end of the announcer's introduction.

"This Christmas, we celebrate with Her Majesty and His Royal Highness from the South Pacific. Summer skies and New Zealanders have welcomed their monarch with joy and exuberance. It has been a truly memorable coronation year for Her Majesty, and we look forward to all that her reign will bring in the new year, and beyond. Happy Christmas to all our listeners around the world, from all of us at the BBC World Service."

We all stood as the national anthem was played and a rousing chorus of "God Save the Queen" rang around the ship. It *had* been a memorable year. In fact, I couldn't believe how far I'd come, and how much had changed over the last twelve months. I had met new friends and reconnected with old, my cookbook was in the making, and I was doing a job I enjoyed. I also had the spark of an idea for a potential partnership with Mason, when and if the timing was ever right. I still thought of Andrea every day, but the sadness was gentler now, and bright tendrils of hope wound through me along with the Christmas wine.

It was late when a handful of household staff returned to the ship, while the others remained at Government House with the queen and the duke. I was surprised when an equerry handed me an envelope. Inside was a single page of writing paper from a hotel in Auckland, and on it, a short message:

Dear Jack,
It was such a pleasant surprise to see you—again! It seems that we are destined to bump into each other once a year, at Christmas time. But if you were serious about meeting again when you're back in London next summer, then I would love to hear from you. I've written my home address at the bottom of this note. Perhaps you could send a postcard or two in the meantime as you sail around the world, just so that I know you haven't fallen overboard!

Keep cooking, chef. I look forward to trying more of your recipes.
Until then, happy Christmas.
Your friend,
Olive
X
PS I didn't really like the gumbo. I was just being polite!

I laughed aloud, and in that moment, I realized that I was already looking forward to seeing her again. As the cheerful banter of the others swirled around me, I promised myself that I would definitely call by her house or send her a note, as soon as I was in London again.

I smiled as I reread Olive's note, folded it, and joined in the merriment as we sang our way—badly—through a list of Christmas carols to end an almost-perfect Christmas Day.

1954

". . . to all of us there is nothing quite like the family gathering in familiar surroundings, centered on the children whose Festival this truly is, in the traditional atmosphere of love and happiness that springs from the enjoyment of simple, well-tried things."

Queen Elizabeth II, Christmas Day 1954

Queen Elizabeth II

Sandringham Estate, December 1954

There truly is no place like home. After so many months away, I had never been happier to return to the familiar surroundings of Buckingham Palace and then quickly on to my beloved Balmoral for the summer. The Commonwealth tour had been a greater success than we could ever have imagined, but it had left us both exhausted. It had also left me with a sense of what life must be like for the big film stars like Marilyn Monroe and Grace Kelly, constantly hounded by the press. I'm not entirely sure I like the attention.

This morning at my desk, I have been looking through some of the film footage I took this year in Scotland; memories of another happy family summer spent together amid the wild and peaceful beauty of the Highlands. These are the days when we make our most precious memories, captured in casual photographs and shaky cine-camera reels. These are the moments I treasure as much as the crown jewels. Charles and Anne seemed to have grown six feet while we were away. I'd missed them horribly, but the months apart have been quickly forgotten with time spent together since our return.

It is lovely to see the children grow to love Balmoral as much as I did as a child. The ponies—William and Greensleeves—stole Anne's heart this summer. She could hardly bear to be away from them when we left. Even Philip is becoming rather fond of the old place, and was ever so amusing at the Highland Games. He still grumbles about the Pathé news cameramen hanging around, but I remind him that a few hours of film to keep the public happy will allow us many more hours of privacy away from any cameras and news reporters.

And here we are, already celebrating another Christmas at beloved Sandringham. I am glad to return. My Norfolk country home is nearly as dear to me as Balmoral.

Philip hasn't adjusted as easily as I have to life back in Great Britain. He came alive at sea, where he most loves to be. His easy camaraderie with the crew warmed my heart. He has even taken to dabbling in the kitchen since our return, inspired by the talented chefs who kept us so well-fed on board SS *Gothic* and dear *Britannia*.

"Oh, hello you," I say when he potters into my study. I have been sorting through the contents of the daily correspondence and my list of matters to attend to.

He drapes himself over a chair, his great limbs sprawling like an octopus as he huffs and sighs like a bored toddler.

"Any plans for today?" I ask, hopeful that he has some.

"Not much. I might shoot something, I suppose. Not much else to do here, is there?"

I peer at him. "Philip. Don't sulk. It is not becoming."

"I'm not sulking. I am simply . . ."

"Bored," I conclude. "Yes, I can see that. Why not take Anne out for a ride? She was asking all day yesterday while it rained. Or take them both out in the carriage. They would enjoy that."

At this, he sits up. He enjoys carriage rides himself, although he goes far too fast for my liking.

"Yes, I suppose I could do that." He lets out another long sigh.

"You miss traveling, don't you?" I say. "No doubt there will be another tour soon."

"I could always go on my own," he says. "Keep the flag flying around the Empire while you keep the collieries and steelworks happy and plant a few more trees."

"Don't be silly. You cannot possibly go on a royal tour on your own!"

"Why not?"

I put down my pen. "Well, because . . . because *I* am the queen and you . . ."

He stands up, hands on his hips. "I'm what? The chap who walks five paces behind you? The fellow who doesn't have a proper job or role to play?"

"Philip, stop it. Of course you do."

"Do I?"

I hate when we have cross words. "Why don't we go for a walk through the gardens and around the lake while the weather is fine?" It is a peace offering.

We both look past the scarlet poinsettias on the edge of my desk and the decorative garland draped around the window casing, to the winter sunshine pouring through the glass. We are fortunate to have a slightly warmer day after the recent frosts.

"Very well," he says. "And then an early lunch. I'm starving. Has Devereux arrived yet?"

"The household chefs are due this afternoon, I believe."

"Good. I have a hankering for a bowl of that gumbo he makes. Bloody delicious."

I scribble a quick note on my desk pad before we go, a reminder to enquire about a possible overseas trip for Philip alone. I hate the very thought of being separated from him, but I hate the thought of him being unhappy even more.

He takes my arm as we leave the study, and I call for my corgis, Susan and Sugar, to follow.

"Are they coming, too?" Philip asks.

"Why don't you ask them?"

"They are dogs, Lilibet! We tell *them* what to do, not the other way around!"

I laugh. "Oh, Philip. If you believe that, next you will tell me that Father Christmas is real."

The dogs bound ahead as we change into our wellington boots, and I round up Mummy and Margaret while the nanny corrals the children. These are the days I love the most. Simple family moments. Excitable dogs. Giddy children. Mummy fussing with my headscarf. Margaret oozing elegance even in a mackintosh. Outdoor clothes and the crackle of a log fire waiting to warm us when we return. And, of course, the love of my life, dear Philip.

At times like this, I feel that I am the luckiest woman in Great Britain. Not because I am queen, but because I am part of a family I love with all my heart.

Chapter 33

Olive

London, December 1954

Frost sparkled on the lawns of Green Park. It was a perfect December morning, a nip in the air, the rosy glow of winter sun turning everything to gold.

Rosie looped her arm through mine as we made our way along Piccadilly back to Broadcasting House. "Come on. I'll treat you to a piece of Turkish Delight from Fortnum and Mason."

"A *piece*."

"Yes! One piece. I'm not made of money! I thought you'd want to celebrate with this being your last afternoon of Miserable Maguire breathing down your neck before you head to Sandringham. You lucky thing."

"I can't wait, even if it means putting up with you-know-who."

Rosie beamed. "I am so proud of you, Olive! This is what you've always wanted. A role on the royal beat—even if it's as Charlie Bullen's assistant!"

I sighed. "The man is insufferable, but if I have to put up with him to get where I want to be, then so be it. I am finally being taken seriously."

My "rather unconventional" but wildly successful reporting

on the Speedbird flight, and my more traditional coverage of the queen's tour of New Zealand had impressed Tom Harding and had even caused Maguire to offer a mild compliment. I'd covered a variety of stories since, including the terrible BOAC airplane crash in the Mediterranean, and Roger Bannister's incredible four-minute mile at Oxford University. I'd approached Tom about covering a story on Marilyn Monroe and Joe DiMaggio's wedding, and on a new American rock 'n' roll singer called Elvis Presley, but he considered them to be overseas news stories and wanted my focus to remain on home affairs. Although home affairs were far less interesting, I was finally getting noticed. Things were starting to go my way—with work, at least.

My quick trip to the other side of the world last December had taught me a great deal. Mostly, that I didn't care for turbulence—or for air travel at all, especially after the terrible de Havilland crash in the Mediterranean shortly after I'd returned home—but it had also taught me that, apart from my job, it was my family who made me the happiest. Absence really had made my heart grow fonder. If I'd loved Lucy to bursting before I'd left, I loved her twice as much by the time I returned.

But over the past year, my heart had also felt an absence in another direction.

Toward Jack.

How was it possible to miss someone I'd barely spent the sum total of a week with in the last two years? But miss him, I did. Especially when his postcards arrived with a line or two about their latest port of call, and a silly remark about still not having fallen into the sea. He had even sent a postcard from Balmoral while he'd worked there over the summer, but somehow another year had passed without our meeting. I'd found myself thinking about him more and more, and as I'd watched

Lucy turn another year older, I felt his absence in her life more acutely than ever.

Apart from my parents, Rosie was the only person who knew the truth about Jack. She understood my anguish about protecting Lucy, and yet she also knew how my feelings for him had developed.

And now there was another complication: Peter Hall.

Unreliable as ever, he'd disappeared off the face of the earth again after contacting me last year. His job as an airline pilot meant that he was often away, but even that wasn't an excuse. And then, after months of silence, he'd telephoned a few weeks ago, suggesting we meet at The Thirsty Dog for old times' sake. When the day came, he'd failed to show up, and I'd returned home embarrassed and annoyed with myself for ever thinking he might have changed. A few days later, a bunch of red roses had arrived, with an apology.

Dearest Carter,
Can you ever forgive me for letting you down? My mother took a nasty fall. Had to rush to the hospital. Give me a chance to make it up to you? I'm at the address below. Staying with my mother until she's back on her feet.
P x

At first, I wasn't sure if I wanted to forgive him, or give him another chance, but something about the Christmas season and the approaching end of another year on my own made me nostalgic and sentimental, so I'd telephoned and agreed to meet him.

"I suppose a certain someone will be at Sandringham again this year?" Rosie said now, as we turned into Fortnum's. "Do you think this might be the opportunity to tell him about Lucy?"

I sighed. "I don't know. And, there's another slight complication."

Rosie looked at me through narrowed eyes. "What have you done now?"

"I've decided to give Peter another chance." I knew she would disapprove. I prepared myself for her objections.

"Oh, Olive. Are you sure?"

"Not really, but he apologized for standing me up last week. His mother had a fall."

Rosie rolled her eyes. "He's using his mother as an excuse now? Sounds like Peter Hall all right."

"There's no harm in seeing him, is there? Maybe he's changed?"

At this, Rosie laughed. "I'm not sure men like Peter are capable of changing."

"Well, I'll never know if I don't go and see, will I?"

"And if he *has* changed? What then?"

"Then I'll have a bit of harmless fun with him. God knows I could do with some."

Rosie stopped walking and looked at me. "But if you're having fun with Peter, where does that leave things with Jack?"

"It leaves things exactly as they are now. There's no chance of anything developing between me and Jack. He's far too busy to commit to a relationship—let alone fatherhood. Jack is such a huge complication, Rosie. I just want a bit of fun. Is that so terrible?"

"Sex, you mean?"

I batted her arm. "Rosie May!"

"Deny it all you like, Olive. I know you and Peter have unfinished business, so fine. See him. Sleep with him, if you must. But *please* be careful. Don't jeopardize whatever you might be able to salvage with Jack for the sake of a quick roll in the hay with Hall. This could all go exactly as you want it to. But it could also go horribly wrong."

We walked on. "Trust me, Rosie. I know what I'm doing."

Going to see Peter was really more of an attempt to forget about him than it was an intention to reconnect with him. I felt that I needed to see him to test my reactions and, perhaps, to test his. I hoped I would find him to be the same unreliable Romeo he'd always been, that I would be disappointed by him, relieved to discover there wasn't the slightest spark of attraction.

The Highgate address he had given me meant taking the underground across London. I doubted myself at every stop and nearly got off several times.

Finally, I made my way out of the station and up the hill. With its eighteenth-century architecture and parks and abundance of trees, Highgate was a pretty part of London. I passed the cemetery and Highgate School. Cyclists whizzed by. Groups of friends stood outside bakeries and greengrocers, stamping their feet and rubbing their hands against the crisp December air. It was a stunning winter's day.

Too soon, I arrived at the address at Mill Crescent. I took a deep breath, walked toward number 6, and knocked on the door.

A woman around my mother's age opened it. She had a pleasant face and a warm smile. "Can I help you, love?"

"Hello. I'm here to see Peter?"

"Ah yes. He mentioned a friend would be calling. It's so good of him to stay while his mother recuperates." She pulled the door fully open. "Come in, dear. He's in the front room. I'm his aunt—I shan't get in your way."

I stepped inside, and she showed me into a neat little room. "A friend here to see you, Peter. Be nice. I'll put the kettle on."

Peter was hunched over a table, doing a jigsaw puzzle. It had been so long since I'd seen him and yet, it suddenly felt like no time at all had passed.

"Hello, stranger," I said.

He turned and put his hands on his hips. "Olive bloody Carter! Now there's a sight for sore eyes." He walked toward me and planted a kiss on my cheek. "You look great," he said. "Were you always this pretty?"

He didn't look too bad himself. He was tanned and healthy and his new moustache suited him.

I pulled off my gloves and hat. "I believe I was even prettier back then."

At this, he laughed. I remembered his laugh, loud and hearty.

"It's good to see you, Olive. Really good. I wasn't sure you'd come."

"Neither was I."

We looked at each other for what felt like forever, until his aunt returned with the tea, poured us a cup each, fussed about some cake, and eventually left us alone.

"Likes to know who's who," Peter whispered. "Keeps tabs on me, and any visitors."

"And do you have many?" I asked as I took a sip of tea. "Visitors?"

He pushed his hands through his hair. "No. Which is why she's so eager to know who *you* are!" He looked at me again. "Christ, Olive. I've missed you."

"Liar."

He held up three fingers. "Scout's honor. I really have." He took a packet of cigarettes from the table. "Do you smoke?"

I took one and leaned forward to get a light. "Not often."

"Are you one of those 'only after sex' girls? Shame we never got that far."

"Peter! Stop it."

He laughed. "Stop what? Flirting with you? Never!"

"This is a nice house," I said, desperate to change the subject. I could already feel his old charms working on me.

"Our family home. I'm staying for a week or so, until Mother is back on her feet."

"Peter Hall, the good Samaritan. Who would ever have thought it?"

"I wasn't so terrible, was I?"

I nodded. "You were rather in love with yourself. And with any pretty girl who happened to look your way."

He smiled ruefully. "You're right. I was young and irresponsible. Selfish."

"And you're now a responsible, reputable pilot. How things change! I think you're very brave. After experiencing air travel, I'm quite happy to never go up there again. Especially after that terrible crash last January."

"The de Havilland flight from Singapore to London? I was supposed to pilot the return flight."

"Oh, gosh, Peter. How dreadful. I covered it for a news report. I don't think I'll ever forget it."

"Bloody awful business. We can't live in fear of everything though, can we? It's no good living in what ifs. Might as well lock the door and never step foot outside again." He took another drag on his cigarette. "Do you ever hear from the old gang?"

"Only Rosie. We work together. And I . . . ran into Jack recently."

"Jack Devereux! Blimey. Haven't heard that name in forever. Dull Devereux. How is he? Still boring as hell?"

"Don't be mean, Peter. He's making quite a name for himself as it happens, as a chef in the royal household." It suddenly dawned on me that Peter wouldn't know about Andrea. "Oh, you probably didn't hear."

"Hear what?"

I paused before continuing. "Andrea died, two years ago. A tragic accident in that awful fog."

"Bloody hell. That's rough. Sounds like Jack's been through a lot. And poor Andrea—she was a nice girl." He took another long drag on his cigarette. "Anyway, tell me about you! How the hell have you been?"

We talked for a while about casual things, not straying too far into the past, ignoring the obvious questions about the present. I told him about my role at the BBC, and my recent promotion.

"So, is there a husband on the scene?" he asked. "I presume someone has snapped you up!"

I shook my head. "Then you presume wrong."

"I'm surprised. Heard you'd run off to Cornwall with some new chap you'd met. Maybe I should have snapped you up while I had the chance."

"Maybe you should."

"My mother's greatest disappointment is that I haven't married and had kids. She's desperate for grandchildren, but I keep telling her I'm not the family man she wants me to be. Marriage and children—scares the hell out of me."

"I think it scares the hell out of most people, growing up, facing responsibilities." I stubbed out my cigarette, regretting having it at all. The taste of nicotine was awful in my mouth. I took a breath, knowing what I wanted to say, but aware of what would probably happen if I did. "I don't have a husband, but I do have a daughter."

Peter raised an eyebrow. "You *have* been busy. Didn't have you down as the fallen woman type."

"Oh, I'm full of surprises, Peter." I opened the locket around my neck to show him the photograph I kept there. "This is Lucy."

I was testing him, checking for a reaction, as I always did with men I met. Did they like children, or would they run a mile at the thought of courting a woman with a daughter? I watched Peter closely.

He leaned forward and lifted the locket from my chest, his fingers brushing my skin lightly as he did. "She's cute," he said as he studied the photograph. "The same eyes as her mother." He closed the clasp of the locket, let it fall gently against my chest, and lifted his gaze to meet mine. "What happened? Some lovable rogue leave you in the lurch?"

"Something like that, yes."

"Well, it's none of my business. And it doesn't scare me off, if that's what you're thinking."

We talked for a while. It was strange to be drinking tea and eating cake with Peter Hall. He was different from the wild party boy I remembered.

"Anyway, I'd best be going," I said as we drained the last of the tea. "Thank your aunt for the tea and cake."

He smiled with that easy charm he'd carried when I first met him. "I hope we can do this again, Olive. Or maybe swap the tea for a drink and dancing? I really have missed you." He reached for my hands. "We were good together, weren't we? And I was a fool to let you go."

"You didn't 'let me go,' Peter. I left of my own choice."

He held his hands up in mock surrender. "I didn't think I'd get a second chance, but maybe I was wrong?"

The lilt of hope in his question hung in the air between us as I scribbled my telephone number on a piece of paper.

A smile lit up his face when I handed it to him. "Is that a yes? A second chance?" he said.

"It's a telephone number, for now."

As I walked down the garden path, he called out, "She's beautiful, your daughter. Takes after her mother. If the father is still around, he's an idiot for walking out on you both."

I turned to look at him, then closed the gate behind me and walked down the street, the thump of my heart matching the beat of a sudden heavy rain shower against the pavement.

Chapter 34

Jack

Buckingham Palace. London, December 1954

Ipulled several pans of roasted vegetable and Gruyère bread pudding from the oven, and sliced the hearty dish into squares for the staff. I couldn't wait for them to try it.

"Morning, chef," I said to Max, as he reached for a plate and sat with the others at the staff table.

"Princess Margaret will be joining the children for afternoon tea today," Max told us. "Jack, I'd like you to be on the sandwiches. Mason and Gerald will work on the pastries and biscuits and Lenny will assist me with the ordering today."

"Yes, chef," we all said in unison.

"The footmen are off today so, Jack, you can set up the tea cart."

"Yes, chef."

I was relieved it appeared to be an easy day. We were preparing to leave for Sandringham in a few days, and it had already been a hectic few weeks of guests and dinner parties for the royal family, which meant a busy time for us in the kitchens.

After nearly two years at Buckingham Palace, I still hadn't gotten used to its grandeur and opulence, or the fact that I *lived* here. It was a little astonishing every time I crossed paths with someone whose face was often in the newspapers: Princess Margaret, mostly. Whenever I looked out over the rich red carpets of the Grand Hall, the creamy panels of the frescoed ceiling, and polished marble floors, I felt a sense of pride—and perhaps some guilt at being a former American Navy boy serving a British monarch. I wasn't a royalist, or particularly interested in kings and queens and the nobility, but I was interested in a steady salary. And I was happy here—at least as happy as I could be while not running my own restaurant.

I'd thought about opening my own place a lot over the past year as I worked diligently on my cookbook. It seemed like the logical next step, and yet, I didn't know where I would find the money, even if Mason and I combined resources.

Since the Commonwealth tour and the summer in Balmoral, it had been business as usual in the kitchens at Buckingham Palace. The rationing of meat had, at last, ended, bringing a flood of new dishes we'd been forced to sideline for years. And lately, Max had given me more responsibilities. I was assistant saucier now and had been given a book of recipes to memorize. I regularly spent extra time in the kitchen after-hours, practicing when time and supplies allowed, experimenting with a few of my own ingredients, creating my own unique recipes. Citrus-herb marinade, silky hollandaise with a bite of hot chili, sherry and dill cream, bourbon-butter crumbs for baked oysters. I wasn't in New Orleans anymore, but the ingredients of my childhood had stayed with me. In the last few months, I'd created sauces I would never serve the royal family, testing them on the kitchen staff instead when it was my week to make the staff meal. All the while, I carefully documented each ingredient, the measurements, and notes about flavors, textures, and cooking times. One day, I hoped they'd come in handy.

That afternoon, when lunch preparations were finished, I

wheeled the tea cart loaded with a tiered silver tray of teatime treats to the less formal family room where the family had afternoon tea. As I made my way along the labyrinth of corridors, I marveled at the grand hallways decorated with vaulted ceilings and the impressive collection of portraits and paintings that had been passed down from one generation to the next. I glanced at the luxurious rugs from the Orient and the beautiful decorative tables polished to a shine.

Eventually, I reached the family room. Prince Charles, Princess Anne, and Princess Margaret entered the room ahead of me. Either I was late, or they were early. Nanny Lightbody—the children's nanny—followed. We all avoided her like the plague in the kitchens, because she was forever interfering with the children's meals and was a general nuisance.

I pushed the tea cart inside, being careful not to look in their direction. I'd been taught not to stare at the family, or even to greet them unless spoken to first. Still, I couldn't help but glance at the children, who were chasing each other around the room until they were told sternly by their nanny to sit down. Prince Charles was six years old. His sister, Anne, only four. The nanny would have her work cut out for her, trying to make sure they sat still and ate their meal.

"Your mother would have your hide if she saw you running in here like that. Sit down, you two," Princess Margaret said. "And try to be quiet. I have a dreadful headache."

I smiled to myself as I carefully unloaded the items on the cart to the sideboard. Rumors were flying about Princess Margaret and her wild social life since her lover, Peter Townsend, had been unceremoniously dispatched to Brussels. Apparently, he'd proposed to Margaret but the queen had refused to grant the couple permission to marry, and the whole palace had heard the sisters quarreling. Princess Margaret wasn't exactly known for being discreet with her emotions.

"Hello. I've never seen *you* before." Princess Margaret's voice drifted across the room. "New here, are you?"

I turned and dipped my head, as I now knew was the appropriate etiquette. "I've worked here for almost two years, Your Highness."

"Really? And do you have a name?"

"Jack Devereux."

"Well, Jack Devereux, it's awfully nice to meet you." She fluttered her eyelashes at me. "Where *have* they been hiding you?"

"In the kitchens, Your Highness. And the pleasure is all mine," I said, feeling my neck heat as her eyes followed me across the room to the door. I paused, wondering if I should say anything more or be on my way.

"You sound as if you're from the American south," she added. "I hope to visit there one day."

"I am, ma'am. From New Orleans originally, though I've lived in London now for nine years."

"Goodness, you gave up all that heat and sunshine for dreary old London? There must have been a good reason." Princess Margaret leaned forward on the heel of her hand, her stunning blue eyes intent on mine. "Is she very beautiful?"

If I didn't know any better, I'd have said she was flirting with me. Though her reputation had preceded her, it was hard to parse out what was true in the gossip rags and what was fabricated. Andrea had always complained about how unkind the newspapers were to women in particular. Margaret was beautiful, with her vivid blue eyes and charming smile. I could see why so many men fell for her.

"Aunt Margaret, can I have *this* many biscuits?" Princess Anne held up four fingers, staring at them to make sure she'd held up the correct number. She really was an adorable little girl, with her shining blonde hair tied neatly with ribbons.

"Have as many as you like, dear."

The nanny tutted. "You may have one, Miss Anne, after you eat a sandwich."

Little Anne stuck out her lip in a pout but scooted behind her aunt as she filled her plate. I smiled as Margaret secretly slipped her a second biscuit.

"Enjoy your meal, Your Highness," I said, ducking into the hallway, anxious to be out from under her heated gaze and back in the safety of the kitchen.

Anne raced after me. "Would you like a biscuit, too?" She held out a pale oval of shortbread with one end dipped in chocolate. The chocolate had begun to melt where her little fist held it.

I smiled broadly at her. "Thank you, Miss Anne. I'd like that very much." I accepted the half-melted cookie.

The nanny appeared behind her. "Young lady, come back here and sit down, at once!" she said, shepherding the princess inside and to her seat once more.

I chuckled to myself, and as I headed back to the kitchen, I thought again of what it might be like to have children racing around my own house. I found myself strangely sad to think that I might never know.

My thoughts inadvertently turned to Olive and her daughter, Lucy, and how difficult it must have been for Olive to raise the child on her own. I thought, too, of the handful of postcards I'd sent to Olive from the remainder of the overseas tour, and from Balmoral that summer. I hadn't seen her since those few days in New Zealand, but I'd thought of her often. More often, it seemed, as time passed.

With the demands of my job becoming all-consuming, the weeks and months had a way of racing by, and it was nearly Christmas again. I wondered if Olive might be at Sandringham this year.

I wondered what I might do about it if she was.

Chapter 35

Olive

London, December 1954

Seeing Peter had left more of an impression on me than I'd anticipated. Infuriatingly, I found myself still wildly attracted to him, but there was something else, something beyond the physical pull that had first brought us together back in 1945. He'd changed; softened considerably. The way he was helping his elderly mother and aunt was so considerate, so unlike the Peter I'd known, and that was as attractive as any of his physical traits. Perhaps I had misjudged him all those years ago, and since Jack and I didn't seem to be moving forward, and I was lonelier than I wanted to admit, I didn't see the harm in getting to know him again.

Despite the ways in which Peter had changed, I still didn't expect him to telephone the very next morning.

"How about a walk?" he said.

I smiled into the receiver. "How about a, 'Hello, Olive. It's Peter. How are you?' Are you always this abrupt?"

He laughed. "No point talking about the weather. Can't be bothered with all that small talk nonsense. Waste of time, and life is short. So, how about it? A walk. You and me. Green Park. This afternoon."

The Peter I remembered didn't take romantic walks in parks.

The Peter I remembered wouldn't have telephoned for at least a week.

We arranged to meet at Canada Gate an hour later. Lucy was at a friend's birthday party, so I had a few hours to spare.

"Where are you off to?" my mother asked, noticing that I'd changed my outfit and added a touch of rouge and lipstick. "And who are you meeting?"

"I'm going for a walk with a friend."

"The friend you went to visit? Was it him on the telephone just now?"

I wound my scarf around my neck. "Yes, Mum. And his name is Peter Hall. Do you want to come along as my chaperone?"

"No need for sarcasm. I'm only interested, love. We both want you to be happy."

I kissed her cheek. "I am happy, Mum. I'll only be a couple of hours. I have to pick Lucy up later."

"We could collect her? To give you time, if you need it?"

My poor mother was so desperate for me to find a man to settle down with that she would do anything to help.

"Mum, it's fine. I'm taking a quick walk with Peter, and then I'll be home. I have to pack for Sandringham anyway."

Deflated, she threw her hands in the air and pottered through to the kitchen. "I don't understand you young people. You have no sense of urgency."

London looked so pretty that afternoon, the gray stone buildings warmed by a soft golden sun. Faces glowed beneath the crisp chill in the air. Colorful winter coats and fur-trimmed hats added a dash of elegance to the usually drab streets. Shop windows had been dressed in their finest festive displays and the scent of roasting chestnuts and cinnamon laced the air as I passed the wine merchants and bakeries.

I made my way toward Constitution Hill and Canada Gate— and there he was.

He'd brought me a Christmas rose from his mother's garden. "See! I'm not all bad, am I?"

I smiled as he lightly kissed my cheek. "Perhaps not," I conceded.

Our conversation flowed easily, as it always had. There was no hidden agenda with Peter, no secrets to guess. He was an open book. What was more, he didn't have a deceased wife to complicate things—and I had no secret I was keeping from him.

When we'd walked for a while, we found a bench and sat down.

"This is nice, isn't it?" Peter said. He looked at me with that disarmingly playful smile in his eyes. "I'd really like to start again, Olive. Do things differently this time. Do things properly. I couldn't stop thinking about you yesterday. Couldn't wait to see you again. What do you say?"

"I say it's getting cold, and I could do with a cup of tea."

He pulled me up from the bench. "Lyons' Corner House then. Come on. My treat."

He was, it seemed, impossible to resist, and the smile on my lips was impossible to hide as he turned and gently kissed me. For a moment, I hesitated, but then I gave in to the urge to kiss him back, and we lingered in the thrill of each other as people walked by.

"Tea for two, madame?" he said, smiling as he offered his arm.

"I can't stay long. I promised Lucy we would decorate the Christmas cake this afternoon when she's back from a friend's birthday party."

"And I have to pack. I'm off again first thing. Long-haul to Singapore."

"Do you ever get tired of jetting off from here to there, with no real time to settle anywhere?"

"Suits me down to the ground—ironically! I'm not one for settling, Olive. You know me."

I smiled weakly. "Yes, Peter. I know you."

Chapter 36

Jack

London, December 1954

With only a day left before we were to leave for San-dringham, we were given a few hours off between the tea service and a light evening meal. I pulled on my coat and hat, ready for some fresh air.

"Where are you headed off to?" Mason asked.

"Going for a walk. I'd like to do a little Christmas shopping, pick up something for my nephews, and for Ryan and the family." What I didn't say was that I planned to walk by the building on Richmond Street that I'd hoped to buy with Andrea one day. If I worked up the nerve, I might even look into the pricing. I'd thought about the restaurant so often since we'd returned to England, and I'd yet to visit it. After another restless night, I decided I couldn't put it off any longer. It was time to face it, time to make some decisions, time to inch forward no matter how difficult or painful it may be.

"Mind if I come with you?" Mason said. "I'd like to pick up a few things as well. Can't have you showing me up in front of Ryan, armed with more presents than me!"

Though I was looking forward to a little time alone, perhaps

Mason should come with me to see the building. As potential partners, and all.

"Sure," I said. 'Come with me."

We joined the holiday throngs along Piccadilly, and Regent Street. Though the chill of winter nipped at my nose, it was a bright afternoon. We spent some time at a toy store, where I chose a doll with blinky eyes for Ivy and a fire engine for her little brother, along with some toy soldiers for Andrea's nephews. I had seen so much of them when she was alive that I still thought of them as family. I also still sent a card and presents each Christmas. It was an aching pleasure to keep in touch with Andrea's family— the last thread linking me to her.

As I left the shop, I whistled, "Oh Christmas Tree" and, for the first time that season, I felt a little bit festive.

Next, we crossed the street to Hatchards. As we opened the door, a cheerful cluster of bells jingled. The creaky, multifloor bookstore was a favorite of mine. I'd spent a pretty penny on books there over the years. Inside, I climbed the staircase to the children's books and picked out a few before selecting a couple of novels for Maggie and Ryan. With my arms full, I headed to the cashier's table.

As I wound through the artfully arranged displays, a leather journal caught my eye. Flowers and vines were carved into the soft surface and the pages were edged in gold. I put my stack down and flipped it open. On the first page it read, "This book belongs to _____." I imagined Olive's curled script on the line. She could use it to write notes for her radio pieces.

I closed it, ran my hand over the cover, and brought it to my nose, inhaling the rich leather scent. Someone had made it by hand.

I hesitated a moment, wondering if she'd like it, or if she might think it odd if I got her a gift, especially since we hadn't seen each other in almost a year. Did friends buy each other such sentimental items? But as I imagined her look of surprise and delight when I gave her the journal, I couldn't help myself. I tucked it under my arm along with the rest of the books. I'd ask the cashier to wrap it in Christmas paper and add a ribbon, too.

"Find everything you need?" Mason asked. "I spent a fortune." He held up a stack of books.

I smiled. "I did, too." As we left the store, I finally mentioned the last stop on my list. "Do you remember the old building I told you about, for our restaurant?"

"Of course," he said.

"How about we take a look, since we're out?"

He grinned. "What a great idea! Maybe it will inspire us to sit down with pen and paper and make a proper plan."

The idea of seeing the building again thrilled me, but as we neared Richmond Street, my heart skipped in my chest. I hadn't been back to the area since the week we'd returned from Balmoral that summer, and it still brought up a surge of emotions. So much of my old life had played out on this street, and so much of what I'd hoped for my future was wrapped up in the bricks of that one building.

We turned the corner, passing a row of charming little shops and boutiques, including Howard's Florist which—unusually— was closed, and there it was.

"That's it," I said as I stopped directly opposite the building.

The red brick, and the faded white window trim was as lovely as ever, even if it needed some serious sprucing up, but there was one thing about it that had changed. The "For Sale" sign was gone.

I felt a stab of pain. I was too late.

"It's sold," I said, not bothering to hide my disappointment.

Mason studied my expression and glanced back at the building. "It is perfect, isn't it?"

"Was," I said. "It was perfect."

Mason placed his hand on my shoulder. "I'm sorry, Jack. I know you've had your heart set on that place for a while. But there's bound to be plenty of other places we could make work. Chin up. We'll find something when the time is right."

I nodded. It was a nice thought, but I didn't know where or how we'd ever find a more perfect location. The truth was, it felt as if this was it, and we were at the end of the line. The dream I'd harbored for so long was over. It was time to let it go.

"Should we head back?" Mason held up his shopping bags. "These are heavier than I thought."

"You go on," I said. "I'll walk on my own for a bit. I need to clear my head."

"Of course. You sure you're all right? Maybe a pint would help?"

I smiled. "I'm fine. I just need to brood for a while."

"See you back at the palace then."

That was why Mason was a good friend and would be a great partner—he didn't pressure me, or push; he gave me the space I needed when the time arose.

I stood for a while, gripped by sorrow and regret. Eventually, the chill in the air got the better of me. I turned up the collar of my jacket and glanced next door to Howard's Florists. A light had been switched on inside, and the door was slightly ajar. I pushed the door open a little further and stepped inside. The familiar bell rang above the door.

"Hello?" I pushed my hands into my coat pockets and waited for Mrs. Howard to appear. "Mrs. Howard?"

A man I didn't recognize peered around the door to the back room. "Can I help you?"

"I just wanted to say hello to Mrs. Howard. She knows me. Jack's the name. Jack Devereux. Is she around?"

The man stepped into the main shop. "You haven't heard?"

I felt a knot form in my stomach. "Heard what?"

"I'm afraid Alice—Mrs. Howard—passed away last week. I'm her solicitor. The shop will be put up for sale. I'm itemizing the stock."

"I—I didn't know," I said, stunned. I couldn't believe it. She'd seemed well when I last saw her. A wave of sadness washed over me. She'd been such a dear old woman, and she'd been so good to Andrea, too. First, the restaurant had sold, and now this. I really was closing the book on my former life. "That's awful news."

"I'm so sorry to have to tell you. Was there something particular you wanted to see her about?"

I shook my head. "I used to live close by, and my late wife used to work here. We'd always chat whenever I stopped by. I just wanted to wish her a merry Christmas." Even as I spoke, I still couldn't believe the awful news. "Is there anyone I can send my condolences to? I know she didn't have children of her own."

"There is a reading of her will this afternoon. If you'd like to leave your address and telephone number, I can contact you with funeral details once we know the family's wishes."

I scribbled my information onto a sheet of paper and passed it to him. "That would be much appreciated. Thank you."

"Buckingham Palace," he said as he read the address I'd provided. "That's not what I was expecting."

I smiled lightly. "I'm a chef there. Actually, I'm leaving for Sandringham tomorrow, so I'll add those details, too."

As I turned to leave, I took a last look around the little shop. "I'll sure miss her. And this place. It was part of our Christmas traditions to pick up a sprig of mistletoe from Howard's. The street won't be the same without her."

I strolled for a while, wrestling with my emotions until I reached the cemetery. I had to see Andrea. It was still difficult to go there, but the pain lessened a little as the months and years passed. *Years.* The thought caught me by surprise. How had it already been two years without her?

Afterward, I walked aimlessly until I reached Green Park. My mind full, and a now-familiar ache of loss in my chest, I sat on a bench for a while and watched the sky as the colors shifted. Late afternoon in winter brought streaks of gray-blue and silvery violet, with a hint of pink that edged the clouds as the sun sank lower. It would be dark soon.

Slowly, I walked the path winding between the magnificent London plane and oak trees. I'd always liked this park; it was less fussy, less manicured and far less crowded than St James Park. Something about that appealed to me, the notion that perfection in nature happened all on its own. And I needed the soothing balm of nature now.

A few hundred yards ahead of me, a couple sat beside each other on a bench, deep in conversation. My heart squeezed at the sight. It caught me off-guard, the longing to be one of a pair again; to while away a winter afternoon in the park with someone I loved.

As I drew closer, the man reached for the woman's hand, and as they stood, he leaned forward to kiss her. I caught a flash of auburn curls, a familiar winter hat and scarf. Olive? And was that . . . Peter Hall? It couldn't be. They couldn't be seeing each other again, could they?

I turned quickly in the opposite direction and walked to Canada Gate and Constitution Hill.

It had been nearly a year since I'd last seen Olive, and months since we'd been in contact. There was every possibility she was in a relationship with someone. She was a beautiful woman in every way. Why wouldn't she be with someone? And why was I so bothered by the thought?

A stab of something unfamiliar made me catch my breath. I hadn't felt it in so long that I hardly recognized it.

Jealousy.

Undeniable and uncomfortable.

And I wasn't just jealous that Olive was with Peter Hall of all people. I was jealous that she was with someone other than me.

Chapter 37

Olive

I thought about Peter's kiss as I prepared for my trip to Sandringham. It had felt so lovely to be wanted by someone, to spend time with someone where I could just be myself, even if that someone was possibly the least reliable man on earth.

"Do you really think he's changed?" Rosie asked when I told her about going to see him at his mother's house. "I mean, *really*? Are you sure he isn't putting on an act? You know how he is."

"I know how he *was*. I really don't think he's pretending, Rosie."

"Well, I suppose a leopard can change its spots after all. We were only kids back then. Nine years is a long time to grow up."

We walked along the embankment, a violet winter sky above us.

"And he was lovely when we met in the park again yesterday."

Rosie stopped in her tracks. "You've already seen him again?"

"He telephoned the next day, said he couldn't stop thinking about me. I didn't have time to tell you. I wasn't even sure if I would go, or if he would show up, but I did, and it was lovely. We got on really well. He took me for tea."

"Ahh. I see."

"What's that supposed to mean?"

"You're falling for him again, aren't you?"

I tucked my arm through hers. "I'm not sure. Possibly? Yes. I really think things could be different this time. I even told him about Lucy. He hardly blinked."

"And what about Jack?"

I'd thought about Jack so much, gone over all the moments we'd shared in the past, and the brief encounters we'd had more recently, but what was there really between us? One night together nine years ago and a few looks exchanged last Christmas that I might have misread? Peter was full steam ahead, and there was something exciting about that.

"I haven't even seen Jack since last Christmas. He might be with someone for all I know. Peter is here now. He's a safe bet."

Rosie huffed out a long breath. "A safe bet! How absolutely intoxicating. How could you possibly resist?"

I nudged my elbow into her ribs. "You know what I mean. And I'd forgotten what a good kisser Peter is!"

"When are you going to see him again?"

"After Christmas. We've arranged to meet when I get back from Norfolk."

We walked on a little further until we reached the underground station, where we parted.

Rosie kissed me on the cheek. "I'll see you when you're back from Sandringham then. I just want you to be happy, Olive. If you see Jack at Sandringham and get the chance, maybe you should talk to him? Tell him the truth?"

I let out a long sigh. "I don't know, Rosie. I'll have to see how things are. I might not see him at all."

"Well, you know what I think. Better to tell him now than regret it later."

Part of me knew she was right but a bigger part of me was also terrified of his reaction. I was stalling for time.

By the end of the week, I had a head cold that left my nose as red as Rudolph's.

My mother had been especially kind in recent weeks and had offered to take me to Lyons' Corner House for a cup of tea and a cherry bun.

"You look nice, love," she said, as I poured the tea.

"I look dreadful." I took a large bite of my cherry bun. I'd forgotten how delicious they were.

"Something keeping you awake at night?" she asked. "You do look a little tired now that you mention it."

"I'm just busy at work."

At this, my mother burst into tears.

"Mum, whatever has happened?" I pulled a handkerchief from my handbag and passed it to her.

Eventually she composed herself. "I'm sorry, love. It's Christmas. It always makes me sentimental."

"I thought Christmas made you happy."

"It does. Christmas was when I first met your father. He was so romantic back then. We had our first kiss in the snow in Regent's Park." She hesitated, her eyes still swimming with tears. "He hardly seems to notice I'm there half the time these days. All the romance has gone. Marriage has become an endless cycle of washing your father's underwear and finding his bloody slippers. Bangers and mash for tea in front of that bloody television he can't look away from." She wiped her eyes. "I want to feel special again. Like I matter."

"You do matter, Mum." I covered her hand with mine. "Of course you matter."

"I feel invisible most of the time."

We talked for another hour, by which time we'd worked our way through two more pots of tea and two cherry buns each, and I'd hatched a plan to bring a bit of romance back into my parents' lives. I remembered the way Jack had talked so passionately about food when we'd spent time together on SS *Gothic*, and how he firmly believed that a good meal in the right setting could bring people together.

"You and Dad should go somewhere nice—splash out on a fancy dinner."

"I can't even remember the last time we went out to eat. Your father isn't one for a fuss."

"You leave Dad to me. When we're finished here, we'll go and find you something nice to wear."

"Now? Today?"

I laughed. "Yes, Mum. Now! Today!"

She smiled. "I suppose I could have a look."

After sending Mum home with two new dresses, I booked a table for two at Maison Jerome for that evening. I continued with my Christmas shopping then, picking up some books and a jigsaw puzzle for Lucy, a new shirt and tie for Dad to wear, and a new lipstick from Woolworths for Mum. I saw a lovely notebook in Hatchards that I almost bought for Jack to keep his recipes in, but I put it back. I didn't want to come across as too keen. We were simply friends. That was all. I picked up a woollen scarf instead and made my way home.

Despite complaining that he would miss his favorite television program, and that he wasn't particularly hungry anyway, Dad washed and shaved, while I ironed his "funeral" trousers, as he called them. He forced himself into the new shirt I'd picked out for him, even though it was a little on the snug side. His smart new tie looked lovely. He even splashed on the aftershave Mum had bought him two Christmases ago and which had been gathering dust ever since. It smelled of leather and pine and made my eyes water.

I smiled as I gave him a kiss on the cheek. "You look lovely, Dad. I don't know how Mum will ever resist you!"

He fussed with his tie and tugged at the collar of his shirt. "Feel like a bloody idiot, dressed up to the nines."

Mum looked especially lovely. "Not bad, eh?" she said as she gave us a twirl.

My dad couldn't take his eyes off her. "Not bad at all, Barbara!" He put his arm around my shoulders. "Thanks, love."

"Right, I'll leave you two lovebirds to it. The table is booked for seven, so don't be late. And don't stay out too late either— remember you'll have Lucy for the next few days."

I hurried Lucy into her coat. I'd promised to take her to see the Christmas lights on Regent Street.

Lucy and I waited at the end of the road until my parents left the house, arm in arm as they walked to the bus stop. A promising start.

Lucy grabbed my hand. "I wish you had someone to take you out somewhere nice, Mummy."

"Oh, I don't mind, love. I like it best when we have our family tea together." I paused for a moment. "I have a friend whose job it is to cook tea for the queen. Did you know that?"

She stopped and stared at me. "Really? She cooks tea for the queen?"

I laughed. "Yes, really. *He* does. My friend is a chef in the kitchens at Buckingham Palace. And at Sandringham. He works there every Christmas." I let out a long guilty breath, glad to have finally plucked up the courage to even mention Jack's name to her, but conscious of what I wasn't telling her about him.

"He must be very rich and posh."

I laughed again as I thought about Jack. "Well, not quite."

"I wish I could go to Sandringham with you, Mummy."

"I know, darling. But when I go there, I'm very busy and have to work, so you'd be ever so bored. You'll have more fun here until I get back. Anyway, come on. Let's have a race. Last one to the pond is a sack of coal!"

I set off at a sprint but let Lucy catch me, pretending to be winded and have a stitch and staggering the last few yards. I gasped dramatically as she overtook me. She was almost able to beat me now without my pretending to struggle. My little girl was growing up, and I was so proud of her. I was proud of myself, too. It hadn't been easy to raise her on my own, but we'd muddled through, and would keep muddling through. Together.

We watched the ducks as they slipped on the frozen pond, laughing until tears streamed down our faces. This was where I was happiest. With my girl, just the two of us. Maybe we didn't need anyone else at all.

That night, when I went to tuck her up in bed, I found her Christmas list on her bedside table. What she'd written broke my heart.

Dear Father Christmas,
I would like
1) a typewriter for my stories
2) a dog of my own
3) a daddy, so that Mummy doesn't have to be sad

My darling girl. So sensitive and caring. I tried to hide my emotions from her, but clearly I hadn't done a very good job of it recently. If only it was as simple as Father Christmas delivering a daddy down the chimney, but it was going to be a little more complicated than that.

Tomorrow, I would travel to Sandringham to spend another Christmas in the company of the queen and, unfortunately, in the company of Charlie Bullen. But it was neither of them my thoughts turned to as I laid my head on my pillow. There was only one name that kept running through my head, one face I saw when I closed my eyes.

Jack.

It was always—had only ever been—Jack.

Chapter 38

Jack

Sandringham Estate, Norfolk. December 1954

I still couldn't believe the news about Mrs. Howard. I struggled to imagine her absence in the neighborhood where she had been such a friendly face for so many years. I also hated to think of my beloved old building belonging to someone else. What could possibly flourish inside the charming red-brick walls if not the dream I'd tended to like a treasured garden for years? Why hadn't I grabbed hold of the dream sooner? I shouldn't have wondered and waited for so long. It was a lesson—a cruel lesson—to seize the moment, to be impulsive, rather than worry and calculate the risks, as I always did and always had.

With everything that had happened in the last week, I was relieved to finally leave London for Sandringham, where I hoped to put these new disappointments behind me for a while. When the charming Norfolk villages and the beautiful gardens and glimmering lake of Sandringham Estate came into view, my sadness eased a little. It was good to be back in these peaceful surroundings, away from the stiff formality of Buckingham Palace, and the disappointments that life kept throwing at me in London.

I was looking forward to seeing Ryan and his family, too—and

I was mostly hoping to see Olive. I thought of the journal wrapped in pretty Christmas paper in my suitcase and my nerves flared. I hoped it wouldn't make things awkward between us, that she'd be pleased to know I was thinking of her. Perhaps she might even take the hint that I would like to see more of her, even if I hadn't yet managed to make that clear.

After a busy day and a very late evening setting up for the arrival of the royal family, Max took pity on us and gave us a start time of midmorning. We all needed a good night's sleep before the parade of guests arrived and the Christmas festivities were in full swing.

But I didn't sleep late in the staff quarters. Instead, Mason and I packed up our gifts—I brought my cookbook, too, because Mason insisted I show Ryan and Maggie—and we set off to their house to meet them for breakfast. It had been too long since I'd seen them, and I wanted to seize the opportunity while I could.

As Mason drove us toward their charming home in a nearby village, I admired the morning sun that swept over the beautiful Norfolk countryside, sending golden light dancing on every field, every copse of trees, every rooftop. I'd never been a country boy, always drawn to the bright lights of city life, but I was learning to appreciate the silence and solace these quiet country lanes offered. I'd loved my time at Balmoral Castle in the Scottish Highlands that summer. I'd felt restored there, among the heather-clad hills. And I felt restored here, too. Maybe this city boy would settle for a quiet country life one day.

At Ryan's, I tried to help Maggie in the kitchen but was shooed away to play with Ivy, and little Adam, who was fast approaching his second birthday. Ivy was wild with excitement at the prospect of Christmas, and Adam was finally steady on his feet and needed watching closely. Ryan, too, zipped around the house, glad that Christmas was nearly here.

Eventually, the sausages, bacon, and eggs were served, and we gathered around the kitchen table.

"Show them your cookbook," Mason prompted me as we all ate hungrily.

"You're working on a cookbook?" Ryan asked.

My old uncomfortable timidity arose, and I shrugged. "I've been pulling a few recipes together."

"It's amazing," Mason insisted. "Show them."

I pushed my collection of notes and recipes across the table toward Maggie.

I watched her face as she turned the pages and commented on the unusual ingredients and dishes she'd never heard of. "This is wonderful, Jack. Truly. It's unique and it's . . . so entirely *you*."

"Thank you," I said, smiling as she passed it to Ryan.

As he opened it, a sheaf of papers fluttered to the table.

"Oh, those aren't part of the book," I said, gathering them into a pile. "They're recipes for Olive. I haven't sent them to her yet."

Ryan raised an eyebrow at me. "Recipes for Olive? Olive Carter, I presume? You two are still in touch?"

I took a slug of tea. "On and off. More off, actually."

"He likes her but won't admit it," Mason added.

"Of course I like her. We're friends."

"I think it's sweet that you're writing recipes for her. When will you see her again?" Maggie asked.

"She'll probably be at Sandringham with the BBC for Christmas. At least, I think she will. She's covered the beat in the past, but we haven't spoken in a while."

Ryan grinned. "Does our boy have a crush?"

"All right, all right," I said, laughing. "We're friends, I told you that. Leave a man to his own business!" I pushed up from the table and carried my dish and several others to the sink.

Maggie met me there. She laid a hand on my forearm. "You like her. Very much." It was a statement, not a question.

Though surprised by her earnestness, I nodded. "I do. As I said, she's a friend. It has been nice to reconnect."

"By the look on your face, I'd say you'd like to be more than friends."

I shook my head. "It doesn't matter anyway. I think she's with someone else."

"Do you *know* she's with someone else?" When I didn't reply, Maggie looked at me pointedly. "You should tell her how you feel. You deserve to be happy after . . . well, you know."

After Andrea, she was about to say.

"She'd want you to move on," she said, her tone gently encouraging. 'I just want you to be happy. You deserve it."

"Thanks, Maggie. I'm working on being happy again."

"Good." She kissed my cheek, and we joined the others at the table where, thankfully, the subject had changed.

"Mason was telling me how much you're impressing the team at Buckingham Palace," Ryan said. "You seem very happy there."

"I am, though . . ." I shook my head. "You know how I've always wanted to run my own restaurant? Well, the building I'd dreamed of buying is either sold or off the market. Either way, it's gone."

"There are bound to be others," Ryan said. "Don't give up hope."

"That's what I said," Mason added. "We'll find something."

Maggie raised an eyebrow. "We?"

"You two going into business together?" Ryan asked as he dropped a lump of sugar in his tea.

"We've been talking about it," Mason said. "Which is why Jack took me to see the building."

"I'm glad to hear it," Ryan said. "You two would make a great team."

"One day, maybe." I shrugged. "If we can ever manage to save enough."

Ivy climbed into my lap then, sticky hands and all. "Will you read me your book, Uncle Jack?"

I smiled. I'd always had a soft spot for Ivy, and she knew it. "Oh, this is just a boring book about food, sweetheart. Why don't we open some presents instead?"

She squealed with delight as I pulled the wrapped packages from my bag and handed them to her. She tore open the paper, instantly stroking the doll's shiny hair and making her eyes open and close. She liked the books I'd chosen for her just as much.

As I watched Ivy turn the pages, I glanced at Maggie and Ryan, and at little Adam with mashed egg all over his face, and I was filled with warmth to be part of this simple family moment. I finally realized something I'd never truly admitted to myself, even when Andrea and I had tried for children: I wanted a family.

"We have to get back," I said, standing up. Mason rose from the table, too.

"What do you say to Jack?" Ryan prompted Ivy.

"Thank you, Uncle Jack," she sang.

"You're welcome, kiddo." I kissed the top of her head, then turned to Maggie and kissed her cheek. "And thank you, for breakfast."

She smiled. "Don't be a stranger, Jack. And remember what I said. You deserve every happiness."

I wished them all a merry Christmas as I followed Mason to the door, thinking about all that Ryan and Maggie had said, about the restaurant and Mason, about Olive. Thinking about how much I still missed Andrea.

But, as we drove back to Sandringham Estate, a new revelation struck me. I'd missed Olive, too, this past year. It had taken twelve months, a conversation with my oldest friends—and seeing Olive with another man—to realize it, but if I were to ever have a chance with her, I needed to seize the day, make a move.

Maybe this Christmas would be the one.

Maybe a little luck and Christmas magic would bring her to my door.

Chapter 39

Olive

My parents' romantic meal was a great success until it turned into a complete disaster. They'd chosen a shrimp starter and were both struck down in the night by awful food poisoning. I woke to discover them both as sick as dogs. There was no way they could look after Lucy, and there was also no way I could back out of my role as Bullen's assistant at Sandringham.

There was only one thing to do. Lucy would have to come with me, although what on earth I would do with her when I got there, I didn't know.

I couldn't bear to involve Maguire, so I took a chance and placed a call directly through to Sandringham House and asked to speak with Mrs. Leonard. When I explained my predicament, she was very understanding.

"I'll ask Evans to bring you directly to your cottage. Your daughter will have to lie very low, I'm afraid. Perhaps I will ask Nancy or one of the other girls to sit with her while you're busy."

"That's ever so kind of you," I said. "She's very well behaved. She'll be no trouble."

"Leave it with me, dear. I'll inform security to expect you both."

"Thank you, Mrs. Leonard. I really didn't know what else to do."

She paused slightly before responding. "I understand how challenging your situation is, Miss Carter. I have absolute admiration for any woman raising a child on her own. We'll see you a little later today."

Lucy could hardly contain her excitement when I explained that she was coming with me to Sandringham.

"And we're really spending Christmas with the queen? In a castle? Will there be ponies? And dogs?"

"In a sort of castle. And yes, there will be lots of ponies. *And* dogs!"

She chose her best dresses and her favorite teddy bears and talked nonstop all the way to the train station, and all the way to King's Lynn. Thankfully, Charlie was driving himself there. My plan was to get Lucy into the cottage before he saw me. He would never even know she was there.

It was a relief to find Evans waiting at the station. He was as pleasant and chatty as ever, and was great with Lucy, who couldn't take her eyes away from the car window as we got closer and Evans turned through the gates. As we rolled along the sweeping driveway and Sandringham House came into view, Lucy squealed with excitement.

"Look, Mummy!" she shouted. "It's a real palace. And there's a flag on the roof!"

Evans chuckled as I shushed her. "No need to be quiet, Miss Lucy," he said. "I still get excited by the view, even after all these years."

Once we'd parked, he helped carry our luggage inside and wished us well.

"She's a live-wire that one!" he said. "Reminds me of my great-nieces and -nephews. Children make Christmas, don't they? Mrs. Leonard will pop down in a while. She said to make yourselves comfortable."

Lucy ran around the cottage, inspecting the comfortable bedrooms and the little kitchen, everything tastefully decorated in the style of a cozy country home. A toy bear had even been placed on the pillow of the bed in the smaller bedroom, a tag tied around his paw with the name *Lucy* written in beautiful looping script. Dear Mrs. Leonard taking extra care, I presumed. Everything was so considered here. Not too austere. Not too simple. Just right. I was Goldilocks, lost in a fairytale.

I bent down to undo the top button on Lucy's scarlet coat and took off the black velvet beret my sister had given her for her birthday. She looked like a Victorian Christmas card.

I wrapped my arms around her and pulled her toward me. "I love you, Lucy Carter." I loved her so much I felt I would burst. She was my world, my constant through everything. A gift I hadn't known I'd wanted and now couldn't imagine being without.

She giggled as I blew raspberries into her ear. "I love you, Mummy Carter."

Just then, there was a knock at the door. I opened it to see a young woman armed with a stack of jigsaws and board games.

"Hello, miss. I'm Nancy. Mrs. Leonard asked me to call down to you." She smiled at Lucy. "And you must be Lucy. I brought some games and jigsaws for us to do together. Do you like jigsaws?"

I was so grateful to Mrs. Leonard. Finally, I could relax a little to know that Lucy would be in safe hands while I worked.

"Lucy loves jigsaws. She'll be no trouble," I said. "You will be a very good girl, won't you, Lucy. You can stay here with Nancy while I go and do my job."

I wasn't even entirely sure what "my job" would entail. Tom had made it very clear that I was to assist Charlie. What he hadn't made clear was what I would be assisting Charlie with. I was due to meet him in the breakfast room in thirty minutes.

I arrived four minutes late.

"I was about to send out a search party," Bullen said as I rushed into the room. "The tea will be cold."

A tray of tea and scones sat on the table. I was starving but resisted the urge to dive straight in.

"Sorry about that. The cottage I'm staying in was a little further away than I'd remembered."

"Not held up by your daughter then?" He stared at me. "Most unusual for a royal reporter to bring their child to work with them."

How did he know Lucy was here?

I felt color rush to my cheeks, but I refused to apologize, or explain, or make an issue of it. I sat down in the seat opposite him. "Did you want to run through a schedule? Discuss ideas. Or would you like me to take notes?"

Clearly annoyed by my refusal to bite, he removed a typed sheet of paper from his briefcase and handed it to me. "I've underlined the tasks assigned to you. I shall mostly be spending time with the duke. I'm doing a feature on him this year. The palace is keen to elevate his profile."

I ran my eyes over the items I'd been assigned.

1. Short piece on the floral arrangements and florists
2. Short piece on the royal children: milestones, first Christmas with their mother in two years, etc.
3. Short piece on the royal Christmas cake

"And who am I to interview about these matters?" I asked, trying to control the irritation in my voice. He'd tasked me with small trivial items, while keeping the important things for himself. Of course he thought women could understand nothing beyond children, flowers, and cake. After three years of working diligently, and covering the royal family's Christmas in some way or other, I deserved more.

"You're the budding reporter, aren't you? Great friends with Her Majesty?" He stood up to leave. "I have no doubt you'll find the right sources. But, if you find you are struggling, I could always help."

I would rather chew on a wasp than ask Bullen for help. "Oh, I shall manage perfectly well. I've spoken with one of the florists before," I said. "And, as a mother, I can fully relate to the difficulty of being apart from your children. As for the Christmas cake, I have a friend in the royal kitchens as it happens, so there will be no problem there."

He huffed out a breath. "Well then. I have planned your time wisely."

"Apparently so." I stared at the tea and scones on the table. "Is jam first the correct etiquette for scones, or cream first? I'm never sure."

He shrugged. "Personal preference. But if you want a tidbit for your little write-up, I believe the queen puts the cream on first."

Little write-up! I stared at him, then scooped up a spoonful of jam, added a dollop of cream on top, and took a defiant bite.

I waited for him to leave before I let out a frustrated breath and threw my notebook onto the table. How was I ever going to get rid of him? I had so much to prove, so much more than anyone else, because I was a woman, and a mother.

I walked to the window and looked out across the manicured lawns and gardens. It really was so beautiful here. I watched as festive garlands were hung around the doorway, and staff rushed to and fro, busy in their tasks to make the place perfect. My attention was drawn to a couple of men carrying a hamper, both of them laughing as they struggled and maneuvered awkwardly beneath its weight.

Jack.

I stood to one side, in case he spotted me. My stomach flipped as a smile spread to my lips. He looked happy and relaxed, just as he had on SS *Gothic*. Get a grip, Carter, I told myself. But there was no denying the flutter of excitement at seeing him.

Just then, I heard footsteps behind me, and turned to see Her Majesty. I dipped into a curtsey before rushing to pick up my things and get out of her way. "Ma'am."

"Ah, Miss Carter. I heard you were coming. I hope the accommodation is suitable."

I assured her that it was more than suitable. "Mrs. Leonard has thought of everything."

"And your daughter is quite settled?"

Even the queen had heard about Lucy being here? The familiar sense of dread I'd carried ever since Lucy was born surfaced again. Would I be found out? Would my status as an unmarried mother be revealed? Would everything I had worked for be taken away from me?

"Yes, ma'am," I replied. "She is rather impressed to be at a real palace."

At this, the queen offered a slight smile. "What age is she?"

"Eight and a half, ma'am. The half is very important."

"Does she like dogs?"

I nodded. "She loves dogs, but we can't have one because my mother reacts to their hair."

"She can play with the corgis then. In fact, it is rather appropriate for her to be here. The theme of my speech this year centers on Christmas being very much a children's festival."

"That sounds lovely, ma'am. The driver, Evans, was just remarking on how Christmas is made by children."

"Indeed." She walked to a shelf and pulled a book from between the spines. "Inspiration," she said, "for this year's speech.

It is hard to believe another year has passed since we were in New Zealand."

"Yes, ma'am. The year has flown."

She looked at me. "Are you very busy?"

Should I say yes? No? I settled on something in the middle. "I'm never too busy for you, ma'am."

"Would you mind listening to what I have so far? It seems that you are quite the lucky charm now. I fear some great calamity might befall me if I don't run through the speech with you before the big day."

I smiled, thrilled she should consider my opinion so important. "Of course, ma'am."

"Jolly good. I am in the study next door."

We stepped inside and she pulled some pages across the desk as she sat down.

I lost track of time, listening intently, making small supportive comments and offering the occasional piece of advice. It was almost a familiar routine now, and I was increasingly comfortable, and confident, in her company.

We were interrupted by a knock on the door and Mrs. Leonard was shown into the room.

"Ah. Good timing. We were just finishing," Her Majesty said.

"Very good, ma'am. I wondered if I might borrow Miss Carter for a moment or two."

"Is everything all right?" I realized how long Lucy had been with Nancy. I hope Lucy is behaving herself."

Mrs. Leonard smiled. "Everything's fine. Lucy and Nancy decided to go exploring."

I groaned. "I'm so sorry. I did tell her to stay in the cottage."

"Well, she's now in the kitchens, being treated to bonbons and cinnamon apple puffs. And I can hardly say I blame her. The smell has been tormenting me all day!"

I stood up. "Honestly, that child could charm her way into the vaults holding the crown jewels."

I curtsied to the queen, who was feeding a treat to the corgis, then hurried after Mrs. Leonard. "I hope she isn't causing any bother. I'll take her straight back to the cottage."

"Not at all! She's a delight. She's helping one of the chefs—the American fellow."

A rising sense of panic flared in my chest. She must be with Jack.

I hurried to the kitchens, and there she was, kneeling up on a stool, cutting out stars from scraps of pastry, her tongue stuck out to one side as she concentrated.

I stood for a moment in the doorway, my heart in my mouth as Jack patiently instructed her, only helping when she got in a muddle.

I moved forward, propelled by an instinct to interrupt them. I wasn't ready to confront this. I wasn't ready for whatever this might mean for all of us. In my haste, my elbow knocked a pot of spoons from the windowsill and sent them spilling onto the floor in a terrible clatter.

"Mummy!" Lucy scrambled down from the stool and ran over to me. "I'm making pastry shapes for the mince pies. Look!"

"I can see that, darling. But I did ask you to stay in the cottage, didn't I?" I tried to keep my voice steady, not to show the depth of my reaction.

"But it was boring there, so Nancy said we could come up to the house for a look around. Mr. Jack is a chef. He makes all the queen's food!"

"*All* the queen's food?" I looked at Jack, who offered a quizzical smile.

"I'm a very busy man," he said. "It's good to see you again, Olive."

Did he lean toward me to kiss my cheek in greeting, or was I imagining it? Either way, the moment passed as I reached for Lucy at the same time to lift her down from the stool.

"It's good to see you, too, Jack." Surely he could hear the pounding of my heart. "Thank you for keeping her busy. I hope she hasn't been getting in your way."

He smiled. "She makes a great sous-chef. You're welcome in my kitchen anytime, Lucy."

She beamed at him, and I felt like my heart would burst with love and fear. I didn't know how I would ever share my enormous secret in a way that they would both understand, and forgive me for keeping from them.

I gave Lucy a meaningful stare. "Anyway, I'm sure Mr. Jack has a million things to be doing without bored little girls getting under his feet." I told Lucy to tidy her things and wash her hands and thanked Jack again. "Sorry about this."

"There's no hurry. How long are you here for?" he asked.

"A few days. I'm assisting Charlie Bullen."

"Too bad you're not the one holding the reigns."

"Any chance you could give him some undercooked prawns? Add a drop of something poisonous into his soup?"

He laughed. "I'll see what I can do."

"I've been tasked with doing a piece on the royal Christmas cake. I don't suppose you could help me with that?"

"Not my area, I'm afraid. But I'm sure Brian over there would be more than happy to bore you with tales of life as a pastry chef and the delicate craft of sugarwork."

Was he trying to put me off? "Thanks awfully. I'll ask him."

There was a moment, a beat. Neither of us knew what to say.

Lucy broke the silence. "Can I help you again tomorrow, Mr. Jack?" She pulled her hand from mine and threw her arms around his legs.

He stood as stiff as fire irons in Lucy's embrace. I, too, seemed to freeze. Could he see it: his brow, his cheekbones in her face? Did some part of him instinctively know?

"Come along, you. Mr. Devereux is very busy." I took Lucy's hand and hurried her out of the kitchen. I only remembered to breathe again when we were halfway across the lawns.

"Are you cross, Mummy? You seem cross."

"No, darling. I'm not cross."

"Why are you walking so fast? Don't you like Mr. Jack?"

I stopped and bent down so that our eyes were level. "I do like Mr. Jack, darling. He's very nice, and it was very kind of him to show you how to make the toppings for the mince pies. But it was a surprise to see you in the kitchen, that's all."

"I like surprises. And I like Mr. Jack. He talks all funny!"

"I like surprises too, darling."

But no matter how often I'd imagined it, or how often I'd hoped for it, nothing had prepared me for the surprise of seeing Lucy and Jack together.

How differently would Jack see her when he knew the truth?

And how differently would he see me for keeping the truth— and Lucy—from him for all these years?

If only I could turn the clock back.

If only I could have told him from the start.

Chapter 40

Olive

London, November 1945

Rosie insisted I go on the next group outing to take my mind off things, but I really wasn't in the mood. Andrea had to pull out at the last minute to help out at the florist's shop she was now working at, and Peter was ill, so it was just Jack, Rosie, me, and a chap called Arthur from the pub who Rosie was sweet on at the time. We spent the day in Windsor Great Park, admiring the castle and imagining living there like the royal princesses. Rosie still didn't believe that I'd seen Princess Elizabeth in the conga line on VE Day, but I knew I had, and it was a moment to remember.

Jack didn't understand our fascination with the royal family. He found all the traditions stuffy and old-fashioned.

"You're very quiet today," he said as we strolled along. "Everything all right?"

"I'm fine," I said.

He offered me a small smile. "Liar."

I shook my head. "You wouldn't understand."

"I definitely won't if you don't tell me."

I hated him for being so blissfully unaware of the situation. I *couldn't* tell him. That was the problem.

"Women's troubles, that's all."

He pushed his hands into his trouser pockets. "Ahh, I see."

We walked on in silence for a while.

At last, he said, "You should talk to Andrea. She's good in a crisis. She's so calm and sensible."

Jack and Andrea. Like fish and chips and salt and pepper. The perfect pair.

"You two are still madly in love then?" I asked. "Still getting married?"

He laughed. "Of course we're still getting married! She's so excited about it all. It's all set for Valentine's Day."

"And you? Are you excited?"

"Not in a bride-to-be way, no. But about building a life together, yes."

"A life, and a family, I presume. Little Devereux children running around."

At this, he let out a sigh. "Hopefully not for a while, although don't tell Andrea I said that. She's keen to start a family immediately, but I'm not ready for the responsibility of parenthood. Couldn't afford a family right now on my wages anyway, even if I wanted one."

As we passed a grove of silver birch trees, their golden leaves rustling in the breeze, my thoughts returned to VE Day, dancing with Jack in the jazz club, meeting Andrea in the fountain in Trafalgar Square. I wondered what might have happened if I hadn't pulled her along as part of our group. Would it be Jack and Olive, the perfect couple, planning our wedding?

"I hate to see you so quiet, Olive," Jack continued. "It's not like you. Is Peter giving you the run-around again? I could knock some sense into him if you like?"

I smiled half-heartedly. "I'm not sure that would make a difference. Things are cooling off between us, actually."

Jack stopped walking. "Sorry to hear that. If he's not treating you right, then he's an idiot. He clearly doesn't know a good thing when he sees it." He seemed to check himself and looked at the ground.

"I'm a good thing, am I? I'm not so sure about that."

Jack looked at me and let out a breath. He reached forward and brushed a tear from my cheek. He let his thumb linger there a moment, at the edge of my lips, just as he had before he'd leaned in to kiss me three months ago. My heart raced beneath my cardigan.

"You're definitely a good thing, Olive. Don't ever forget it."

But *he* had already forgotten it. I wasn't a good enough thing to steal him away from his darling Andrea.

Just then, Rosie ran up to me and grabbed my hand.

"Arthur just asked me out! We're going to the pictures later!"

Whatever might have been said between Jack and I was blown away with Rosie's excitement and a cold breeze that sent a flurry of leaves tumbling along the path ahead.

I couldn't keep my pregnancy a secret forever, no matter how much I tried to hide my morning sickness, or how carefully I dressed to conceal my bump. My typing pool supervisor was the first to notice, dispatching me unceremoniously on the basis that pregnant women *could* not, and *should* not work, let alone the scandalous matter of my being an *unmarried* pregnant woman.

"You will be paid until the end of the week," she said. "And do stop sniveling. These situations are easily preventable, *Miss* Carter." Her eyes fell to my empty ring finger, and she gave a sniff of disapproval. "You have nobody to blame but yourself."

My mother was horrified, worried about what the neighbors would think, and shocked that I had been so careless. She took to her bed with a migraine.

"You can move back in here until we work out what to do about it," she called from the top of the stairs. "I'll send your father round to your flat to pick up your things."

"But Mum, I don't want . . ."

"I won't hear another word about it." She slammed the bedroom door.

I lay on the sofa and listened to her crying for an hour.

Among the group of friends, I kept up the pretense for as long as I could, but I felt different around them as my freedom slipped away with every half pint of lager I forced myself to drink. When I couldn't hide my condition any longer, I made up endless excuses for not joining everyone—a cold, a touch of the flu, too tired. I finally broke things off with Peter before he found out. The truth was that I was ashamed, and afraid of my friends' pity and judgment being added to everyone else's.

Besides, if anyone in the group discovered I was pregnant, Jack would most likely realize the child was his. And how could I say anything when it would surely break him and Andrea apart? I wouldn't be the one to end someone else's happiness. I couldn't do it.

I had never felt more alone.

Rosie kept urging me to tell Jack.

"What good would it do?" I said. "Telling him isn't going to change *this*, is it?" I pointed at my stomach, still not quite able to believe another person was growing in there. "He doesn't want a baby any more than I do."

Rosie was furious about it all. "But it isn't fair that you have to deal with it on your own, Olive. *He* should take responsibility. He is half of the reason you're expecting after all, unless you're the Virgin bloody Mary."

I looked at her and burst into laughter for the first time since I'd found out I was pregnant. I laughed until I cried, months of emotion pouring out as Rosie held me in her arms and told me it was going to be all right, that things would work out, as they always did.

I was grateful for her unwavering friendship and support, but I didn't believe her. This wasn't something that worked itself out, like an argument, or making a muddle of something at work. This was a permanent, life-changing situation. One that everyone and the whole world would not only judge me for, but one that would make my life far more difficult, even if it wasn't fair. It had already happened at work, and I knew worse was to come. I was terrified.

I moved back home, into my childhood bedroom. All my plans for a successful career at the BBC, all my dreams of a bright future, abandoned.

My mother made arrangements for me to go and stay with a relative in Cornwall until the baby was born. I had avoided the dreaded mother and baby homes, but I was being sent away nevertheless.

Shunned by society, banished from my home, I was as lost and afraid as a person could be.

Chapter 41

Jack

London, December 1945

It had been a whirlwind romance between Andrea and me. After her initial reserve, everything suddenly clicked into place. We talked easily and for hours, spending every free minute together. What we enjoyed most was spending time alone, in a corner booth in the back of a pub, learning everything there was to know about each other. I felt as if I'd known her my entire life.

One chilly December night, I walked her home after an evening of dinner and dancing.

"I've been a little worried about Olive," Andrea said as we stopped outside her boarding house. "It's strange that she hasn't introduced her new boyfriend to the gang, don't you think? She doesn't seem the sort to abandon her friends."

Olive had been noticeably absent the past few weeks. When I'd asked about her, Rosie had mentioned that Olive was dating someone new that she'd met at work. I was pleased she'd finally ditched Peter Hall, but I couldn't help but miss her when the group got together. Everyone liked Olive. It was impossible not to like Olive.

"I'm sure she's just enjoying being with her new beau," I said.

"You know what it's like to fall in love, no time for anyone but each other. She'll be back, in time."

"I hope you're right."

"She and Rosie live near the fish and chip shop where I work. Why don't I stop by tomorrow on my way, make sure all is well? It would be no trouble."

"Would you?" Andrea asked, sliding her hands beneath the lapels of my coat and gently tugging me closer. "I think that would be lovely. Put our minds to rest."

"Of course."

She leaned up onto her tiptoes to kiss me. "And yes, I do know what it's like to fall in love. And lucky me that I found gorgeous you!"

I smiled as our lips met, and we lingered in a kiss. "I'll see you tomorrow."

"Goodnight, darling," she said and disappeared inside.

I walked back to my own place, thinking about our conversation. Some nagging part of me wanted to see Olive, new man on the scene or not. I wanted her to know that we all missed her.

The following morning, I headed to work earlier than usual. When I reached Olive and Rosie's flat, I knocked on the door and waited a moment.

As the door swung open, I felt the smallest letdown to see Rosie, not Olive.

"Jack? What are you doing here?"

"I'm headed to work, and I thought I'd stop by to say hi to Olive. Is she home? We haven't seen her in a while."

Rosie studied my face a moment before replying, "She's not here, Jack. She's gone."

"Gone?"

"Moved out."

"Oh." I felt my face fall. "Where to?"

Rosie looked anxious and awkward. "Sorry, Jack, but I promised Olive I wouldn't tell anyone."

I laughed, a little nervously. "But it's me! Surely you can tell me?"

Rosie shook her head. "I'm sorry. I promised."

"I understand. I guess that would explain why she hasn't been around lately. And neither have you, come to think of it. I just thought . . . I don't know what I thought. I wanted to say hi. Let her know she was missed."

"It was kind of you to check on her," Rosie said, her voice soothing. "But she isn't likely to be back anytime soon."

It all sounded so final, so unlike Olive. "Well, if you see her or talk to her, will you tell her I stopped by? And if she ever wants to call, she knows where to find us."

"Us?"

"Andrea and me."

Rosie nodded. "Right. Of course."

As I turned to go, Rosie grabbed my arm. "Jack, wait. I . . ."

"Yes?"

"Nothing." She released my arm. "See you sometime soon."

As I walked away, I wondered what Rosie had wanted to say, and where Olive had gone. The only explanation I could imagine was a family incident, something terrible, perhaps, that had made her pack up and leave so suddenly. Or maybe she'd fallen head over heels with the new guy and they'd run off together. I shook my head. That didn't sound like her either.

As I continued toward work, it occurred to me that I might never see Olive again. And at the same time, I realized that I cared for her more than I'd dared admit.

But I was engaged to be married to the woman I loved.

Olive and I were a moment. Andrea and I were a lifetime.

Chapter 42

Jack

I watched Olive lead her daughter out of the kitchen. Lucy's long blonde braids were tied with ribbons, and the lapels of her coat were smeared with flour. I'd never been great at judging children's ages, but I figured she was about seven, the same age as Ivy—a cute kid, and precocious with adults. But what struck me most of all was that she was the spitting image of Olive. Pretty and friendly and clever, like her mom.

I wondered, for a moment, what her father had been like. It must have been incredibly difficult for Olive to lose a husband and then find herself raising Lucy on her own. The world wasn't kind to single mothers. This, I knew, from my own mom and our difficulties when I was little. She'd had her share of faults, but she'd truly struggled and that counted for something, despite our fractured relationship these days.

I placed the remainder of the stars and hearts that Lucy had made with the leftover scraps of dough on a sheet pan and slid them into the oven. I'd bake them and ice them, drop them off at their cottage later along with Olive's gift.

Max skirted in behind me to collect a utensil he needed. "Seems you're a popular man. Who was the little girl helping you earlier? It's not usually permitted to have a child in the kitchen, but I thought I'd let you off, as it's Christmas."

"She's the daughter of an old friend. I somehow ended up babysitting."

"You were very patient with her. Children exhaust me. I'm glad I never married, or had children."

"Too busy for them, chef? Married to the job?"

At this, he laughed. "Something like that, yes!"

"I'm about to finish up here," I said, changing the subject. "Do you need me to work on anything else before I head to my room?" I was looking forward to wrapping up my chores for the day so that I could deliver Olive's gift and say a proper hello.

"You're a free man," Max said. "Go and get some rest."

I heaved a sigh of relief. "Great. See you bright and early tomorrow."

Outside, I walked quickly, savoring the perfect winter night. Stars gleamed overhead and my breath puffed out in little white clouds. My thoughts turned in circles around Olive as I walked. Suddenly I was nervous to see her. Our short encounter in the kitchens earlier had been awkward. She'd seemed surprised to see me, and a little irritated with Lucy. I hoped Olive liked the gift I'd bought her—and I hoped it wasn't too much.

I remembered that impulsive night so many years ago when things had turned passionate between Olive and me. Both of us had accepted that it was a one-time thing, unfinished business from VE Day. My feelings for Olive back then had been confusing—I was attracted to her, to be sure, but it was Andrea, with her tender, steady ways, who I fell in love with. Andrea was so similar to me, and after the uncertainty of war, we'd both craved the stability we found in each other.

But Maggie was right: Andrea would want me to be happy. I might be too late—Olive might be with Peter now, for all I knew—but I needed to tell her how I felt.

I walked around the lake, past the willow tree that lay dormant for the winter, past a bench placed in the perfect spot to watch the ducks on a summer day, and on to the cottages, balancing the plate of treats for Lucy. Along with the pastry hearts and stars Lucy had made to top the mince pies, I'd added jam biscuits, gingerbread men, and shortbread shaped into angels. Children, I was learning, were easily pleased and there was almost nothing better in the world than their excitement at Christmas.

As I approached Olive's cottage, the windows glowed through the drawn curtains and the happy sounds of laughter and music emerged from inside. Without pause, I knocked on the door. In an instant it swung open with a whoosh of warm air.

"Mr. Jack!" Lucy shouted, her cheeks fire-engine red.

Olive filled the doorway behind her. Her eyes were bright, her hair mussed. She looked radiant.

"Jack! What a surprise! We were just dancing. I'm a little out of breath!"

"I hope I'm not bothering you. I have something for you both."

"And I have something for you as it happens. Come in."

I stepped inside the cottage and saw at once the cluttered dining table, overflowing with crafts. Paper streamers, tinsel, cut-out stars and snowflakes sat in heaps, ready to be placed on a Christmas tree.

"We're decorating the tree," Lucy said. "Want to help us? It has to be ready for Father Christmas, or he won't leave me any presents."

"You're right," I said, laughing. "I brought your pie dough, baked and iced, and some other treats."

Her already-round eyes widened. "Mummy, can I have some?"

"You can have two and no more. You'll make yourself sick."

I laughed as Lucy gobbled down two angels, a jam biscuit, and one of her own creations, in one minute flat.

"That's enough, young lady." Olive carried the plate of goodies into the kitchen and transferred them into a tin.

She stepped into the bedroom then, emerging a moment later holding a package. "I hoped I might see you here. I got you a little something." She smiled shyly.

I found myself grinning, relieved she'd bought me something, too.

"Open it!" Lucy said, as eager as if it were a present for her.

I laughed at her enthusiasm and opened the paper carefully.

"Just rip it!" Lucy squealed.

"Calm down, love," Olive said. "Let Jack open it the way he wants to. It's his gift."

I played on Lucy's childish impatience, opening the paper teasingly slowly, then tore through the rest quickly. A navy scarf uncoiled and landed in my lap. I picked it up and wound it around my neck, appreciating the soft yarn against my skin.

"It's perfect. How did you know I needed a scarf?"

"Lucky guess. I remembered you were always complaining that England is too cold."

"Open yours," I said, handing Olive my present.

She opened the paper—and gasped. "Jack! It's beautiful." She turned the red journal over, running her hands over the etchings in the leather.

"I thought you might use it to take notes, for your reports and articles."

"It's wonderful. Thank you so much." She held it to her chest, a wide smile on her face.

"Now open Peter's present, Mummy," Lucy said. "Mummy's other friend gave her a present, too!" she added, turning to me.

271

My warm smile froze. So it *was* Peter I'd seen with Olive in the park recently. Again, I felt a stab of jealousy dampening my spirits.

"We need to finish the tree and get you to bed," Olive said suddenly. "We'll leave the rest of the presents until Christmas Day."

"Well, ladies," I said, eager to be on my way. "I have a very long day tomorrow, so I'd better get to bed myself."

"Thank you again, for the journal," Olive said as we walked to the door. "I love it, truly. It was so thoughtful of you."

"I'm glad. I guess I'll see you around over the next few days?"

"It seems like I'll be working flat out if I am ever to prove myself to Charlie Bullen. I suppose you'll be up to your eyes, too?"

"Working round the clock." I offered a rueful smile. How I wished she wasn't tangled up with Peter Hall again. "Well, goodnight."

"Goodnight, Jack," she said.

"Goodnight, Mr. Jack," Lucy called after me.

I waved at Lucy and turned to go, warring with my feelings, embarrassed that I'd thought Olive might be able to see me as something more than a friend. Now I knew the truth for sure: Peter was courting Olive, and I had no business butting in, not now. We were friends, nothing more. Always had been, always would be.

I walked through the falling snow, alone once again, back to my room in the staff quarters. My earlier enthusiasm lost; my hopes deflated.

When I opened the door to my room, I noticed that a large envelope had been left on the desk, addressed to me, care of Sandringham House. I picked it up and tore it open. Inside was a smaller packet with a label on the front that read: *For the attention of Jack Devereux*. Something inside clinked.

Puzzled, I fished out a set of keys and a handwritten note.

Dear Jack,
Knowing you—and dear Andrea—has been a highlight of my
final years. You are a talented and wonderful young man, and
though tragedy has befallen you, I know you will one day find
your way again. In fact, I hope my gift will help you do just that.

I have been unwell for a while, but I have chosen not to
bother anyone with the news. There is something beautiful
about living a life right until the end, without any sorry looks
and tearful farewells. As I reach my final days here in the hos-
pital, I have a chance to set my affairs in order—something I
should have done a long time ago. You see, I have been keeping
a secret. One I should have told you about years ago, but I
wasn't yet ready to let go.

Inside this package are the keys to the building on Richmond
Street. I have put off every potential buyer that has shown inter-
est through the years, because in my heart, I knew they weren't
the right fit for such a special place. I never had children of my
own, and now, as I look back on my life, I realize I've known
someone deserving of the building all along. You, dear boy. I
have watched you admire it and love it as much as my late hus-
band, Walter, once did when it was a thriving restaurant in his
name. I know it will be in good keeping and will thrive once
again, in your hands.

We can't bring the things we've cherished with us when we
go, but we can leave them in the care of others who have loved
us and will remember us. What a blessing.

The sum of money I have also left will, I hope, help you
repair the old place.

Bring it back to life, Jack.
Fill it with love, laughter, and delicious food once again.
With great affection, always,
June Howard

My eyes stung as I read the letter for a second and a third time. I couldn't believe it—the building I'd yearned for had belonged to Mrs. Howard all along. And now it was mine.

Gratitude washed over me as I clutched the keys tightly in my hand. This dear woman had made me believe that Christmas miracles do happen. I couldn't wait to tell Mason, and Ryan and Maggie, and Olive—so many people—but for now, as I watched the snow fall beyond the window, it was a Christmas gift to savor quietly as I whispered a thank you to the stars.

1956

"Of course it is sad for us to be separated on this day, and of course we look forward to the moment when we shall all again be together."

Queen Elizabeth II, Christmas Day 1956

Queen Elizabeth II

Buckingham Palace, August 1956

I watch the children as they play with the dogs, and count my blessings. They fill my heart with such joy.

My eyes stray to a photograph on my desk, a candid moment captured between Philip and I in New Zealand. It is hard to believe that it has been two years since we returned from the Commonwealth tour. Since then, it has been a thankfully peaceful time without too much travel or upheaval, and I have enjoyed being more present in the children's young lives. They grow so alarmingly quickly! I've suggested to Philip that it might be time to add another to the family soon. He hasn't yet responded on the matter.

A great deal of my time is now taken up with the grown-up children in my government. They are forever squabbling and falling out. I do miss dear Winston terribly. He was a steady hand, albeit difficult at times. Anthony Eden is a different character altogether. I sometimes wonder when we might have a woman as our PM. I long for the day.

Apart from the pressing matters of government business, family affairs occupy a great deal of my time. Philip has been in better spirits of late, having launched his Duke of Edinburgh Award, but I still worry for Margaret. It breaks my heart to see her so unhappy, but I must admit, I was relieved when she finally announced she did not intend to marry Peter Townsend. I had hoped we could put the whole sorry episode behind us. With my sister, it was never going to be quite so simple.

"Are you ever getting up?" I ask as I enter her room and pull the curtains back. "It's nearly eleven."

She groans and turns away from the light. "Go away. I only went to bed at six."

I perch on the edge of the bed and reach for her hand. "Don't be cross with me, Margaret. I can't bear it."

She rolls over and pulls up her eye mask. "Good. Then you know how horrible it is to be hurt by someone you love."

Despite the seriousness of the conversation, I stifle a laugh.

"Whatever is so funny?" she says.

"You look terrible! You look like a panda with your mascara halfway down your cheeks."

She pulls herself upright and leans against her many pillows. "I wish I was a panda, then I could roam the mountains of China and nobody would ever find me."

"*I* would find you. I wouldn't stop looking until I did."

She reaches for her cigarettes and lights one, purposefully exhaling in my direction.

"Besides, I would smell you out easily enough," I add, wafting my hand in front of my face to dispel the awful smoke. "Come on. Get up. We're having lunch with Mummy, remember?"

At this, she groans again. "Must I?"

"Yes. You must. We would be thoroughly miserable without you." I lean forward and kiss her cheek. "I do love you, Margaret. I hope you know that."

"Yes, Lilibet. *You* love me. It is that wicked queen inside that doesn't."

There is nothing much I can say in response. I leave her to sulk and make my way downstairs.

So much has already happened in the first few years of my reign, both in public and in private. As I walk through the many rooms and look upon the portraits of those who have reigned before me, I wonder how long I will be queen. Winston firmly believes I will out-reign Victoria, having come to the throne so young. After so many years of instability, firstly with my wayward uncle and then with the unexpected death of my dear father, I do hope he is right. I'd like to become a reliable rock for these dear nations. Steady the ship, as Philip might say.

Yet, I do worry. The world is changing at a rapid pace, and there are those who challenge the relevance of a monarchy in modern society.

"Ah, there you are." Philip strides into the library. "I've been looking for you everywhere."

I glance at my husband. "Is there some emergency? It is not often you seek me out these days."

He smiles and plants a kiss on my cheek. "Oh dear. Her Majesty is feeling neglected. Off with my head, is it?"

"Don't be silly, Philip."

"I was looking for you because the artist is here. You are sitting for a portrait, remember?"

"I was trying to forget." I let out a long sigh. "Very well. I may as well get on with it."

Just then, the children barrel into the room, along with the dogs. I smile at their noise and exuberance, a welcome relief from the worry and formality of other matters.

How strange it is to think that one day Charles will be king and will walk these ancient corridors, considering the portraits of past monarchs, just as I have done. Mine will hang among them as Queen Elizabeth II, but it is in the private family albums, among the simple snapshots of family holidays and in more candid private moments, where he will see the real me.

Mummy.

Elizabeth "Lilibet" Windsor.

Chapter 43

Jack

London, August 1956

I reached for the set of keys on my nightstand and followed Mason outside. It was our day off from our duties at Buckingham Palace and, like all our free days now, we headed straight to the restaurant.

Our restaurant.

I still couldn't quite get used to the idea, couldn't believe the dream was—finally—becoming a reality. It had been a year and a half since I'd opened the note from Mrs. Howard, and discovered she was leaving her husband's restaurant to me. My initial excitement had been followed by many months of frustration and delay, thanks to an estranged brother who'd contested Mrs. Howard's will, causing legal headaches for her lawyers, and plenty of anxiety for Mason and me. When, at last, the verdict was decided in our favor nearly a year later, we had finally been able to start the extensive renovations the building needed to be at her best again.

As Mason and I walked, a steady warm drizzle pattered against the pavement. London rain, I called it. By the time we arrived, we were both soaked, and I was more than a little grouchy. I needed a decent night's sleep, but my mind kept me awake, turning over all the things we still had to do. Today's tasks were to go over the inventory lists, and deal with some persistent plumbing issues. I couldn't wait to work on our menus and fire up the ovens, decorate the tables, and stock the wine cellar—but all in good time.

I was increasingly grateful that I wasn't embarking on the project alone. Mason was at the center of every decision, and we were tirelessly working together on all of it; with his classical French training and my flair for spice and invention, we made a great team. We'd not only become good pals these last few years, but he was proving to be an excellent business partner. He'd been amenable to my leading as head chef and him being the second as sous-chef, but we both agreed he had veto power over menu items. A good compromise.

We spent long hours hunkered down together, drawing up plans, gutting the building, finding electricians, carpenters, plumbers and other tradesmen, and managing the necessary paperwork. At every stage of the renovation, we seemed to hit another snag. The heating had rattled so loudly that I couldn't hear myself think, so the ducts had needed cleaning. Pipes, ceiling tiles, and damaged flooring had been replaced. Every problem, every mishap and setback had cost money, adding to the growing tab. The money Mrs. Howard had left was almost gone.

We'd lost so much time to legal battles and repairs, and had plenty more still to do, but at last we were able to think about opening in the fall, or early the following year at worst. In the meantime, we continued to work hard in our roles at Buckingham Palace. It was a godsend to live in the staff accommodation, allowing us to save our wages as the money from Mrs. Howard quickly dwindled. On days off, we dedicated ourselves to the restaurant.

As I stepped inside and flipped on the lights, the smell of fresh paint rushed my senses. We'd had the walls painted a warm butter yellow, the wainscoting white, and the mahogany chairs were dressed with elegant burgundy cushions. Colorful paintings of scenes from the streets of New Orleans decorated the walls—a jazz band, the famous two-story building with curled iron railings on the corner of Bourbon Street and Toulouse, and a picture of a Garden District plantation home with a large oak tree dripping with Spanish moss that I'd saved from Grandpa's restaurant. The crowning piece was a brass chandelier in the middle of the room. Every detail made me beam with pride.

"Cup of tea?" Mason asked, rubbing his hands together. "I'm parched."

"Me, too. Sounds great."

We sat together for hours with the ledger, adding up costs, making predictions for the next few months, recording totals in the margins until my head ached. We'd conferred with other chefs we knew, picking their brains for a sense of likely running costs and customer numbers. I really disliked the business end of things, but I knew it was important, so I made myself concentrate.

Eventually, a knock at the front door gave us an excuse to take a break.

"Must be the sign," I said, jumping down from my stool. We were expecting the delivery of the new sign to hang above the entrance outside. I couldn't wait to see how it looked.

"Jack Devereux?" the man asked as I opened the door.

"That's me."

"We're here to mount the sign, if you're happy with it."

Mason joined us. "Let's have a look then!"

We'd talked through the design weeks before so everything should be in order, though not much had gone right during the renovation process so far. I hoped, for once, our luck would turn.

I held my breath as the man removed the burlap cloth. The large gilded sign was stunning, the script of the writing perfect. My heart skipped in my chest. Emotion welled in my throat.

I looked at Mason, who was smiling broadly. "It's perfect. Let's mount it."

We went outside to watch the men at work as they decided on the safest way to lift it. Two of the workmen yanked on a pair of ropes fastened to a pulley, while two others balanced on ladders either side of the door. Carefully, slowly, the sign was raised into position.

I crossed the street to see how it looked. "Move it a foot to the right!" I called.

"I think it looks fine as is," Mason said, flicking a cigarette butt to the ground.

"If you cross the street, you can see it's off-center," I replied. As the men hoisted the sign into the proper position, I shouted, "That's it! Perfect!"

Hanging the sign was about the only thing that had gone smoothly since we'd begun renovating.

"You were right." Mason clapped me on the back. "Finally, it looks like a restaurant."

"It sure does," I said.

It was perfect. A sense of pride and emotion washed over me as I admired the beautiful new sign, and the name we'd chosen for our new restaurant.

Andrea's.

It had never been anything else to me, and Mason had been generous to agree that it was the right choice. It was an elegant name for an elegant restaurant, and I knew she would have loved it.

"All right, partner," Mason said. "I'm heading out to the suppliers."

"Great. Be tough with them about the prices. I'll try out a few sample recipes. Start thinking about the menu," I said.

Since Mason would be gone all afternoon, I'd decided to

spend the time experimenting with recipes for our rotating menu of daily specials. The kitchen was, at last, mostly stocked with cookware and utensils, or at least enough for the items I looked forward to cooking: shrimp étouffée, pepper pot beef soup, and beignets filled with coconut rum cream, among dozens of other dishes.

I crossed the cobbled street that led to our front door, passing a pair of black lampposts that we'd positioned on either side of the arched entrance, exactly like those that decorated the French Quarter. A touch of home.

I'd scarcely made it through to the kitchen when a familiar face appeared in the small round glass window of the back door.

Olive, all smiles.

I waved her inside.

"I was just passing and thought I'd look in to see how it's all going," she said. "I wasn't sure you'd be here on a Saturday. You really *are* putting in the hours. It's looking great though."

"It's even better from the front," I replied. "Come on. I've something to show you."

Olive had been so happy for me when I'd told her about Mrs. Howard's gift of the dilapidated old building. She understood more than most people what it was like to chase a dream. We'd seen each other a handful of times over the past year and a half, but not nearly as often as I'd have liked. Between the restaurant and the day job at the palace, my free time was limited, and she was busy making her mark at the BBC.

She was also busy with Lucy. And Peter. I still hated the thought of them together, but it seemed as if things were reasonably serious between them. I kept expecting to hear of their engagement. I'd tried to give up on the idea of anything more than friendship with Olive, and yet, every time I saw her, I found myself wishing things were different.

She hurried behind me as I rushed through the restaurant and out of the front door.

"Where are we going?" she asked.

"Close your eyes!" I guided her across the road, then turned her so that she was facing the restaurant and told her to open her eyes. "Ta-dah!"

She took a moment to respond as she looked at the new sign above the door.

I folded my arms across my chest and admired it again. "What do you think? It's perfect, isn't it? The color was Mason's idea."

She nodded as she stared at the gold and burgundy sign. "It's perfect, Jack. She would love it."

I saw the effort in her smile. The tone of her voice didn't carry her usual enthusiasm. "Should we have painted it blue?" I asked, suddenly unsure. "That was my other thought. We still have time if you think—"

"No, I mean it. It *is* perfect. All of it. The color. The script. The name." She pushed her hands into her coat pockets. "Anyway, I'd best be on my way or I'll be late."

"Going anywhere nice?" I couldn't help myself asking.

She hesitated a moment. "The pictures. A matinee with Peter."

Of course she was going with Peter. "Well, I won't keep you. And I've plenty to do." I tried to keep my voice light, even though my reaction was anything but.

As she turned to go, I remembered a promise I'd made to her. "Wait, I offered to teach you how to cook something for your dad, remember? So he can surprise your mom for her birthday? How about next week?"

"That would be great, if you're not too busy."

"Never too busy for you, Olive." Even as I said it, we both knew it wasn't true. We were always too busy for each other, it seemed, especially lately.

"What delights have you in store for us?" she asked. "Something hot and spicy from the Deep South?"

"Of course! By the time we're finished, you'll be fully converted to Cajun spices and marinades. No more boring English food for your family!"

"I doubt it. They're highly suspicious of spicy food."

"That's because you Brits don't know how to cook it! If I teach you how to make the dishes yourself, you'll see them differently. *Taste* them differently. You'll never eat dry meat pasties or bland mushy peas again." I held out my hand. "Deal?"

Olive put her hand in mine and shook it as her face finally brightened. "Deal, chef. See you next week then."

With that, she hurried off down the street. I stared after her, the feel of her hand still in mine.

Chapter 44

Olive

ndrea's. Of course. It was the perfect name for Jack's restaurant, the sign beautifully crafted in her favorite colors of burgundy and gold, the perfect way to honor his wife. So why did it upset me so much? How, after all this time, did Jack still have such an effect on me? Why did I still have feelings for a man who, infuriatingly, didn't have the same feelings for me?

I had no claim on Jack. I'd made that clear when I decided not to tell him I was pregnant with his child, and now that he had met Lucy and I'd still not told him, I had potentially made everything much worse. I felt sick with nerves whenever I saw him, unable to find the words or the courage to tell him. Besides, his heart was clearly still with the only woman he would ever truly love.

I tried to put Jack out of my mind as I made my way to Leicester Square to meet Peter. He'd suggested dancing, and I'd suggested the theater. We'd compromised and settled on matinee tickets for a new musical film.

Peter was already waiting outside. He looked irritated, as if he'd waited a month for me to arrive.

"Sorry I'm late!" I called as I hurried toward him.

He gave me a half-hearted peck on the cheek. "I'd honestly be surprised if you turned up on time. What kept you today? High tea at Highgate? A crisis at the castle? I could write the headlines for you at this stage."

Peter found my role as assistant royal reporter highly amusing.

I ignored him. "I was with Jack, actually. He was showing me the new sign for the restaurant."

"Restaurant? Pile of rubble, isn't it? If he ever opens it will be a miracle."

He was so dismissive of Jack's ambitions, but I didn't have the energy to argue with him. "Shall we go inside?"

I adored the film. Peter fell asleep. As I glanced at him slumped in his seat, I found myself wishing Jack was sitting beside me instead. Jack wouldn't have fallen asleep. We would be laughing about something funny we'd both noticed.

The unavoidable truth was that the more time I spent with Peter, the more I realized we had almost nothing in common. It had been a fun year of roses and cocktails and shows in the West End, but I'd never lain awake at night thinking about Peter. I never wondered what he was doing when we weren't together. Perhaps most telling of all, I'd never dreamed of being intimate with him. There was only one man who occupied my thoughts that way: Jack.

As the tumultuous love affair played out on the screen in front of me, I felt as if it was my life the actors were portraying. Why was I with Peter when I was thinking about Jack all the time? Why couldn't I forget about Jack and be happy with Peter? I was gripped by a sudden sense of panic. What was I doing?

When the film was over, Peter suggested we go to The Thirsty Dog. It was strange to be back there, the empty spaces in our conversation filled with memories of the gang of friends laughing and joking, making wild plans for our future, but also tainted by the memories of how suddenly it had all ended for me.

I took a sip of my lager and lime. It tasted bitter and flat. "I think the barrel needs changing."

Peter took a sip and declared it to be fine.

Maybe it wasn't just the barrel that needed changing.

Suddenly, I couldn't bear to be there any longer. I made an excuse about wanting to get home.

"Lucy had a temperature earlier. I'd like to get back to check on her."

"Now? We've only just got here."

I could tell Peter was irritated. "I'm sorry. I'd feel better if I went home."

"Fine. I'll walk you to the tube. There's always something with that kid, isn't there? Always something to be worried about."

His words cut through me. "I'm her mother, Peter. It's my job to worry about her."

I'd been careful to keep Lucy separate from my relationship with Peter until I was certain it was going to last. He'd never seemed particularly interested in spending time with her anyway. He liked me a lot, but not enough to take on what I brought with me.

We stepped out into the rain. For a long time, neither of us said anything.

We stopped at the entrance to the tube station.

Peter pushed his hands into his coat pockets. "I'm sorry, Olive. I forget sometimes that you have a kid to get home to."

He spoke about her as if she were a new puppy I'd recently brought home.

As I looked at him, his face lit by the streetlamps, I felt nothing.

"We don't have to do this, Peter. If it's all too much? You know, with *the kid*."

"I do care for you, Olive. It's just . . . I'm not sure I'm cut out for this."

"Then maybe we should both take some time to work out what it is we *are* sure of."

"Maybe we should."

I made my way down the steps to the underground, careful not to slip on the tiles that were slick from the rain, and all I felt was a sense of relief. The illusion of happiness I'd tried to create with Peter over almost two years of casual dates, with long intervals between, had finally been revealed for what it was.

Peter had been a distraction, a smokescreen.

Suddenly, I could see clearly.

Chapter 45

Jack

Mason and I were pleased with the restaurant sign, and the last of the renovations were going smoothly. It wouldn't be long before we'd leave our roles at the palace and set out on our own, masters of our own fates. We had warned Max well in advance, and he was behind us all the way. We'd now begun looking ahead to opening the restaurant within the next couple of months, though we knew the timing would be tight.

I swallowed hard at the thought. As thrilled as I was, I was also nervous. Would anyone want to eat at our new restaurant? More importantly, would they like it? Londoners likely hadn't eaten red snapper topped with Cajun fried oysters, or pepper biscuits with honey butter, or chocolate cinnamon buttermilk cake. "*Epis*,"— spice—Grandpa would say in his thick Creole accent, "*awakens the senses, brings one to life.*" And I would certainly awaken my customers' senses with the dishes I'd planned. Mason and I had toiled over the menu offerings, making sure each dish was unique, substituting ingredients that were common in Louisiana but weren't available in London. I sometimes worried the menu was *too* unique, but we were both willing to take that chance.

Mason poked his head inside the kitchen. "Olive is here."

We'd both been working around the clock, and my energy was flagging, but I couldn't wait to see Olive. Spending time with her would be a welcome distraction.

"Have you asked her out yet?" Mason said as he pulled on his coat. "She really is a great-looking girl."

I took spices from the cupboard. "So? Not everything has to be about that."

At this, Mason laughed. "Usually ends up being about that though, doesn't it?"

"She's with someone else anyway."

"You should muscle your way in."

"Maybe I will," I said. "Anyway, beat it, will you. I need to get to it." I set down the spices and met Olive at the entrance as Mason made a tactful exit.

"Hi," she said. "Sorry I'm late. Again!"

My stomach flipped as she entered the room. She was dazzling in a simple pink cashmere sweater, her hair a cascade of soft waves around her face, her cheeks pink from the exertion of walking in the heat of a summer evening.

"You're right on time." I opened the door wide. "We definitely said . . ." I checked the clock, "twenty-five past."

She groaned. "Sorry! I'm a disaster." She tripped over a crate of wine as she stepped inside. "Oops. Hope that's not the good stuff."

I laughed. "Graceful as always, I see." I moved deftly around the counter and poured her a glass of wine. "For you, ma'am."

"Why, thank you, kind sir." She spoke with a pretend upper-class accent and a playful smile. "So, what's cookin', chef?"

"We're making something simple that your dad can easily follow. A few ingredients, quick to pull together, delicious."

"That sounds perfect. What's it called?"

"A po' boy," I said.

"A *what*?"

"It's short for 'poor boy,' a sandwich the Martin brothers of New Orleans made at their coffee stand to feed the streetcar union strikers back in the 1920s. It's become something of a classic. Oysters are everywhere—cheap, or free—in Louisiana, if you know how to catch them, just like crawfish."

"Oysters? Aren't they supposed to be an—"

"Aphrodisiac. Yes."

"Are you trying to woo me, Mr. Devereux?"

I glanced at her. "Maybe?" *Yes*, I wanted to say. *Yes, I am.* But my timid nature got the better of me. "They'll help your dad woo your mom for sure!" I pointed to a cutting board and a large knife. "Time to get to work! First, we'll slice the lettuce, tomato, and onion."

As she began slicing, I stood beside her, peering over her shoulder, showing her what to do. She didn't even know how to hold the knife properly.

She looked back at me, meeting my eye. "I can chop vegetables, Jack!"

I could make out every fleck of gold in her amber eyes. "It isn't chopping, it's slicing, and if you keep at it like that, you'll cut your fingers clean off." I showed her again, placing my hand on hers as I winced at her haphazard hacking. I paused for a moment as I realized how close she was. The scent of her perfume. Her breath fanning across my cheek. I met her eye for a moment, studying her beautiful face.

"I think I've got it," she said, looking away.

I removed my hand swiftly, cleared my throat. "Great."

She followed my instructions without her usual light-hearted chatter, and when the oysters were perfectly fried and nestled on a smear of rich remoulade, lettuce, tomato, sliced dill pickles, and crusty bread, she waited for further instructions.

"That's it," I said. "You've done it perfectly."

"It can't be perfect. I'm a terrible cook."

"Not this time."

She met my eyes again. "Well then, you must be a good teacher. I suppose we should eat these."

"I suppose so."

We sat at the new staff table that had been delivered the day before and ate in silence. I wondered what she was thinking. She had a serious air about her this evening, as if something was on her mind.

"Is everything all right?" I asked. "You seem a bit . . . distracted?"

She shuffled slightly on her stool. "I just have a lot on my mind."

"Work? Bullen still being an obnoxious pain in the ass?"

She smiled. "Always. This is delicious by the way," she said, after taking a large bite. "Really, Jack. I'm so glad you're opening your own place. London needs your food."

"Thank you. I hope you're right."

We talked for a while about her parents, and how she longed for them to be happy with each other again.

"They could use a bit of romance and adventure in their lives, that's for certain," she said. "But every time I think they're making progress, they slip back into their old routines. Hopefully, these oysters will work some magic on them."

"Well, now that you know the recipe, let's hope your dad will agree to making it for your mom. A little spice can go a long way. In recipes, and in life."

She smiled. "A philosopher as well as a chef!"

"Well," I said. "It's late and I need to get some sleep. I have another long day at the palace tomorrow and then I need to put in a serious shift here if we're ever going to open on time. This was fun though. We should do it again sometime."

"I'd like that."

As she rose to leave, my desperation grew. I had to do something, say something, or at least try to spend more time with her.

"Would you like to come over on Saturday, for Mason's birthday? We thought we'd have it here, now that we have a stocked kitchen. Well, close enough for a party anyway. Should be a good time. You could bring Rosie . . . or Peter, if you like?" I was testing her, trying to get a reaction by mentioning him.

She hesitated. "That sounds like fun. I'll need to see if my parents can watch Lucy."

"Of course."

"What time?"

"Eight o'clock?"

She nodded. "I'll do my best. Thanks again, for tonight. And no fingers lost!"

I had so many more things I wanted to say, but for now, the hope of seeing her at Mason's party would have to do. I watched her as she walked through the kitchen, nearly tipping over a tray of polished spoons in her adorable clumsy way.

Olive Carter, I thought, you have no idea what you do to me.

Chapter 46

Olive

I'd enjoyed my cooking lesson, even though Jack gasped at the haphazard way I chopped the onions and shrieked as I added too much salt. He was so measured and exact, just as he'd always been. Jack was a man of recipes and measurements, everything carefully considered, which was why it was so hard to find the right time to tell him about Lucy; to turn his life upside down.

But I was getting closer to telling him. I could also feel the two of us getting closer. I'd noticed the way he'd looked at me, the way he'd smiled at me, the way he hesitated rather than pulled away when our hands briefly touched, or our feet knocked together beneath the table. Maybe something more would happen between us at Mason's party.

For now, I had my parents' love story to resurrect.

I'd liked Jack's suggestion of a po' boy, but decided it was best not to explain the aphrodisiac part to Dad. He'd agreed to cook the dish for my mother, even though he thought it was a silly idea, trying to impress her with food.

"But don't you see, Dad. She's been cooking for you—for the family—half her life. This will mean more to her than any fancy restaurant. Trust me."

"A few oysters isn't going to stop my hair thinning, or trim these extra inches from my belly, are they?"

"It's not about that, Dad. It will show her that even with thinning hair and a thickening waist, you still love her."

He muttered as he started to chop the parsley. "Doubt it very much."

No matter how much Dad doubted it, I knew there was part of him that hoped this would work. Him and Mum were made for each other. I sometimes wondered if it was my fault they'd grown apart in recent years. Having me and Lucy in the house certainly didn't help. That was why I was determined to try and bring them back together.

I took everything from the fridge and set it out on the countertop, just as I'd seen Jack do. "Preparation, preparation, preparation." We followed his careful instructions until the oysters were perfectly fried and nestled on a smear of rich remoulade, lettuce, tomato, sliced dill pickles, and crusty bread.

"You need to remind each other why you fell in love in the first place," I said as I pulled out the old photograph albums from the sideboard. "Look through these together, remember what fun you used to have. Look at you both on your wedding day. You look so young!"

"We *were* young. And madly in love."

I gave him a hug. "You're still the same people inside, even if the outside has got a little tatty. You can fall madly in love all over again. I know you can."

By six-thirty, he was washed and shaved and dressed smartly. I set the kitchen table, added candles to old wine bottles, turned the main lights off, and switched on the fairy lights I'd draped around the banisters.

Lucy came bounding downstairs. "Mummy! It looks so magical!"

I was pleased with my work. "Not bad, eh?"

My dad put his arm around my shoulders. "Not bad at all, love. Thank you."

"Mum will be back from Auntie Jean's soon. Have a glass of wine to steady the nerves."

"Can't remember the last time I was nervous with your mother— probably the first time I took her out, when we were twenty-one."

"Good. Then pretend you're twenty-one again, you old romantic!"

While I'd been busy helping Dad prepare everything, I'd hardly left any time to get myself ready for Mason's birthday party at the restaurant. I settled on a simple knitted two-piece in teal and added an enthusiastic layer of makeup to hide the dark circles under my eyes. I kissed Lucy goodnight, told her to behave herself and to not interrupt the dinner party, wished Dad good luck, and hurried to the bus stop to meet Rosie.

We made our way to Richmond Street together. I was stupidly nervous, partly about seeing Jack, and partly about how the night might end if I found the courage to tell him about Lucy. Rosie understood my apprehension.

She reached for my hand. "Just see how the night goes. And try to enjoy yourself. We're going to a party, not an execution."

The restaurant looked lovely and welcoming as we turned the corner at the top of Richmond Street. The sign was lit up, and the replica lampposts illuminated the entrance. Inside, candles flick-ered on every table, the soft lighting adding to the atmosphere. The smell inside was delicious.

Jack rushed to take my coat and added a peck on my cheek.

"I'm so pleased you made it," he said. "You look beautiful. Did you do your hair differently?"

My heart squeezed at his compliment, but I claimed to have hardly made any effort at all.

"I brought Rosie. I hope that's all right?"

"Of course!" Jack gave Rosie a warm hug. "It's so good to see you—it's been years. I must admit, I was expecting Peter," he added, turning back to me. "But Rosie is much better."

"Peter and I broke up."

Jack's brow lifted in surprise. "I'm sorry to hear that."

"No need to be sorry. I'm not. Peter and I have run our course."

Jack hesitated a moment as a smile danced in his eyes. "So, how are things going at the *other* restaurant?" he asked. "Everything going well for your dad?"

I laughed. "I think he's ready. I'm not sure he'll get the full five-star review in the papers, but he's giving it a good try."

"That's all it takes. An effort." He reached for my hand and tucked it into the crook of his arm. "Come on over and join the others."

I did my best not to lean into him, but all I could think about was his nearness and the flicker of surprised happiness that had passed over his face when I'd said Peter and I had parted ways. Maybe things were moving in the right direction with Jack after all.

"Happy birthday, Mason," I said, as Rosie, Jack and I joined the others at the table. I added a crimson lipstick mark to the collection on Mason's cheek. I'd enjoyed getting to know him on the odd occasion when I'd called in at the restaurant. He seemed to be a good partner for Jack.

"Thank you for coming," he said, and introduced me to a few of his friends who I hadn't met before.

"I'd hoped your brother might be here," I said. "I was looking forward to seeing Ryan again after all these years."

"Busy with the family in Norfolk," Mason replied, although he wasn't really looking at me. "Are you going to introduce me to your friend?" he asked, his eyes fixed on Rosie.

"Rosie May," she said, not bothering to wait for me to introduce her. "Pleased to meet you."

A smile lit up his face. "The pleasure is all mine, Miss May."

Rosie took the empty seat beside him. "You didn't tell me he was *this* good-looking," she whispered to me.

I kicked her under the table and took the glass of wine Mason was holding out to me. "Try not to be too obvious," I whispered in reply.

But that wasn't Rosie's way. She didn't dither and doubt, or hold back, like I did. I smiled to myself as she commenced her confident flirtation, which Mason instantly responded to with plenty of his own.

Jack appeared at my shoulder. "Is this seat taken, madam?"

My heart leaped at his voice. "It is now." I patted the seat in invitation for him to sit down. "Besides, don't you own every seat in the place? You can take as many as you like!"

He laughed. "I think I'll stick to this one."

I was glad he'd chosen to sit beside me. "It all looks so lovely, Jack. And whatever you're cooking back there smells delicious."

His sea green eyes danced in the candlelight. "The old place cleans up nicely, doesn't it?"

"Mrs. Howard would be so proud," I said. "You and Mason have done a wonderful job with it all." I was sure Andrea would be proud, too, but I couldn't quite bring myself to say it.

"Speaking of which . . ." Jack turned and tapped the rim of his glass with his knife. "A toast, to the birthday boy."

We all raised a glass to Mason and sang a boisterous round of "Happy Birthday."

The evening passed in a cloud of happy chatter, laughter, and excited talk about plans for the new restaurant. We all drank too much wine, and toward the end of the evening, when someone put a Buddy Holly record on the gramophone, we all got up from our tables and danced as if we didn't have a care in the world.

It was a perfect evening, made even more perfect when Jack and Mason insisted on escorting Rosie and me home. We took the bus and parted ways at the top of my street, exchanging goodnights, Mason and Rosie heading one way, Jack and I, the other.

I swayed a little as Jack walked me the rest of the way, laughing as life carried us along, our wayward feet swept up in the happy atmosphere of the evening, the easy hum of wine settling in our bones and drawing us to each other. I let my head rest against his shoulder. My inhibitions were numbed, my doubts and indecision left at the restaurant door. And I so very much hoped he'd had as wonderful a night as I had.

Too soon, we reached the garden gate of my house. Both of us paused; uncertain, unsure.

"Well," I said.

"Well," he replied, his eyes soft as his gaze settled on mine.

"That was a lovely evening, Jack. Thank you."

"Thank *you*," he said. "It was all the lovelier with you there. And Mason and Rosie seemed to hit it off."

"Didn't they just!"

We looked at each other for a moment, neither of us moving, neither daring to break the spell of the wonderful evening. And suddenly I didn't want to wait any longer. I knew how I felt about Jack, and as the streetlamp threw a pale glow across his handsome face, I reached onto my tiptoes, and kissed him on the lips, gently, tentatively.

Though he stood stock-still, he didn't pull away.

I closed my eyes, leaning into him, our breaths quickening as our lips explored each other's. We lingered in the moment, my heart thumping beneath my dress, a sense of inevitability washing over me as I remembered the first time we'd kissed years before, and the delicious night that had followed.

When I opened my eyes, his were still closed.

"I'm sorry," I said, my voice catching in my throat.

"What for?" He opened his eyes, a smile dancing at the edge of his lips.

"For that. I'm a little drunk, I think."

He laughed. "You think?" He touched my cheek with soft fingertips. "Don't be sorry, Olive."

I took a deep breath. "Jack, there's something I need—"

A small voice at the front door caught our attention. "Are you coming in, Mummy, or are you going to kiss Jack allllllll night?"

I turned to see Lucy in her nightie, a knowing smile on her face. My little girl—*our* little girl—was growing up.

A foolish grin on his face, Jack waved to her. "Hello, Lucy."

She waved back shyly. "Hello."

"I'd better go," I said, suddenly flustered. It was all I'd ever wanted—the three of us together—and yet it all felt wrong in that moment; deceitful even. The weight of my secret pressed down on me. Why couldn't I just tell him?

He stuffed his hands into his coat pockets. "Olive?"

"Yes."

"Don't be sorry," he said quietly. "About the kiss. I'm not. Could we do this again, maybe? Meet next week, for another cooking lesson? I could help you make a cake for your mum's birthday?"

"I'd like that." I started to laugh lightly, the wine and the moment going to my head. "But we don't always have to cook something! I'd like to meet you anyway."

My stomach was a swarm of bees, my heart racing as I walked up the path. I hadn't planned to kiss him, and I was a little embarrassed to have been caught by Lucy, but I couldn't deny how excited I felt, and how I'd yearned for it to go beyond a kiss.

Lucy met me at the door.

"Did you have fun at the party, Mummy?"

"I did, darling. And you should be in bed fast asleep." I turned to close the door. Jack was already halfway down the street. I longed for him to turn and wave.

As if reading my mind, he stopped beneath a streetlamp and lifted his hat, circling it above his head.

I smiled as I closed the door.

"I like Jack, Mummy. He's silly."

Dear sweet Lucy. If only she knew.

I lifted her into my arms. "I like him too, sausage. Now, to bed!"

I lay awake for hours that night, remembering his look, his touch, his smile in the dark.

There was no point denying it anymore. My feelings had gone far beyond liking Jack.

I was, once again, in love with him.

Chapter 47

Jack

Olive danced around my thoughts all week. All I could think about was our laughter together, the fun we'd had at Mason's party, our kiss, her soft lips and the twinkle in her eye—but I still couldn't seem to let go and throw caution to the wind. I was glad—relieved—she'd broken things off with Peter, but leaving that aside, it had still felt strange to kiss someone who wasn't Andrea. I so desperately wanted to be able to move on, but maybe I wasn't ready.

Mason and I had both put in another long week of double-shifts, working between the palace and the restaurant. We'd been forced to reprint the restaurant menus, the cutlery had been delivered—missing half of each set—and we'd started on the beverage menu. There would be wine and beer for sure, but it was a matter of deciding on which ones.

I stepped outside Andrea's for a breath of fresh air and to calm my mind. I stooped under the leaves and tucked myself against the stone wall with a mug of tea. Max had said he needed to talk to me later, that big news was afoot at the palace, and that I might be needed for a special job of some kind. I couldn't imagine doing a single thing more—I was overworked as it was. But I also didn't want to let down my boss, the man who'd had faith in me from the beginning, and the patience to teach me so many new skills. Whatever it was, I would do my best to fit it in.

When I'd finished my tea, I headed back inside.

"Hey, can you help me with these deliveries?" Mason said.

"Be right there," I replied, making my way toward the staircase.

But as I lifted a large heavy box from the pile on the ground, a loud boom, followed by an ear-splitting screeching sound, reverberated through the restaurant. After it, came a worrying gushing noise.

Mason looked at me. "Is that . . . ?"

"Water!" I shouted.

We dropped the boxes and raced toward the back of the restaurant.

"Son of a—"

Water was gushing from the restroom in a steady stream and pooling in the hallway.

"It must be a burst pipe." I swore loudly. How could another thing have gone wrong?

Mason darted to the linen closet, calling over his shoulder. "I'll get some towels. You get the breaker in the basement!"

I raced toward the basement door.

"And bring up a bottle of whisky!" Mason called after me, laughing. "I'd say we'll need a drop after we get this sorted."

For the hundredth time that year, I was glad I'd chosen him as my partner.

It was a long day and a late night at Andrea's with all the plumbing chaos. With so much on my mind, I'd been unable to sleep, staring at the ceiling in my room at Buckingham Palace for hours before I'd finally gotten up and worked on the cookbook to distract myself. It was nearly finished. When I finally fell asleep, I'd only managed a few hours of rest before my alarm clock woke me.

Despite my fatigue, I arrived on time for my shift the next morning. We'd promised Max we wouldn't let our restaurant preparations get in the way of our work in the royal kitchens.

"Morning, chef," I said, rubbing my eyes.

"You look like hell, Jack," Max replied.

Max never beat around the bush, but I appreciated that in a person. "Yes, chef. I'm sure I do. It's been a long eighteen months."

He nodded. "How close are you to opening?"

"We were hoping for October, but we've now had a plumbing setback and need another inspection. Several of our major appliances have been back-ordered, too." I sighed. "Looks more like an opening early in the new year."

"That works out in our favor then," Max said.

"How so?"

"This is what I wanted to talk to you about. The duke is going on a tour. He'll be speaking at the opening ceremony of the Olympics in Australia, and while in the southern hemisphere, stopping in Antarctica to visit the British station there. We leave in October."

"We?"

"Can't go on a royal tour without one of my best chefs, can I. What do you say? I know you have a lot on with the restaurant, but how about one final sea voyage before you quit the palace for good?"

I was honored to be asked, but my mind raced with all that going on the tour would entail, especially not being around for the final stages before our grand opening at the restaurant. Then again, all the major decisions had been made—the place was decorated, the menus finished. All that was left were inspections, a few major appliances, and to order the food. There was also the advertising; we'd need some time for that. Still, it made me uneasy to think of leaving at such a crucial time.

"Is Mason going with us?" I asked, chewing my bottom lip.

"He'll stay here, help run the kitchen for Her Majesty at Sandringham over Christmas, and manage the staff who stay behind." A smile flickered in his eyes. "I wasn't sure you would ever forgive me if I took you *both* away from the restaurant."

"Thank you, Max. I'm honored that you would think of me."

I worked hard the rest of the afternoon. I knew Mason would fully support Max's decision, and it was good to know I had a trusted partner with whom I could leave the last of the details for our opening. But there was someone else who filled my thoughts: Olive.

Just as we were getting close, I was leaving. We'd arranged to meet in a few days' time so I could help her make a tiered birthday cake for her mother. I'd have to tell her I was leaving then. I hoped she would understand—that she would wait for me and give me a chance to take her out properly when I returned. And yet, hadn't we had so many chances already? Doubt chipped away at my confidence as I gathered up the ingredients I needed for my next dish.

We would have to make the most of the weeks we had together until I left. I had to prove to her that I was worth waiting for— that *we* were worth waiting for—and that no matter how long it took, it would be worth it in the end.

Chapter 48

Olive

London dazzled beneath a generous late summer sun as I made my way to Andrea's after work. The clear blue skies lifted my mood after a rather tense meeting with Tom Harding. I'd been following up on a story about John Grigg—Lord Altrincham—and his outspoken criticism of the monarchy which had left rather a bad taste in royal mouths.

I'd dug out an archive piece from the coronation year where he'd claimed the monarchy was outdated and lacked relevance in post-war Britain. His thoughts about how the new queen might modernize the monarchy had been quietly ignored at the time, but I was interested in exploring his opinions. Tom was nervous about it. He felt it was too controversial and that the BBC's relationship with Buckingham Palace was "far too important to damage by dabbling in the thoughts of titled peers with too many opinions."

I would leave it for now, but there was a growing mood in the country that the royal family were too distant and unrelatable. It was the elephant in the room; an issue that would have to be addressed sooner or later, and I wasn't afraid to tackle it, even if Mr. Harding was.

I tried to forget about work as I arrived at the restaurant and

CHRISTMAS WITH THE QUEEN

knocked on the door. I felt at home there now. I'd even stopped noticing the sign above the entrance.

"Hello? Jack? Hellooooooo?"

"In here!"

I made my way through to the kitchen where Jack already had everything perfectly organized, the ingredients and utensils we would need to make mum's cake arranged in neat lines.

"What's so amusing?" Jack asked, noticing the smile on my face.

"You! You're such a chef, Jack! Do you ever make a mess, or spill anything? You would be horrified if you saw the state of the kitchen when Dad and I made the po' boys."

He laughed. "Yes, I probably would. You know me, Olive. Creature of habit. Once a chef, always a chef." He handed me an apron. "Anyway, if it took a messy kitchen for your dad to impress your mum, then I'm glad."

"Turns out my dad can be quite the charmer when he tries. And not a bad cook, either. He's taking mum away for a night next weekend, as a birthday treat. It's almost sickening to see them flirting with each other over the cornflakes every morning."

"Love finds a way after all. Louisiana food. Can't beat it! That po' boy really worked its magic!"

"It certainly did."

"Well, good for you for not giving up on them. Even when they'd almost given up on each other."

"Yeah. Good for me." I pushed my hands into my coat pockets. It seemed that while I was always fixing everyone else's love stories, I was terrible at fixing my own.

Jack stopped and looked at me. "You okay? That's the face of an Olive who has something on her mind."

Silence puddled between us as I shifted awkwardly on my feet. "Jack, about the other night. There's something I need to tell you . . ."

"It's fine, Olive. We were both a little happy, or merry, I suppose you English would say."

"*Too* merry." A light blush rose on my cheeks as I remembered how forward I'd been. "It was a fun night though."

"It was, and—well, I'd hoped we might have more like it."

"Hoped?"

He took a deep breath. "There's something I need to tell you, too. I've been appointed to accompany the Duke of Edinburgh on his tour to Australia. I just found out a few days ago."

My heart sank. I'd heard about the duke's tour, having been briefed on it just that week. I'd wondered if Jack would be sent as part of the staff, but had hoped not. "Gosh, Jack. That's exciting for you!"

"It is. A great honor. But it's also a shame, about the timing."

"Will you have to delay the opening?"

"We weren't going to make the fall anyway. We're planning for next spring now instead." He hesitated. "But it's also a shame because . . . well, I felt things were maybe . . . developing between us?"

It sounded like a question, as if he were looking for confirmation from me. He was so painfully shy, so uncertain.

"I thought so, too," I said softly. "It seems we are destined to be ships passing in the night." I tried to force a smile.

A little of the light in his eyes faded. "It seems that way, doesn't it."

"And you'll be away for Christmas," I added.

In quiet moments alone, I'd allowed myself to imagine a family Christmas this year, all of us together: Jack, Lucy, and me. Now, he wouldn't even be on the same continent. It was this constant uncertainty that made me so reluctant to tell him about Lucy, and to tell her about Jack. Even as Jack and I had become closer, I'd been careful to maintain a distance between him and Lucy. He was sweet with her, and asked about her often, but I couldn't bear to bring him into her life only to have him leave on another long tour. I had to make sure he would be around for her, for both of us.

"Shall we get on with this cake, then?" I said.

He looked a little deflated. "Sure. Let's get to it. First you need butter and sugar."

I followed his instructions, trying to concentrate, but my heart wasn't in it.

That was that then. Jack was heading halfway around the world and there was nothing I could do about it.

"You didn't beg him to stay, did you?" Rosie peered at me over the top of her spectacles. She'd called around to wish mum a happy birthday. "You're not living in a Bergman film, Olive. People don't really go rushing to train stations to declare their undying love for each other."

I sighed and finished the last of my sandwich. "Of course I didn't beg him to stay. I told him I was happy for him. He offered to cook me a Christmas dinner before he leaves, since he won't be here over Christmas."

"Well, *that's* romantic. You wouldn't catch many men offering to do that. Most men I've been out with can't even be bothered to make me a slice of toast, never mind a Christmas dinner."

I smiled. "Surely Mason can do better than a slice of toast. How's it all going?"

A dreamy look crossed her face. "It's wonderful. He's wonderful. Everything's wonderful. I think he's the one, Olive, and it's all thanks to you."

"Me?"

"It was you who dragged me along to his birthday party. Matchmaker Carter strikes again!"

"Yes. Good old Matchmaker Carter, fixing everyone's love life and making a holy mess of her own. Nothing much changes, does it?"

"A mess? I'd say you've made more of your life than any of us. Look at what you have. A great job. A beautiful daughter. A man who clearly adores you, even though the two of you can't seem to ever work it out."

I looked over at Lucy, playing happily in the corner of the sitting room. Rosie was right. I hadn't made a mess of things. I'd made the best of things, just as I'd promised Lucy I would the day she was born on a blustery spring day in Cornwall.

"You're so brave, Olive. I don't think I could have done what you did."

Was I brave? I certainly hadn't felt brave at the time.

In those wild windswept weeks before Lucy's arrival, I had been absolutely terrified.

Chapter 49

Olive

Cornwall, January 1946

Since discovering I was pregnant, my life had not been my own. Decisions were made without my input. Arrangements were put into place without consulting me. I was to stay with my mother's aunt Mary, in her cottage in Cornwall until the baby arrived, at which point it would be given up for adoption.

I had no say in the matter.

"Your father and I have talked about it," my mother said as she washed the dishes and I dried. "We've decided it's for the best."

"Best for who?" I asked. "Best for me and the baby—or best for you, so that you don't have to deal with the gossip and shame?"

She slammed a saucepan onto the draining board. "You'll do as you're told, Olive. Clearly, you are not able to make sensible decisions for yourself, so we'll have to make them for you."

"Do you agree with this?" I asked, challenging my father.

He could barely look at me. "I'm sorry, love. What else can we do? It's for the best."

We hardly spoke on the long journey down to Cornwall. I'd said I would take the bus and the train, but my father insisted on driving me. He wept when he said goodbye.

"Let us know how you're doing, love, won't you?" he said. "Let us know when the little one comes."

I was hidden away like Rapunzel in her tower. It was a punishment to have been sent to Cornwall, and yet being there gave me space to think, and reflect. My parents were partly right; I had paid the consequences for my actions. I'd lost my job and my friends. And I knew that if I'd stayed at home, I would only have been stared at and shunned by the judgmental ninnies my mother befriended. But I fundamentally disagreed with the decision they'd made for me to give the baby up for adoption. And while I had tried to forget about Jack, I hadn't come to terms with the fact that he was married, unavailable, and out of my life forever.

Cornwall was beautiful. Its wild rugged beauty quickly stole my heart. Through the cold winter months, as my body changed, and simple tasks like putting on my shoes became a ridiculous ordeal, I watched the brooding skies and walked along stormy beaches. The salty air invigorated me, the wind filled me with hope and determination.

By the time the spring came, I had decided to keep the baby. I knew it wouldn't be easy to navigate life as an unmarried mother, but I also knew that I couldn't bear to part with my child. Whatever happened, it would be the two of us together.

She was born in May, my perfect daughter forged from salt and wind. I couldn't have loved her more—or been more afraid of how our lives would work out.

An hour after she was born, I telephoned my parents.

"I had the baby, Mum. A little girl."

She was silent for a moment. "Is she well?"

"She's perfect."

"And you?"

"I'm fine. And Mum, I'm keeping her."

I heard her cover the mouthpiece and speak to my father. I heard the muffled words, "*a little girl.*"

My father came to the telephone then. "I'm coming to bring you home, love. Both of you. I'll be there tomorrow morning."

Men had let me down and disappointed me my whole life, but not my father. He was the only one I could ever rely on.

I held my daughter in my arms and told her it would all be fine. "We'll be all right, little bear. We'll muddle through, together."

She gazed up at me, blinking, and I knew that whatever lay ahead for us, love would see us through.

Chapter 50

Jack

The final weeks of summer had turned to autumn, and now, in only two days' time, I'd be leaving with the duke and his crew to sail to Australia. But first, there was a very happy occasion to celebrate: Mason and Rosie's wedding.

Mason had fallen hard for Rosie after they'd met at his birthday dinner. He'd proposed shortly after, and the date was set. Nobody was surprised at how quickly it had all happened. Rosie and Mason were made for each other and, as he'd said to me, "When you know she's the one, you know she's the one."

I had felt the same way about Andrea. The only difference now was that I knew there can be more than one love of your life. If you're lucky.

We were both relieved, in part, to put the grand opening of Andrea's on hold, until he'd honeymooned and enjoyed a few months of wedded bliss, and I'd returned from the royal tour.

And so, on a beautiful autumn day, I took the train to Cornwall to watch my dear friend and business partner marry the love of his life. But it was Olive my thoughts turned to as the train wound along the coast. This would be the last time I'd see her for several months, so I had to make it count.

With Peter finally sidelined, we'd spent a little more time together when our schedules had allowed: a few cooking lessons, a walk in the park, a trip to the zoo with Lucy. She was a sweet kid, easy to be around, and I wished I'd had more time to get to know her. I promised myself I'd do that, and more, as soon as I returned.

Now that I was about to head away for several months, I felt a sense of urgency to tell Olive what I'd slowly come to accept and could no longer deny: that I was in love with her, that she had stolen my heart, and that a part of me had always loved her.

One more day, and I could tell her everything.

The morning of the wedding dawned with clear skies and beautiful sunlight. I dressed in my nicest suit and met Ryan, Maggie, and the kids to walk to the church together.

Ryan gave me a warm hug. He looked sharp in his suit. "Can you believe my little brother is getting married?"

"Yes, I can! And thank God! He's been a lovesick puppy these past weeks."

Maggie kissed me on the cheek. She looked beautiful in a pale blue A-line dress with her red hair swept atop her head. "We've missed you, stranger!"

"I've missed you, too. Life has been a little crazy! And I can't believe how much those two have grown!"

Maggie smiled as Ivy and Adam inspected their new surroundings. "Yes, and too quickly. The years go too fast. I've told Ryan it'll be time for another soon!"

Ryan raised his eyebrows at me. "Right. Time to go!"

We laughed and set off down a narrow, cobbled lane.

It was to be a simple affair at the church and, afterward,

champagne, cake, and finger food in the local pub—the perfect kind of wedding as far as I was concerned. The old Anglican church was draughty but beautiful with its towering stained-glass windows, flickering candles on the altar, and bouquets of white and pink flowers tied with ribbon at the end of each pew.

I joined Mason and the other groomsmen in the vestibule while the guests were seated and, soon, the bridesmaids joined us there. Rosie's sister, another friend I didn't recognize, and Olive, radiant in a pastel-pink chiffon dress that complemented her figure, her creamy skin, and the lush auburn waves around her face. My heart turned over in my chest as her eyes met mine.

"You're stunning," I said.

She fussed with her dress. "I look like a meringue."

"A very pretty meringue!"

"You're not too bad yourself, out of the chef's whites for a change," she said.

Lucy was a flower girl. She twirled for me. "Do you like *my* dress?"

"Oh, yours is the prettiest of all, Miss Lucy. You look like a princess."

She beamed, revealing a gap in her teeth, and I thought her the most adorable kid I'd ever seen.

Just then, the organ pipes struck up.

When the service began, I escorted Olive down the aisle until we parted ways to stand on either side of the bride and groom. The service was touching, and as I watched Mason and Rosie exchange their vows, I couldn't help thinking back to my own wedding day. Andrea and I had been so happy, so full of love and life and hope, just as Mason and Rosie were. Just as I wanted to be again. I looked from the happy couple to Olive. My stomach dipped as her lips curved into a small smile.

After the ceremony and the traditional confetti-throwing

outside the church, we gathered at a local pub, filling the place to the rafters. A pianist began to play, and everyone was merry as we grazed on sandwiches and plenty of wedding cake, three tiers and beautifully decorated in sugar roses. All Mason's own work.

As the day wore on, Rosie gathered the female guests for the traditional bouquet toss. She scanned the crowd, and I thought I caught a wink before she turned her back and launched her bouquet over her head. She threw it too high, and it ricocheted off the rafters, landing at Olive's feet. Olive scooped it up and held it over her head, laughing as the other ladies clapped. Rosie stepped down from her perch on a chair and slung her arms around Olive, kissing her cheek. They laughed and shared a private comment, and I couldn't help but wonder what it might be.

When the pianist began a slower number, I held out my hand to Olive. "Care to dance?"

She slipped her hand into mine. "Love to."

I pulled her into the circle of my arms and, as the music continued, she drew closer, until only an inch or two remained between us.

"What a beautiful place Cornwall is," I said. "There's something wild and romantic about it. Have you spent much time here?"

She hesitated for a moment. "Cornwall is where Lucy was born. I hated it when I first came here, but I loved it by the time I left." Her eyes misted over. "I haven't been back since."

I imagined she was picturing the event in her mind, thinking about Lucy's father. "Ah. I see. It must be strange to be back."

"A little," she admitted, "especially since . . ." Her words trailed off.

"Especially since what?"

"Nothing." She shook her head.

I didn't press, but followed her gaze to Mason and Rosie, wrapped up in each other, moving slowly to the music.

"Do you really think there's only one person for everyone?" she asked.

I hesitated for a moment and then told her the conclusion I'd come to in the last year, the words I'd been wanting to tell her.

"I used to believe that. Now, I think the heart is capable of much more." I gathered her hand and held it to my lips. "You swept back into my life and made me happy in a way I never thought I could be happy again."

Without hesitation, I cupped her face with my hands, peering into her beautiful eyes, inhaling the scent of her intoxicating perfume. In another breath, I pressed my lips against hers. I felt her respond, moving toward me as the other guests fell away around us, and it was just the two of us. Her eyes filled with so much hope I could hardly bear it. She felt the same way I did, I could see it all over her face, so why was there still this hesitation?

"Olive, I think . . . well, *I know* I'm—"

"I have to tell you something, Jack." She gazed up at me, a look of fear in her eyes as she blurted out the words. "It can't wait another minute."

My smile hid my sense of trepidation. "Sounds serious!"

"Jack, please. Don't joke. Not now."

"Do you want to go somewhere more private?"

She hesitated. I saw her glance over to where Lucy was dancing with Ivy. "Yes," she said.

I gathered our coats, my stomach shifting with unease at her tone, her serious expression. I couldn't imagine what was so important that we needed to leave the wedding reception, but I tucked her hand in the crook of my arm and led her outside.

Chapter 51

Olive

My heart hammered against the fabric of my dress as we left the pub. We crossed the road to a grassy bank that sloped downward and then dropped sharply, becoming a stark, rocky cliff that faced the ocean. Despite the sun overhead, the wind blew off the heaving waves below and whipped around us, tossing my hair into my eyes and biting against my cheeks. I remembered this wind, the raging emotions that had seemed to swirl within me beneath the wild Cornish skies as I'd waited for Lucy to arrive. I remembered everything from being here before: the fear, the isolation, the sense of abandonment and loneliness.

I wanted things to be different now. I wanted Lucy's life to be different now.

When we stopped, I turned to face Jack. He studied my face as if searching for an answer there.

He reached out, cradling my cheek in his hand. "What is it, Olive? Whatever it is, I promise I'll help you. Are you sick?"

I shook my head. My stomach lurched with unease, heaving and rolling along with the ocean swell below. I took a deep breath. It was now or never, and never wasn't an option anymore.

"It's about Lucy."

"Is *she*—"

"She's well, don't worry. It's . . ." I looked down at my hands, wishing I could change things. "It's about her father."

Jack frowned. "Her father?"

My knees shook. My mouth was as dry as a desert.

Jack smiled encouragingly. "Please tell me, Olive. It can't be as bad as you think. I'm made of strong stuff."

A gust of wind buffeted us both. I grabbed Jack's arm to steady myself. "I don't know how else to say this, Jack. And I'm sorry." I took another breath and let the words rush out of me. "I'm not a widow. There was never a husband. It's you, Jack. You're Lucy's father."

The words swirled on the stiff breeze around us, echoing and repeating with the crash of the waves below.

Time seemed to stand still as he stared at me, speechless.

"That night, all those years ago, when we were together . . . You remember?"

He nodded slowly and ran his hands through his hair as he took a step back from me. "Of course I remember. But . . . are you sure?"

I nodded. "She's yours, Jack. There was nobody else. Peter and I never . . . I was planning to tell you the night you announced that you and Andrea were engaged."

He stared at me. "Oh, God, Olive. Why didn't you say something?" He turned to face the ocean.

"How could I? How could I possibly tell you?"

"Did anyone know?"

"I confided in Rosie. And, of course, I couldn't hide the pregnancy from my parents, though they never knew who the father was. My mother was so ashamed she sent me away here, to stay with her aunt. They wanted me to give the baby up for adoption. I was so confused and alone and afraid, Jack. And then Lucy was born and when she looked at me, I knew I couldn't bear to spend a day without her. I walked these wild cliffs of Cornwall and felt fortified by the beauty here, strengthened by the love I felt for her. By then, you were married, and I'd lost touch with the group. It was just me and Lucy. It was always just me and Lucy—until then there you were, at Sandringham, of all places."

I felt nauseous, dizzy with anxiety and yet light-headed with relief. Finally, my secret was out in the open. All the years of dread and worry, of wondering what to do, what to say, whether I should look for him, write to him. In the end, I hadn't needed to search for him at all. He'd simply walked back into my life, carrying a tray of tea and scones in the queen's country home. It was unbelievable, and yet, even then, in those first moments of surprise at seeing him again, I'd felt the inevitable pull of fate.

"Say something, Jack. Please."

He placed his hands on his head and let out a long breath. "I don't know what to say, Olive."

"When Lucy was born, she was the image of me. My nose, my lips. There was no trace of her father in her. But I see it now. More and more." I reached for Jack to touch his face. He recoiled as if burned by a flame.

His face crumpled as shock and disbelief took hold. "Jesus, Olive, why didn't you tell me? How could you keep this from me? From her! All this lost time with her—with my *daughter*."

Tears flowed down my cheeks, unchecked. "I'm sorry. I'm so sorry, Jack. I wanted to tell you, but I didn't know how. You and Andrea were so in love and happily married. You'd moved on from whatever we could have had. What good would it have done to ruin your life by telling you I was having your baby? I was afraid you would reject me. Reject us. When my family sent me away to Cornwall, I tried to forget about you and resign myself to life as an unmarried mother. You were happy. So was I, in time. And so was Lucy. And she was what mattered most of all."

"Ruin my life? What the hell gives you the right to decide what might and might not ruin my life? That was *my* decision to make, not yours. And since then? You've had so many chances to tell me. *For years.* I've spent time with her, Olive! Gotten to know her!"

I grabbed his arm. "Jack. Please, I—"

He held up a hand to stop me and turned to walk away.

"Jack—" His name came out as a sob as I ran after him. "I didn't mean to hurt you. I tried to tell you so many times but something always interrupted us. You were grieving for Andrea when we met, and then you went away for so long, and you've been so busy with your job at Buckingham Palace, and then the restaurant . . ."

He turned on the spot. "But none of that matters! Don't you see? All this time. I can't . . ." Tears streamed down his face as the happy laughter and music of the wedding reception leached through the open windows behind us. "Go back inside, Olive," he said. "I need some time alone."

All the fight left me. I didn't want to pretend anymore. "I tried to tell you, Jack. Truly, I did. But, maybe, if I'm honest . . ."

He threw his hands in the air and laughed hysterically. "There's more? I thought you'd already been honest?"

"I wanted to be enough. I wanted you to love me for *me*, not just because of Lucy. I'm so proud of her, and so proud to be her mother, but . . . it's so hard. It's so hard to be everything for her. I just wanted to be Olive again. The girl you danced with, all those years ago."

He looked at me. "I'm not even sure who you are anymore. Maybe you're not the person I thought you were—the person I thought I'd fallen in love with."

"Love?"

"Yes, Olive. Love."

As I watched him walk away from me, my heart broke into a thousand pieces, and I saw my future walk away with him, too.

I knew he would never forgive me.

And I knew I would never forgive myself.

I'd kept the truth from him for too long. I had found Lucy's father, and then I'd lost him all over again.

Queen Elizabeth II

St. Mary Magdalene Church, Sandringham, December 1956

I miss Philip terribly. I take no solace from the golden hue of December sun flooding through the stained-glass windows, no joy from the song of a mistle thrush outside, no pleasure from the peaceful solitude of my beloved church. Everything feels less without him here; smaller and quieter. Myself included.

I take a moment alone with my thoughts and my prayers before returning to the house and the children and the business of the crown. I am not ashamed to admit that it sits heavy at times, especially now. I wonder what life Philip and I might have known if we had followed our hearts and settled on the beautiful island of Malta, as we'd planned. But plans are not permanent—they are fleeting moments, a whisper on the wind, a mere possibility. Nothing more. Those of us who see our plans fulfilled might consider ourselves very fortunate indeed.

I make my way back to the house. It is a short stroll along the gravel path that crunches pleasingly beneath my shoes. Soon, the pathways will be lined with local well-wishers, come to catch a glimpse of their royal family as we make our way to church for the Christmas Day service. It is my favorite part of the day, a welcome break between the endless parade of rich food for breakfast and lunch, and a rare opportunity to mingle with local parishioners and to pray and give thanks in our beautiful church.

I call Susan to follow me. She has found something fascinating in a hedgerow, which will no doubt result in her eating, or rolling in, some foul thing. She trots along at my ankles. I can't help but smile at her jaunty gait. I envy her simple existence.

Back in my study, I push papers around on my desk and let out a long sigh. Susan lies at my feet, chocolate eyes trained on mine, entreating me to suggest another walk before the light fades. I lean down and rub her velvet ears.

"You miss him, too, don't you?"

She tilts her head slightly, still waiting for the magic word.

I smile. "Soon. I have all these papers to sign first."

She rests her head on the tips of my toes. It seems we all must wait for the thing we want the most.

The fire spits and crackles pleasantly in the grate as I work. I have asked for it to be banked high, and the heat is a joy at my back. Philip would declare it "bloody stifling" and pull off his jumper dramatically.

I smile at the thought. Dear Philip. He loves nothing better than a stiff breeze in his cheeks, a nip in the air, preferably a howling gale.

I am happy he is back at sea, taking charge of matters, pulling on the loose threads of a naval career he so loved. Philip is like an ocean wave himself, restless and petulant, pulled by forces beyond his control. I know it bothers him at times to live in my shadow, to walk two steps behind, to give me the space to be queen. So it is fitting that he has this time to be himself, to simply be Philip again, and not a Prince, or a Duke, of anything.

I hope he will be happier when he returns, and that *we* will be happier as a result. Those around me seem to falter at the slightest disagreements and rush to the divorce courts, but there can be no such outcome for Philip and I. We must find a way to make our differences work, because our marriage is not simply about the two of us.

I reach for the photograph on my desk, taken at Balmoral five summers ago, the wind pulling my headscarf, his hands resting on the top of his walking stick. A perfectly normal young couple in love, enjoying the splendor of the Scottish countryside. That was the summer before dear papa died. We had no idea what awaited us in the months that would follow.

"One day at a time, Lilibet," my father once said when I'd asked him how one learns to be a king or queen. "One day at a time. That is how."

Chapter 52

Jack

Royal Yacht *Britannia*, Southern Ocean, December 1956

I took it one day at a time. There was nothing else to do.

I was a father. Lucy was my child.

No matter how many times I ran the words through my mind, I couldn't get used to the idea that another part of my life had been running in parallel all these years. After the initial hurt and confusion had crashed over me, anger had come next. Olive had telephoned me at the palace several times before I left England, but I didn't reply. I was hurt, and wanted to hurt her in return.

In the end, I was glad to have left with the royal tour so soon after Mason and Rosie's wedding. Sailing to the other side of the world was exactly what I needed. It had given me space to think, and time for me to digest this new truth that had turned my life completely upside down.

On the upper decks of *Britannia*, I looked out at the sunset that stained the sky with vibrant, fiery hues. I'd enjoyed our time in the South Pacific with its warm winds, vast deep blue seas, and a searing hot sun that beamed over the shimmering waves. At night, thousands of stars had clustered like sand on a shore we could never reach but admired from afar. But our journey became more remote as we sailed toward the waters of the Southern Ocean. I felt isolated, and, at times, intensely lonely so far away from home.

As I had come to expect, the duke was on deck, too, chatting amiably with the crew. A few men had drained half a bottle of scotch, their laughter ringing out into the night. The duke was so different at sea. Although I had seen some parts of his life, I couldn't fully imagine what his days consisted of when he was back in England, but I knew my life had taken an abrupt turn.

I was a father. Sweet, inquisitive little Lucy was my child.

My thoughts kept turning back to this incomprehensible fact, and to all those years ago, when Olive had suddenly disappeared. It now all made sense. There was never a new boyfriend. She'd been sent away to Cornwall to have her baby.

Our baby.

All this time, I'd never known I had a daughter. I'd had no idea that Lucy, the darling little girl I'd come to know, was mine.

I squeezed my eyes closed as my thoughts became a tangled web of memories: the miscarriages and Andrea's death, how lost and bruised I'd been for so long. I'd given up on the idea of children, written them out of my story, but now everything had changed.

I thought of how fate had brought Olive and me together again, only to throw more obstacles in our path over and over, our timing never quite right. Some distant part of me understood why she had held her secret so tightly. The last thing Olive needed—the last thing Lucy needed—was an on-again, off-again father figure. They needed someone who would be there for them always. Someone who would love them.

Love.

I loved Olive. I cared deeply for Lucy, too, and knew it would only be a matter of time before I loved her with all my heart. I didn't know how I could ever forgive Olive, but if I was to know my daughter, I would have to find a way. I had no idea where we went from here. I didn't even know if Olive had told Lucy the truth. What I did know is that they were happy without me. But could I ever be happy now without them?

"How've you won again?" one of the crew shouted, followed by a mix of bragging and laughter.

"He cheats!"

I glanced over at the men, playing some game or other. They were enjoying themselves, but soon, we'd all squirrel away to the warmth belowdecks, out of the wind. We were southbound, and it wouldn't be long before we left the balmier temperatures for the coldest region in the world.

As the Royal Yacht *Britannia* tossed on the sea, I tried to quiet the tumult inside me. Part of me understood why Olive had guarded her secret. After all, I had guarded my feelings about her for too long. I hadn't given Olive the open door she needed to share the most important thing in her life with me. Perhaps we had both left things too late.

I gripped the railing as sea spray wet my face, and a memory flooded my senses.

It was a hot, hazy afternoon, and I was seven years old, sitting in a booth at Grandpa's restaurant with a thick banana and chocolate milkshake.

"What are you doing, Grandpa?"

He was bent over a notebook, scratching down notes as fast as he could think. "I'm writing a recipe. My crawfish étouffée. One day you'll need to make it and if you forget a detail, you can look it up in here."

The étouffée was bubbling on the stove and the thick aroma of homemade stock, cayenne pepper, and onion permeated the air. He'd made it extra spicy, the way most of his customers liked it.

"You're writing this for me?"

"Yessiree," he said, dropping the pen. "You're a natural, son. Your life might take many twists and turns, but don't let that get you down. There are a lot of second chances in life. And one day, you're going to be a great chef. Better than your old grandpa. Now, bring me the bag of rice from the pantry."

I'd hopped up and did as he asked, all the while listening to him whistle a familiar tune.

As the memory faded, my eyes focused on the darkening sky in front of me, the wind in my hair. He was right: I *was* a great chef, and life was full of twists and turns. If you were lucky, it was full of second chances, too.

But would I have a second chance at happiness; at love? That was the only question that remained.

Chapter 53

Olive

Sandringham Estate, December 1956

As the car moved through the Norfolk countryside, I gazed out of the window and thought of Jack. The months we'd already spent apart had only made me miss him more, and I was miserable, despite the approach of Christmas. According to the itinerary of the tour, he would be in the Southern Ocean now, headed for the Chatham Islands, where the duke would deliver his own part of the annual Christmas Day message.

Jack seemed so impossibly far away. Half a day, in fact. I often found myself calculating what time it was for him, twelve hours ahead of British time. His Christmas Day would be over before ours had hardly begun. Just like our chance at being a family was over before it had hardly begun.

Rather than bringing us closer together, as I'd hoped it would, telling Jack about Lucy had crushed him, and now he was halfway around the world, and furious with me. With no way of contacting him, there was nothing I could do but wait for him to return in February, and hope that, by then, he'd had time to understand, and to forgive me. The alternative was too awful to think about.

I let out a long sigh, hardly noticing we'd arrived as Evans pulled the car through Sandringham's gates.

"Not like you to be so quiet," he said.

"Sorry. I was miles away."

"Halfway around the world I'd say, judging by the look on your face."

Did he know? I offered a half-hearted smile. "Indeed."

Inside, I took a moment to pause and appreciate where I was before I headed to the small room that had been set aside for me to work in. An office of my own. It was a far cry from my first Christmas here, blundering around the kitchen and attempting to speak to anyone who would respond to me. I only wished I could tell Jack about it all: how Charlie Bullen had retired—at last—and how Tom had offered me the position of royal correspondent on a permanent basis.

I still couldn't get used to the idea that Charlie's desk at Broadcasting House was now mine. I would never be fond of the man, but I was at least able to respect his years of dedication to the BBC, and to the monarchy. Rumor was it that it had pained him to see the royal family's relevance being questioned, and the way the press increasingly speculated about their private lives, and he couldn't bear to be part of it anymore.

Finally, all the potential I'd shown was being recognized. I had a weekly radio broadcast called *Royal Roundup*, and my more in-depth studies on different members of the royal family had been widely regarded as refreshing and modern. A new take on an old institution. The queen and her staff trusted me, it seemed, and trust went a very long way in securing the smaller details and shared intimacies that allowed me to show the royal family not just as static images on postage stamps and commemorative teacups, but as real people, with hopes and fears, and flaws.

I was working on a piece for a Christmas week broadcast about the duke's tour. My angle was to explore how the temporary space in the royal marriage allowed each to shine individually; Philip especially. For so long, he had been in his wife's shadow, and the strain was starting to show. Gossip was circulating among the Fleet Street columnists about his roving eye, and the palace hoped that a piece in his favor would help his image.

But it was my appointment at three o'clock that I was most looking forward to.

On the dot, I was escorted to the library, where the footman announced me.

"Miss Carter, ma'am."

The queen looked up, her face widening into a smile. "Miss Carter! How can it possibly be this time of year already! Goodness, where do the months go?"

I curtsied. "It's hard to believe, ma'am. But here we are again."

"And I believe that congratulations are in order."

"Ma'am?"

"On your new appointment. I heard about Charlie's retirement. I was very pleased they passed the baton to you."

"Thank you, ma'am. I hope I can fill his shoes."

"More than adequately, I should say." She picked up her papers from the desk. "You will be pleased to know that I have a thorough first draft this year. When I sat down to write it, I knew precisely what I wanted to say."

I settled in the chair opposite, notepad poised on my knee as she read her script aloud.

It was surprisingly tender and moving. There was something especially heartfelt about this one as she spoke about spending Christmas apart from her husband. As I listened to the queen's sentiments about Philip, I felt how closely they chimed with my feelings about Jack.

The emotions I'd tried to keep in check for so long came flooding out.

"Oh dear." The queen passed me a box of tissues. "That isn't quite the reaction one hopes for from a Christmas address."

"I'm so sorry, ma'am. I don't know what has come over me." I dabbed at my eyes and cheeks. "I'm missing someone too, this Christmas. Your words struck a nerve."

"Is that a good thing, or not?"

"Good, ma'am. Your speech . . . it's beautiful." I finally composed myself.

"And perhaps I have you to thank for that."

"Me, ma'am?"

"I have rather enjoyed our time together over these past Christmases. You remind me who it is I am speaking to. I know some consider my life to be very detached from reality, but some things transcend status. A mother missing her children. A wife missing her husband. You remind me of the woman I might have been, Miss Carter. And for that, I am grateful."

I wasn't sure how to respond to such a candid speech and was glad the dogs chose that particular moment to barrel into the room.

"Thank you, ma'am. It is a privilege to be here, to spend time with you."

"A privilege you have earned through talent and hard work. Never forget that."

She stood up and called the dogs over, and I returned to my work with renewed clarity and confidence.

My piece on Philip was scheduled to be broadcast a week later. I was proud of it—and even more proud to see my name in the program listings of the *Radio Times*. I, Olive "Calamity" Carter, had finally made it to the listings alongside David Attenborough, Vera Lynn, and J. B. Priestley. For the first time in months, I felt hopeful, even if I was sick with nerves at the thought of hearing myself speaking on the wireless.

My mother was hysterical with excitement. She insisted on opening a bottle of Asti Spumante to mark the occasion. My radio broadcast was the most exciting thing to happen to the Carter family since I'd won a Scottish dancing medal at school. We weren't a family of high achievers, which meant that even the smallest thing was seen as a great occasion.

My mother grabbed my arm as my piece was announced. "Oh. Oh. She's on, Bob! BOB! SHE'S ON!"

I hid behind a chintz cushion and closed my eyes.

"*Philip, the Duke of Edinburgh, remains somewhat of an enigmatic figure. Not one to easily conform, he walks a fine line between royal tradition and rebellion, always ready to dismiss the rule book and follow his own path. And that, perhaps, has never been more evident than in the first solo tour that he is currently undertaking in the southern hemisphere. But who is the real man who walks behind the queen, and what roles might we see him take on as the queen looks ahead to another year on the throne . . .*"

Lucy looked at me, then back at the wireless. "Is that really you speaking, Mummy?"

"Yes, love. It really is me!"

My mother shushed us both and turned the volume up.

It was all over so quickly. After weeks of hard work, and several attempts to get the recorded piece just right, it was done.

I emerged from behind the cushion.

My father patted my arm. "Very good, love. Well done. You're a natural."

He did his best to hide it, but I saw the tears in his eyes before he excused himself and took a moment in the kitchen. My silly old dad. How I loved him.

How much I longed for Lucy to love her father as much as I loved mine.

On Christmas Eve, I took the package I'd been saving for weeks from the drawer in my bedroom. I was afraid to open it. Jack had left it for me at the hotel in Cornwall. He must have intended to give it to me after the wedding, as a farewell gift before he departed on the royal tour. When he'd left Cornwall suddenly without telling anyone why, Rosie had found it in his room. It had been with me ever since, tormenting me. On the front, he'd written: *Do not open until December 25th!*

Since it would already be Christmas Day where he was, I wasn't technically cheating. I sat on my bed and carefully opened the blue wrapping paper, dotted with miniature whisks and spoons. My hands shook. I hardly dared to know what it was he'd wanted to give to me, or say to me, before I'd ruined everything.

I took a deep breath and unfolded the note inside.

Dear Olive,
I'll be a thousand miles away by the time you read this, sur-rounded by blue skies and endless oceans, missing you and imagining you getting ready for Christmas. Let me guess: you've been to Liberty and Harrods to see the windows, caught snowflakes on your tongue in Green Park, sung carols (badly) in the little church at St-Martin's-in-the-Fields, and bought an armful of books in Hatchards. Did I forget anything? Oh, yes. Your cheeks are covered in glitter after making Christmas cards with Lucy!

I wish I could tell you this in person this Christmas. I wish I could tell you all the things I've been too hesitant to say when I had the chance but, well, the truth is that I love you, Olive.

I love you!

<u>*I LOVE YOU! (yes, I'm shouting!)*</u>

When I get back, I hope we can spend more time together so that I can show you just how much you mean to me. In the meantime, I've been writing down the recipes from our cooking lessons. A silly thing, but I thought you might like them, enclosed here. Perhaps you can try them out while I'm away.

With all my love, and Christmas wishes,
Your Jack
xxx

My heart sang in my chest as I read his words. He loved me. I laughed and smiled, and wiped tears from my face as I read his notes, titled "Recipes for Olive," beneath which he'd listed the dishes we'd made together, with notes alongside them.

Might be too spicy for her. Dial back the heat? Maybe something a little more mellow.

Likes—seafood (pre-shelled, doesn't like to "see their faces and legs"), chicken, beef but only well done (doesn't like the juices).

Dislikes—lamb (too cute), mushrooms (too slimy), parsley (disgusting), olives (ironic).

I smiled as I read on. He had listened to everything I'd said. He had remembered and noted everything I liked and disliked. Nobody had ever taken that much notice of me before.

Jack was always so precise with his recipes, and yet always

willing to make changes and adjustments to get it just right. "It's missing something," he would say as he dipped a spoon into his simmering pot, taking a moment before realizing it was salt, or spice, or a splash of burgundy it was missing.

I knew now, with absolute certainty, what was missing from my life—if only he would forgive me.

Jack.

It was, and would always be, Jack.

Chapter 54

Jack

Royal Yacht *Britannia*, Chatham Islands, December 1956

We disembarked at the Chatham Islands for a brief official visit, before pushing on to Antarctica. The seas had turned rough and many of the more valuable goods—grand pianos, the state banquet silver and china, and the Royal Marine band's instruments—were tied down and stowed. We struggled with meal preparations in the galley kitchen, giving me flashbacks to my time in the Navy.

Despite the pitching and rolling, we enjoyed a relaxed Christmas Eve. Everyone was in good spirits as we hung red and green streamers from the piping and rafters, and along the walls where we could. Someone had thought to play a joke on the duke and drew a ridiculous face on a large gold balloon along with the words, "A Happy Christmas Dukie." We all got a good laugh out of it.

Max and I, and the rest of the kitchen staff, busied ourselves preparing for the Christmas meal the next day. When we'd finished, some went in search of entertainment, but Max and I plopped down in a chair in the lounge and kicked up our feet.

"I have something I want to say to you," Max said.

"What is it, boss?"

341

"First of all, I'm happy for you. For you and Mason. Your restaurant is going to be a roaring success, I have no doubt."

I couldn't help but feel a pang of sadness. I had grown close to Max the last couple of years, in particular while we were away, and this felt like a goodbye.

"I hope you'll stop by on your days off," I said. "Try the house special."

He laughed. "I will! I'll need to satisfy my gumbo cravings. But, speaking seriously, and what I really wanted to say, is that you are an exceptional chef and an exceptional man."

"What's gotten into you tonight?" I asked with a grin.

"I suppose being at the bottom of the world, close to the end of the year, makes a man reflect on things. Do you think you will be ready to open Andrea's once we are back?"

"Mason has been hiring staff while I've been away, and I'll need about a month to finalize things, order the foodstuffs, run through routines and rules with the staff. But nearly everything else was set before I left."

"It won't be the same at the palace without you two. You will be missed."

"I'll miss you, too, my friend." We shook hands and then stood, wrapping each other in a bear hug and pounding each other on the back.

I headed to my cabin, my thoughts drifting to my friends back home, how they would be celebrating Christmas Eve and Christmas Day in the northern hemisphere. Ryan and Maggie with the children, Mason and Rosie spending their first Christmas together as husband and wife, and, above all else, Olive and Lucy.

I wondered if Olive was at Sandringham again. I thought about her kindness and adorable clumsiness. My heart lurched as I pictured her, the tip of her pen poised against her lip as she pondered her words. And I pictured Lucy. Since I'd learned the truth, I'd conjured the image of her sweet little face in my mind a thousand times. How had I missed the similarity? Her light hair and green eyes, the same as mine. How had I missed it all?

As I slipped into sleep, my mind filled with a vision of Olive, smiling in that beautiful, infectious way of hers, and the look in her eyes as they met mine.

An hour later, voices drifted through the cabin and several crew members poured into our shared room in the mess deck.

"Get up!" one of the men shouted. "It's time for the speech!"

I sat up in bed, nearly knocking my head on the bunk suspended above mine. I pulled on a sweater and stumbled into a pair of boots and followed the rest of the crew. It was the early hours of the morning, but we wanted to honor the queen and celebrate with our countrymen.

I joined the crew in the lounge as the duke made a joke, and then shuttered himself away in his private salon. He was to deliver part of the Christmas Day broadcast and didn't seem the least bit nervous.

The broadcast began, as always, with the national anthem, but in a change to usual proceedings, the voice we heard next was Philip's rather than the queen's. He sounded happy and confident, relaxed and assured. We hung on his every word, listening intently, proud of him and of the bond that had formed between us all at sea—the kind of camaraderie that came from sharing an adventure together. It was unspoken, but we all understood the deeper message within the duke's words—that the voyage had changed him, put his loyalties into perspective, and had also changed his views on what was important and what wasn't.

The voyage had changed me, too.

There was a moment's delay when the duke's broadcast ended, and the next voice we heard was the queen's, just as Philip joined us.

I couldn't help but watch his face. As soon as Her Majesty's voice filled the room, instant fondness registered in his usually guarded eyes, and for a moment, they glistened. He clearly missed his wife and family, even if he was enjoying his foray across the world's seas.

I pictured Olive there, too, at the queen's side, and wondered what she was thinking. I was tired of being hurt, tired of being angry. I missed her terribly. I wanted to take her in my arms, but the truth was, after how I'd behaved—leaving her in a whirlwind of hurt and anger, ignoring her telephone calls, and leaving the country for five months—I still wasn't sure how we could move past it all when I returned.

On the last day of the year, a cry rippled through the corridors as we crossed the Antarctic Circle. The duke was setting a record for the royal family with our voyage to the land of perpetual winter, and I was proud to be a part of that moment. I couldn't wrap my mind around what it meant to be sailing to the most remote part of the world. None of us could, and we spent a lot of time theorizing, discussing the stars, the change in sea, sky, and temperature, the sensation of leaving everything and everyone behind.

Being so far away from home affected us all. I became particularly introspective, profoundly moved by the remote landscape. I marveled at the vastness of the world's beauty, at how small I was within its sphere. I understood on a new fundamental level that my pains and joys were mere moments in an ever-moving, ever-evolving world far beyond me, one person, one flicker in space and time. It was comforting to know I was part of something greater, and I found myself releasing the last of my resentments about the way my carefully laid plans had slowly and systematically been turned on their head, one after the other.

"Let's have a celebration, shall we?" Max announced to the staff. "It's New Year's Eve, after all."

In the lounge, several men were sharing cigars, a few wore poorly constructed paper hats, and one of the deckhands was pouring measures of spirits and passing them around. When we all had one, we raised our glasses.

"To breaking records, to traveling to the bottom of the world, to—"

"Going home to our women!" someone shouted.

Laughter broke out and we all clinked our glasses against one another as the duke joined us. He was puffing on a cigar. On this voyage, he'd seemed more alive than I'd ever seen him, even on the previous royal tour. He was brimming with awe and wonder and passion for the natural world. I'd mentioned to Max that I wouldn't be surprised to see the duke spearhead some environmental causes in the future.

"Your Highness, good evening," I said when he sat down beside me. "There's a whiff of cold air around you, sir. Been up on deck?"

"Yes. Bloody freezing. I went in search of a moment alone, but my thoughts seemed to follow me."

"They tend to do that."

"So do headlines, apparently," he added. "Bloody vultures. Always looking to spark trouble on the home front."

"I'm having a bit of trouble on the home front myself, sir."

"A woman?"

I nodded. "It's messy and complicated. I left under a cloud, and now I don't know what to say to her when we return, how to make things right."

His eyes met mine. "My advice? Don't waste another minute. Life is complicated but love is not, and neither is forgiveness. That is more important than almost anything."

His words struck me to my core. He was right. Of course he

345

was right. After all of the rumors that had circulated about his relationship with Her Majesty, he must know a thing or two about forgiveness.

"You're a good man, sir. And a wise one."

He chuckled softly. "I'm not sure Lilibet would agree."

I smiled as a deckhand began singing "Auld Lang Syne," to ring in the new year.

Max came over and linked his arm through mine. "Come on, boy. Sing along. Loud and clear!"

I smiled and offered my other arm to the duke, and we all lifted our hands up and down and shouted our boisterous song to the stars, saying farewell to another year.

Should auld acquaintance be forgot
And never brought to mind?
Should auld acquaintance be forgot
And the days of auld lang syne?
For auld lang syne, my dear
For auld lang syne
We'll drink a cup of kindness yet
For the sake of auld lang syne

As we sang and toasted to old friends, beneath the garlands and tinsel, on the other side of the world from dear old London and everyone I loved, I knew I didn't want to spend another Christmas without Olive, or without my daughter.

When everything else was stripped away, when I let go of all the questions of why things had happened, and why Olive hadn't told me about Lucy until now, what remained was simple: I loved them both.

Philip was right. Life was the complicated part, but there was nothing complicated about love.

1957

"It is inevitable that I should seem a rather remote figure for many of you. But now, at least for a few minutes, I welcome you to the peace of my own home."

Queen Elizabeth II, 25 December 1957

Chapter 55

Jack

London, February 1957

As our months at sea came to an end and we finally headed toward London, I had never been happier to see the dusky gray skies of a city I realized was my true home. But I knew it was far more than that: London was the place where I'd truly become a man—where I'd learned to put my heart on the line for the first time, and where, at long last, I was ready to do it again.

As I dropped off my chef whites and left Buckingham Palace for the last time, I paused outside to look at the iconic building I now knew so well. Even from here, I could almost smell the pastry chef's vanilla sugared almonds, the odor of Princess Margaret's cigarettes, and the scent of furniture polish. I could hear the hum of voices as the maids chattered while they went about their dusting and vacuuming, or the patter of little Charles's and Anne's feet and their accompanying laughter as they raced through the grand, gilded corridors, all the while being chastised by Nanny Lightbody. I had fond memories of the palace, and of my work here, and would miss it more than I had expected. But every season had its time, and I was perched on the precipice of a new one.

My first stop was the post office. I'd tied up the typed pages and handwritten notes of my cookbook together with string and neatly wrapped them in brown paper, adding a letter to the publisher, explaining my background and my experience in the royal kitchens. I hoped they might like it enough to publish it. If not, I was glad to have spent the time writing it all down. A published edition would be this chef's icing on the cake.

Next, I walked toward my old stomping ground, The Thirsty Dog. As I walked past, I remembered the good times with the old gang, and the more painful moments—the last time I'd been there with Andrea before her accident. I'd visited her grave earlier that morning, laid fresh flowers and asked for her acceptance as I moved on with life. I knew that was what she would want for me, and that she would always be with me, no matter what.

I turned and began to make my way toward Richmond Street. Although it was February, a generous sun shone overhead, illuminating the city in golden light. A promise of the spring to come. The streets were bustling with double-decker buses and taxis, the sidewalks with mothers and children and shoppers, friends arm in arm. The air bubbled with happy chatter and the sounds of a city awakening as the last of winter drained away.

I stepped around a puddle that glittered in the sunshine and turned the corner. Howard's Florist came into view, but the faded sign I would have recognized a mile away was no longer there. In its place, there was a shiny new sign. A thank you, from me. The new florist who had purchased the shop had been gracious enough to honor the former owner's legacy.

A lump of emotion caught in my throat as I thought of how much Mrs. Howard would have liked it with its gold swirls and hand-painted flowers; how much Andrea would have loved it, too. I continued on, passing my restaurant—I'd be spending plenty of time there soon enough—but for now, there was something more important I had to do.

I walked onward to Regent Street. When Maison Jerome came into view, I paused briefly outside it. My former employer had never given me a chance, but how different my life would be now had I not followed Andrea's encouragement to look for something better, or if I had resisted Ryan's insistence to follow him to Norfolk that terrible Christmas to take up my position at Sandringham after all. Life turned on a dime, it seemed. What I'd learned since was to cherish each moment; treasure the things I had now.

Finally I arrived at Broadcasting House, home of the BBC. Heart in my mouth, I entered the lobby and approached the desk.

"Can I help you, sir?"

"I hope so. Could you tell me how I might reach Olive Carter?"

"Is she expecting you, sir?"

"No, but . . ." I paused, and smiled to myself. "Well, that's not entirely true. Let's just say that I hope she is expecting me."

Chapter 56

Olive

I stared at the typewriter in front of me, struggling to find the right words for my new piece. The subject matter was tricky, the right tone hard to achieve after the largely negative response to the queen's last Christmas message, which, critics claimed, had painted a false picture of the Commonwealth as one big happy family. It had added to the growing opinion that the royal family were out of touch, and that the monarchy needed modernizing. Philip's antics overseas had also fueled rumors that the royal marriage was in trouble.

But, apart from a touch of writer's block, I was also distracted by the date circled on my desk calendar: the royal tour—and Jack—had returned home yesterday.

"They're back then!" Rosie remarked. "Mason said Jack is as tanned as a leather hide. He's grown an impressive beard, too. Apparently, they had some sort of beard-growing competition while they were away, but Mason wouldn't let him near the restaurant with it, so he shaved it off!"

I sighed. "Boys will be boys." All I could think about was that Jack was back in England and hadn't been in touch. Would he ever contact me again?

"Give him a day or two, Olive. No doubt he's exhausted after the long journey and with the time differences and whatnot."

"I suppose so."

She reached for my hand. "He'll be in touch."

I hoped she was right. I felt sick to my stomach at the thought that he might still be angry with me and not want to see me. Lucy had asked about him several times, disappointed that "my special friend" wasn't around. The tour had been a good excuse, but even she knew that was over now.

Just then, the telephone on my desk rang.

"Olive Carter," I said as I picked up the receiver.

"Someone to see you in reception, Miss Carter. He said you've been expecting him."

My breath caught in my throat. I hardly dared believe it was him.

"I'll be right down." I replaced the receiver and took a deep breath to try and calm myself.

"Olive?" Rosie looked at me, her face hopeful. "Is it him?"

"I think so!"

I hurried out of the office, Rosie's cry of "Good luck" disappearing behind me as I rushed down the stairs, along the corridor and down more stairs, my heart thumping in my chest as I slipped and stumbled. I gasped, steadied myself, hurried to reception, and stopped.

There was nobody there.

I raced to the desk, a sense of panic rising in my chest. "There was somebody here to see me? I'm Olive Carter. Did he leave?"

"He just stepped outside, miss."

I looked through the window, and there he was, the golden light of a low winter sun on his face.

I couldn't believe he was here.

I pushed through the door, heart in my throat.

He turned to face me, love and hope in his eyes. My name fell from his lips, his voice hoarse with emotion.

"Olive."

I ran into his arms. He searched my eyes for an instant, caressing my cheek with his thumb, drinking me in, and the next moment, he tipped my face toward his and our lips met. He kissed me with urgency, washing away all the long months we'd been apart. He kissed me across time, unraveling all the lost years when we'd sidestepped fate. He kissed me as if he'd always loved me, as if there was nowhere else he'd rather be than right here. And I felt as if my heart would burst.

We wiped tears from each other's cheeks.

"Can you love us both?" I asked. "I know it's a lot to ask."

He brushed a curl from my face. "Of course I can love you both. I love you for who you are, Olive. The way you are with Lucy doesn't define you. It just makes me love you even more."

"We'll be all right, the three of us?"

He smiled and pulled me closer. "Of course we will. We're a perfect recipe. Like roast beef, Yorkshire puddings, and gravy."

"Like fish and chips and mushy peas! Like scones and jam and cream!"

"Like shrimp and rice and peppers." He reached for my hands. "The three of us will be more than all right, Olive. We'll be unstoppable!"

He bent his lips to mine again and the whole beautiful, crazy world melted away, and all that remained was love.

Chapter 57

Jack

London, April 1957

When opening day finally arrived, I felt oddly calm. We went about a few last chores, checking the prep stations, polishing the last of the glassware, and meeting with the saucier, grillardin, line cooks, sous-chefs, and maître d' to make sure everyone was confident and ready.

When late afternoon arrived, we dressed in our chef whites and joined the staff for our family-style meal before service began. Everyone was excited to get started. Mason and I had set up a prix fixe menu to ease the staff into the swing of things for the first night. We were serving baked oysters with bourbon-butter breadcrumbs, fresh cornbread, white fish with *beurre blanc* and a pinch of cayenne, mixed vegetables with herbs, a slow-cooked beef dish, and beignets and crème brûlée. An impressive selection of wines and champagne lined the cellar walls. We'd also set aside a special case of champagne for the official toast at eight o'clock.

I sorted through the pile of fresh vegetables, setting aside those that were less than perfect to take home later.

Lucy raced into the kitchen. "I've finished rolling the knives and forks in napkins. What else can I do?"

"You're a great help, kiddo. Here, why don't you help me choose the best of these carrots?" She was keen to get involved, to learn more about everything we were making. My daughter was eager and inquisitive, just like her mother. I hoped she would become a good cook one day, like her father. "Then how about you see if Mason has finished setting up the pastry tray? Maybe you can help him decide where to put everything."

Her eyes widened. "Can I have a slice of that big cake?"

"Maybe later, when we come back to eat," Olive interjected with a laugh as she appeared in the kitchen looking for our daughter.

Our daughter.

It had been surprisingly easy, in the end, to tell her. Olive had done a wonderful job of explaining everything, and when we'd met in the park, Lucy had run to me, and I'd swept her into a huge fatherly hug. We'd all agreed to take things one day at a time, and every day I spent with Olive and Lucy felt more perfect than the last.

I grinned. "I wonder where she gets her enthusiasm."

"From you!" Olive said, leaning in to kiss me.

"From both of us," I said as I wrapped my arms around her and enjoyed the feel of her soft lips against mine. "All right, you'd better be off, too. You're a distraction! I need to focus."

She turned to go, pausing at the doorway to blow me another kiss over her shoulder. "We'll see you tonight. Good luck, darling. You'll be wonderful."

"It's time!" I announced to the crew. "Let's do it!"

The maître d' unlocked the front door. A line of people already stretched down the street. In an instant, the dining room swarmed with guests.

I headed back to the kitchen, where a flurry of activity was well underway. Soon, the opening orders were called as the first tickets arrived. I finished each plated meal with an artful touch before placing them on the pass and calling for service, while Mason ran things in the back. It was frantic, hot, and loud, everyone whirling around the different stations and counters, knocking into each other occasionally, but overall, things ran as smooth as a slick of butter on a hot, honeyed biscuit. I smiled to myself as Mason sang out one order after another, and the maître d' returned again and again to deliver more praise from satisfied diners.

Two hours into the shift, the maître d' poked his head around the kitchen door. "They're here, chef."

I washed my hands, wiped the sweat from my brow, and straightened my jacket before stepping into the dining room. As I looked to the entrance, my heart soared.

The Carters had arrived. Olive's parents, Barbara and Bob, in their Sunday best, and Lucy, pretty in purple and with ribbons in her hair. Olive was stunning in a gold dress that shimmered as she moved, perfect for opening night. She smiled one of her bright, beautiful smiles.

As I approached, I grinned from ear to ear. "You're gorgeous." I kissed her lightly. "And you are too, sweetie," I said to Lucy, before shaking Bob's hand and kissing Barbara on the cheek. "Hello, Mr. and Mrs. Carter. Thank you for coming."

"Oh, you don't have to call us that, dear," Mrs. Carter said. "It's Bob and Barbara to you. We're practically family, after all."

I laughed. "Very well."

"Everything looks amazing!" Olive said. "The tablecloths, the lighting, the paintings. It smells divine, too."

"Let's hope it tastes divine. Follow me. The others arrived a few minutes ago." I showed them to their table where Rosie, Maggie, and Ryan were already seated. "I'll send out some champagne." I signaled to their waiter, who arrived promptly.

"My goodness, it's Evans and Mrs. Leonard!" Olive exclaimed, as she recognized the staff from Sandringham. They were seated at the table across from her. "How lovely of you both to come. And how lovely to see you together."

Evans winked. "We wouldn't miss it. Max told us all about it."

Mrs. Leonard's cheeks flushed a little as she smiled, shyly. "Life can't all be work and no play."

Next, Olive spotted her boss, Tom Harding and his wife, Evelyn. She was so happy to see them both. I knew then that her night was as complete as mine.

I smiled and headed back toward the kitchen, stopping by Max's table on my way. A few of my friends from the palace staff had joined him. "Thank you all for being here."

"We wouldn't miss it for the world!" Max said, shaking my hand heartily. "Tell Mason to come out, too, when he has a minute. We want to congratulate him."

"I will. But I'd better get cookin', or you won't be eating tonight!"

Their laughter followed me as I headed back to the kitchen.

When the time came for the official toast, the staff abandoned their stations for a moment and joined the guests in the dining room. As champagne glasses were distributed, I was nearly overcome with emotion. It was time.

I tapped my fork against my water glass.

"Can I have your attention, please? I'd like to propose a toast." I waited for a moment as everyone turned to face me. "Thank you all for coming to our opening night, and for supporting this endeavor that my talented partner, Mason, and I are deeply proud of. It means more to us than you can imagine to see this dining room full." I met the eyes of Ryan and Maggie, and continued. "I'd like to take a moment to honor my grandpa, who first taught me the power of a great meal and the magic of spices. I hope you're making gumbo in heaven, Grandpa." I paused as everyone burst into spontaneous applause. "I'd also like to say a special thank you to Max Barrington, whose patience and encouragement pushed me to the next level. You're a gracious gentleman, Max, and a great friend." He smiled, and I pushed on. "To dear Mrs. Howard, whose kind heart and generous gift made this all possible, and to all the loved ones who are no longer with us, but who we will always remember. And finally, to my darling Olive and our daughter Lucy. I love you both with all my heart." Olive blew me a kiss. "Now, if you'll all raise a glass to Andrea's. May your stomachs always be satisfied and your hearts always be full. Cheers!"

A chorus of voices rang out in celebration across the crowded room as my eyes searched for Olive's. She was my past and my future.

She raised her glass and mouthed the words, "I love you" as she smiled proudly.

I had done it. We had done it. And we had done it well.

Chapter 58

Olive

Sandringham Estate, December 1957

Evans turned the corner and the now-familiar black gates of Sandringham Estate swung into view. A smile crossed my face.

"There she is, Lucy!" I said, leaning forward to get a better view of the impressive sandstone buildings in the distance, lit by the soft light of early morning. "Like a regal old lady, isn't she!"

Lucy's nose was pressed to the glass in the back of the car. She didn't have to kneel up to see out anymore. She was tall, like her father, and she was growing up fast.

"Will the television people already be here?" she asked.

"I expect so. There'll be lots of cables and wires and lighting to set up before the broadcast."

"Will I be able to watch them get everything ready?"

She was such a curious child, eager to understand how things worked.

"I'm sure we can ask someone. But you're not to get in the way. You were lucky to be invited."

"Glad to be back?" Evans asked, glancing at me in the rearview mirror.

"I am! Sandringham is almost starting to feel like my Christmas home! This is when the countdown starts, when you drive through those big black gates, and I hear the crunch of the tires on the gravel." I thought of how unsure I had been when I'd burst into Tom's office five years ago and had practically begged him to send me in place of Charlie Bullen. "There's something in the air here. It makes me feel like a child again."

Evans pulled the car to a stop, opened his door, and walked around to open mine. As he did, Mrs. Leonard appeared in the doorway.

"Looks like someone's waiting for a kiss beneath the mistletoe," I teased as I took my small case from the seat. Lucy jumped out after me.

Evans blushed. "Don't be starting that nonsense again," he said.

"I will keep saying it until the two of you admit you're madly in love and do something about it! I saw the two of you, inseparable at Andrea's on opening night!"

At this, he threw his hands in the air in mock despair and returned to the driver's seat. I watched him wave to Mrs. Leonard as he passed her, and I saw the smile that lit up her face in response. I wondered if I could concoct a plan to bring them together, as I had for my parents. My thoughts flitted back to Jack's po' boys and his cookery lessons, how we'd laughed as I'd made a mess of everything.

Life was busy for us both at the moment. After the excitement of opening night at Andrea's, and a packed restaurant every night since, summer had tipped toward autumn and a busy season of royal functions and banquets to report on—and now, here we were, racing toward the end of another year, the prickle of Christmas in the air. Jack was joining us later, as a special guest of Max Barrington. He'd—quite rightly—insisted Jack should be served from the royal kitchens as a guest, as a way of thanking him for his years of hard work. Mason had been invited, too, but he and Rosie were spending Christmas with her family in Cornwall.

When I stepped inside, I took a deep breath. It was good to be back. The elegant rooms and long corridors hummed to the sound of festive preparations, the rattle of ladders and the clink and clatter of decorations being hauled here and there. A welcoming fire crackled in the grate. Cedarwood smoke scented the air, mingling with the aroma of clove-studded oranges and fragrant bundles of cinnamon sticks tied with crimson ribbon. No wonder the queen loved spending Christmas here. And yet, this Christmas at Sandringham, everything would be very different with the live television broadcast of the queen's Christmas Day speech.

Preparations were already well underway. The TV crew had arrived the previous day, causing chaos, according to Mrs. Leonard.

"Tearing the place asunder with their cables and microphones and Lord knows what else. Prince Philip finds it all fascinating. Her Majesty isn't quite so enthusiastic. I suspect she's nervous."

Regardless of her nerves, the queen was prepared to embrace change when necessary, to do the right thing for the monarchy. I'd learned a lot from her, but that was perhaps the most important lesson: that what we want, and what we must do, are two entirely different things.

We stepped over snaking wires and long rolls of cable, careful not to tread on or dislodge anything. Two television cameras were already set up alongside several large lights. There was a palpable air of tension about the place.

Everyone was on edge after a few difficult months following Lord Altrincham's latest scathing opinion piece, in which he'd described the queen as a "priggish schoolgirl" and her style of speaking as "a pain in the neck." His words were cutting and personal and had clearly hit a nerve. In response, it had been decided that this year's Christmas message would be televised. Let the people see the queen. Give them access to her home on Christmas Day. It was a risk, but a risk we all hoped would pay off.

Times were changing and, as much as I loved radio myself, it was increasingly considered to be old-fashioned. Having seen how quickly people had flocked to a television set to watch the coronation, the royal family believed they could, once again, use it to their advantage.

"I didn't realize it would be quite so technical," Mrs. Leonard said as we avoided another spooling cable. "I can't help thinking it is all a bit unsavory, all this equipment and intrusion. I worry the intimacy of the Christmas message will be lost among it."

"I think it will be wonderful," I said. "Viewers at home won't see any of the wires and cameras. All they will see is Her Majesty, speaking directly to them. She is the consummate professional. I'm sure she will take it all in her stride."

"Who will take it all in her stride? Me, by any chance?"

I dipped into a curtsey as the queen entered the library. "Ma'am."

She wore a stiff sapphire-blue satin dress, belted at her tiny waist, a string of pearls set off perfectly by the sweetheart neckline. Her perfume was bright and floral—expensive Yardley, no doubt. Only England's finest for Her Majesty.

"Jolly nice to see you, Miss Carter."

"It's actually Mrs. Devereux now, ma'am." I still couldn't stop smiling whenever I used my new name. Mrs. Olive Devereux. Jack said it sounded positively aristocratic.

"Ah. I see. Very good. Such happy news. My congratulations to you both."

"Thank you, ma'am."

"What do you make of the new house guests?" she continued, indicating the television cameras. "They're quite well behaved, but the dogs have rather taken against them."

I smiled. "Not too off-putting, I hope."

"Sylvia tells me I am to ignore the cameras and everyone in the room, and imagine I am speaking to a mirror, or to my husband."

Sylvia Peters, a colleague at the BBC, had been drafted in to coach the queen specifically on presenting to camera. Sylvia was a pro with many years' experience.

"They offered to provide me with something called a tele-prompter," the queen continued, "so that I can read the script, but I have declined."

"Will you keep your notes on the desk, ma'am. Just in case?"

"I will. But I shan't use them. There is little point in having a television camera pointed at me if the audience can only see the top of my head while I read from a script!"

Pragmatic as ever. She'd grown in confidence over the years since I'd first met her. She wore her responsibilities as well as she wore her beautiful Dior dresses. The echo of grief that had haunted her first year on the throne had been replaced by a shimmering sense of purpose and duty. I wished her father could see her. He would be so incredibly proud.

"I believe we shall see a little more of you in the new year," she added. "A television documentary is being planned?"

"Yes, ma'am. We hope to continue the success of the televised Christmas Day speech, to let people know it isn't a one-off and that they can expect to see you on their television screens more often."

She laughed lightly. "Not too often, I hope. Besides, I haven't done it yet. It might be a one-off after all!"

"I doubt it very much, ma'am."

"Well, it is most kind of you to lend your support."

Just then, Prince Philip strode into the room, arms full of books. "I brought a few, Lilibet. Wasn't sure which one you meant. Golly, don't you look a picture! I could . . ."

The queen cleared her throat and busily tidied some papers on her desk. "Don't let me keep you, Mrs. Devereux. Christmas is for family, after all."

Philip turned as he saw me beside the window. "Ah. Sorry to interrupt."

I dipped a curtsey as I tried to keep a smile from my lips. "Thank you, ma'am. Your Highness. And a very happy Christmas to you both."

I returned to my temporary office, where a parcel had been placed on my desk, wrapped in brown paper and tied with a ribbon. On the front was one word. *Olive.* I knew the handwriting.

I opened the paper and gasped. *Grandpa's Kitchen—Wholesome Southern Cooking,* by Jack Devereux. Jack's cookbook! It was beautifully presented, each recipe accompanied by an illustration of the finished dish, and occasional family photographs of Jack and his grandpa, or Jack in his chef's whites, and other memories from his time in the royal household. I flicked through the pages, smiling as I saw a recipe for *Olive's Tomato Soup* and another for *Mr. and Mrs. Carter's Po' Boys.* But it was when I returned to the front of the book and read the dedication on the title page that my heart lurched.

For my daughter, Lucy. The missing ingredient.

The first flakes of snow began to fall as I looked out of the window to see Lucy and Jack, laughing as they chased the queen's corgis around the lawns in the falling snow. He'd made it in good time. I smiled, my heart full of love.

I pulled on my coat and hurried downstairs.

The snow sparkled as it fell, coating the gardens with its glittering, bright beauty, making everything new again.

Lucy called me over, her cheeks alight with a rosy glow, her excited breaths drifting skyward. Our girl was blossoming into a bright and confident young woman.

Laughter filled the air as we scooped up the first dredges of snow and threw snowballs at each other. Jack brushed a lock of hair from my eyes as he took my hands. Suddenly, he spun me around in circles until I was dizzy. I couldn't stop laughing and screamed at him to stop.

"My turn!" Lucy cried, running to join us.

He took her hands, and we twirled and twirled in giddy circles until we fell to the ground, our faces turned to the sky as the lacy white flakes fell around us. The distant sound of church bells and Christmas carols rang through the air.

Jack reached for my hand. "I'm so glad to be with you. With both of you."

I turned my face to his and squeezed his fingers. "There's nowhere else we could be, Jack. There was never anywhere else I wanted to be."

Epilogue

Queen Elizabeth II

Sandringham House, 25 December 1957

The gentleman from the BBC approaches the desk. He speaks in a low whisper, as if afraid to startle me and send me running into the woods.

"One minute to go, ma'am."

The entire situation reminds me of a Balmoral stag hunt. *Tread quietly. Speak softly.* I nod to indicate my understanding, straighten my shoulders, try to ignore the thump of my heart beneath my stiff satin dress. I wish I had worn something less formal. What *does* one wear for one's first television broadcast? My mouth feels horribly dry.

"Might I have some water?" I ask.

My request stirs a flurry of activity. The young woman who has been coaching me rushes forward with a glass of water.

"Anything else, ma'am?" she asks.

I shake my head as I take a sip and wish I had accepted Philip's suggestion of a Dubonnet to settle my nerves.

"You'll be wonderful," she whispers. She takes the glass and steps to one side.

"Thirty seconds."

The man behind the camera adjusts a wire at his feet. I focus my gaze directly at the lens, just as I have rehearsed. I do hope I don't look awful. One never had to worry about such things when one spoke into a radio microphone.

Philip stands off to the right, arms folded, a bemused smile on his face as he leans against a bookshelf. I honestly don't know why I let him convince me that it was a good idea for my Christmas Day message to be broadcast live on the television. He can be terribly persuasive when he sets his mind to something. "We need to modernize, Lilibet," he'd said. "Bring the monarchy right into people's homes. That'll show bloody Lord Altrincham and his bloody opinions."

I try to forget the cruel remarks about my being a "priggish schoolgirl" and steal a glance at a photograph of the children on the desk, and another of Mummy and dear Papa, each item carefully chosen and arranged with exact precision. "Some flowers, perhaps, ma'am? A couple of books?" So much fuss for a few minutes on air.

"Ten seconds. Nine, eight . . ."

I close my eyes, take a deep breath. I have been informed that people at home will see images of the exterior of Sandringham while the national anthem plays.

I think about my grandfather, delivering the first Christmas message exactly twenty-five years ago, his gruff voice crackling over the wireless as if from a different world entirely. I picture Papa sitting at this very desk, stumbling painfully over his words every Christmas Day. It caused him so much anguish; so much worry. "You will do a much better job when it is your turn, Lilibet darling," he'd said after his first Christmas speech. "You'll be an absolute marvel."

"Five, four, three . . ."

I count the two and one silently in my head as I have rehearsed, take a breath, open my eyes, then turn to the camera and smile.

"Happy Christmas."

Authors' Note

As we started to plan our fourth novel together, we knew we wanted to write a historical love story set at Christmas, and soon landed on the idea of following the annual Christmas Day message given by Queen Elizabeth II. As we started writing our first draft in 2022, the queen was looking ahead to her Platinum Jubilee celebrations—an astonishing seventy years on the throne—so it felt very timely to write a novel set during the early years of her historic reign.

Hazel grew up in England, watching the queen's speech throughout her childhood, always at three o'clock on Christmas Day. It was a tradition she continued into adulthood. But, of course, at the start of Queen Elizabeth's reign in 1952, nobody could actually watch her speeches, but, instead, listened on the radio. It was only in 1957 that the—rather brave—decision was made to invite the British public into the queen's home, and broadcast the Christmas Day message through the relatively new medium of television.

When we looked back at those early Christmas broadcasts of the queen's reign, we discovered a young woman who had ascended the throne unexpectedly, and who was faced with navigating a changing society in Britain—and the world—in the post-war years of the 1950s. We also found it fascinating that the Christmas Day speech in 1957 was the first televised speech. We were intrigued by the era and wanted to explore how two ordinary people might become entangled with the royal traditions through their own jobs, and how that might lead them to become entangled with each other. Wannabe royal correspondent Olive, and chef-in-training Jack, quickly jumped off the page and into our hearts. We had such fun developing their will-they-won't-they love story.

As for our research, how could we resist digging into the royal Christmas traditions at Sandringham Estate, and how better to do that than to visit Sandringham in person? We arranged a trip to London to see the famous royal landmarks (and to fit in some essential Christmas shopping in Fortnum & Mason, Liberty, and Hatchards), followed by a train ride to Norfolk, and a bus for our final leg of the trip to the royal estate. As the charming villages, and Sandringham House itself came into view, we knew we'd chosen our topic well.

We spent a memorable day walking the lush grounds and gardens, past the lake with a large weeping willow that hugged its banks, and a bench in perfect position for watching the ducks as we imagined our characters there, holding hands, or perhaps a conversation between Philip and Elizabeth. We took a tour through the surprisingly cozy yet elegant Sandringham home, asking the guides more questions than they'd probably expected. Spot the authors doing research! Then we visited the church where the queen and the royal family attend the Christmas Day service each year. There is nothing quite like being in a place you are writing about, and over the course of a truly special day, we saw our story unfold.

We spent far too much time—and money—in the gift shop, where we oohed and ahhed over the Christmas decorations, cinnamon and clove spiced oranges, trinkets, soaps, gin, and a hundred other things! Then we toasted our book and our special friendship over a delicious afternoon tea. Christmas in October was perfect! We hope we've brought you along on this beautiful journey with us, through the pages of our book.

For fans of our previous books, we hope you have also enjoyed the little Easter eggs we've threaded among the pages for you. We especially loved the full circle of bringing our dear Tom Harding (and Evie Elliott) back from our first co-written novel, *Last Christmas in Paris*. There are a couple of other past characters mentioned, too!

To avoid any confusion (or emails!), we wanted to mention that although Philip was born a prince of Greece and Denmark, he carried the title of Duke of Edinburgh until February 1957 when he returned from his solo tour to Australia and Antarctica, and Elizabeth gave him the title of Prince Philip.

Lastly, we must mention the late queen, Her Majesty, Queen Elizabeth II. To find ourselves writing a novel inspired by her, at a time when her historic reign came to an end, was particularly poignant. When her death was announced in September 2022, toward the end of her Platinum Jubilee year, we were both so moved to see the outpouring of affection for her. We will never forget the images of endless lines of people queuing patiently, day and night, to pay their last respects, or the haunting notes of the bagpipes as the queen's piper played "Sleep, Dearie, Sleep" at the end of her state funeral at Westminster Abbey.

Numerous TV documentaries about Elizabeth's life aired at the time, sharing—for the first time—some very private home movie footage, and the queen's reflections on her life and reign. These touching insights showed a different side to the somewhat detached regal figure we had known for so many years. In writing the pieces in *Christmas With the Queen* set in her own voice, we hope to have captured a little of the more personal, intimate side to this remarkable woman.

Acknowledgments

First and foremost, we must say a very big thank you to our wonderful agent, Michelle Brower, who cheers us on as we brainstorm, research, and write our hearts out. And to Allison Malecha for foreign rights, and all at Team Trellis. We'd also like to thank our U.S. and UK editors, Tessa Woodward and Lynne Drew, and the teams at William Morrow U.S. and Harper Fiction in the UK for their support, the many hours of reading and editing, and creating a beautiful package for our words. Special thanks to Katie Lumsden for her invaluable editorial input, and Olivia Robertshaw for all her hard work.

We must also give a special mention to Lucia Macro, who first blessed the Gaynor/Webb book marriage back in 2015 when we presented her with a somewhat crazy idea to write a novel together. She has been an incredible cheerleader since, allowing our imaginations to roam freely. Lucia commissioned *Christmas With the Queen* several years ago on the basis of a very excited pitch and, although she is now enjoying a well-deserved retirement, we talk about her often and will be forever grateful for her belief in us and our stories.

Thank you, also, to Gill Perdue for sending on the beautiful collection of memorabilia belonging to her grandmother. To see the care and attention that had been taken in gathering all the cuttings from the newspapers to add to her scrapbooks was incredibly touching, and inspired Olive and Lucy's scrapbooking. We are so honored to have them in our care.

To our beloved readers, the many wonderful book bloggers, podcasters, and journalists who support us, and of course the incredible bookstores and librarians who give our books space on their shelves and in your hearts, our stories wouldn't exist without you. Thank you deeply.

And finally, for our families and friends who never cease to make us feel loved—and proud. You mean the world to us.

About the Authors

Hazel Gaynor is an award-winning *New York Times* and *USA Today* bestselling author known for her deeply moving historical novels, which explore the defining events of the twentieth century. A recipient of the 2015 Romantic Novelists' Association Historical Novel of the Year award, her work has since been shortlisted for multiple awards in the UK and Ireland. Her latest novel, *The Last Lifeboat*, was a *Times* historical novel of the month, shortlisted for the 2023 Irish Book Awards, and a 2024 Audie Award winner. Hazel's work has been translated into twenty languages and is published in twenty-seven territories to date. She lives in Ireland with her family.

Heather Webb is the award-winning and *USA Today* bestselling author of ten historical novels, including *The Next Ship Home*, *Queens of London*, and *Strangers in the Night*. To date, her books have been translated to eighteen languages. She lives in Connecticut with her family and two mischievous cats.

Hazel and Heather's cowritten historical novels have all been published to critical acclaim. The *USA Today* and international bestseller *Last Christmas in Paris* won the 2018 Women's Fiction Writers Association Star Award, *Meet Me in Monaco* was shortlisted for the 2020 Romantic Novelists' Association Historical Novel award, and *Three Words for Goodbye* was selected by *Prima* as a Best Novel of 2021. *Christmas with the Queen* is their fourth collaboration.

August 1914. England is at war. As Evie Elliott watches her brother, Will, and his best friend, Thomas Harding, depart for the front, she believes—as everyone does—that it will be over by Christmas, when the trio plan to celebrate the holiday among the romantic cafes of Paris.

But as history tells us, it all happened so differently...

Set in the 1950s against the backdrop of Grace Kelly's whirlwind romance and unforgettable wedding to Prince Rainier of Monaco, *New York Times* bestselling author Hazel Gaynor and Heather Webb take the reader on an evocative sun-drenched journey along the Côte d'Azur in this page-turning novel of passion, fate and second chances...

Three cities, two sisters, one chance to correct the past . . .

New York, 1937: When estranged sisters Clara and Madeleine Sommers learn their grandmother is dying, they agree to fulfill her last wish: to travel across Europe—together. They are to deliver three letters, in which Violet will say goodbye to those she hasn't seen since traveling to Europe forty years earlier; a journey inspired by famed reporter, Nellie Bly.